A SKY OF
PAPER
STARS

A SKY OF PAPER STARS

Susie Yi

Roaring Brook Press
New York

The words that appear in this font depict lines in Korean, and the words that appear in **this font** depict lines in English. *Italicized* words are unspoken thoughts.

1

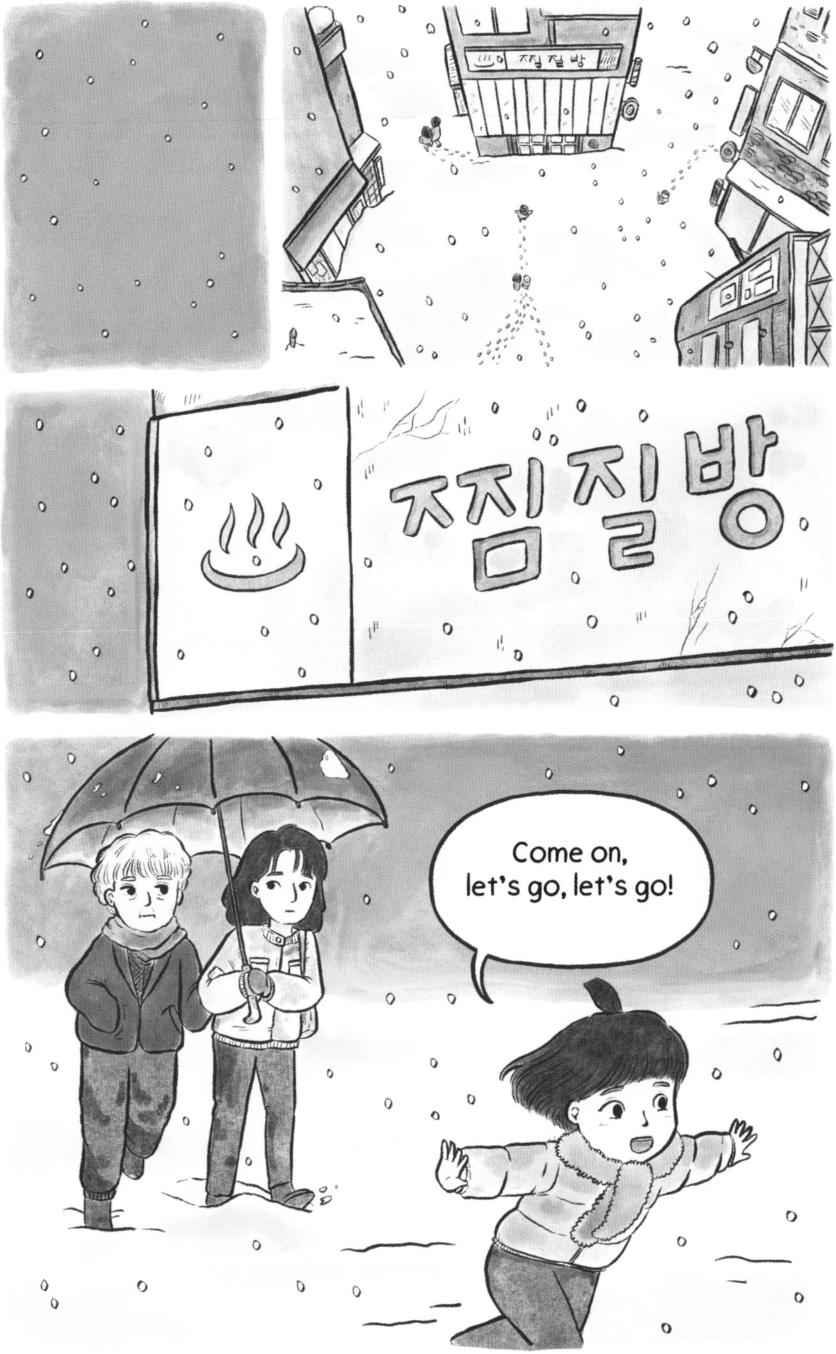
찜질방
찜질방
Come on,
let's go, let's go!

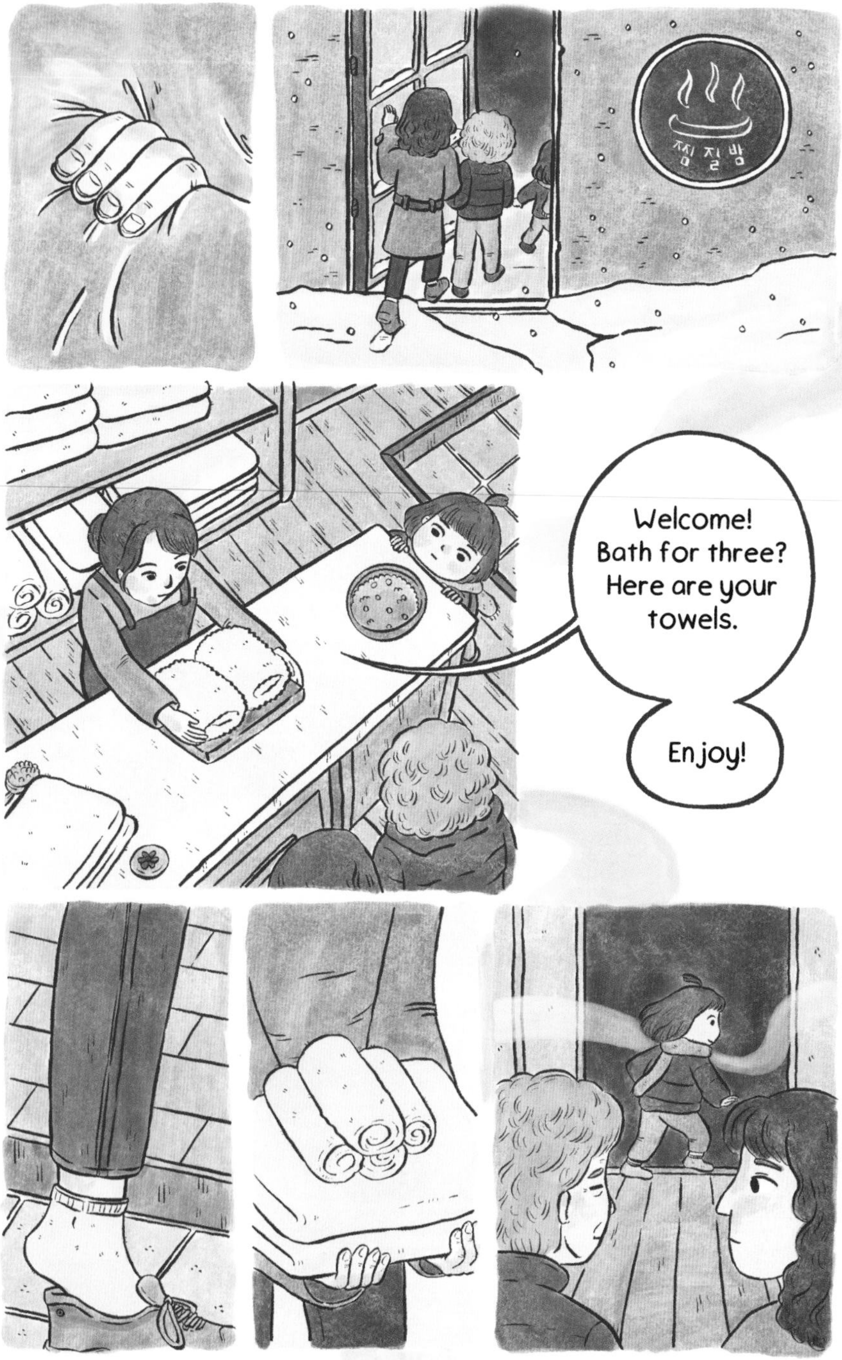
찜질방
Welcome! Bath for three? Here are your towels.
Enjoy!

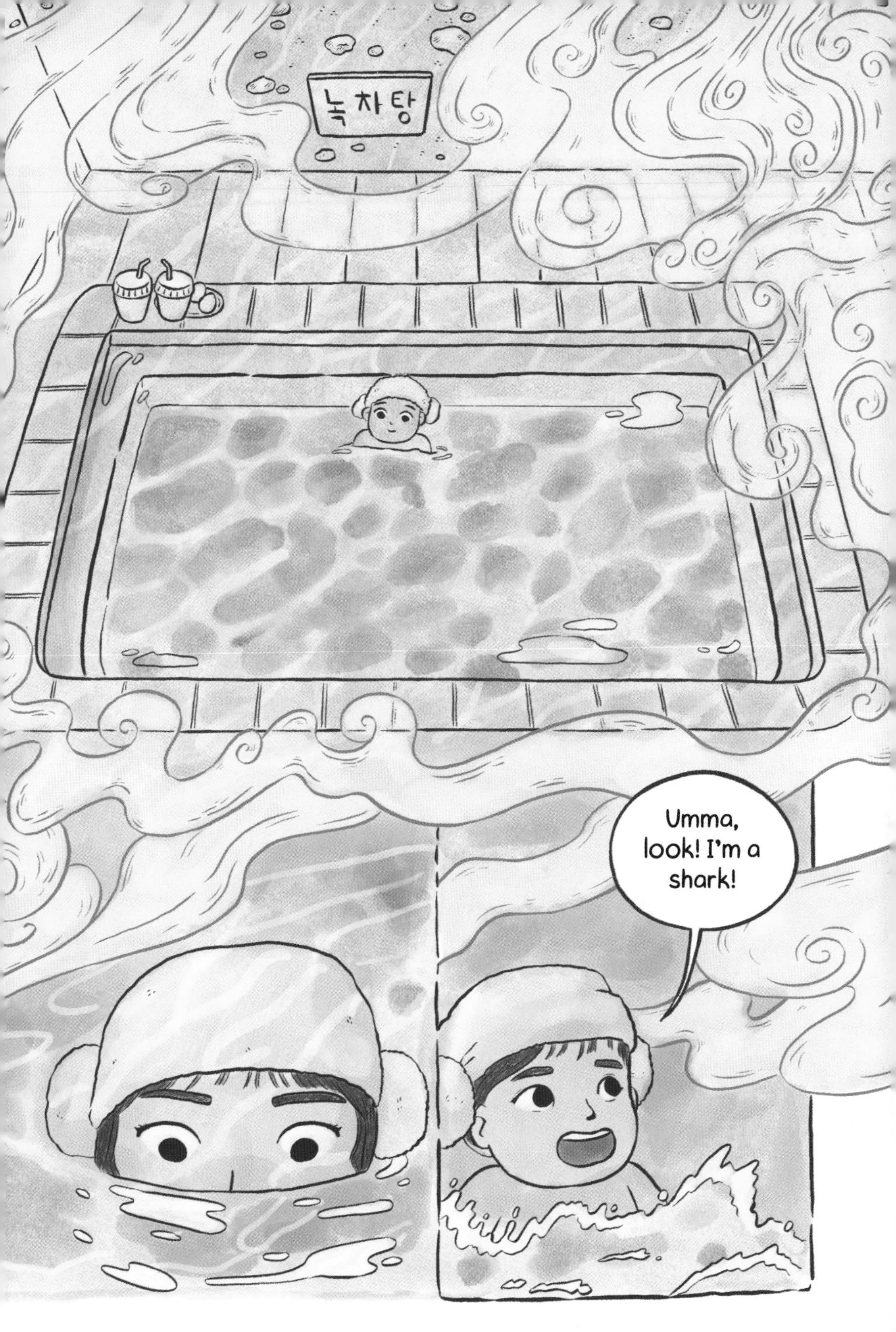
녹차탕
Umma, look! I'm a shark!

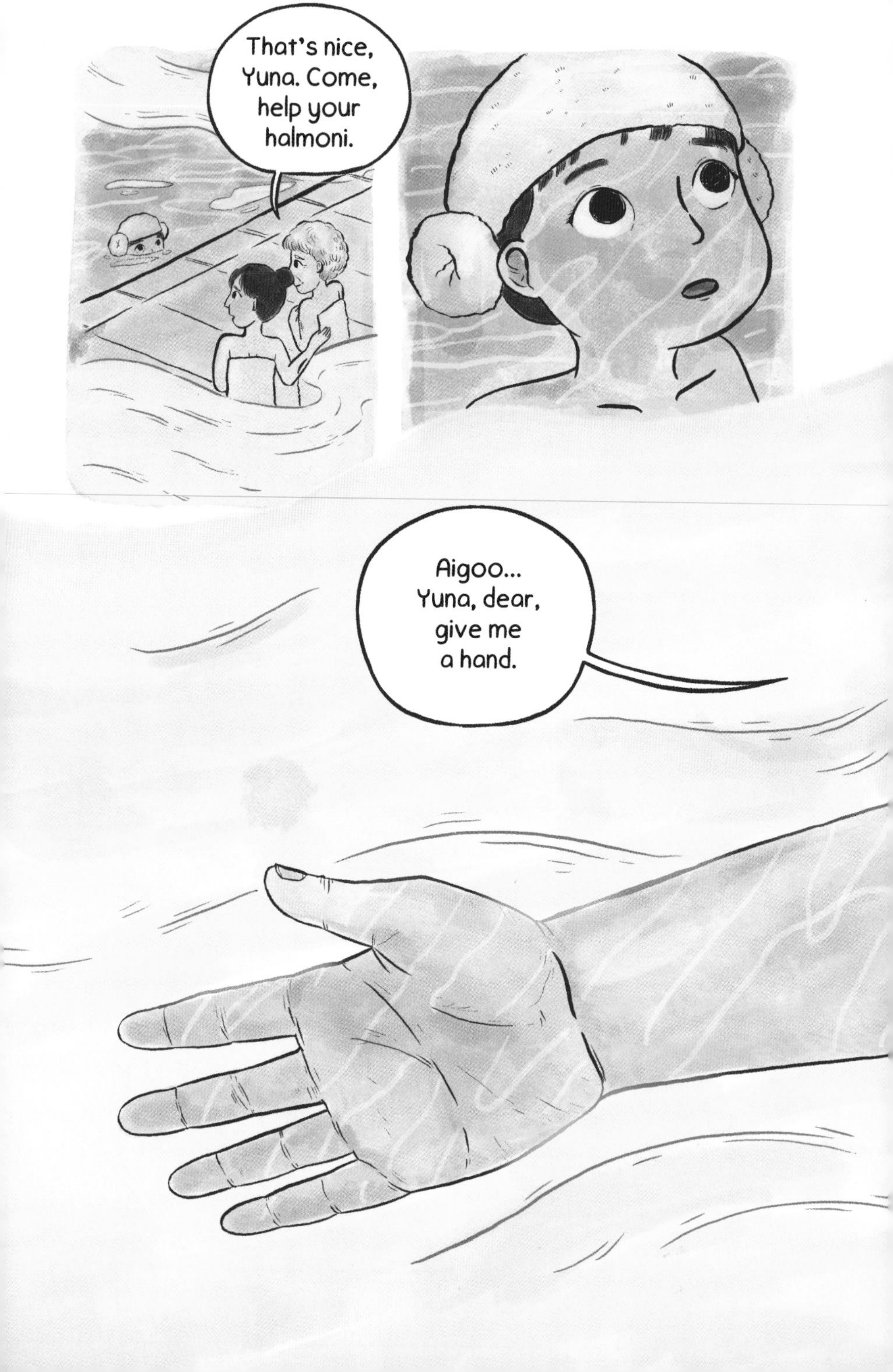
That's nice, Yuna. Come, help your halmoni.
Aigoo... Yuna, dear, give me a hand.

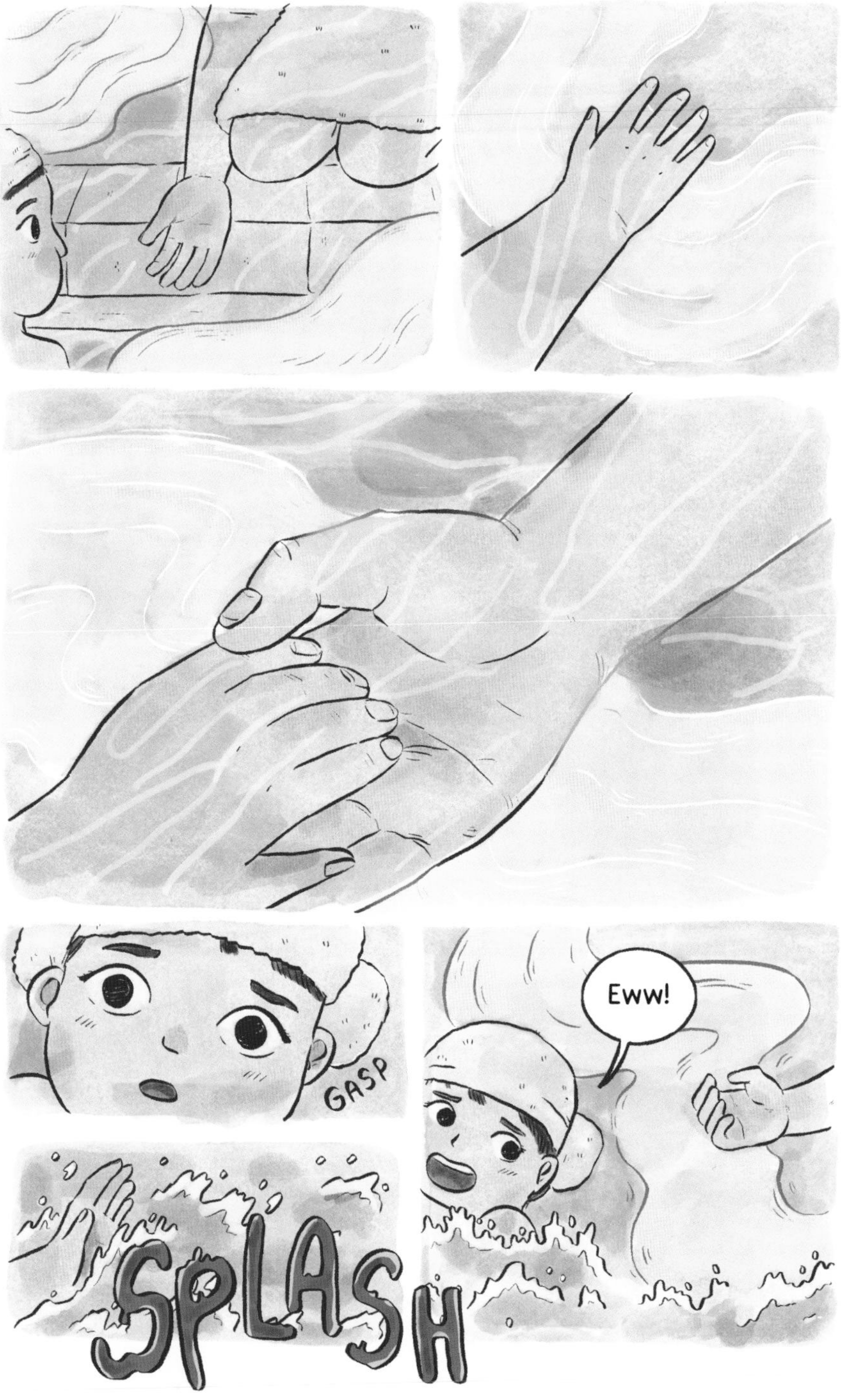
GASP
Eww!
SPLASH

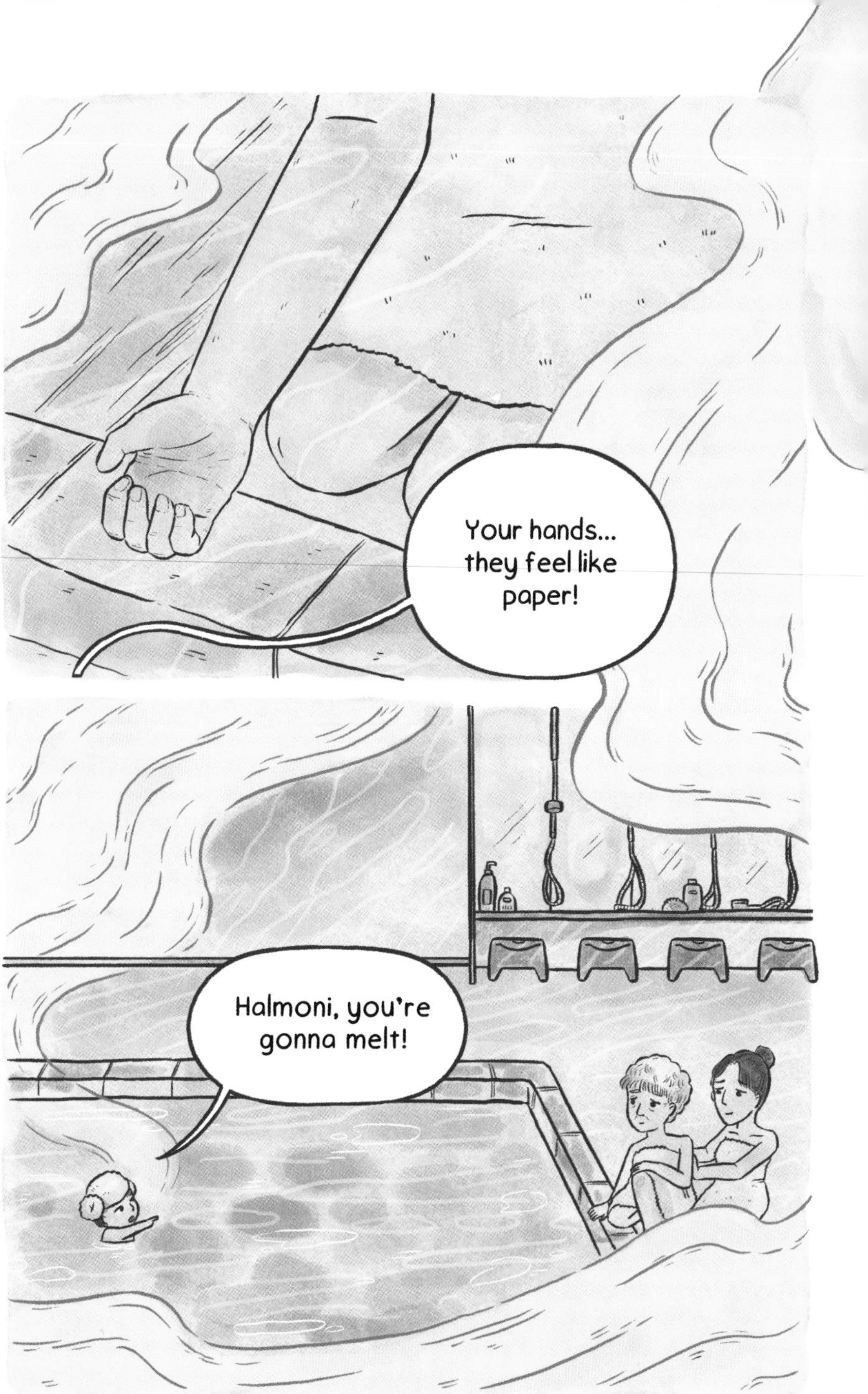
Your hands... they feel like paper!
Halmoni, you're gonna melt!

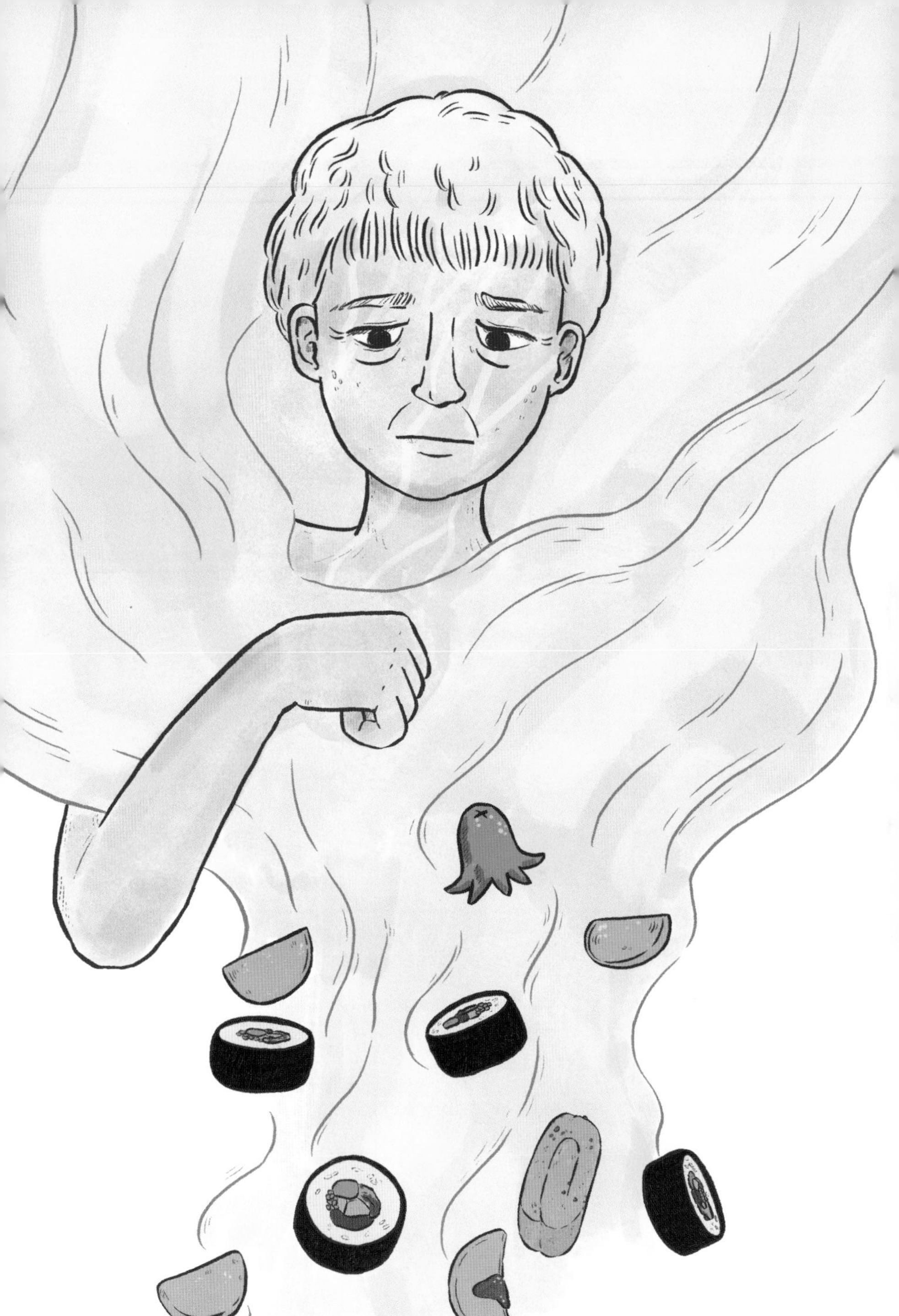

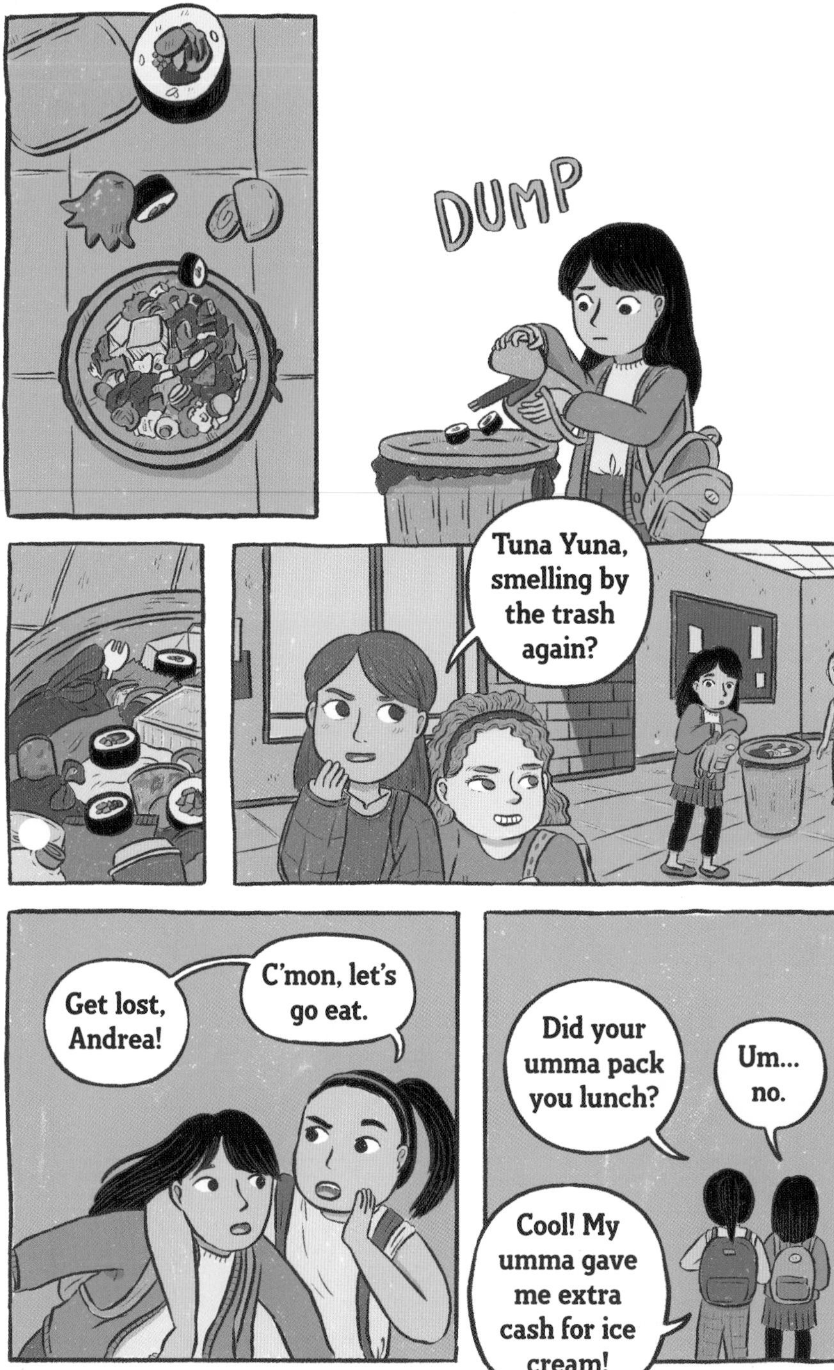
DUMP
Tuna Yuna, smelling by the trash again?
Get lost, Andrea!
C'mon, let's go eat.
Did your umma pack you lunch?
Um... no.
Cool! My umma gave me extra cash for ice cream!

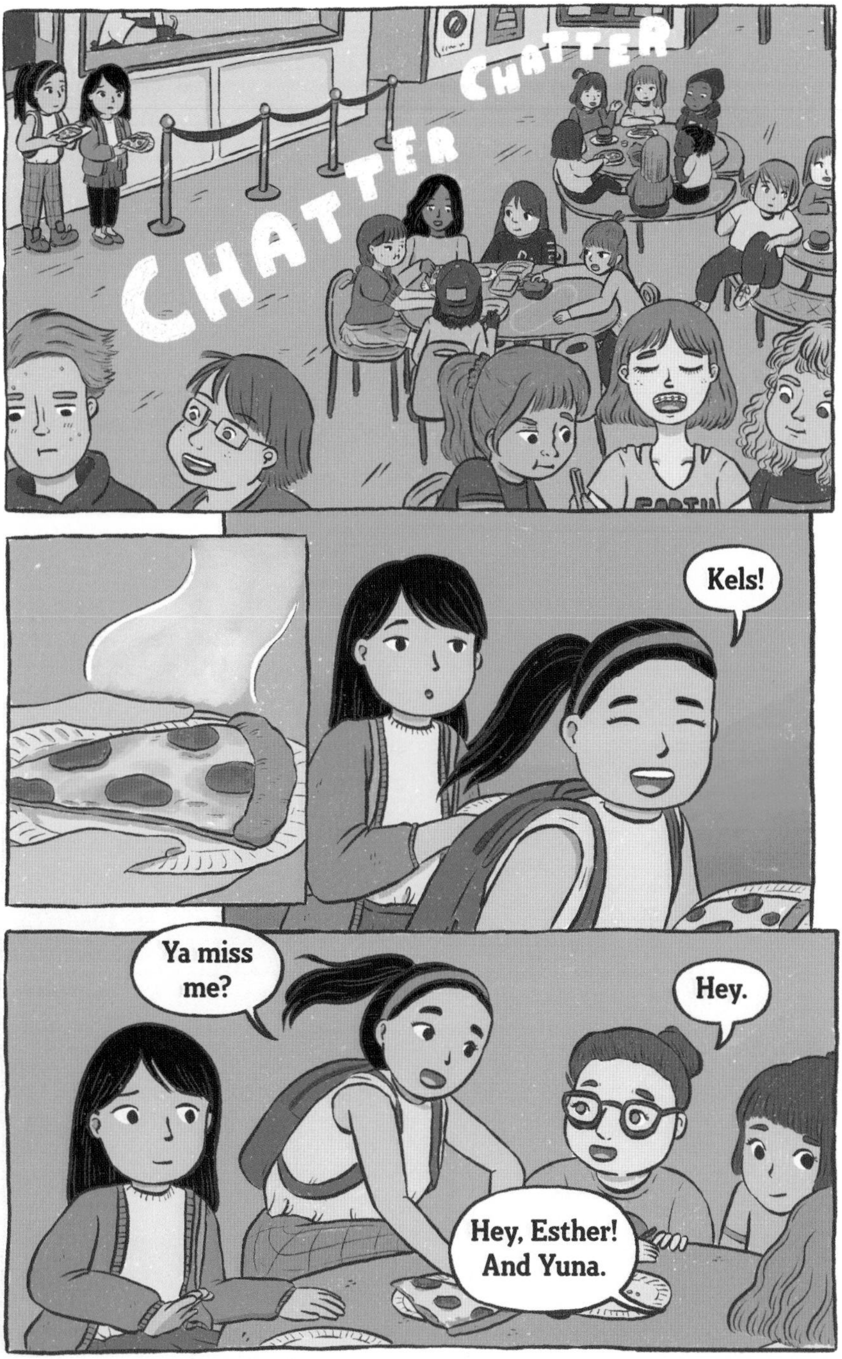
CHATTER
CHATTER
CHATTER
Kels!
Ya miss me?
Hey.
Hey, Esther! And Yuna.

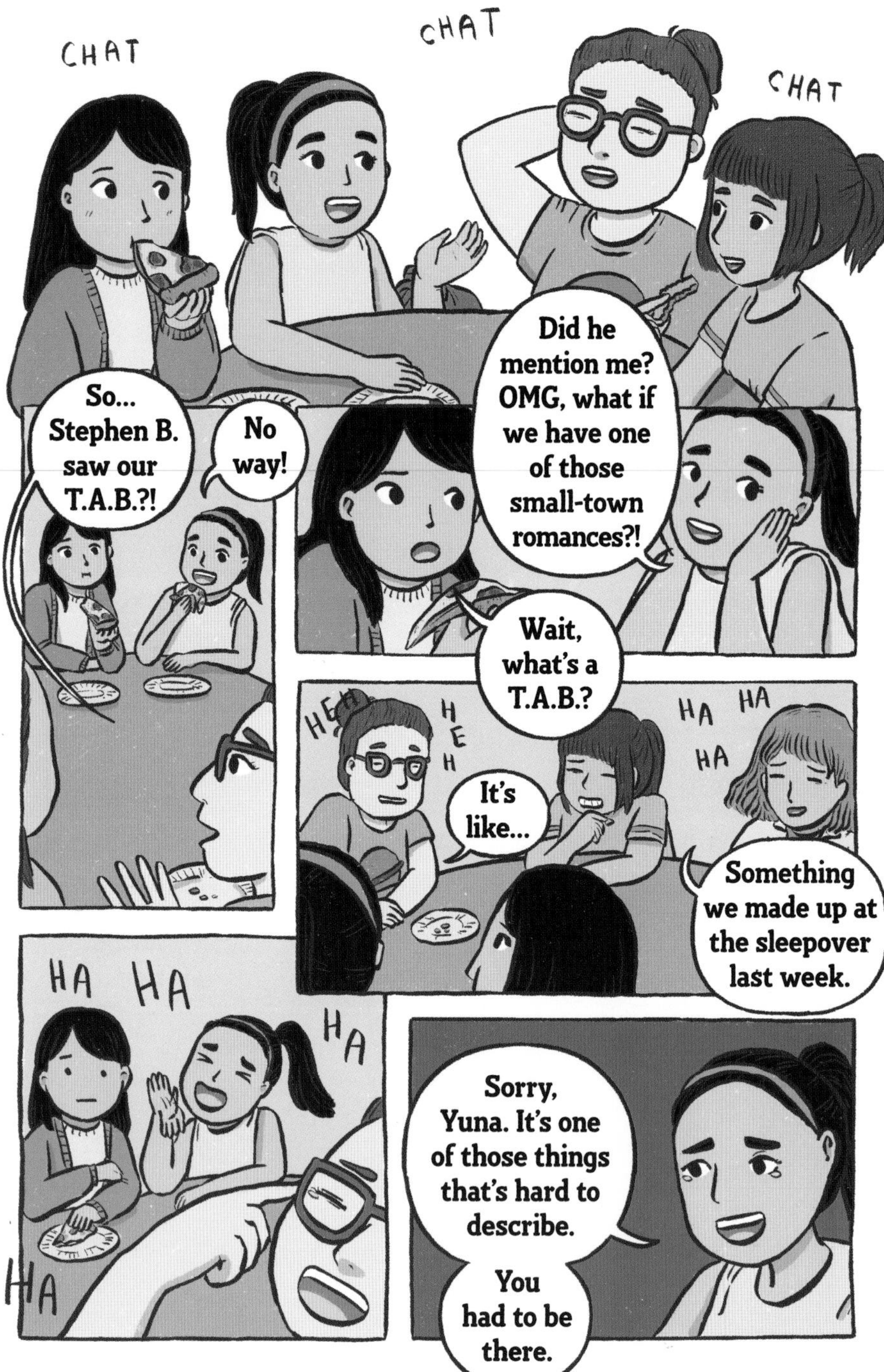
CHAT
CHAT
CHAT
Did he mention me? OMG, what if we have one of those small-town romances?!
So... Stephen B. saw our T.A.B.?!
No way!
Wait, what's a T.A.B.?
HEH HEH
HA HA HA
It's like...
Something we made up at the sleepover last week.
HA HA
HA
HA
Sorry, Yuna. It's one of those things that's hard to describe.
You had to be there.

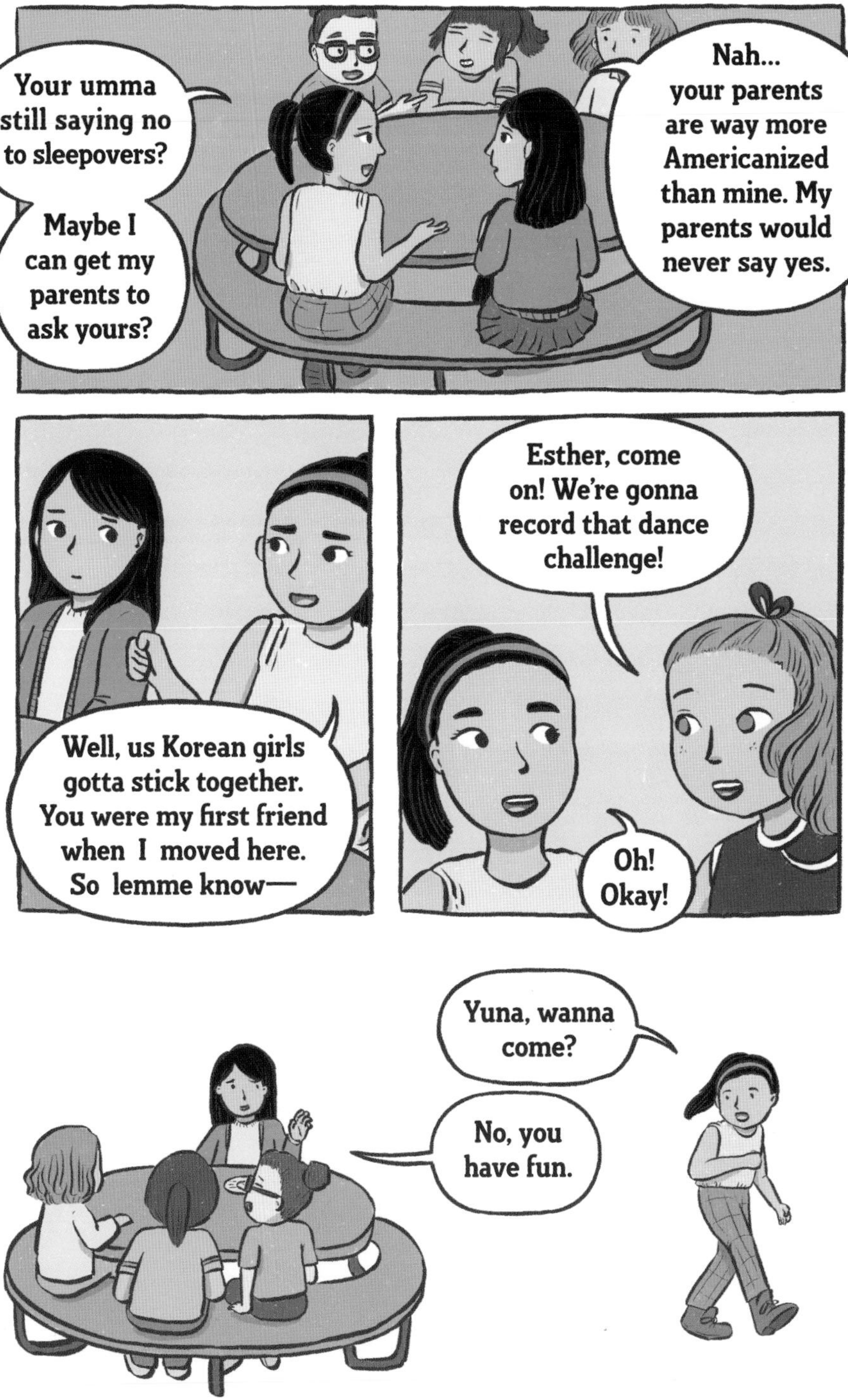
Your umma still saying no to sleepovers?
Maybe I can get my parents to ask yours?
Nah... your parents are way more Americanized than mine. My parents would never say yes.
Well, us Korean girls gotta stick together. You were my first friend when I moved here. So lemme know—
Esther, come on! We're gonna record that dance challenge!
Oh! Okay!
Yuna, wanna come?
No, you have fun.

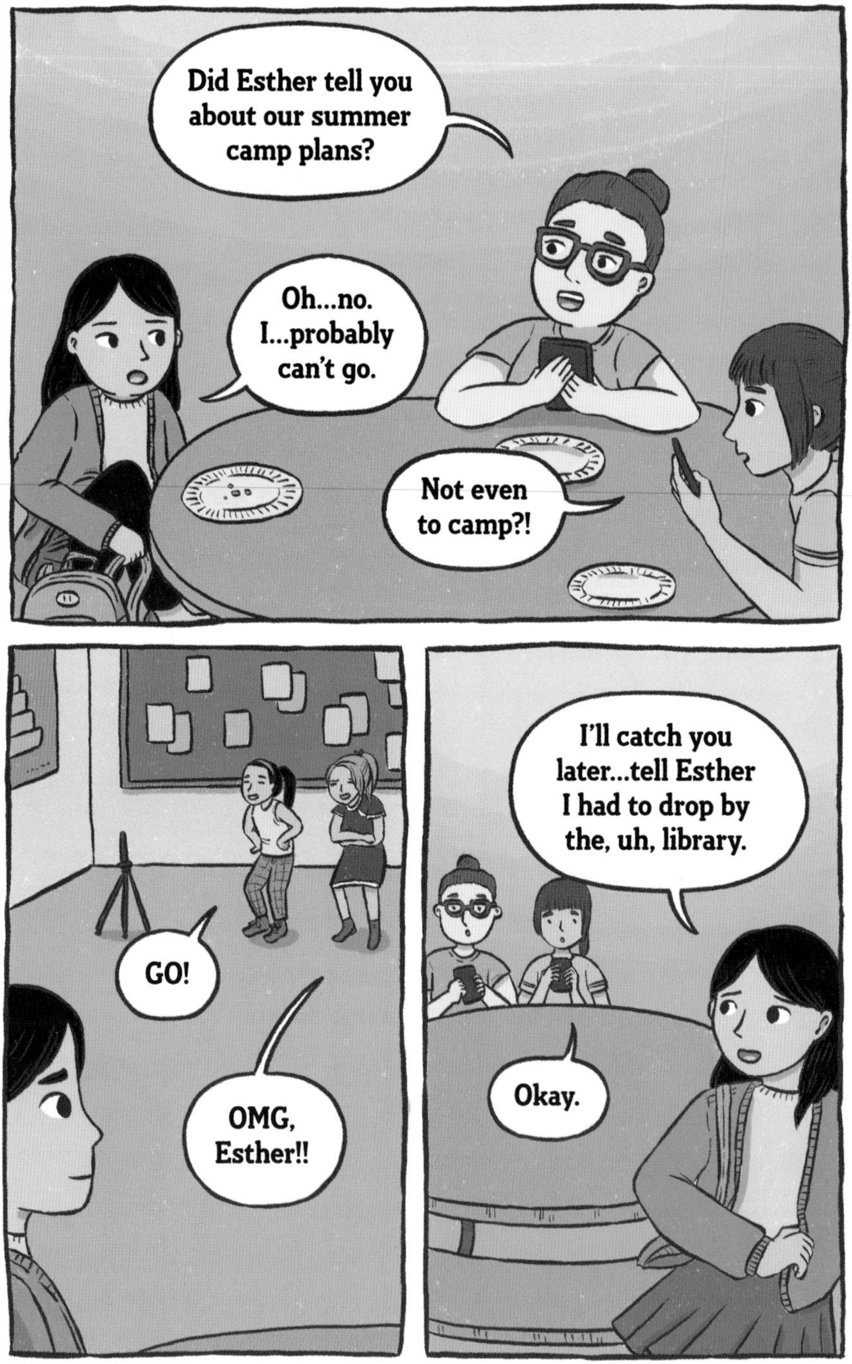
Did Esther tell you about our summer camp plans?
Oh...no. I...probably can't go.
Not even to camp?!
GO!
OMG, Esther!!
I'll catch you later...tell Esther I had to drop by the, uh, library.
Okay.

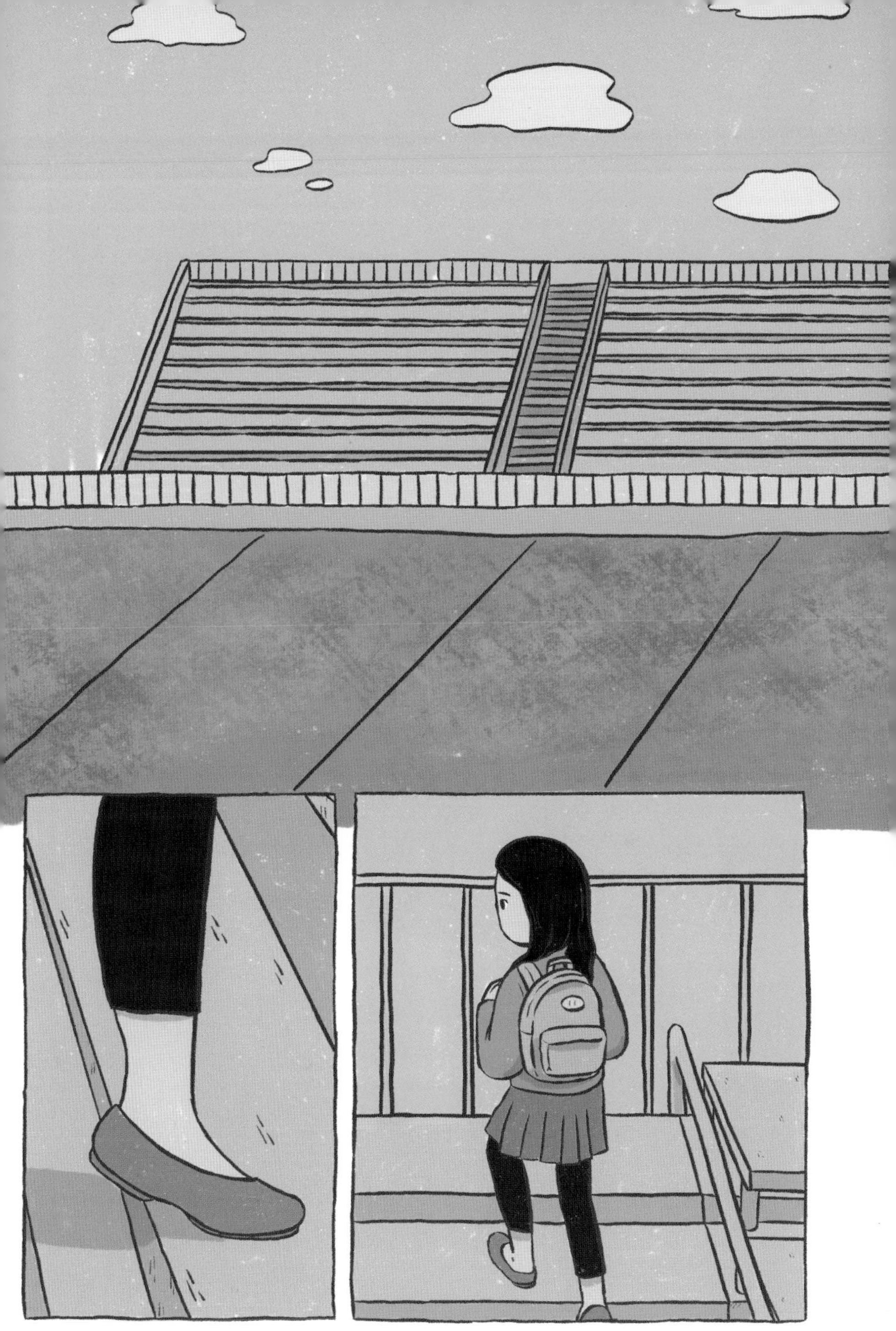

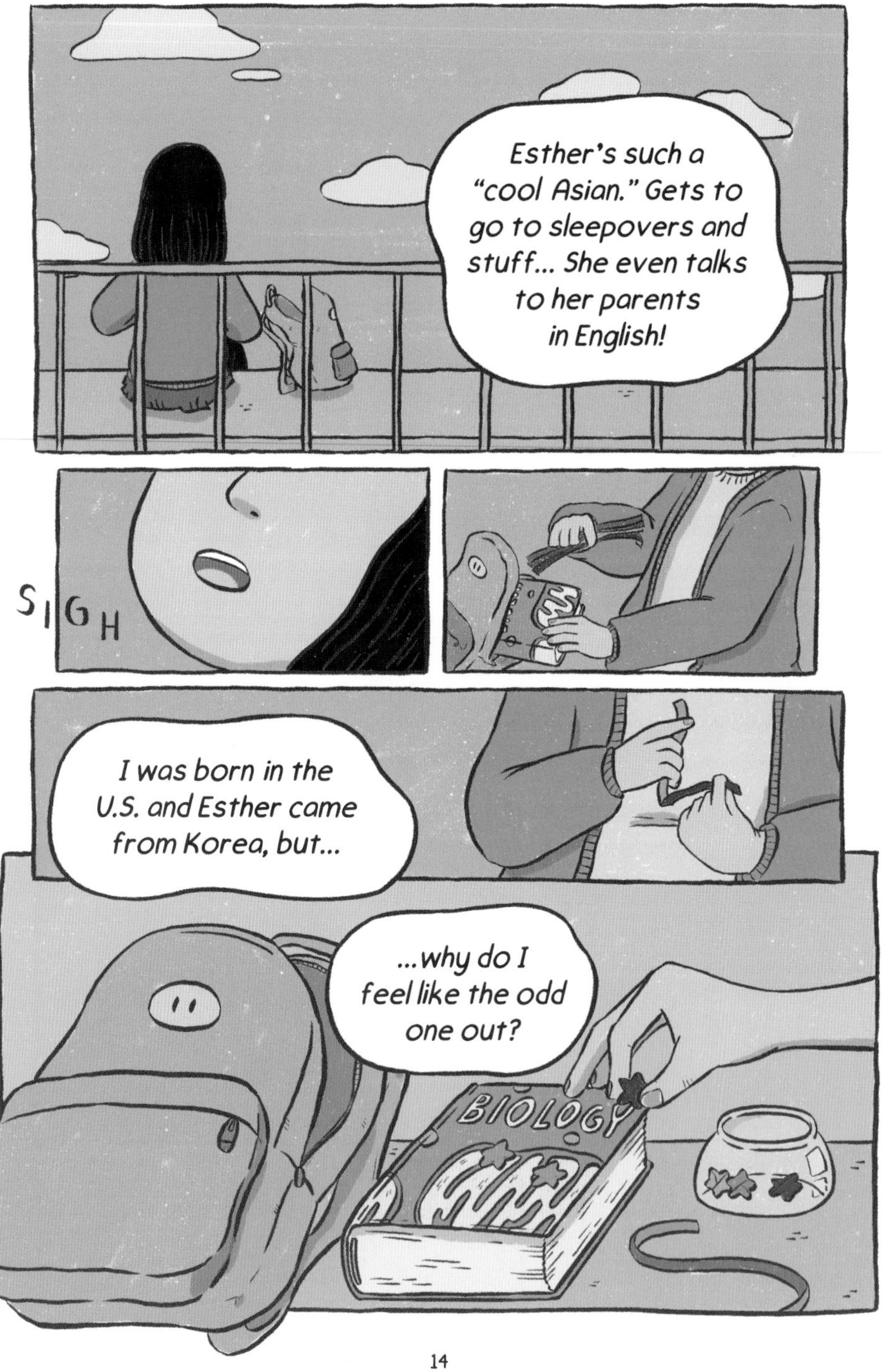
Esther's such a "cool Asian." Gets to go to sleepovers and stuff... She even talks to her parents in English!
SIGH
I was born in the U.S. and Esther came from Korea, but...
...why do I feel like the odd one out?
BIOLOGY

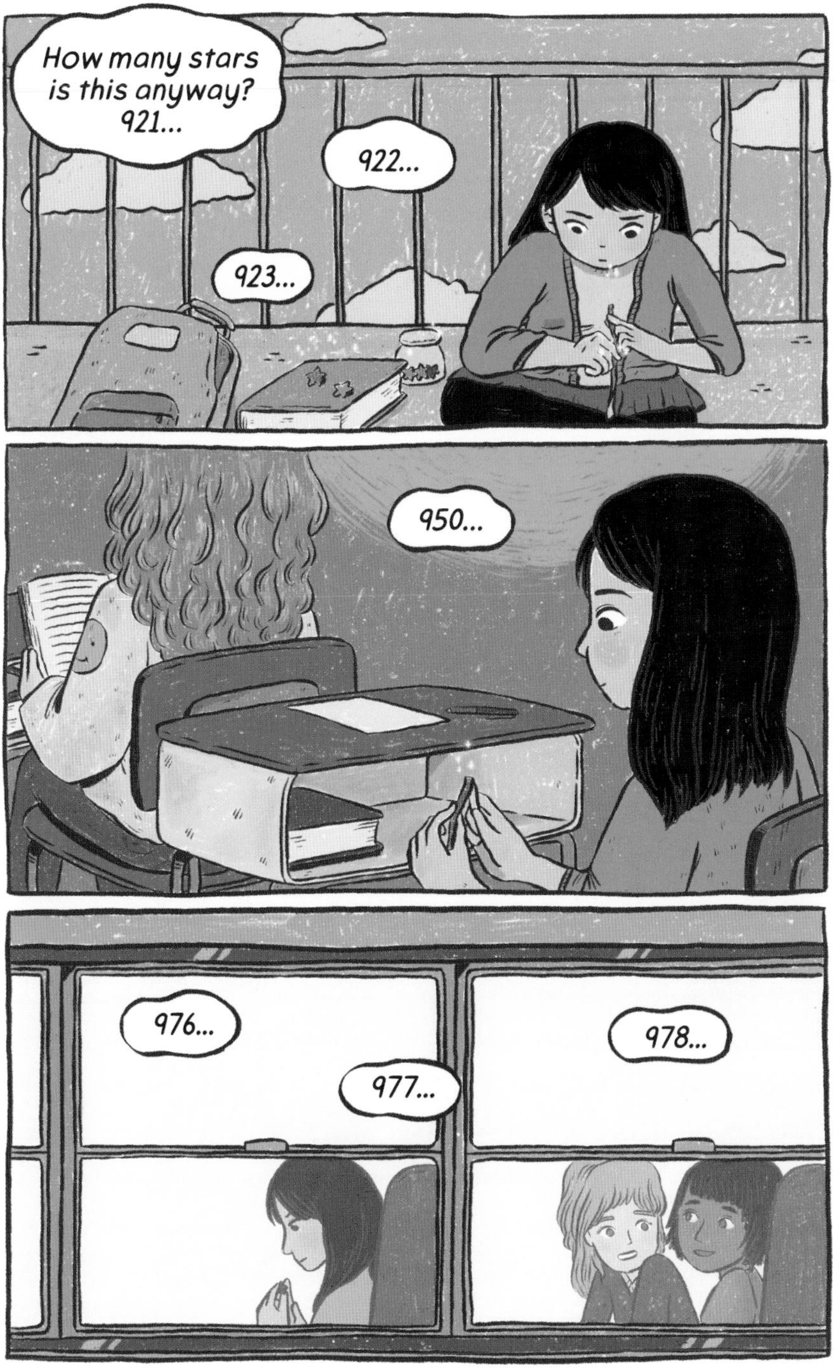
How many stars is this anyway? 921...
922...
923...
950...
976...
977...
978...

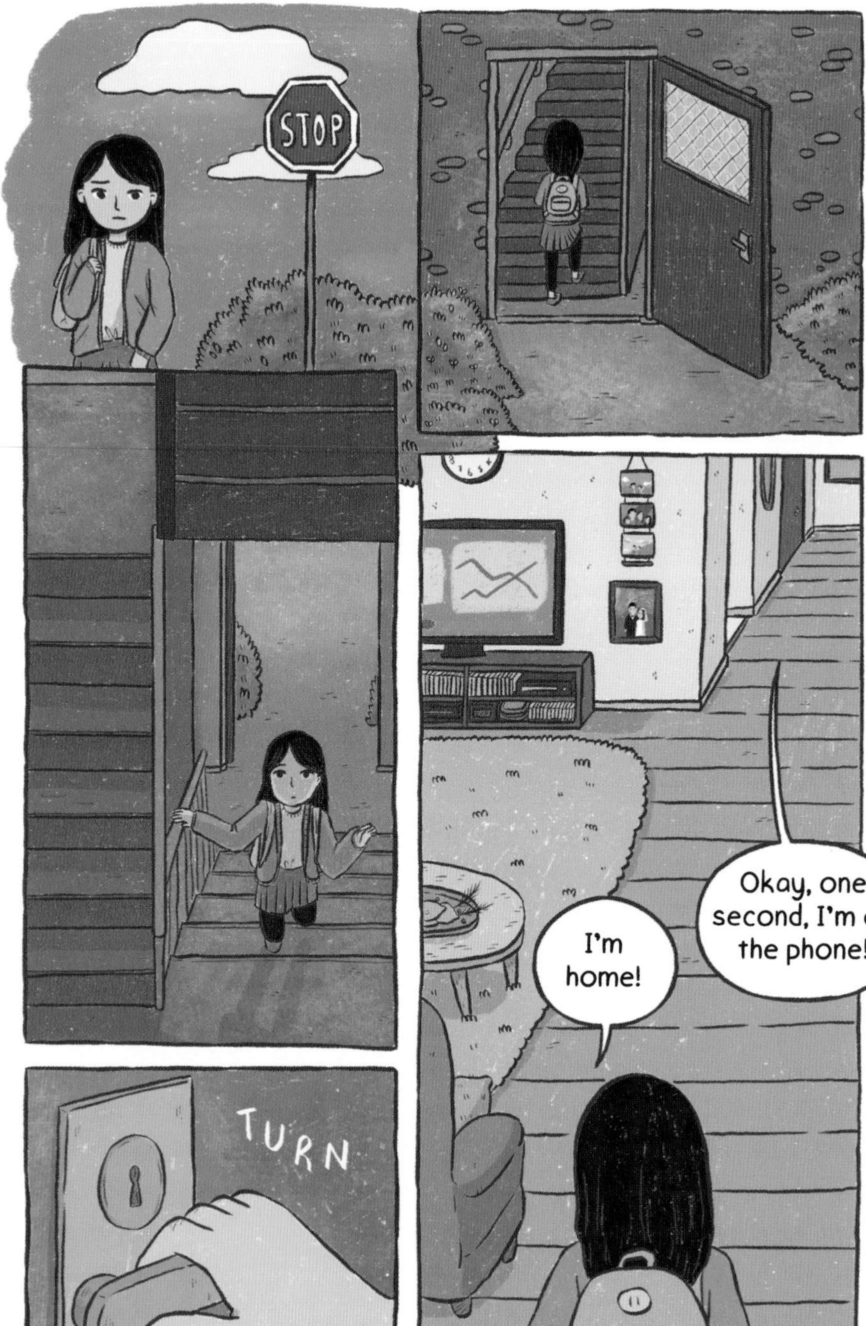
STOP
TURN
I'm home!
Okay, one second, I'm on the phone!

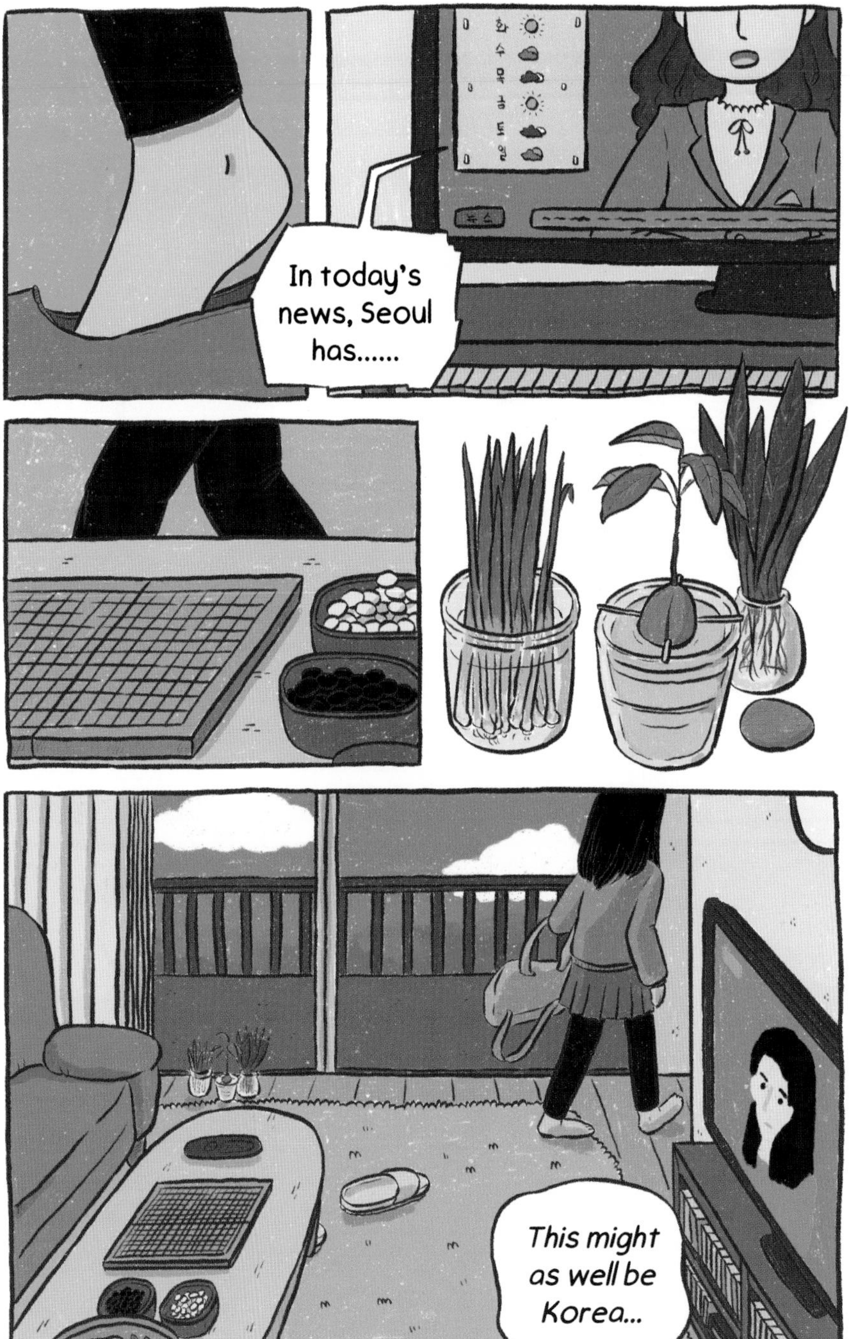

화
수
목
금
토
일
뉴스
In today's news, Seoul has......
This might as well be Korea...

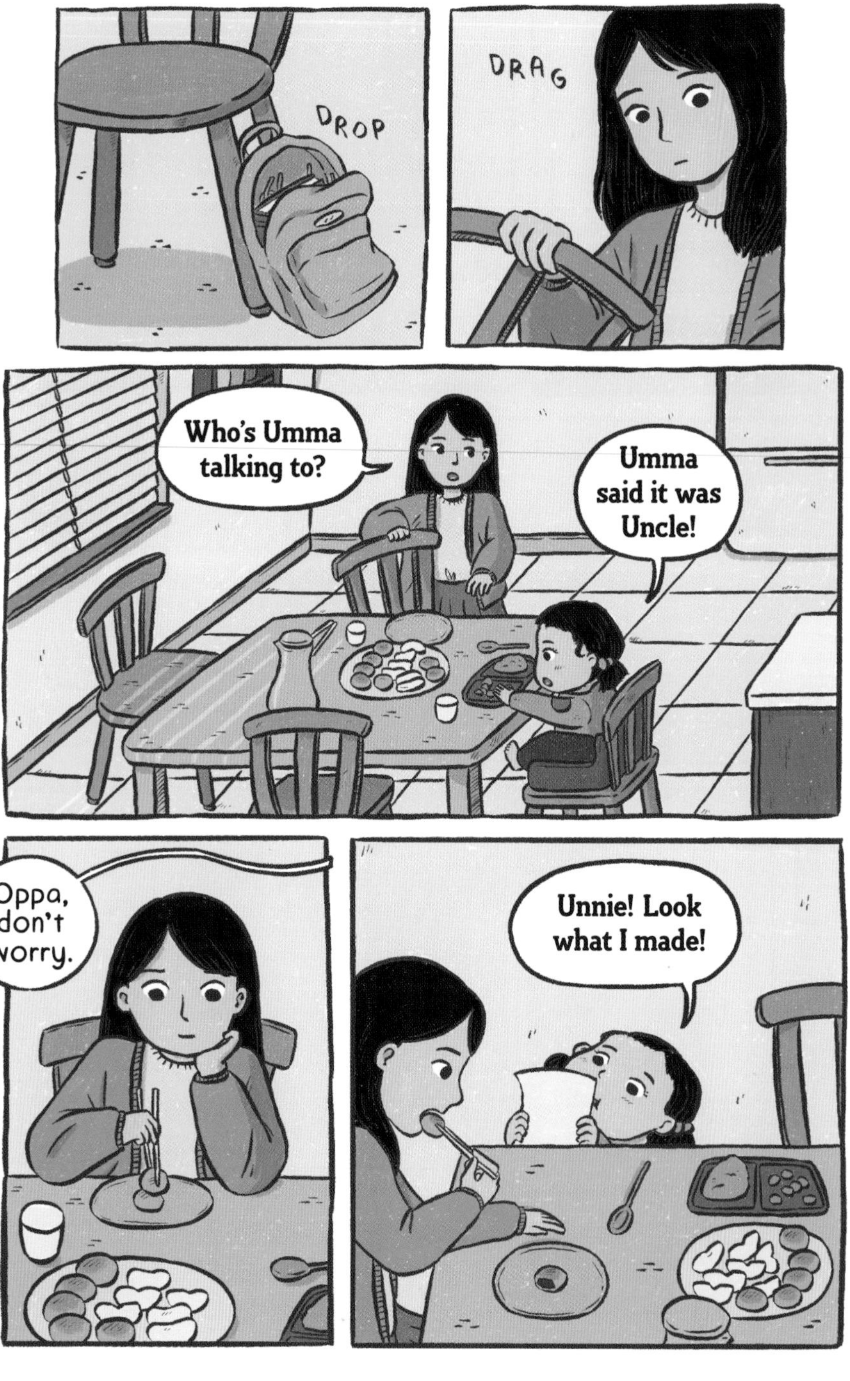
DROP
DRAG
Who's Umma talking to?
Umma said it was Uncle!
Oppa, don't worry.
Unnie! Look what I made!

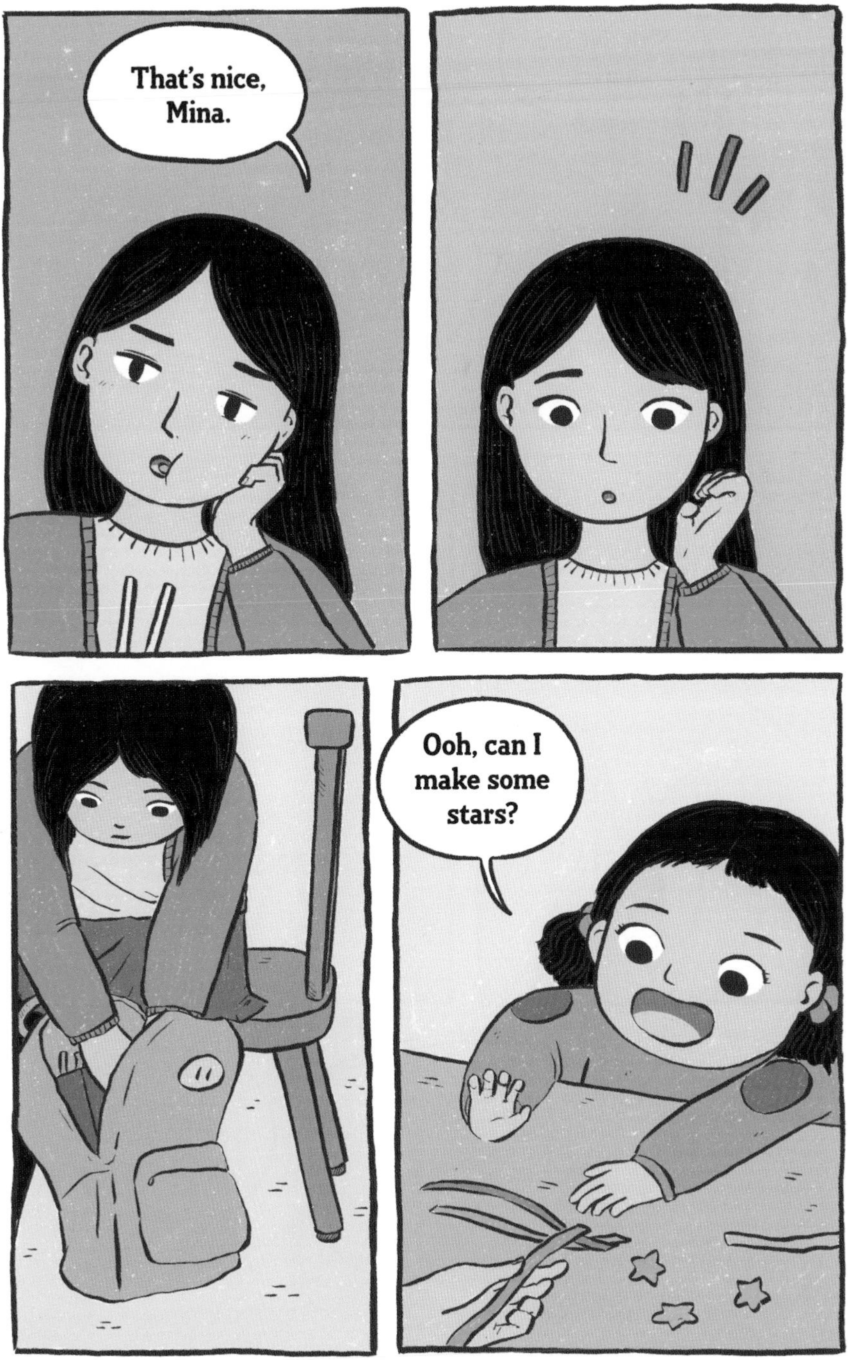
That's nice, Mina.
Ooh, can I make some stars?

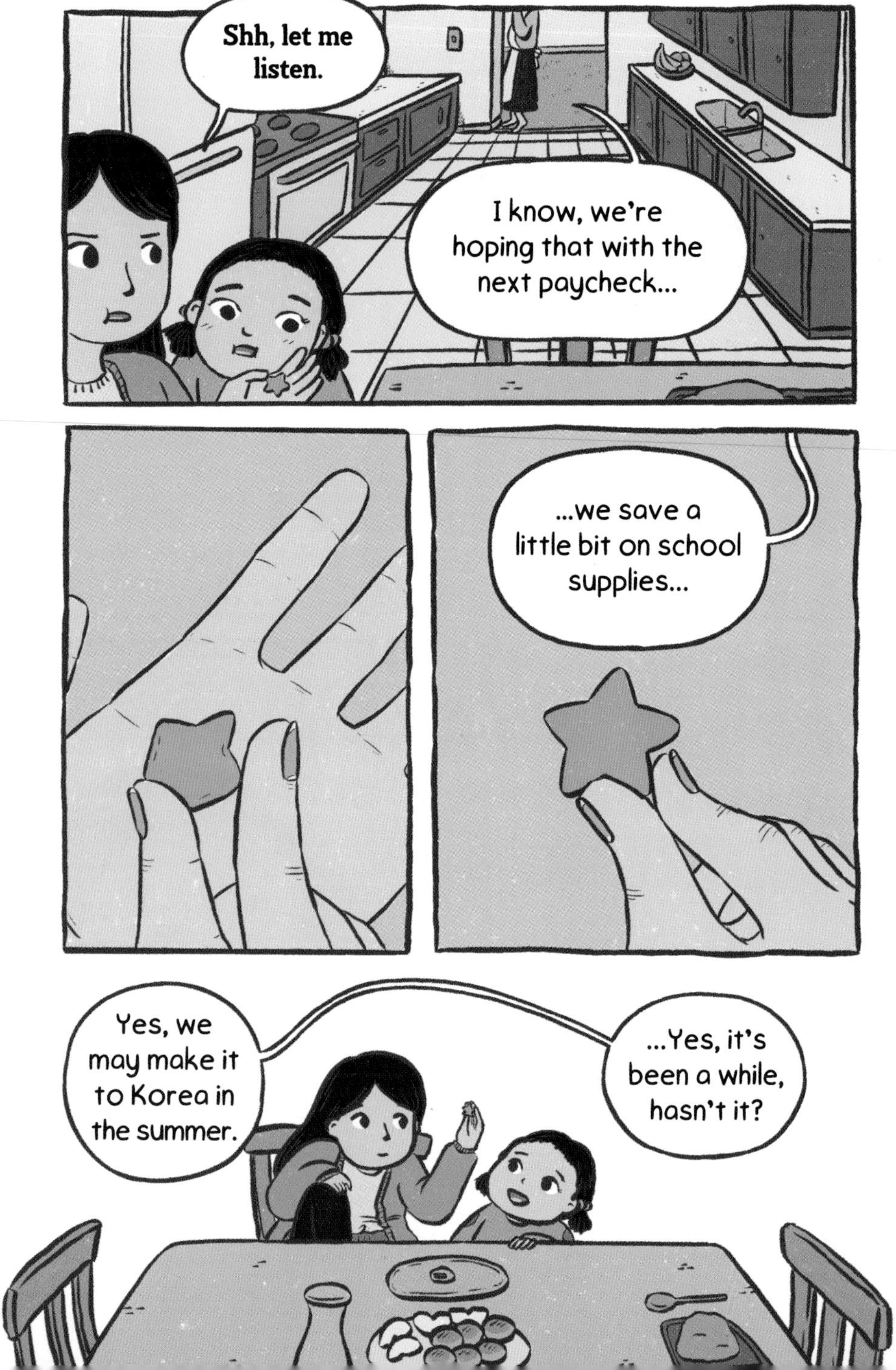
Shh, let me listen.
I know, we're hoping that with the next paycheck...
...we save a little bit on school supplies...
Yes, we may make it to Korea in the summer.
...Yes, it's been a while, hasn't it?

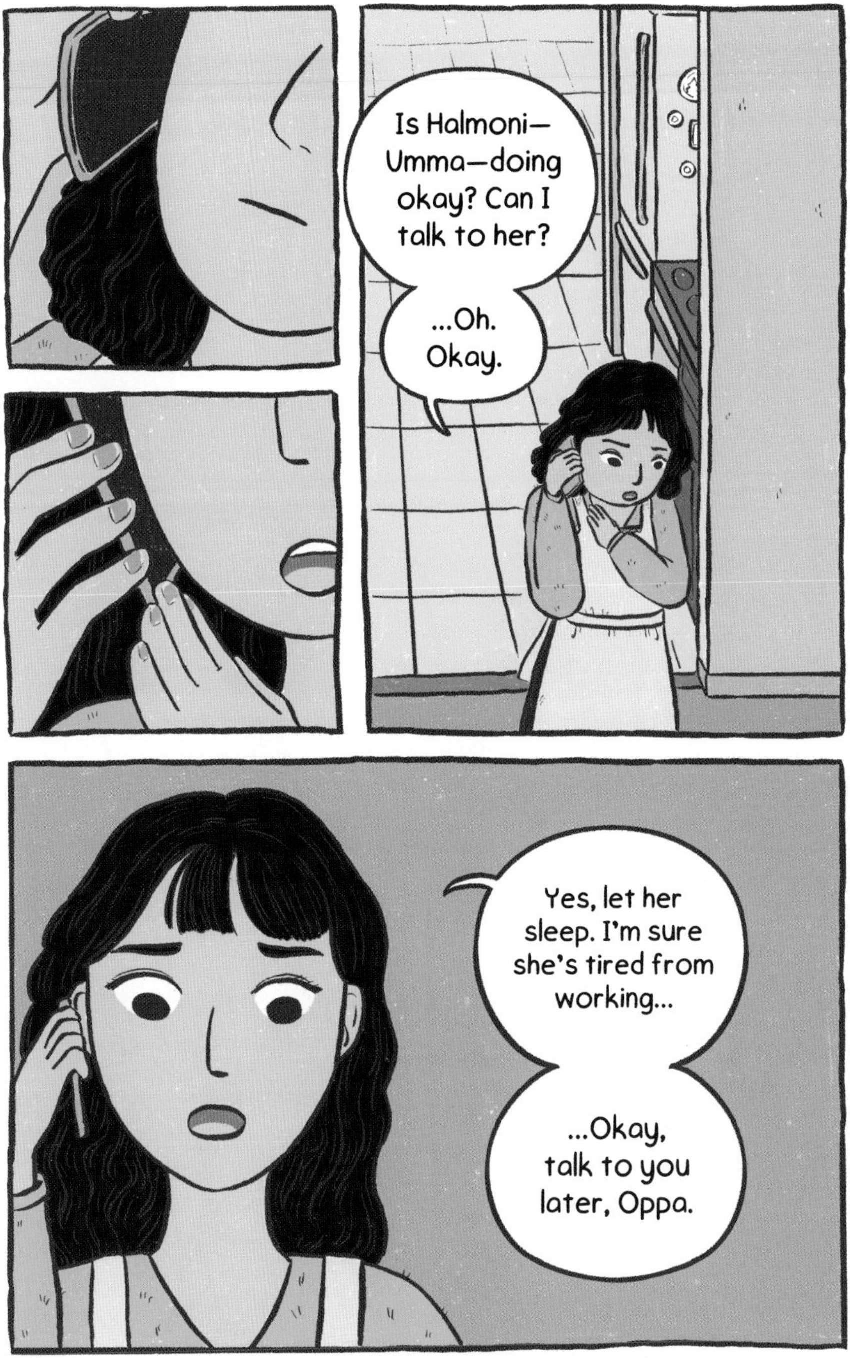
Is Halmoni—Umma—doing okay? Can I talk to her?
...Oh. Okay.
Yes, let her sleep. I'm sure she's tired from working...
...Okay, talk to you later, Oppa.

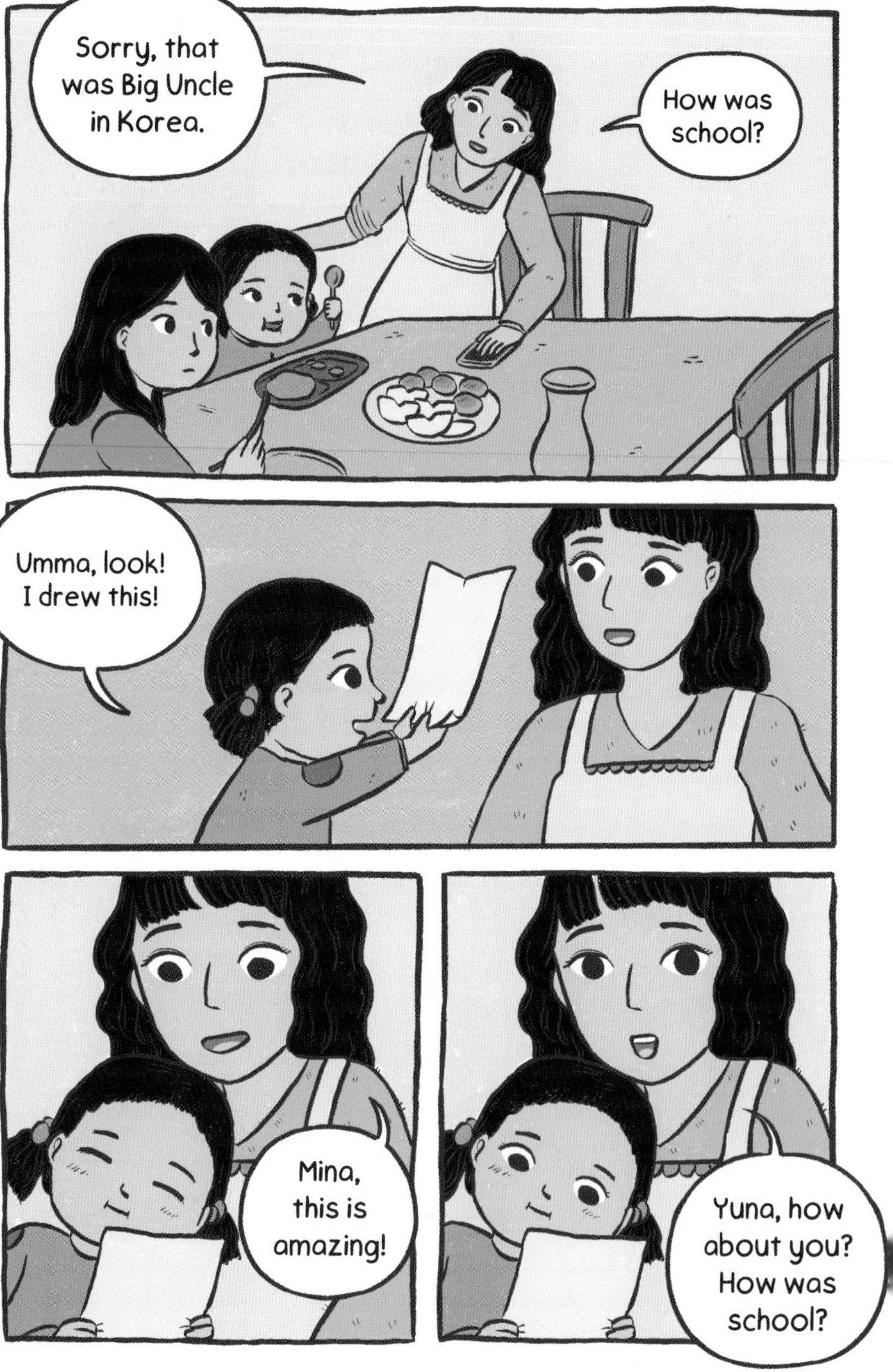
Sorry, that was Big Uncle in Korea.
How was school?
Umma, look! I drew this!
Mina, this is amazing!
Yuna, how about you? How was school?

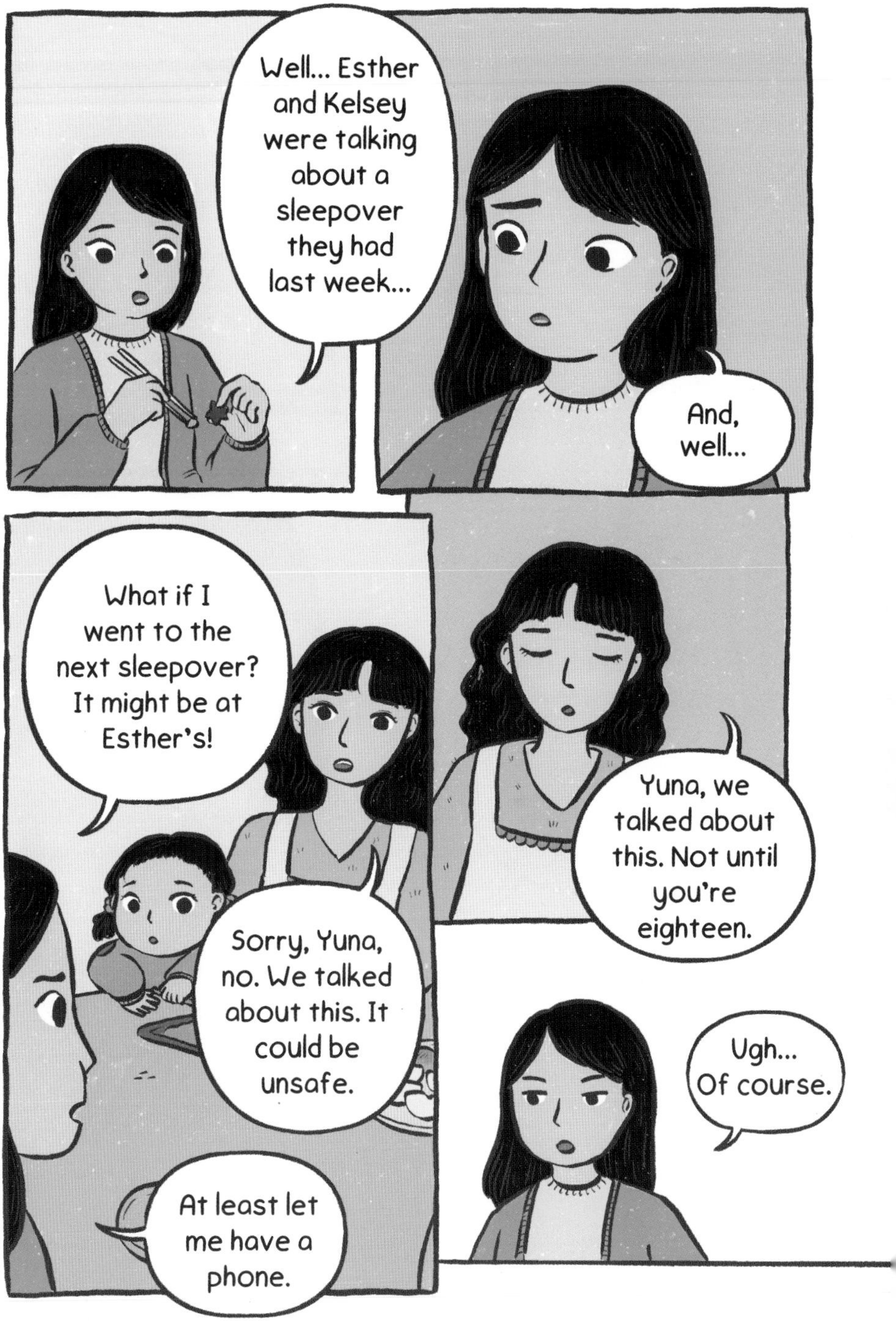
Well... Esther and Kelsey were talking about a sleepover they had last week...
And, well...
What if I went to the next sleepover? It might be at Esther's!
Yuna, we talked about this. Not until you're eighteen.
Sorry, Yuna, no. We talked about this. It could be unsafe.
Ugh... Of course.
At least let me have a phone.

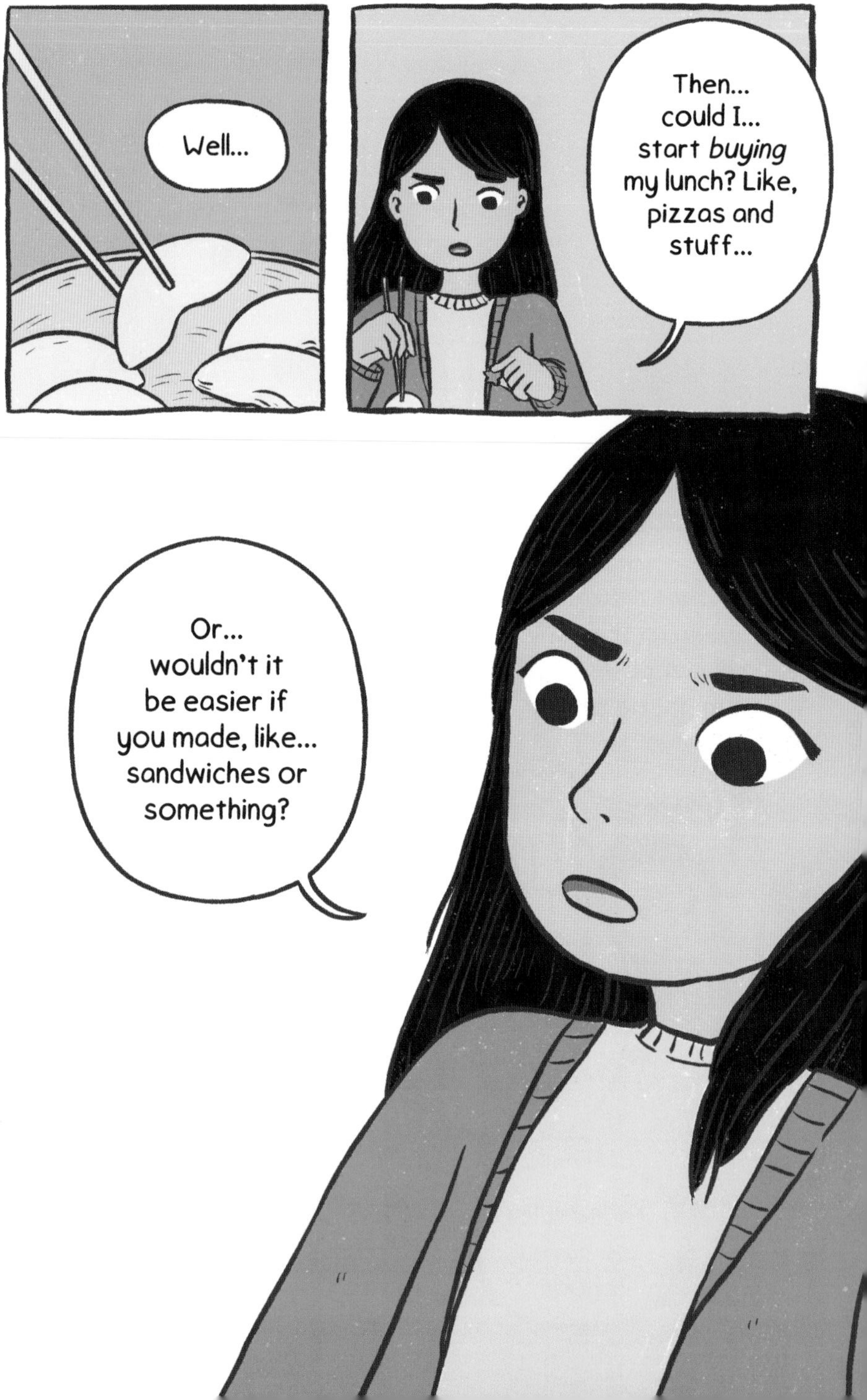
Well...
Then... could I... start *buying* my lunch? Like, pizzas and stuff...
Or... wouldn't it be easier if you made, like... sandwiches or something?

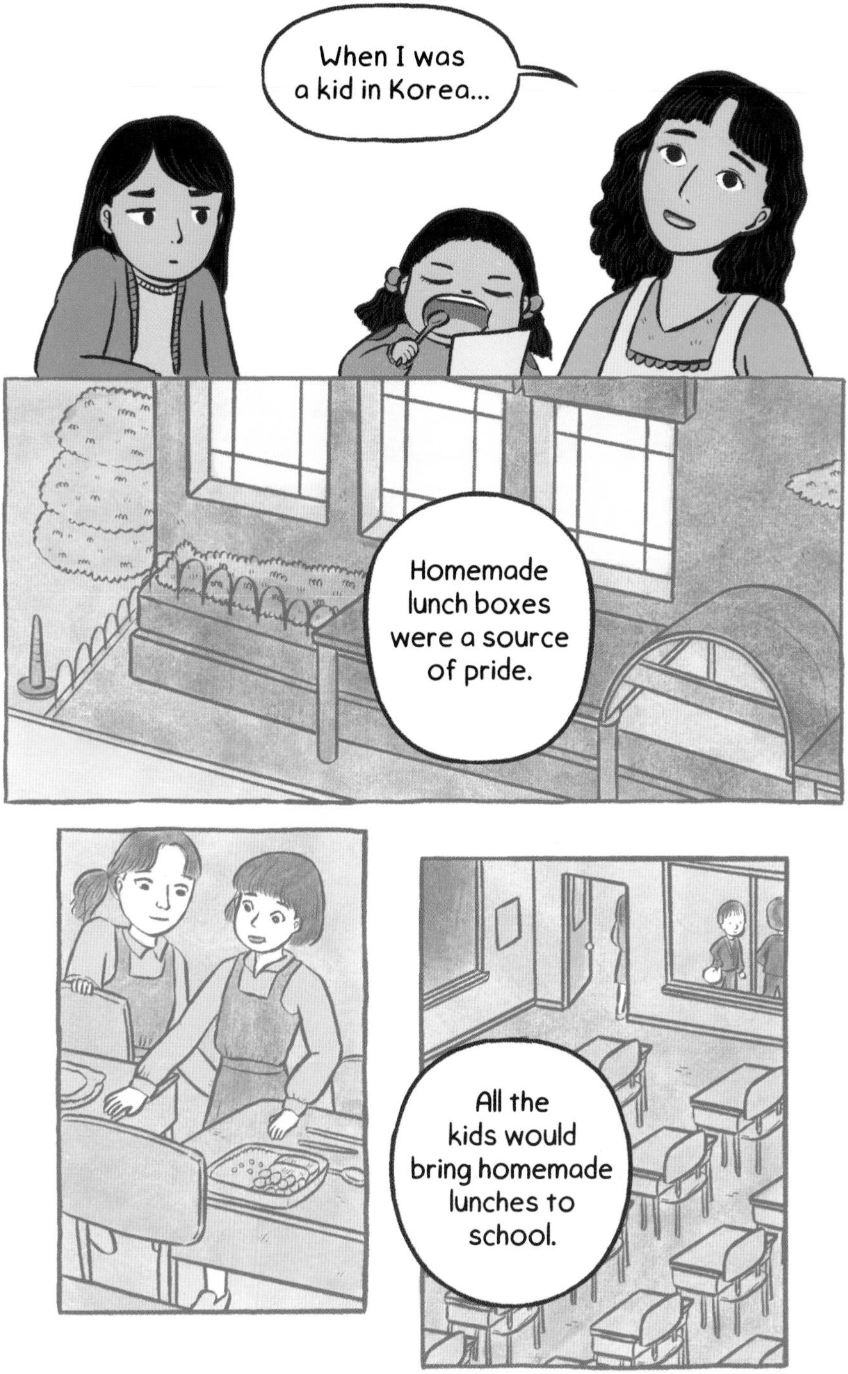
When I was a kid in Korea...
Homemade lunch boxes were a source of pride.
All the kids would bring homemade lunches to school.

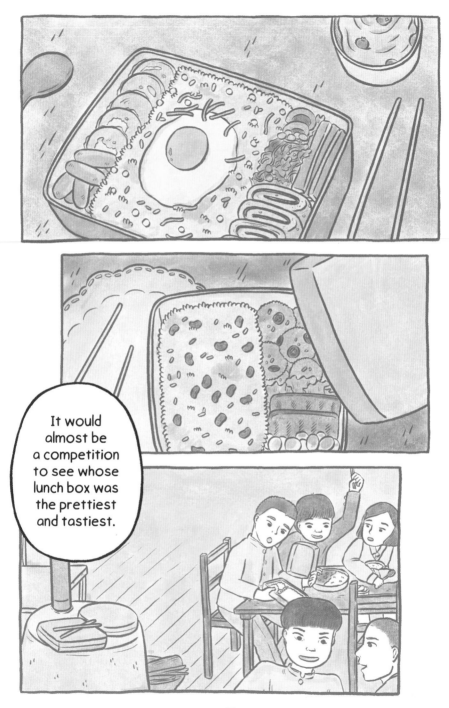

It would almost be a competition to see whose lunch box was the prettiest and tastiest.

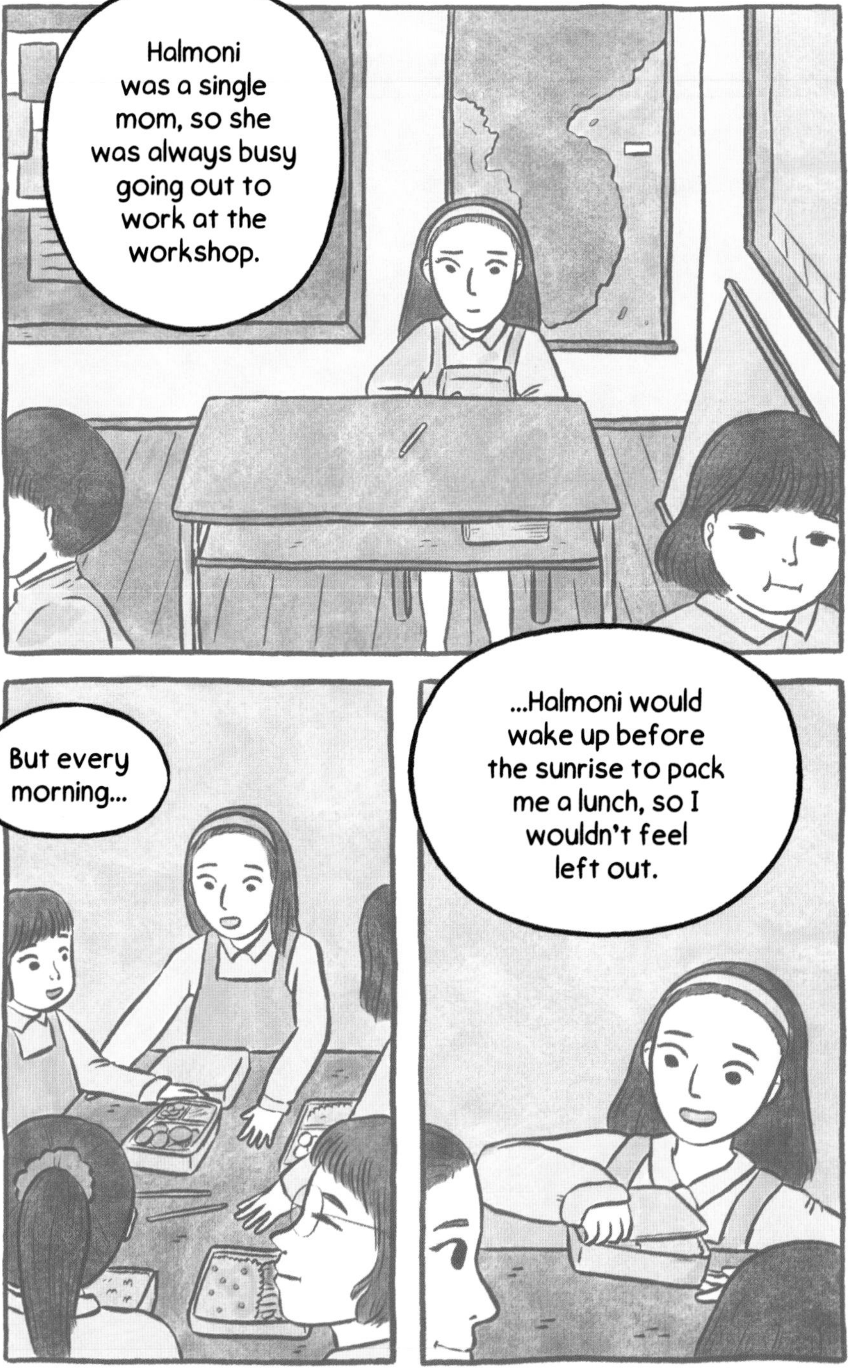
Halmoni was a single mom, so she was always busy going out to work at the workshop.
But every morning...
...Halmoni would wake up before the sunrise to pack me a lunch, so I wouldn't feel left out.

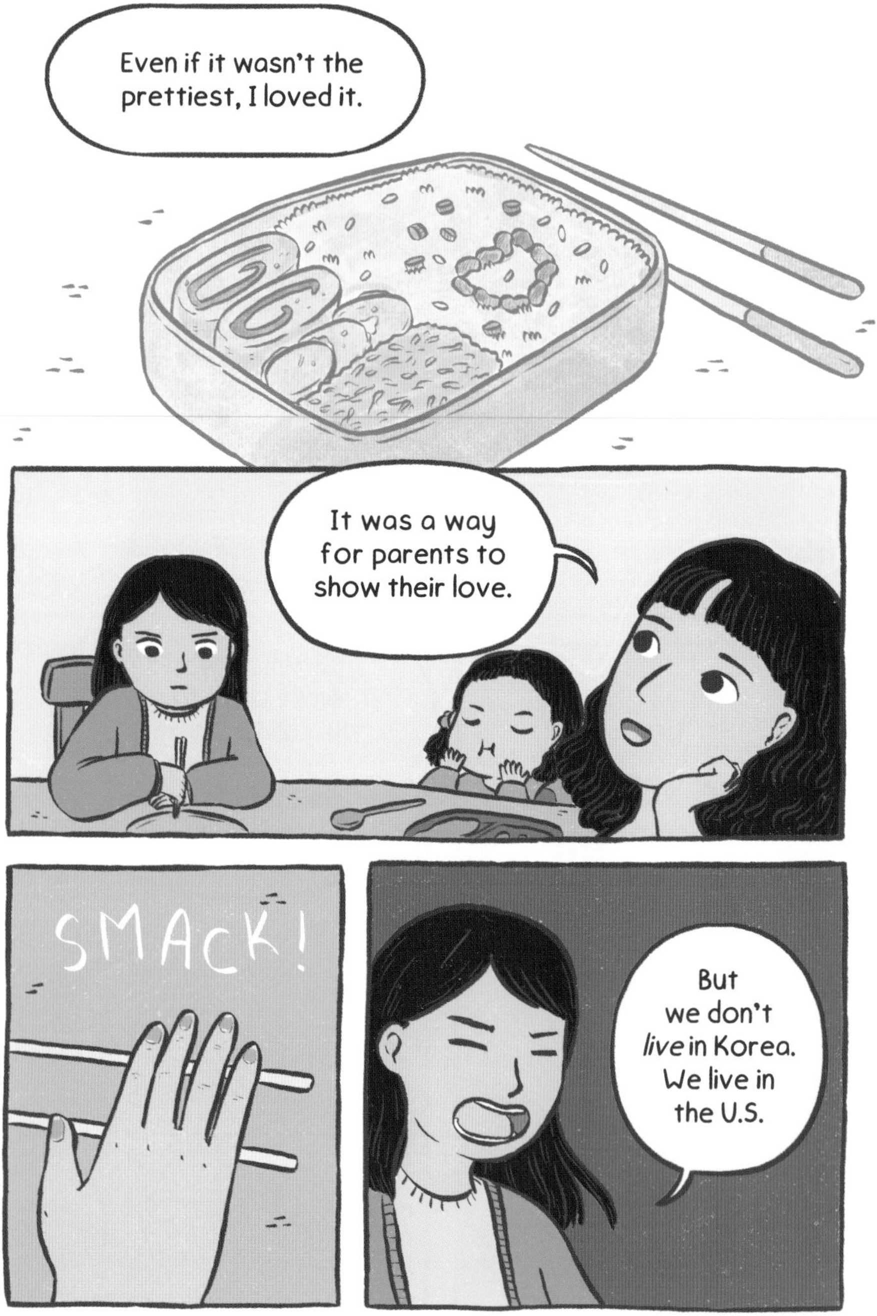
Even if it wasn't the prettiest, I loved it.
It was a way for parents to show their love.
SMACK!
But we don't *live* in Korea. We live in the U.S.

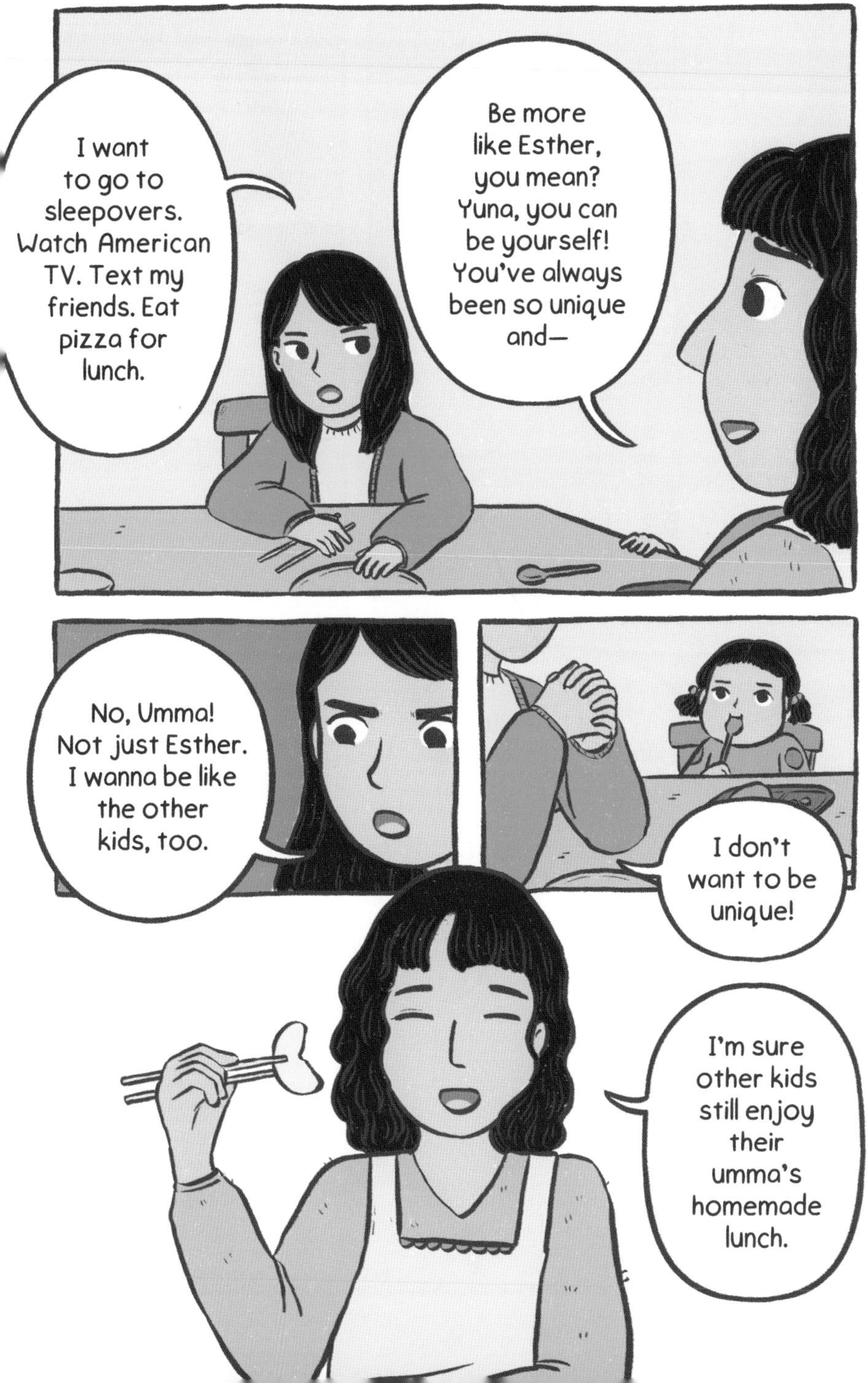
I want to go to sleepovers. Watch American TV. Text my friends. Eat pizza for lunch.
Be more like Esther, you mean? Yuna, you can be yourself! You've always been so unique and—
No, Umma! Not just Esther. I wanna be like the other kids, too.
I don't want to be unique!
I'm sure other kids still enjoy their umma's homemade lunch.

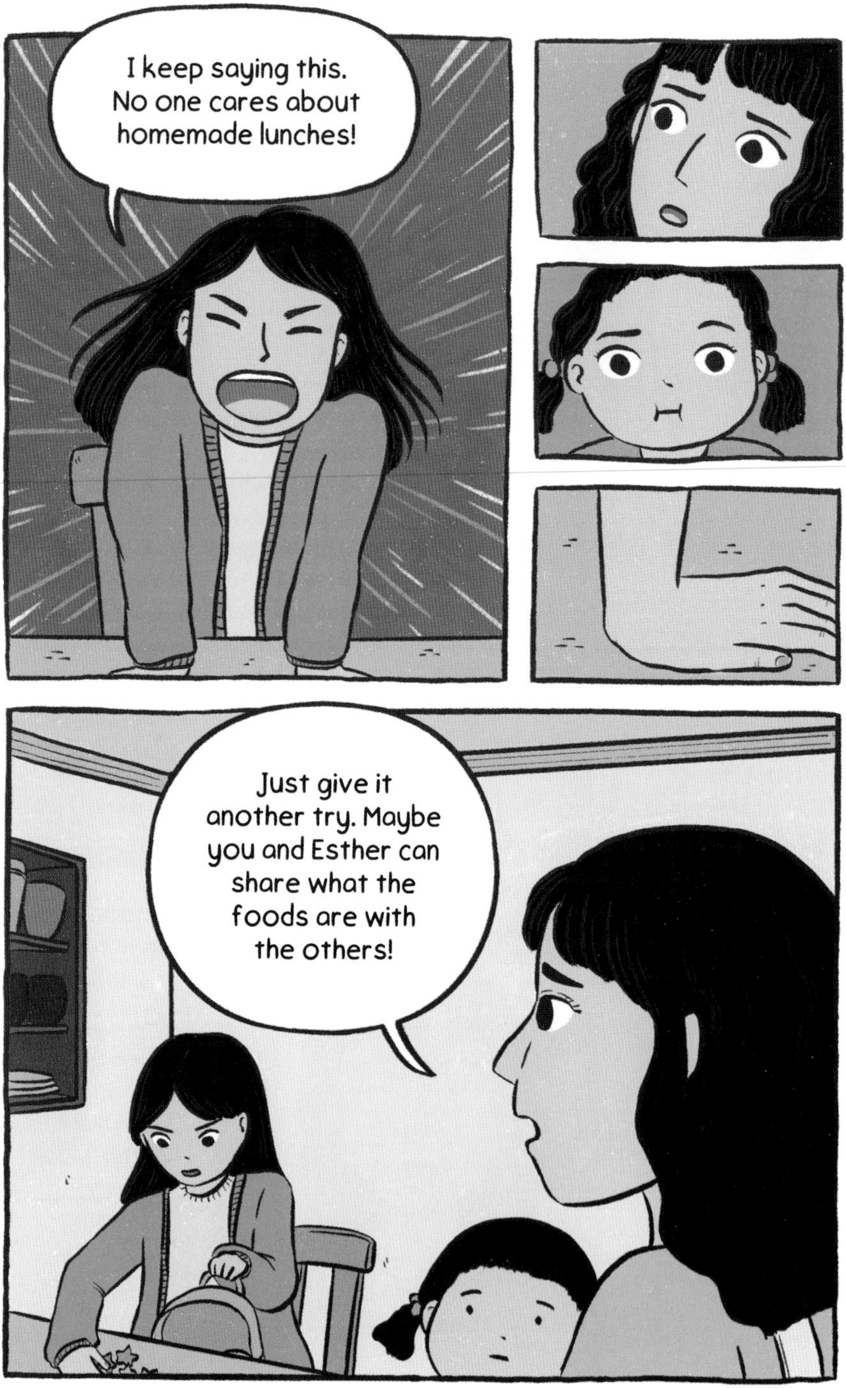
I keep saying this. No one cares about homemade lunches!
Just give it another try. Maybe you and Esther can share what the foods are with the others!

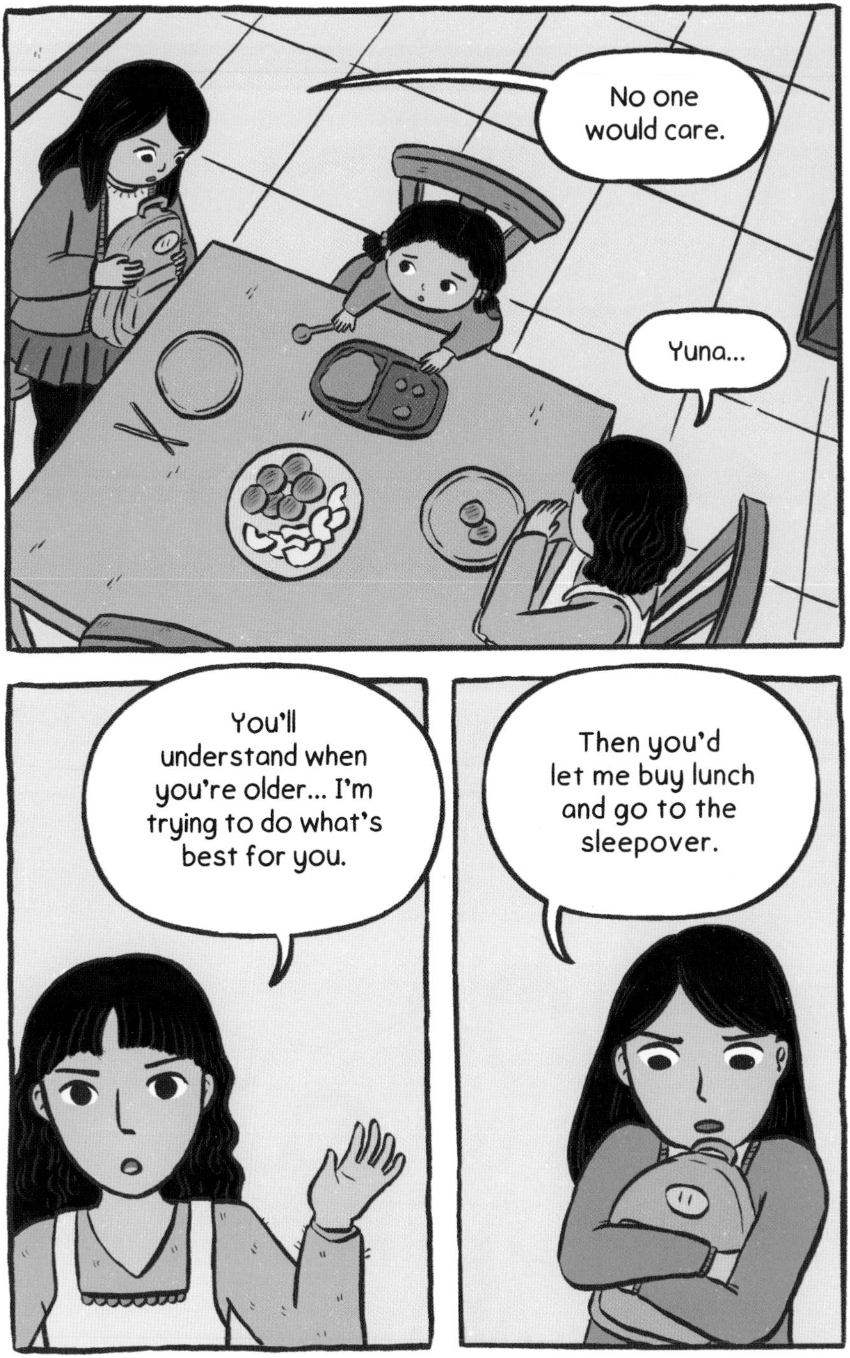
No one would care.
Yuna...
You'll understand when you're older... I'm trying to do what's best for you.
Then you'd let me buy lunch and go to the sleepover.

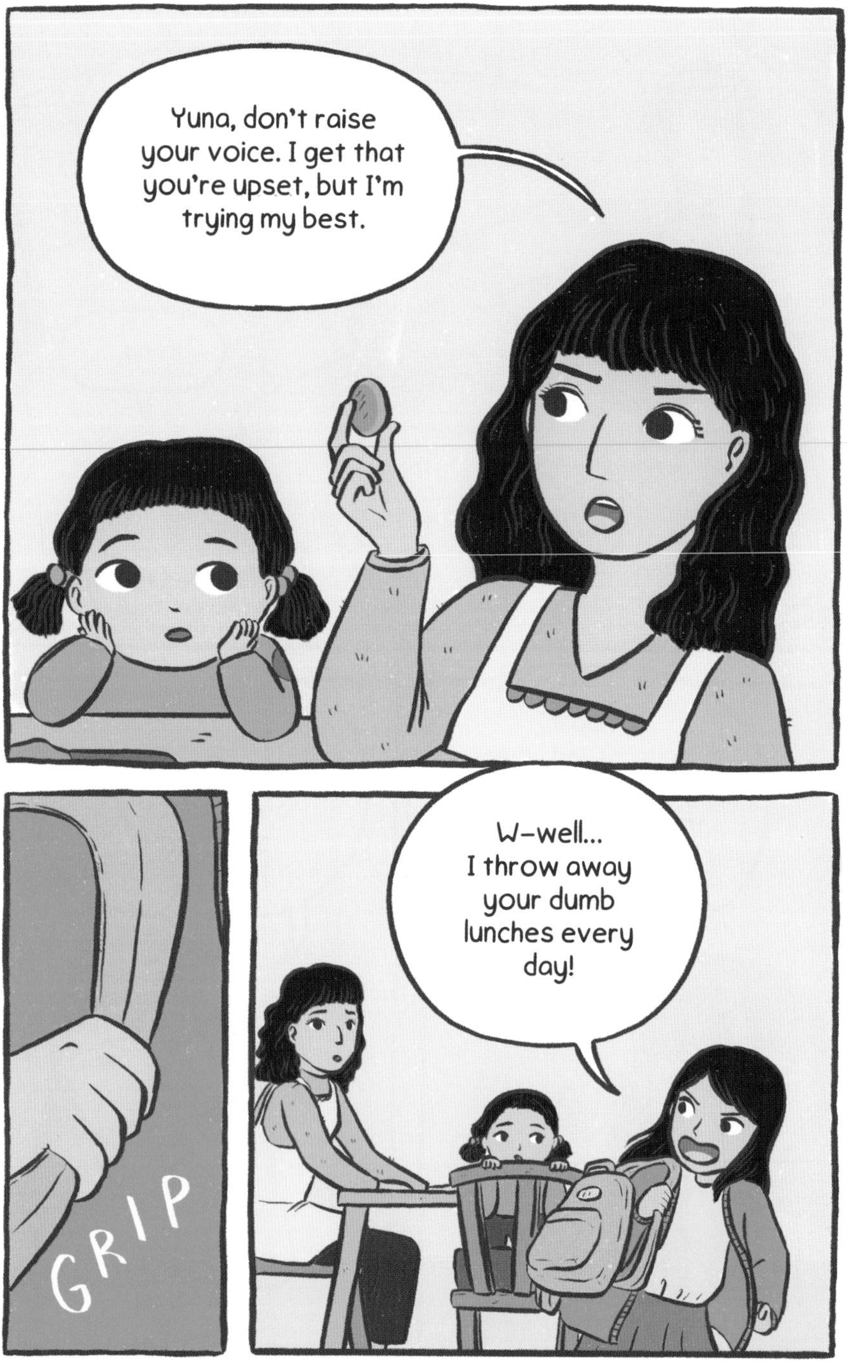
Yuna, don't raise your voice. I get that you're upset, but I'm trying my best.
GRIP
W-well... I throw away your dumb lunches every day!

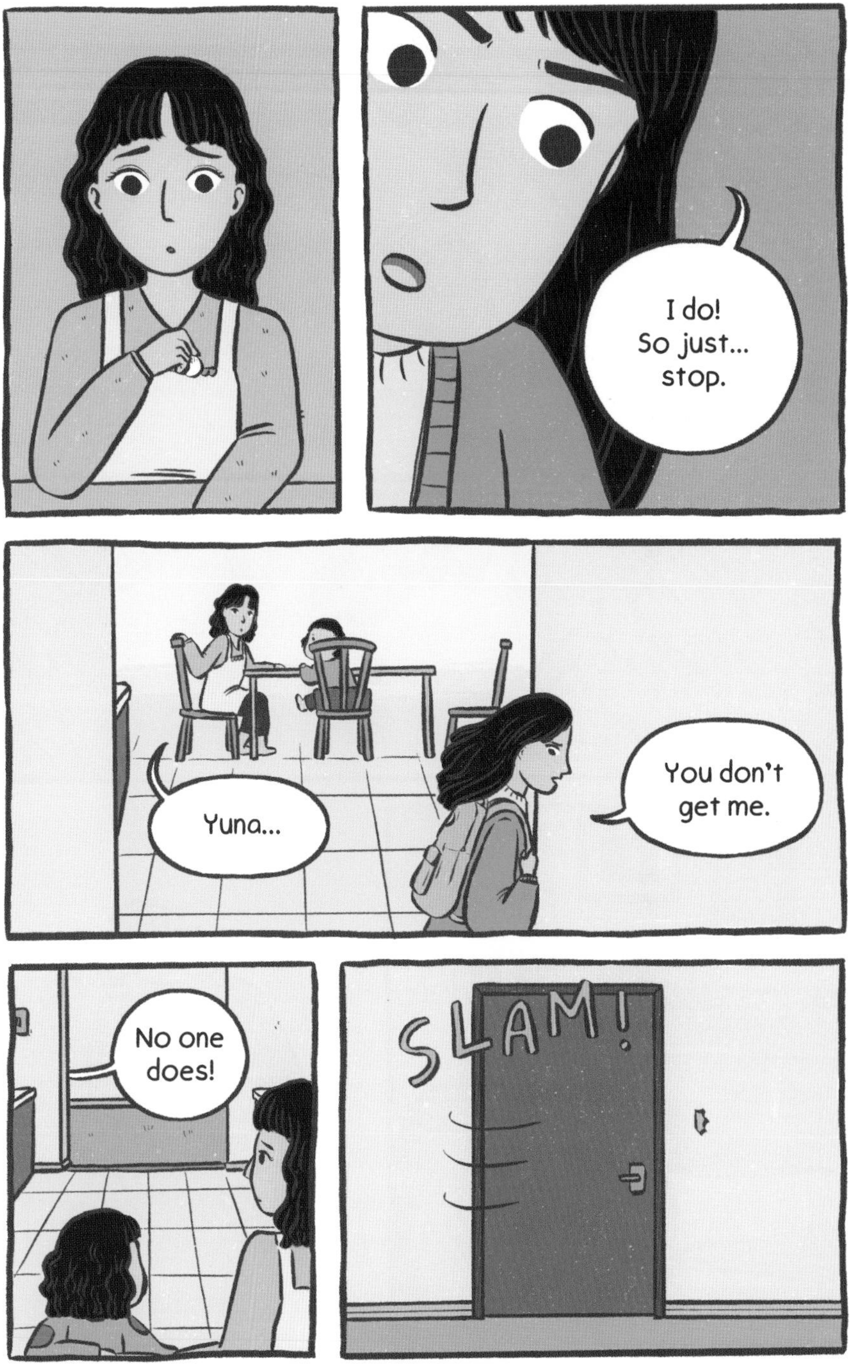
I do!
So just...
stop.
Yuna...
You don't
get me.
No one
does!
SLAM!

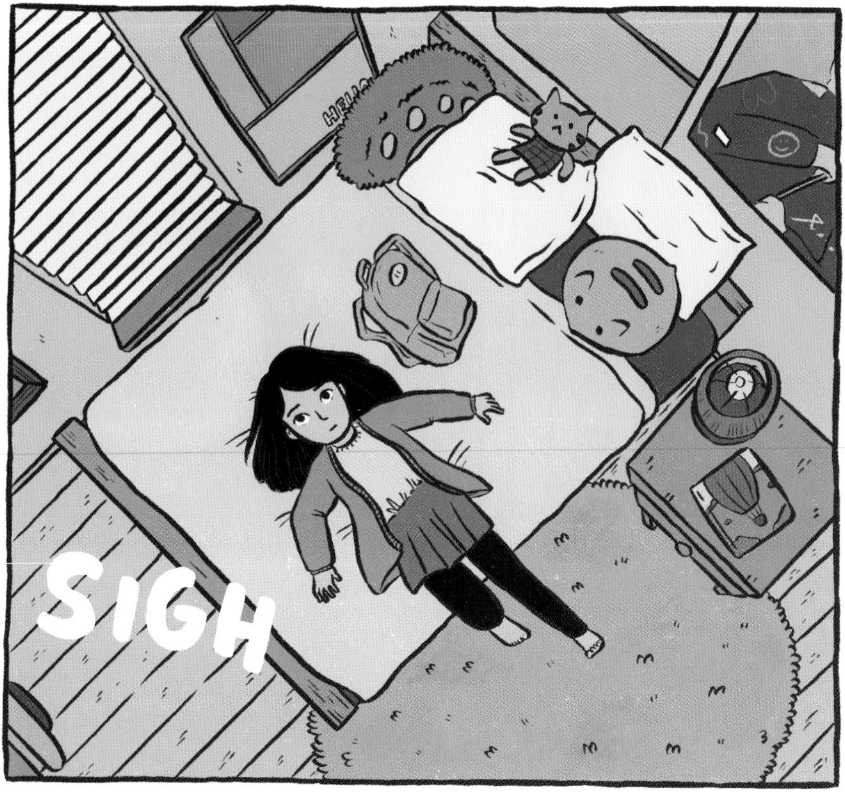
SIGH

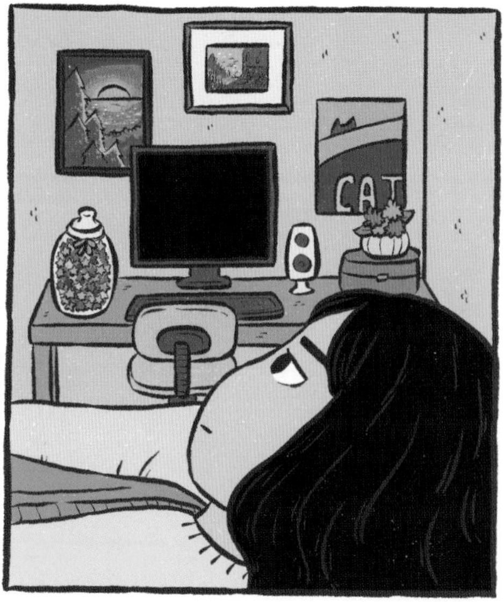
CAT

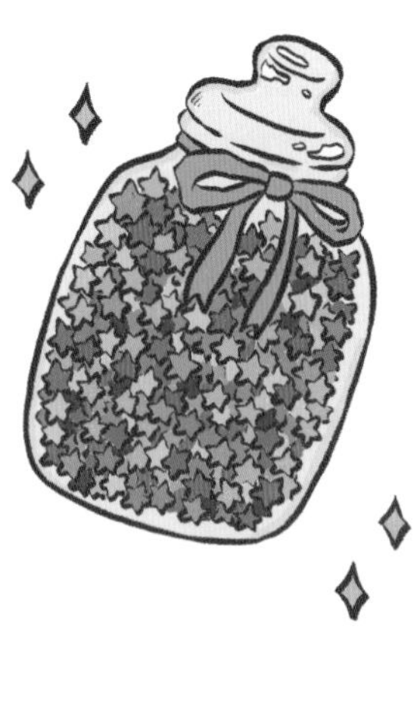

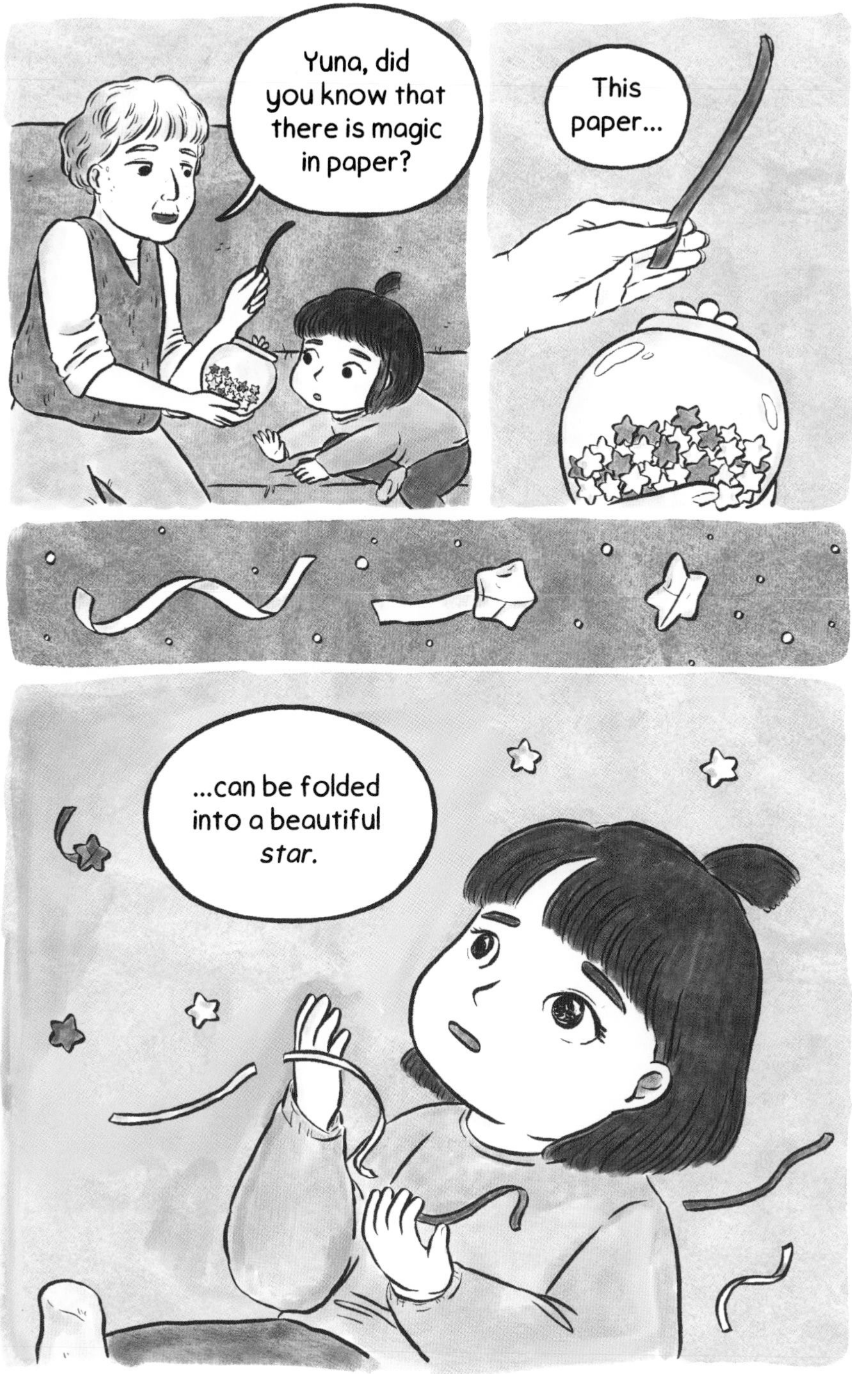
Yuna, did you know that there is magic in paper?
This paper...
...can be folded into a beautiful *star*.

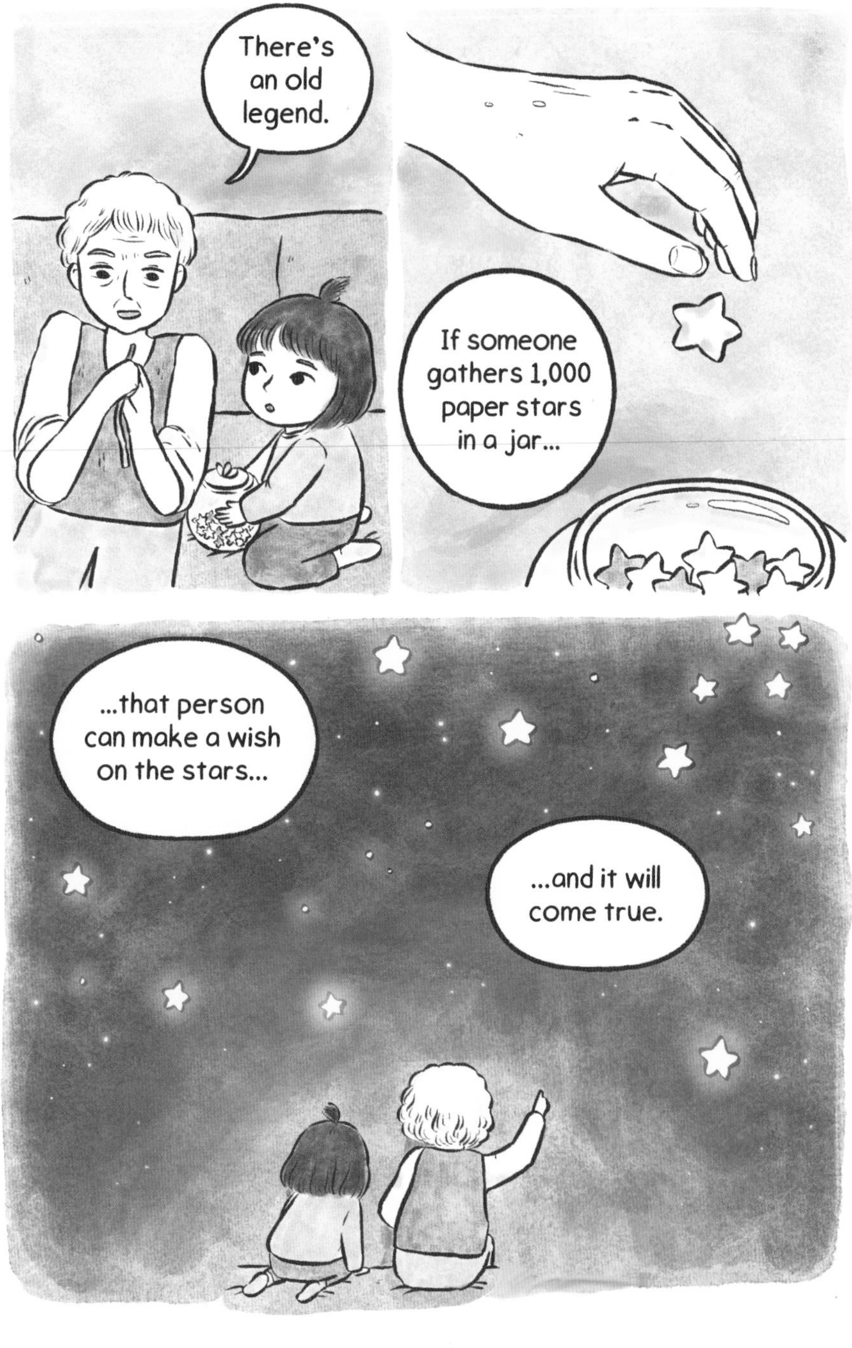
There's an old legend.
If someone gathers 1,000 paper stars in a jar...
...that person can make a wish on the stars...
...and it will come true.

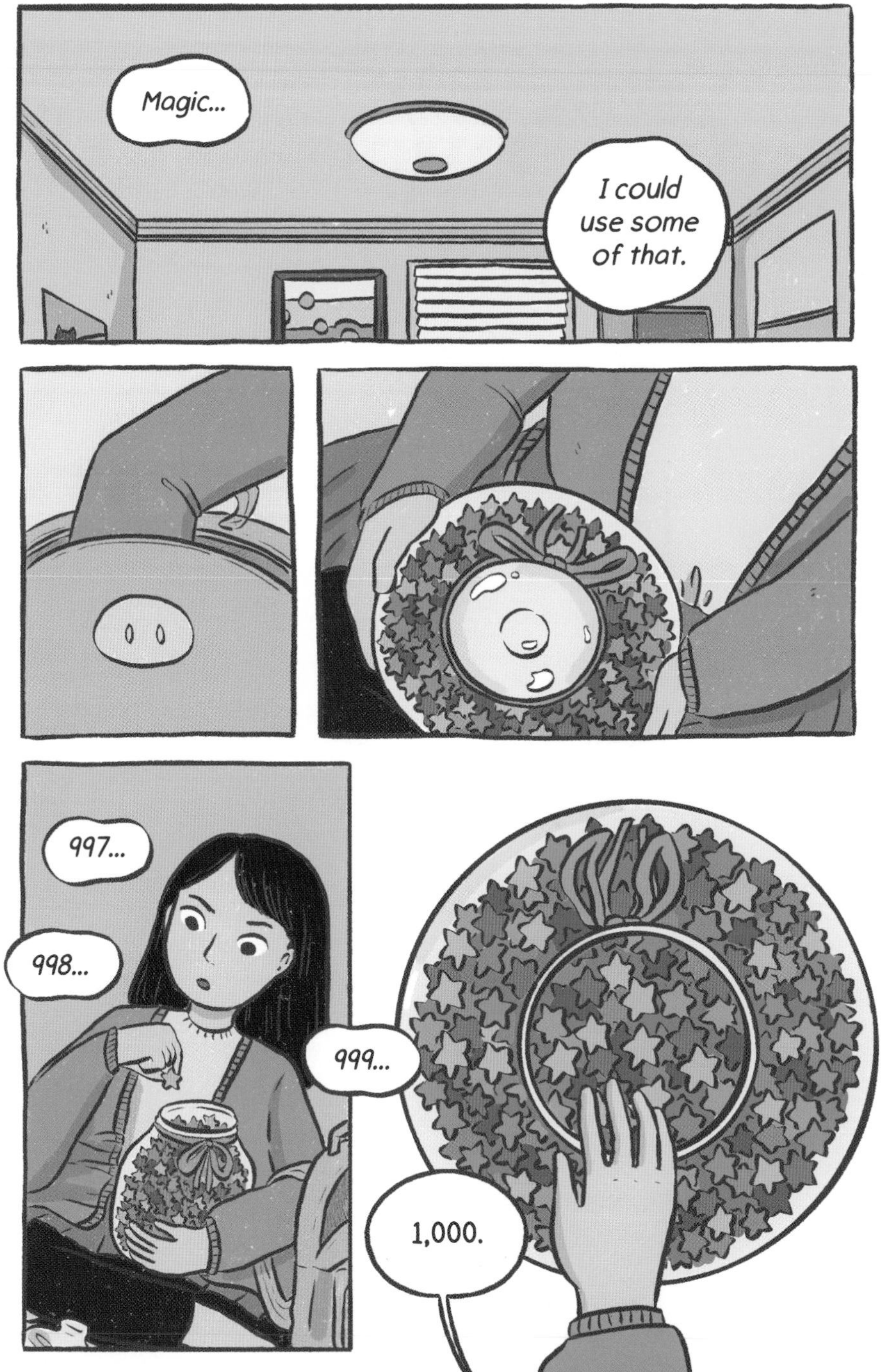
Magic...
I could use some of that.
997...
998...
999...
1,000.

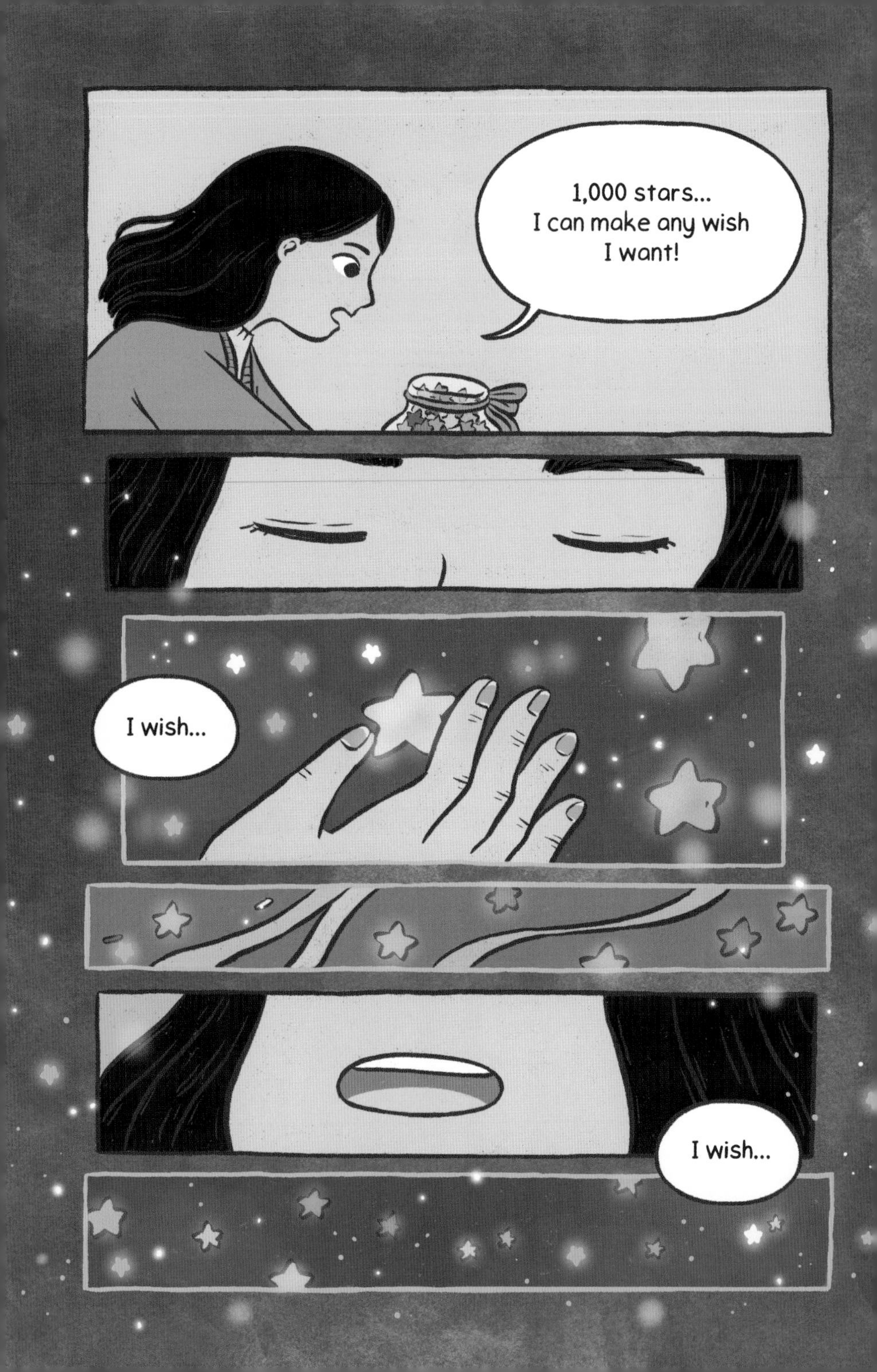
1,000 stars...
I can make any wish
I want!
I wish...
I wish...

I wish...that... we could go back to Korea, and I could be someone else...
...and our family could be normal.
That we would belong. Maybe I could belong...

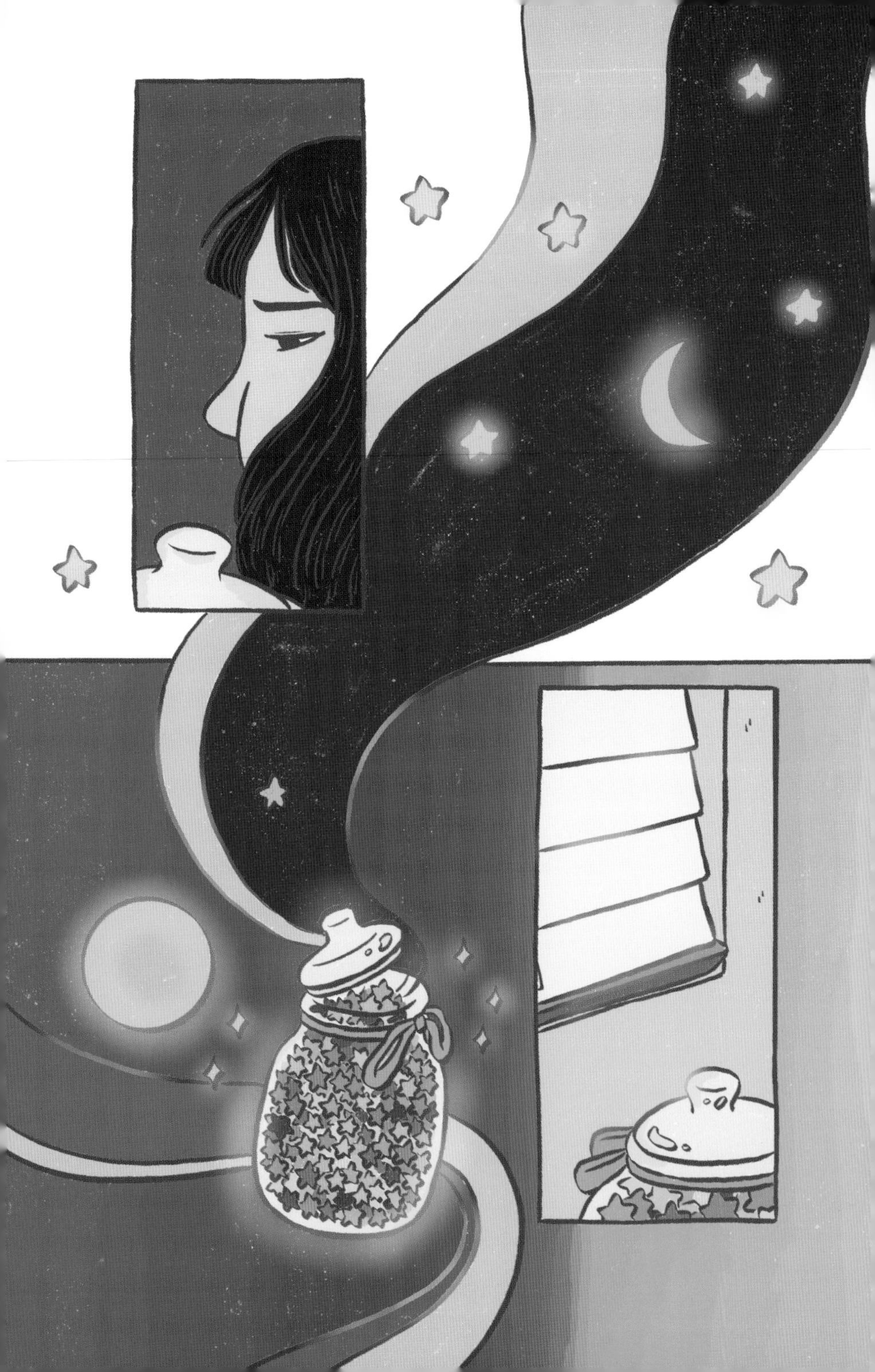

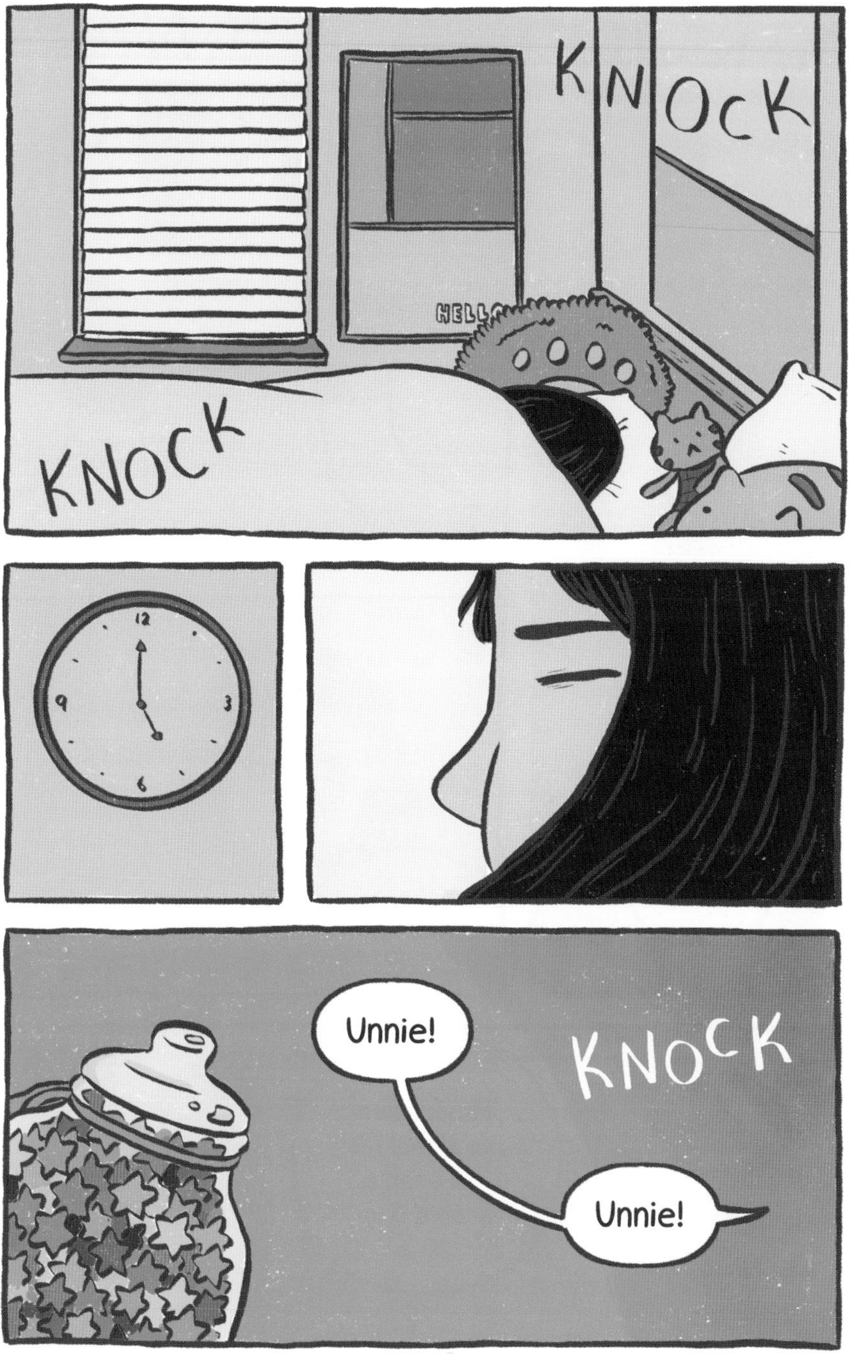
KNOCK
KNOCK
Unnie!
KNOCK
Unnie!

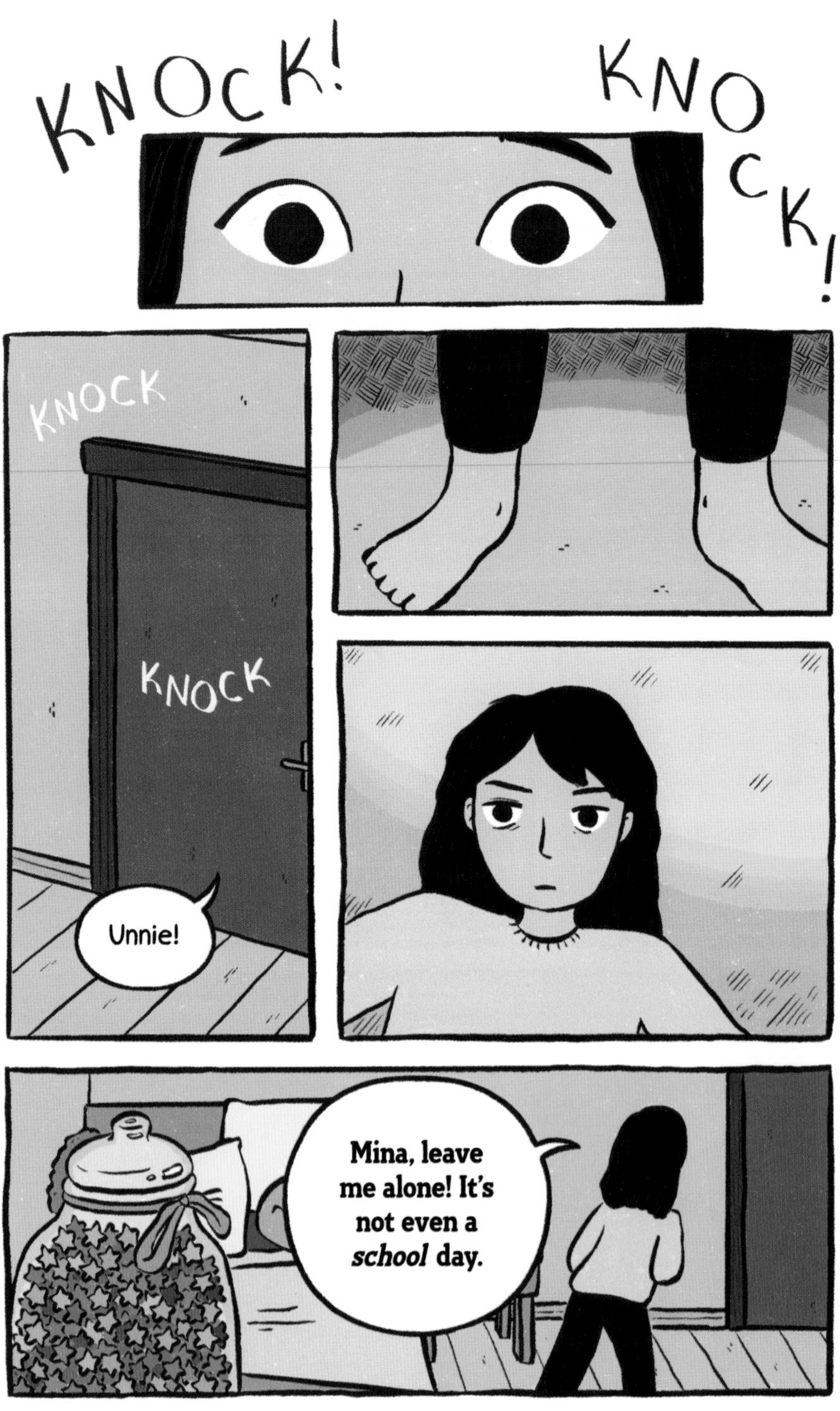
KNOCK! KNOCK!
KNOCK
KNOCK
Unnie!
Mina, leave me alone! It's not even a *school* day.

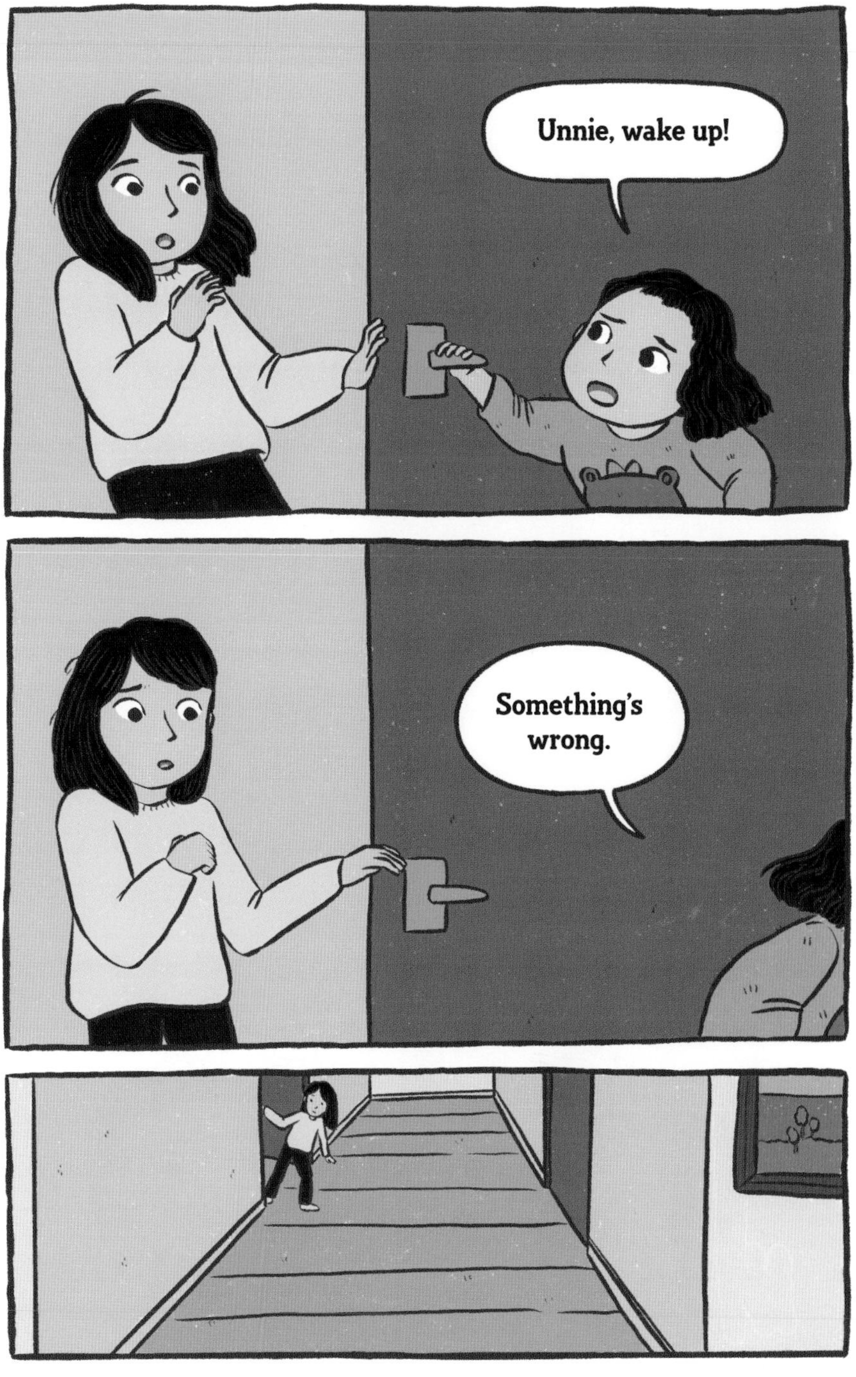
Unnie, wake up!
Something's wrong.

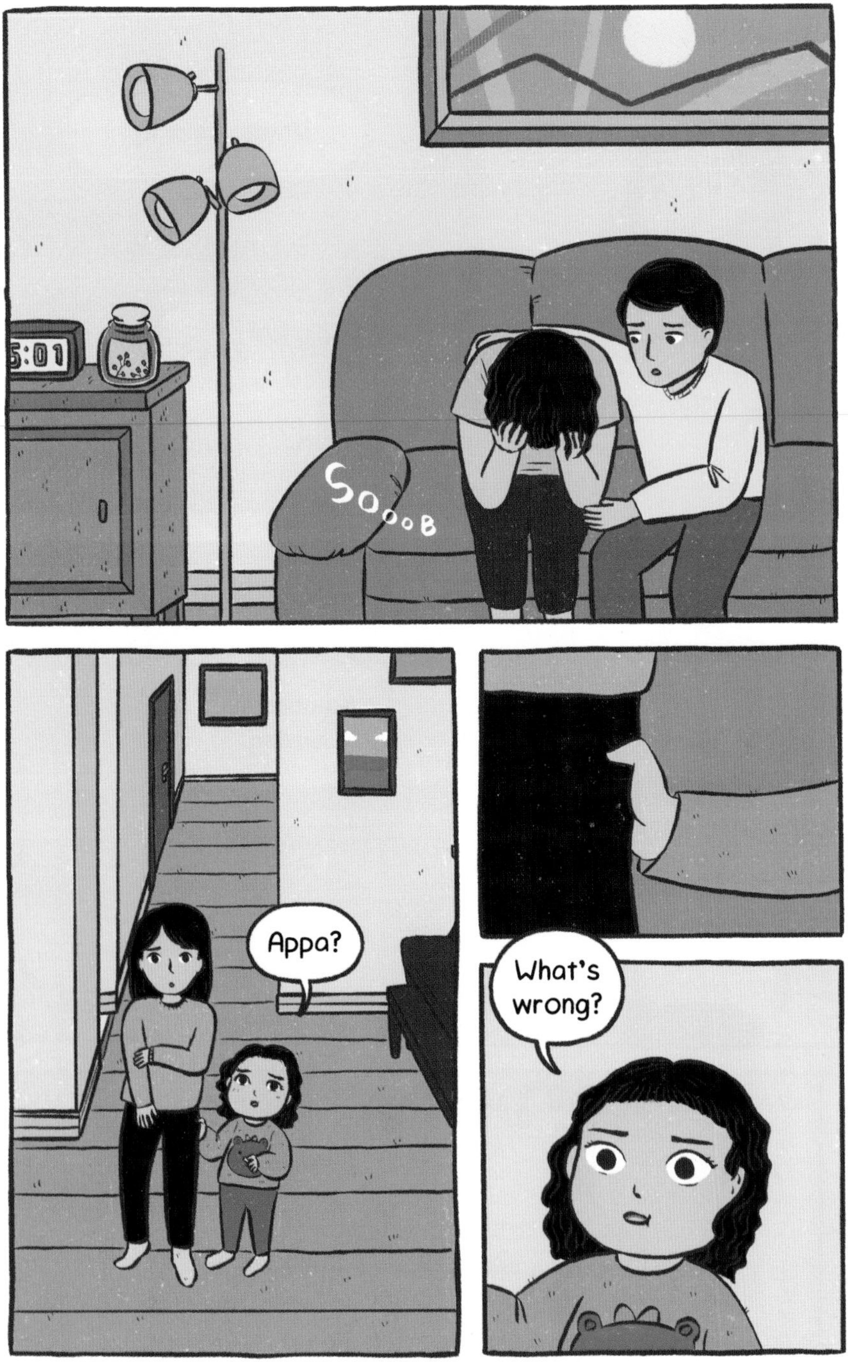
5:01
SOOOB
Appa?
What's wrong?

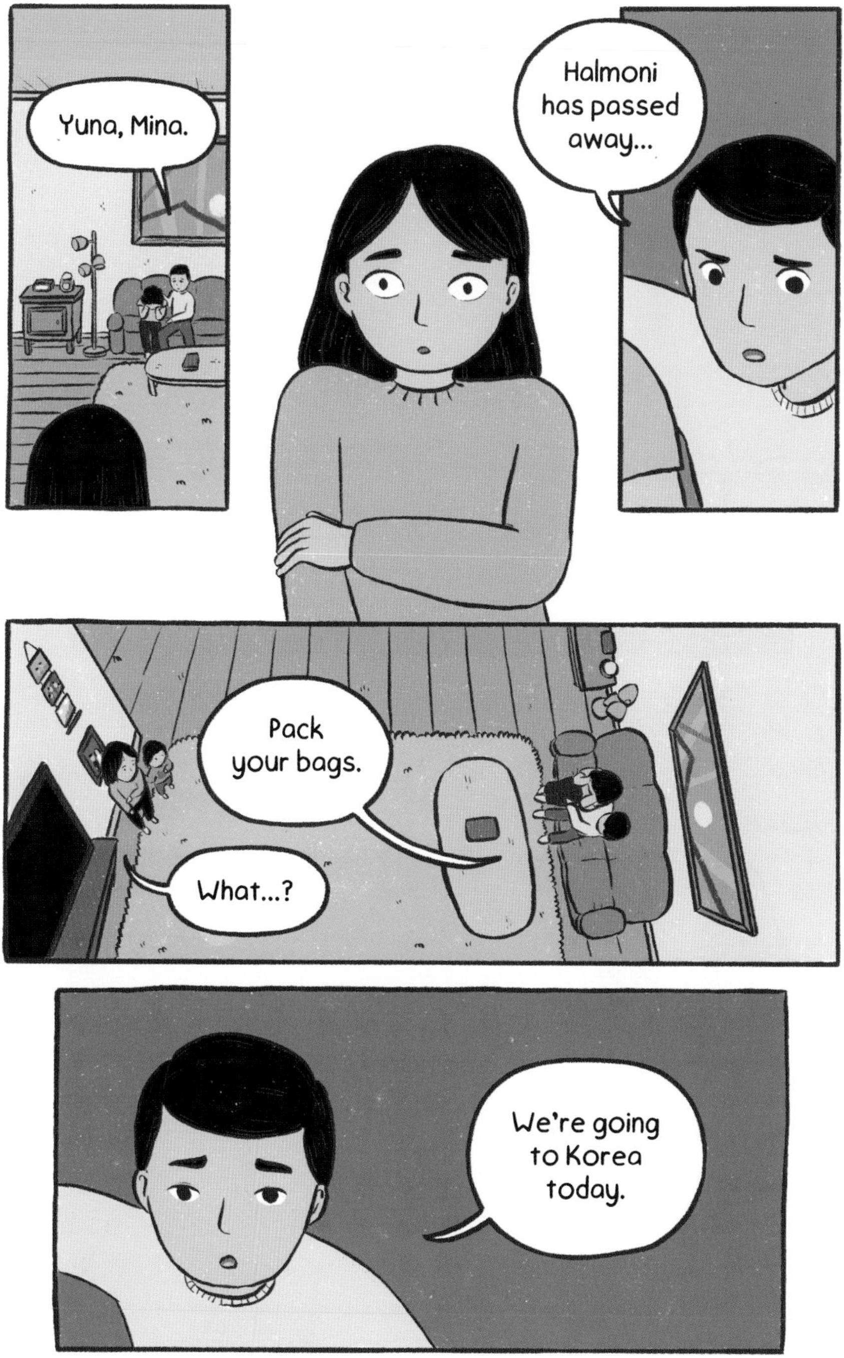
Yuna, Mina.
Halmoni has passed away...
Pack your bags.
What...?
We're going to Korea today.

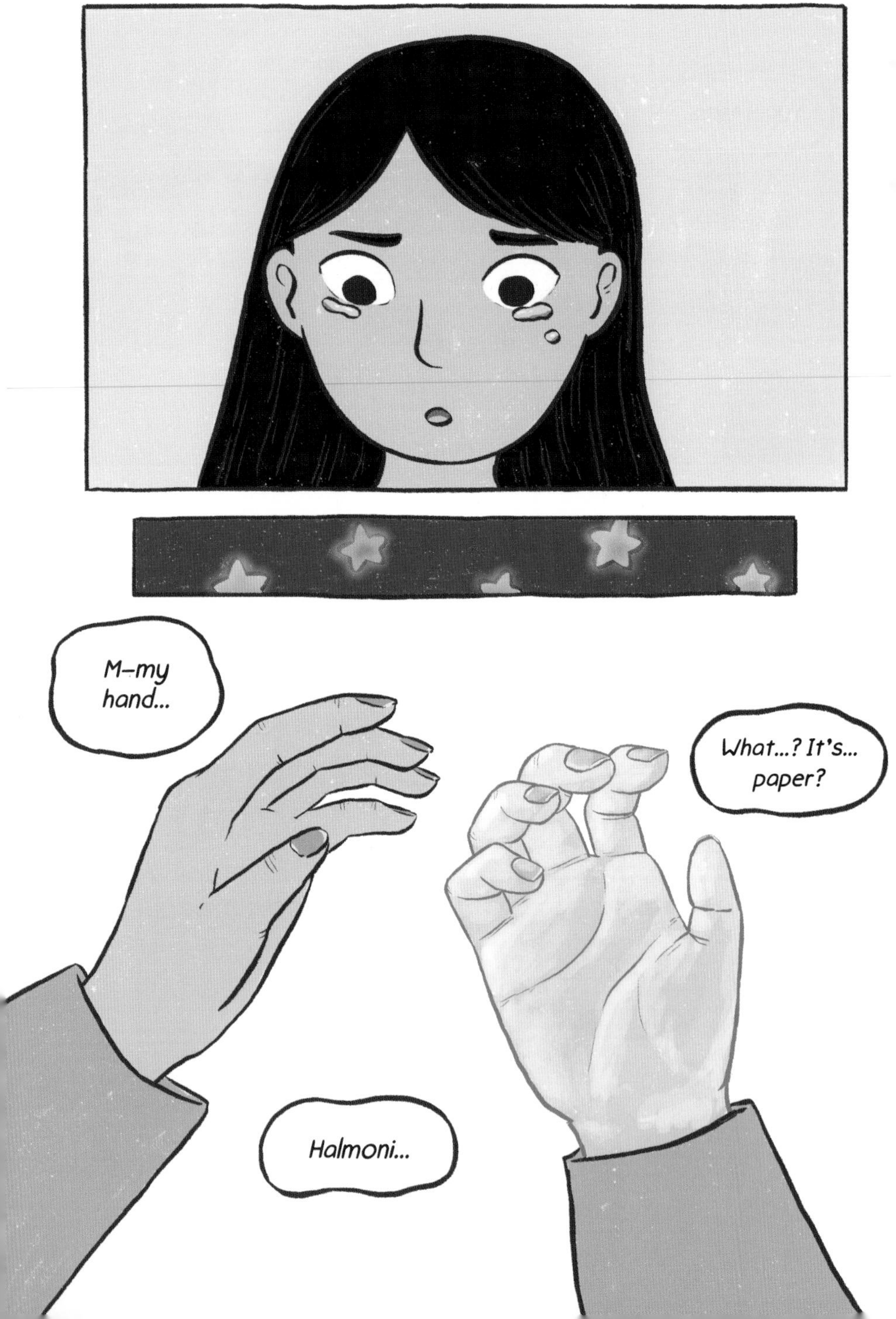
M–my hand...
What...? It's... paper?
Halmoni...

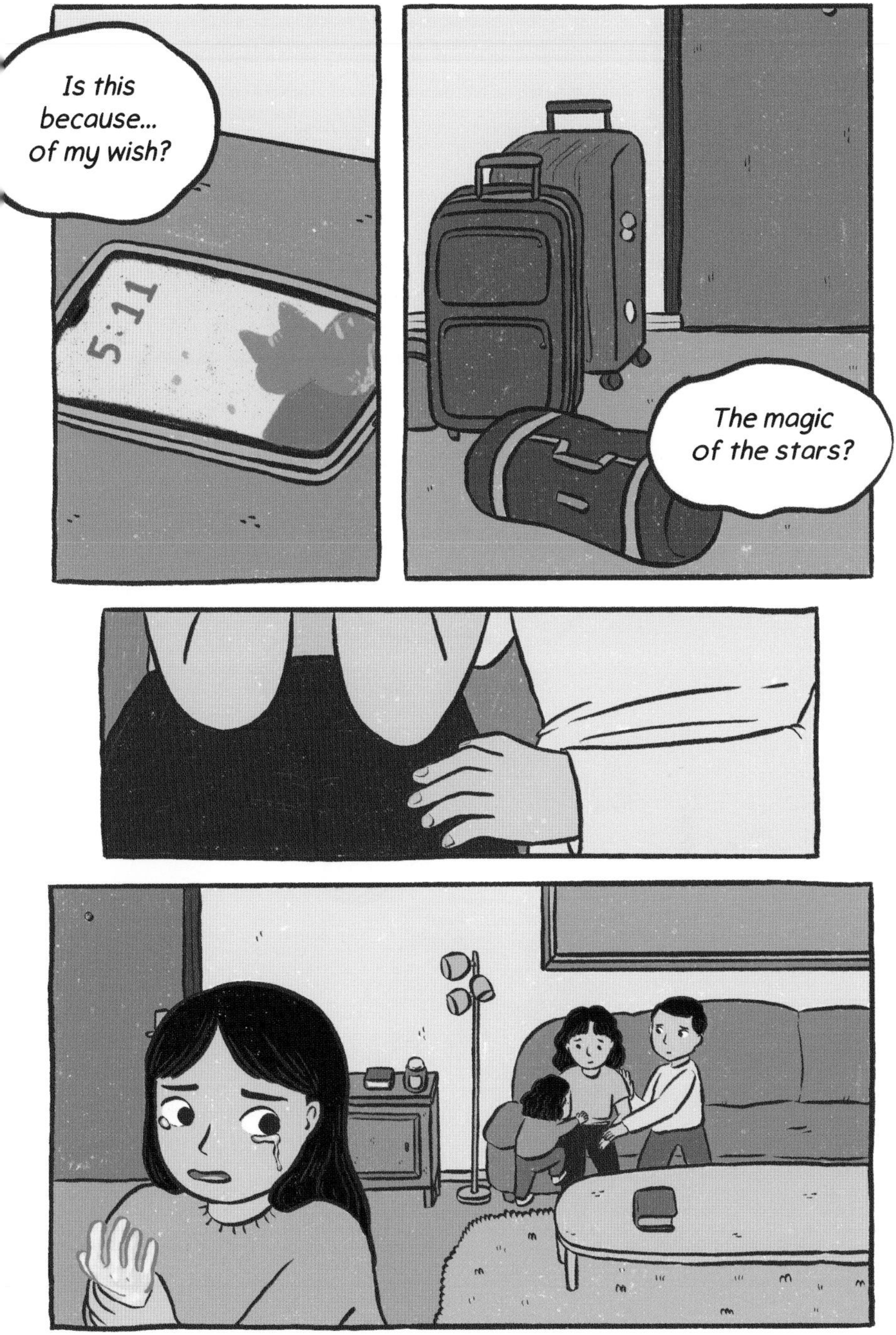
Is this because... of my wish?
5:11
The magic of the stars?

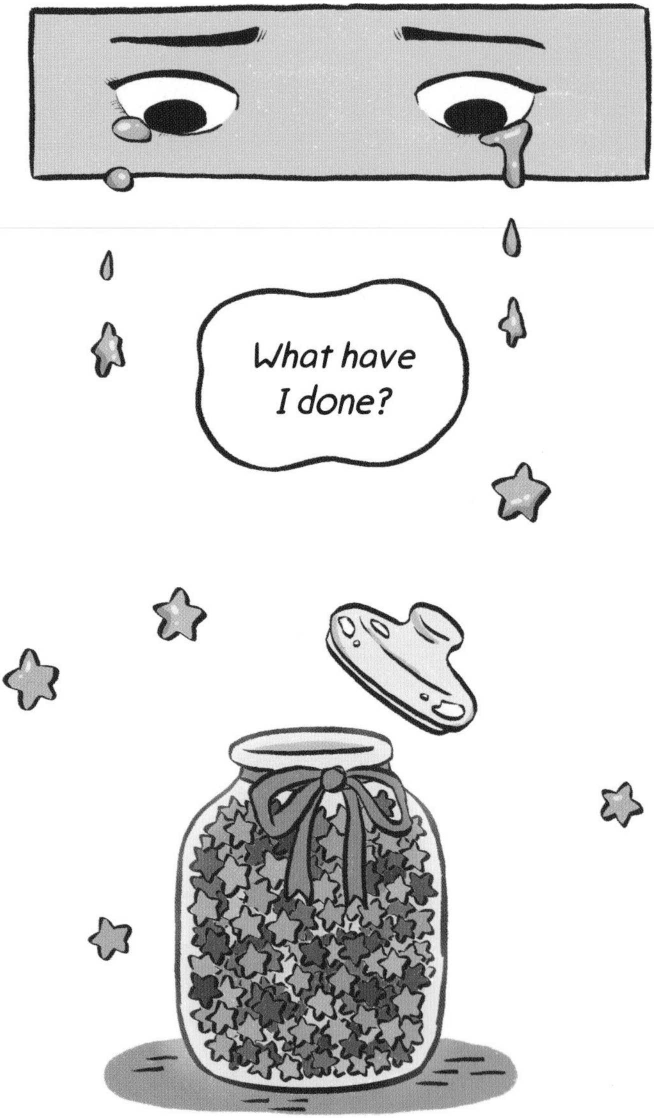
What have I done?

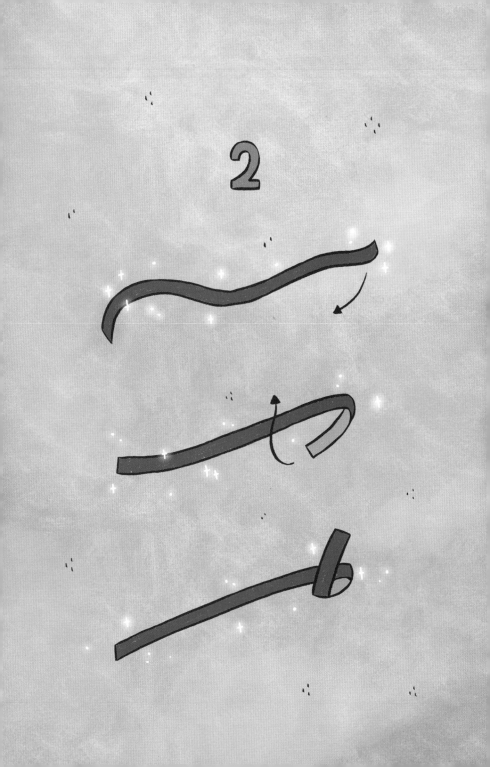

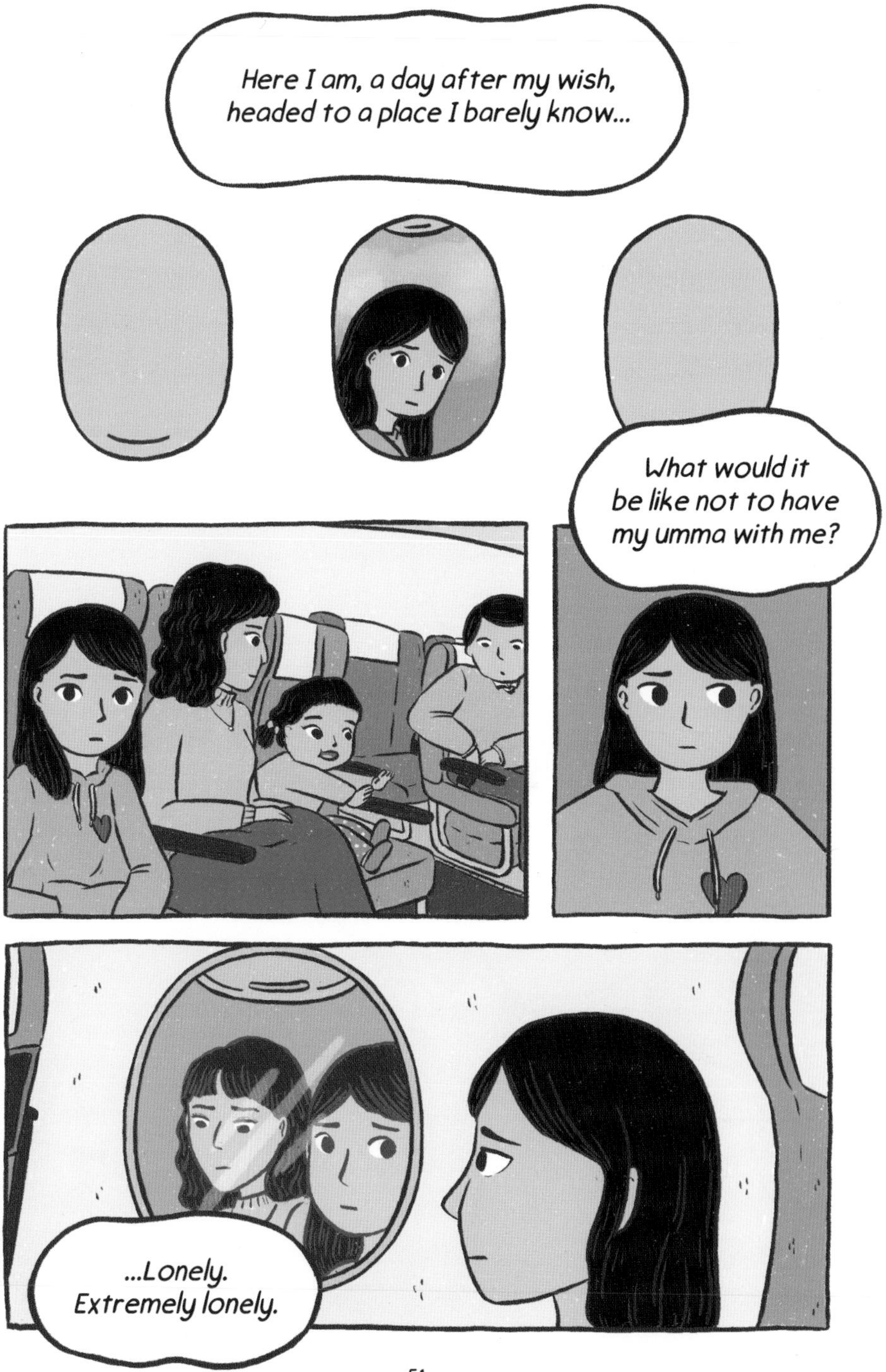
Here I am, a day after my wish, headed to a place I barely know...
What would it be like not to have my umma with me?
...Lonely. Extremely lonely.

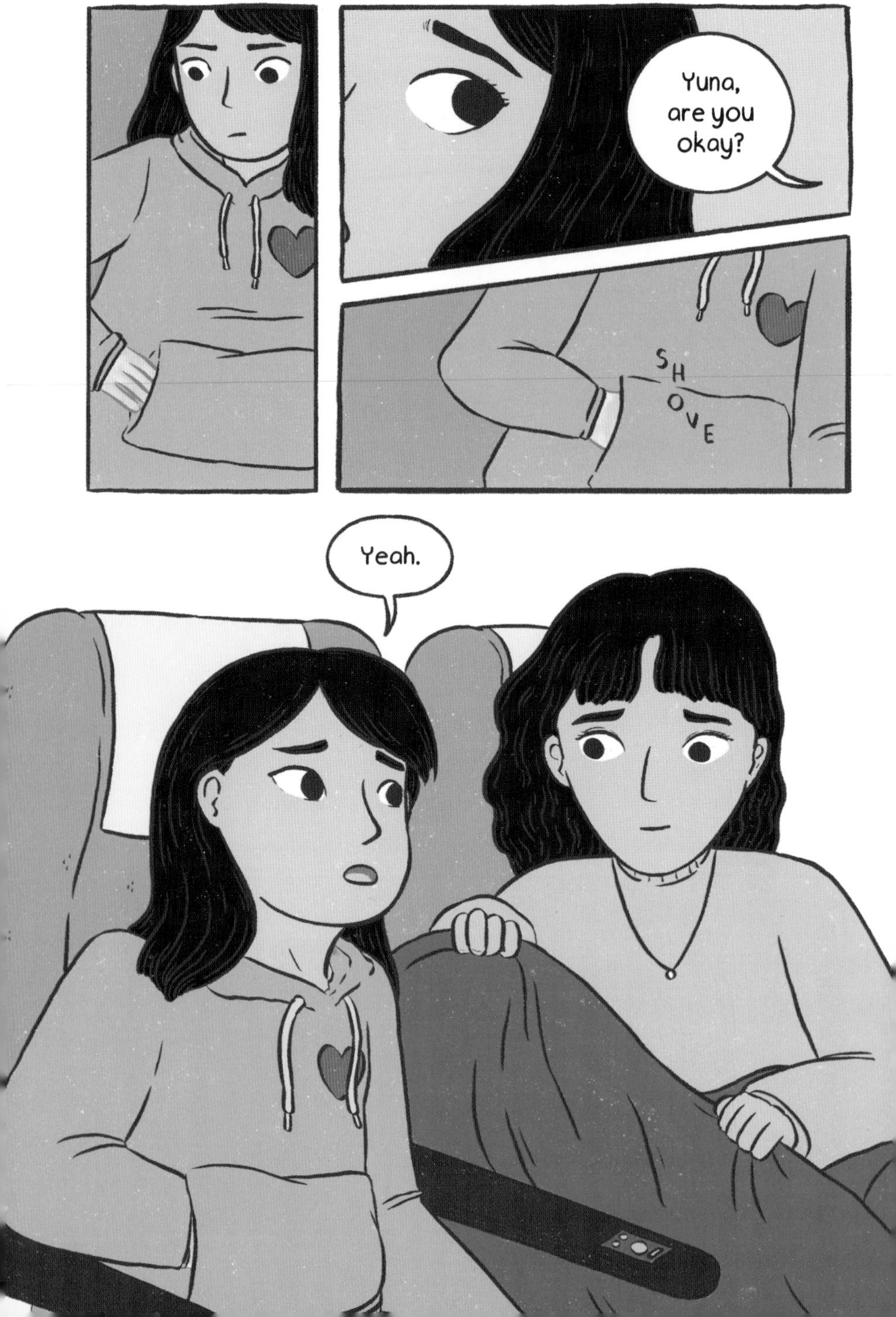
Yuna, are you okay?
SHOVE
Yeah.

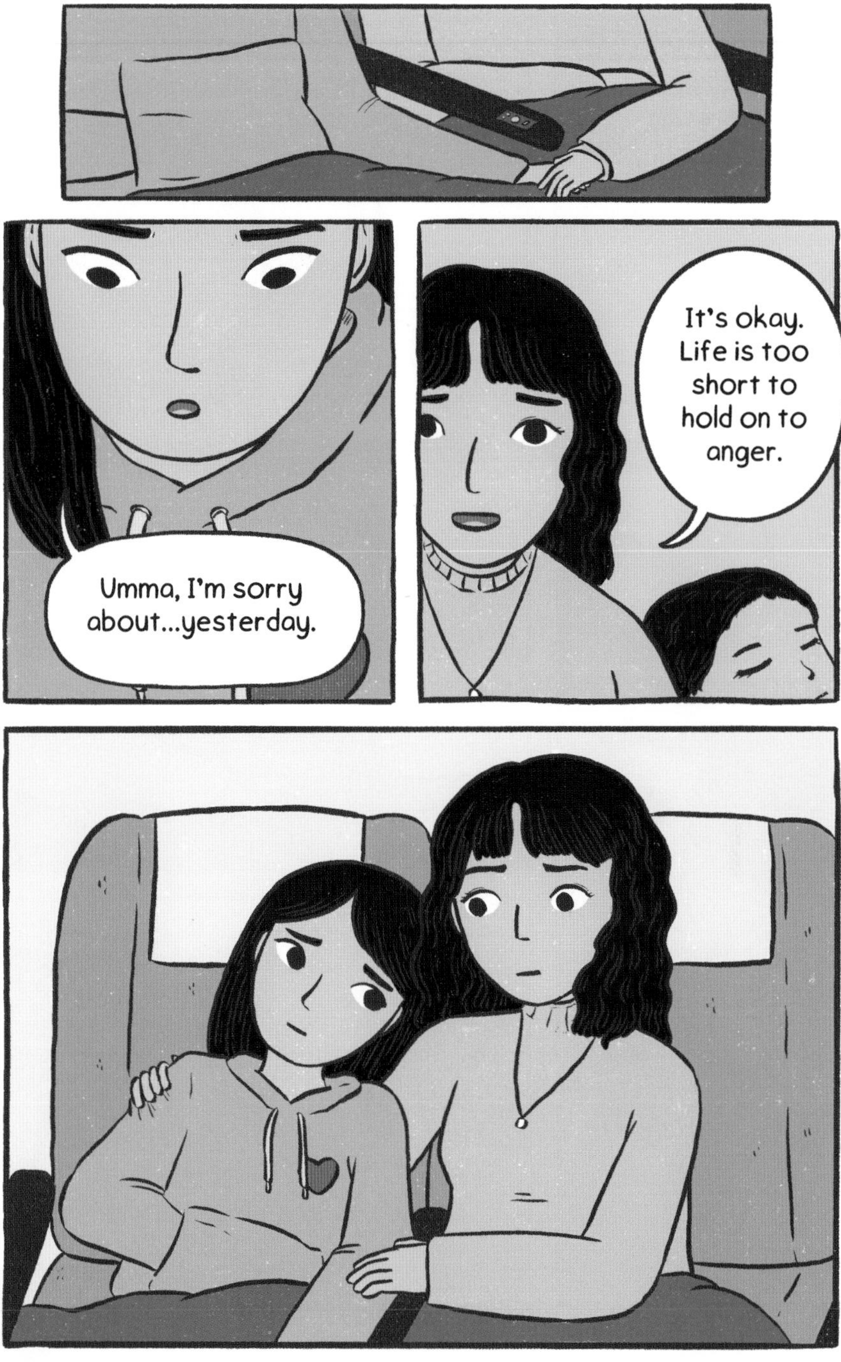
Umma, I'm sorry about...yesterday.
It's okay. Life is too short to hold on to anger.

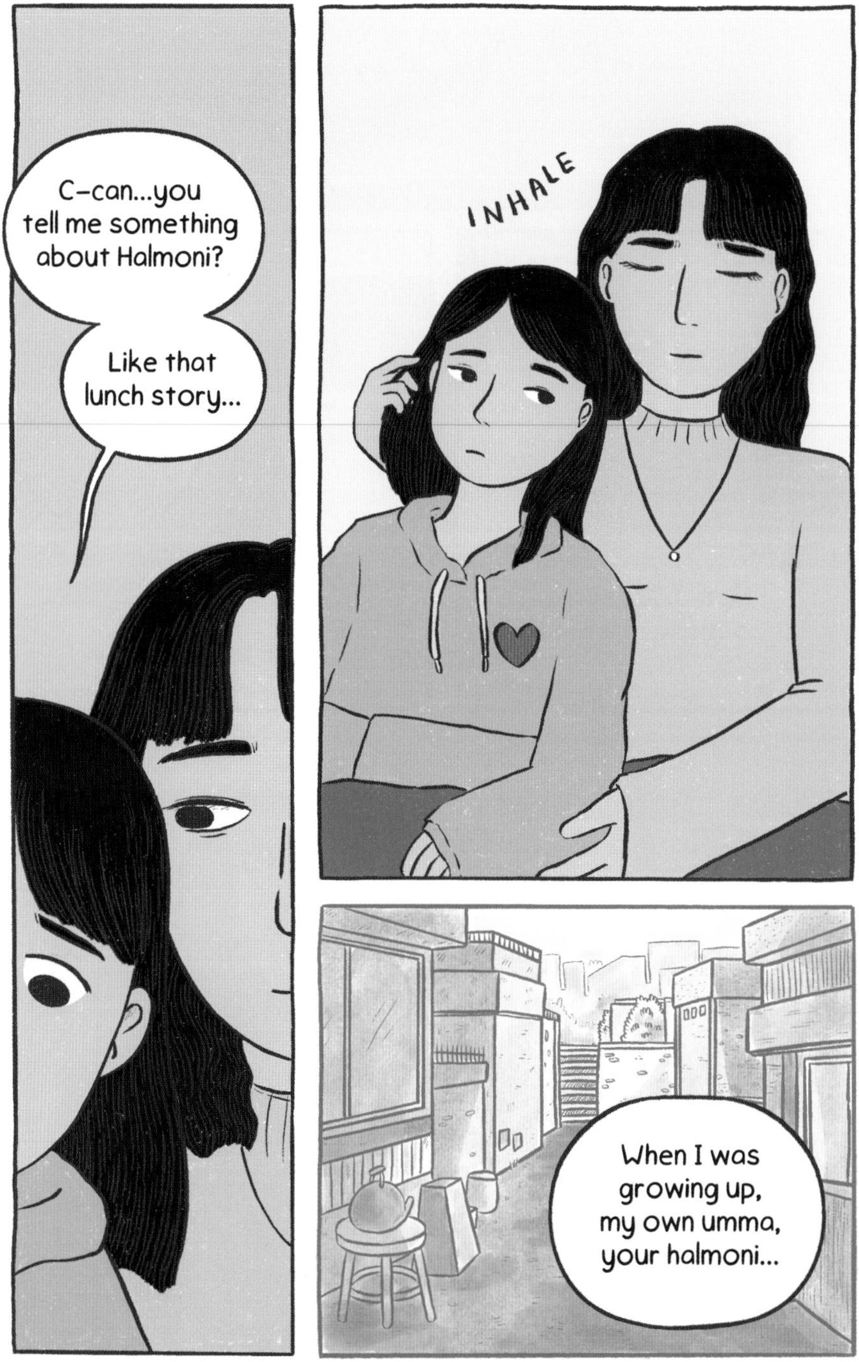
C-can...you tell me something about Halmoni?
Like that lunch story...
INHALE
When I was growing up, my own umma, your halmoni...

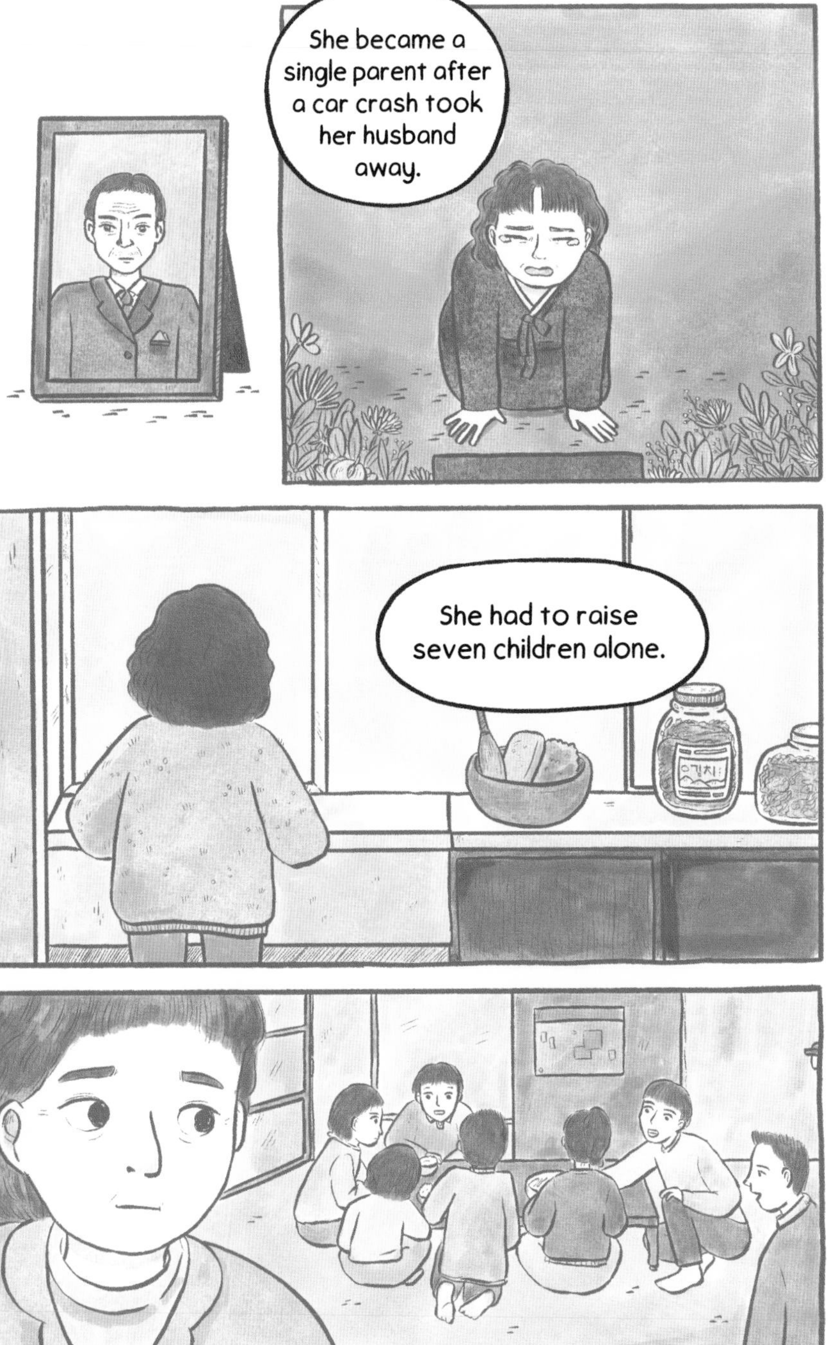
She became a single parent after a car crash took her husband away.
She had to raise seven children alone.

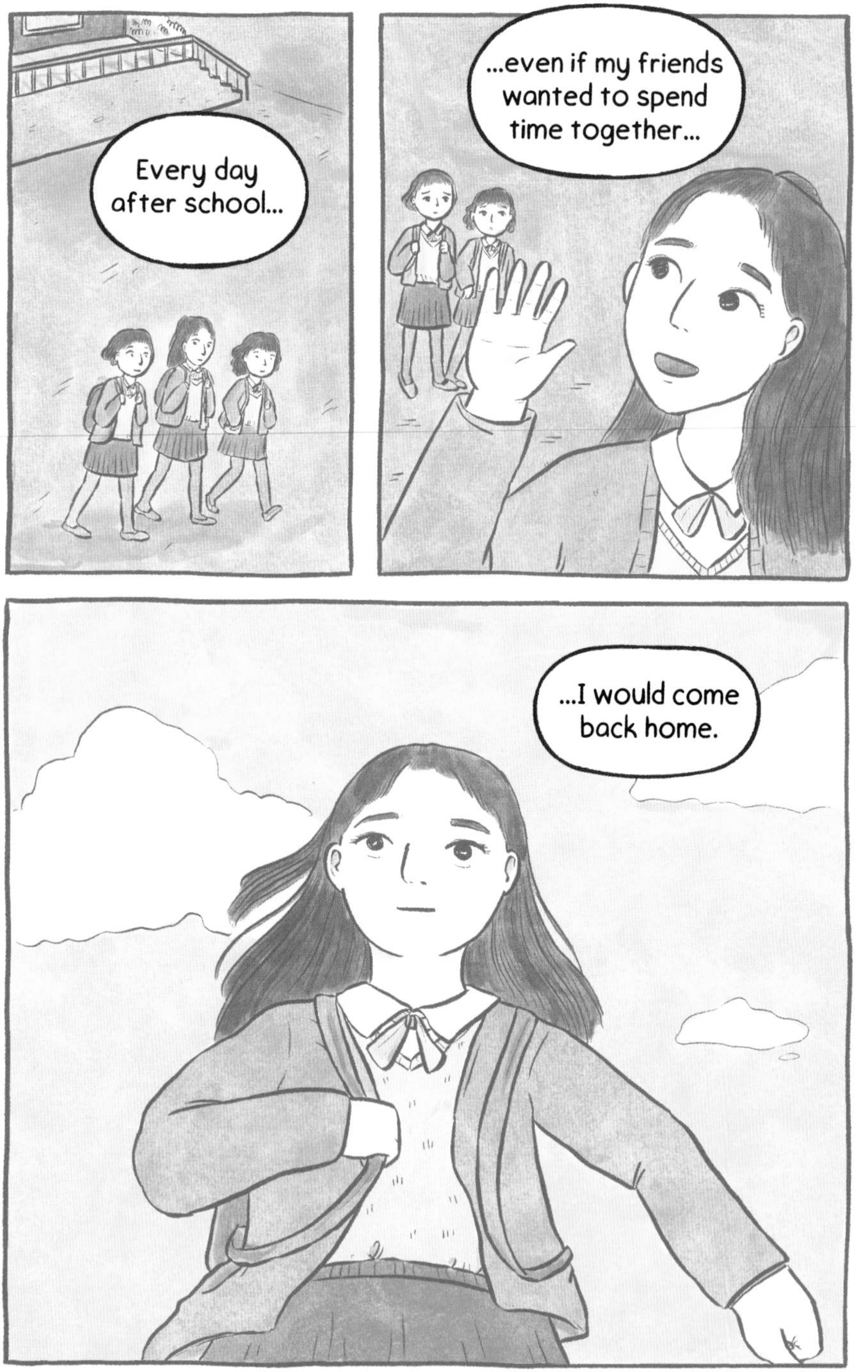
Every day after school...
...even if my friends wanted to spend time together...
...I would come back home.

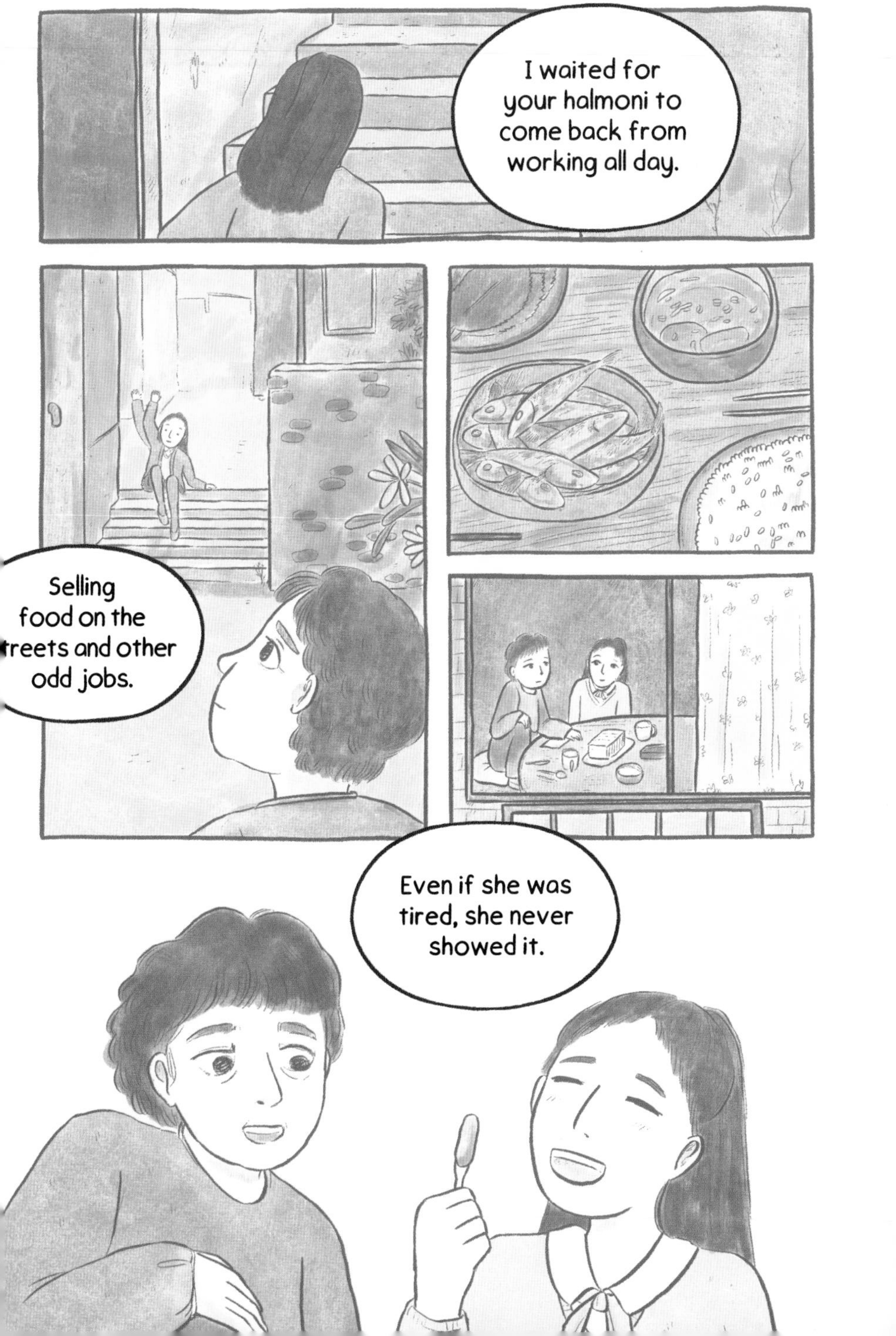
I waited for your halmoni to come back from working all day.
Selling food on the treets and other odd jobs.
Even if she was tired, she never showed it.

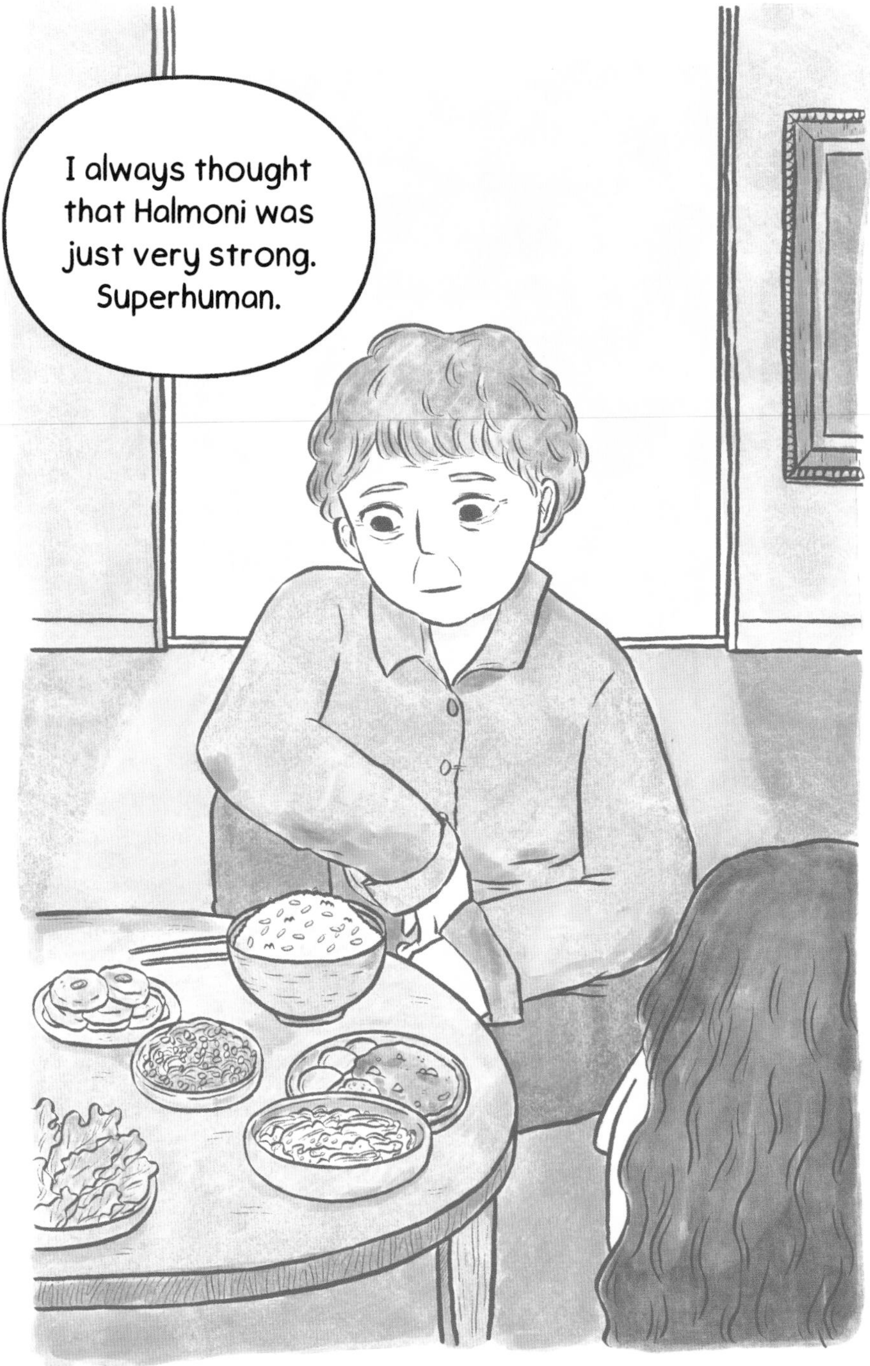
I always thought that Halmoni was just very strong. Superhuman.

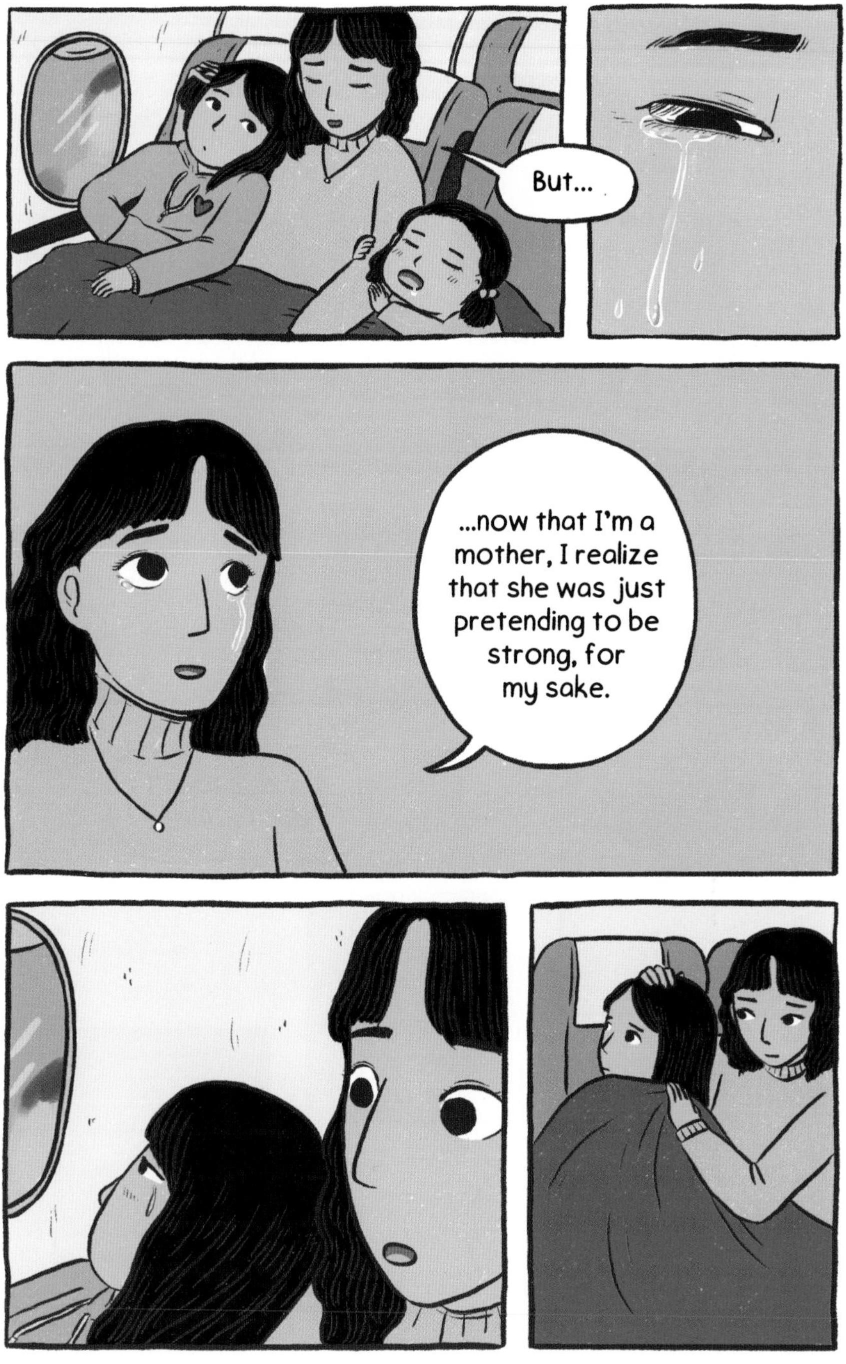
But...
...now that I'm a mother, I realize that she was just pretending to be strong, for my sake.

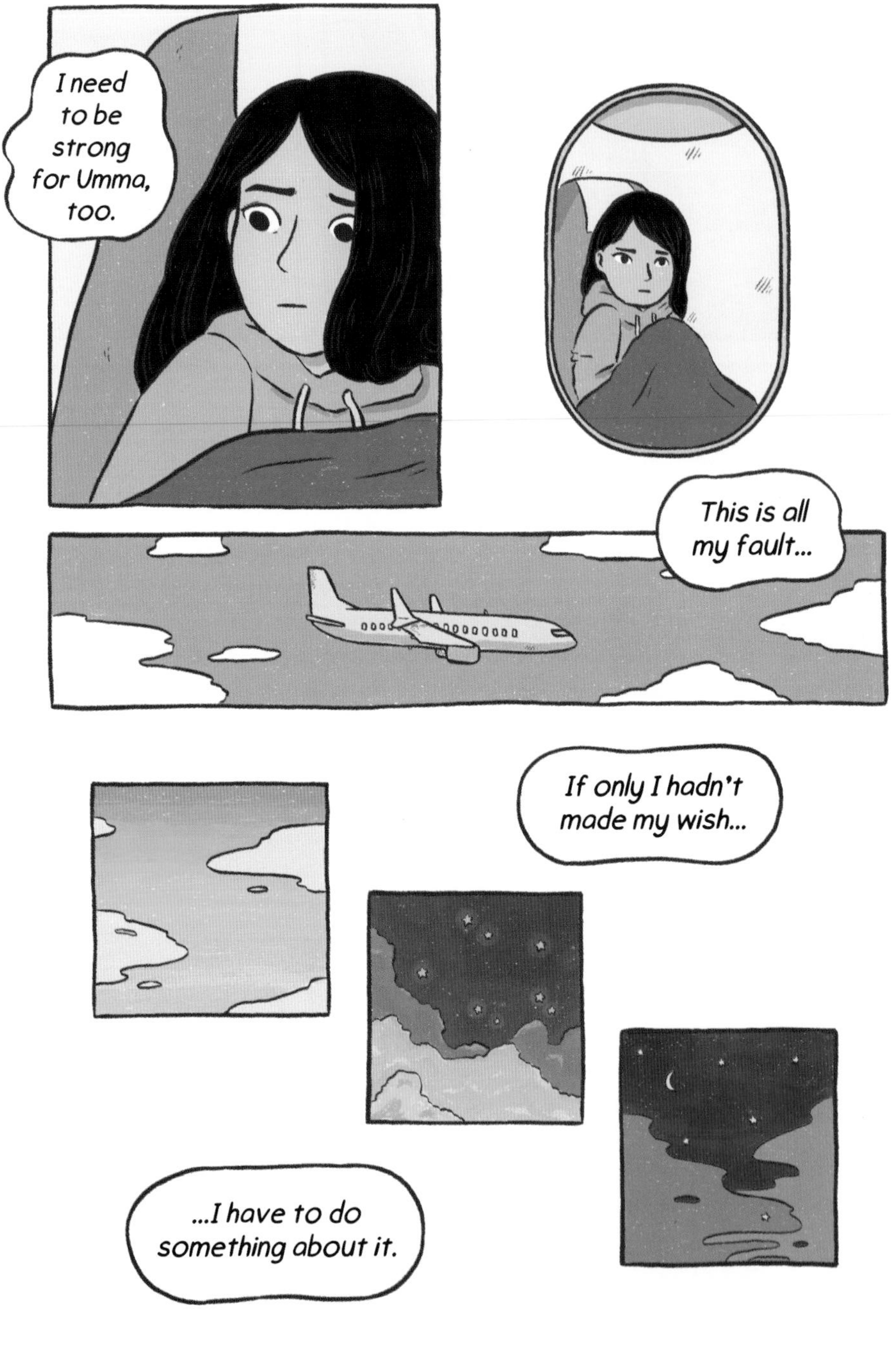
I need to be strong for Umma, too.
This is all my fault...
If only I hadn't made my wish...
...I have to do something about it.

Terminal 2
6
EXIT
EXIT
EXIT
출구

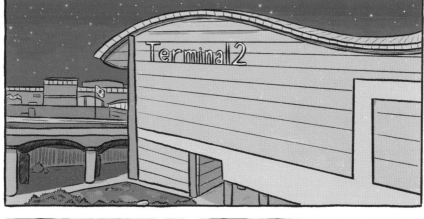

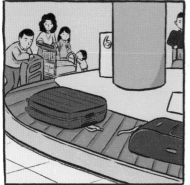

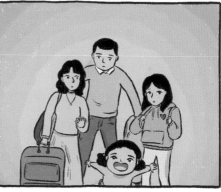

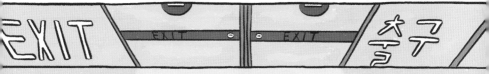

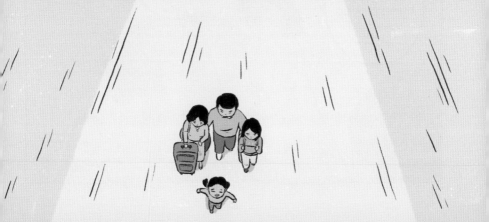

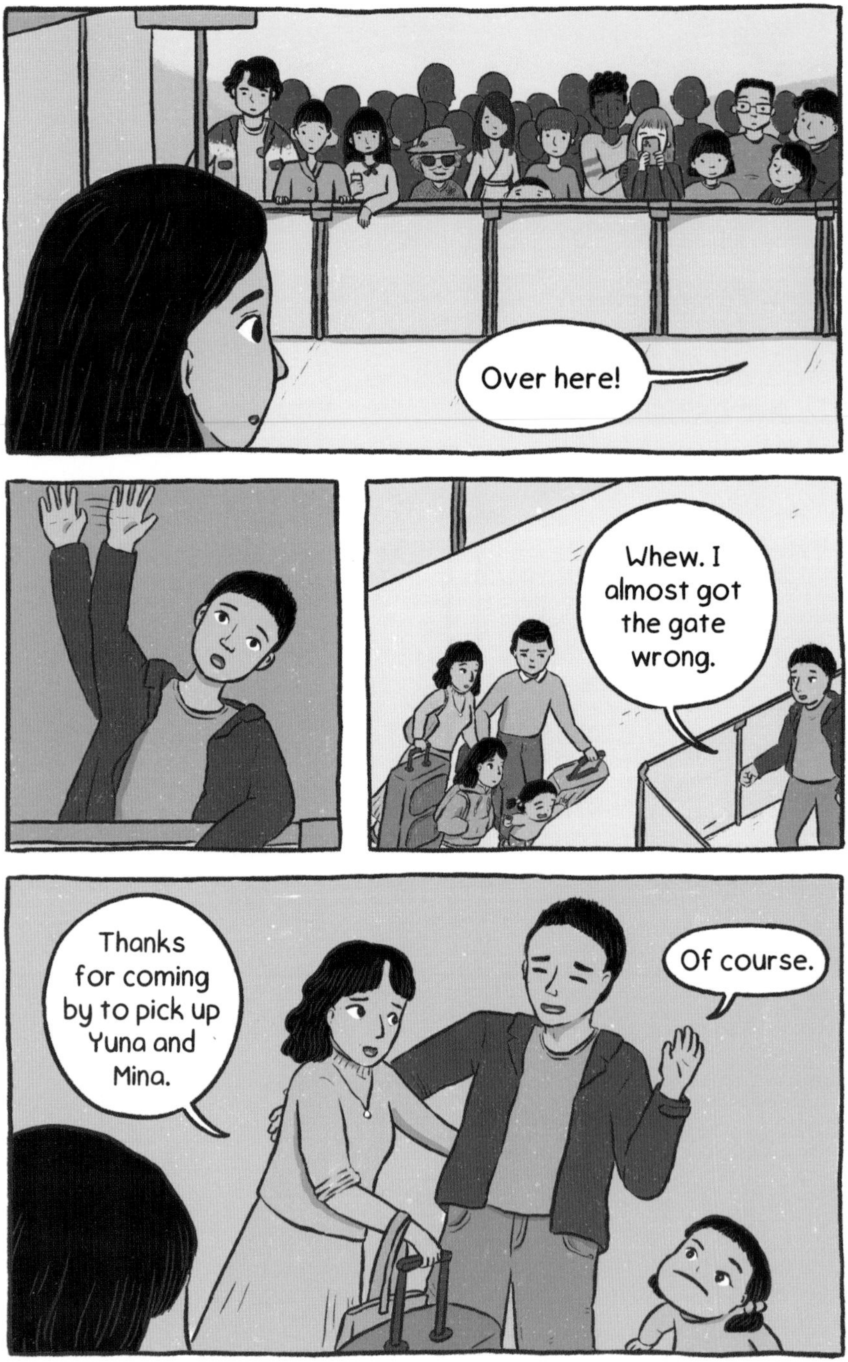
Over here!
Whew. I almost got the gate wrong.
Thanks for coming by to pick up Yuna and Mina.
Of course.

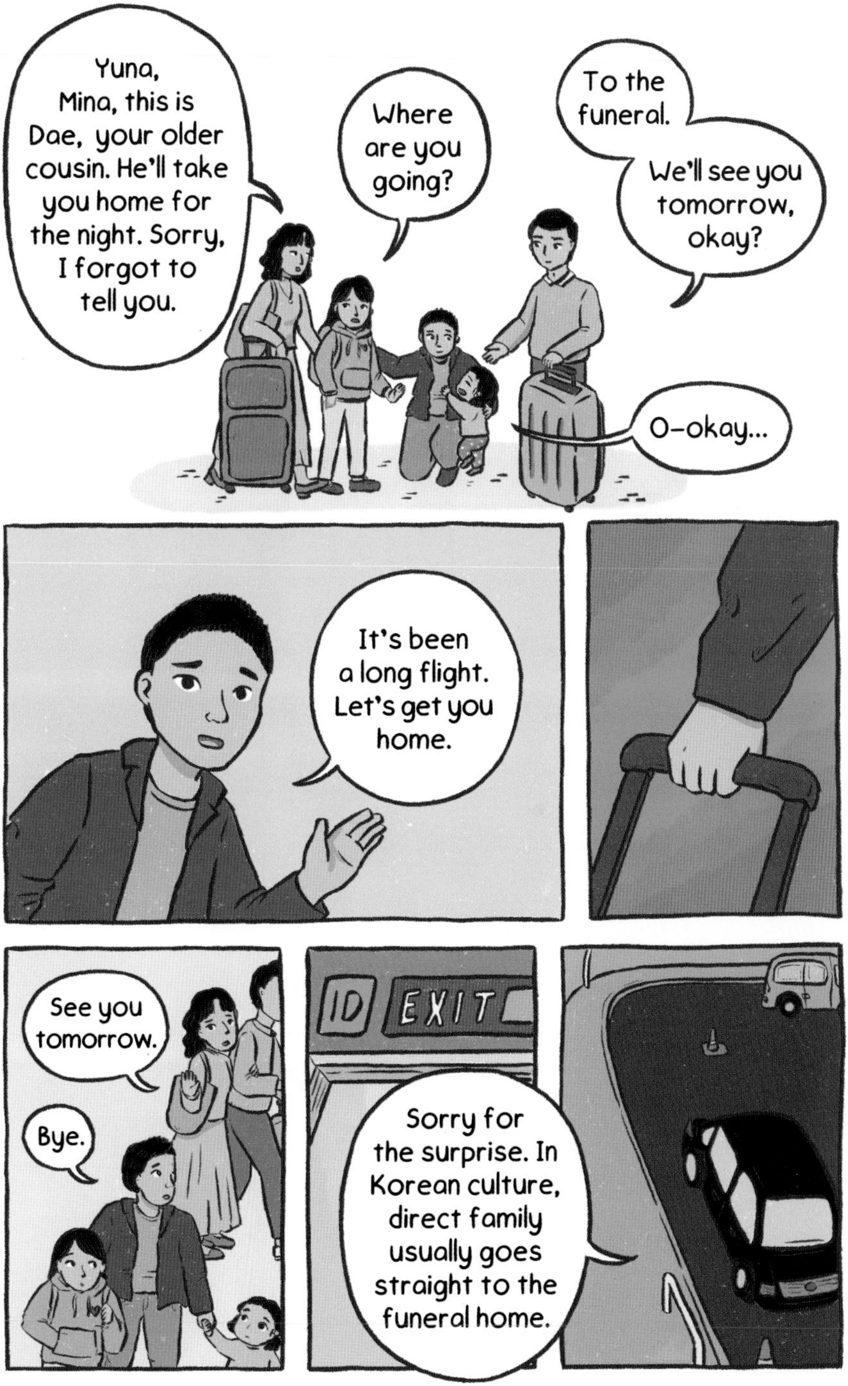

Yuna, Mina, this is Dae, your older cousin. He'll take you home for the night. Sorry, I forgot to tell you.
Where are you going?
To the funeral.
We'll see you tomorrow, okay?
O-okay...
It's been a long flight. Let's get you home.
See you tomorrow.
Bye.
ID
EXIT
Sorry for the surprise. In Korean culture, direct family usually goes straight to the funeral home.

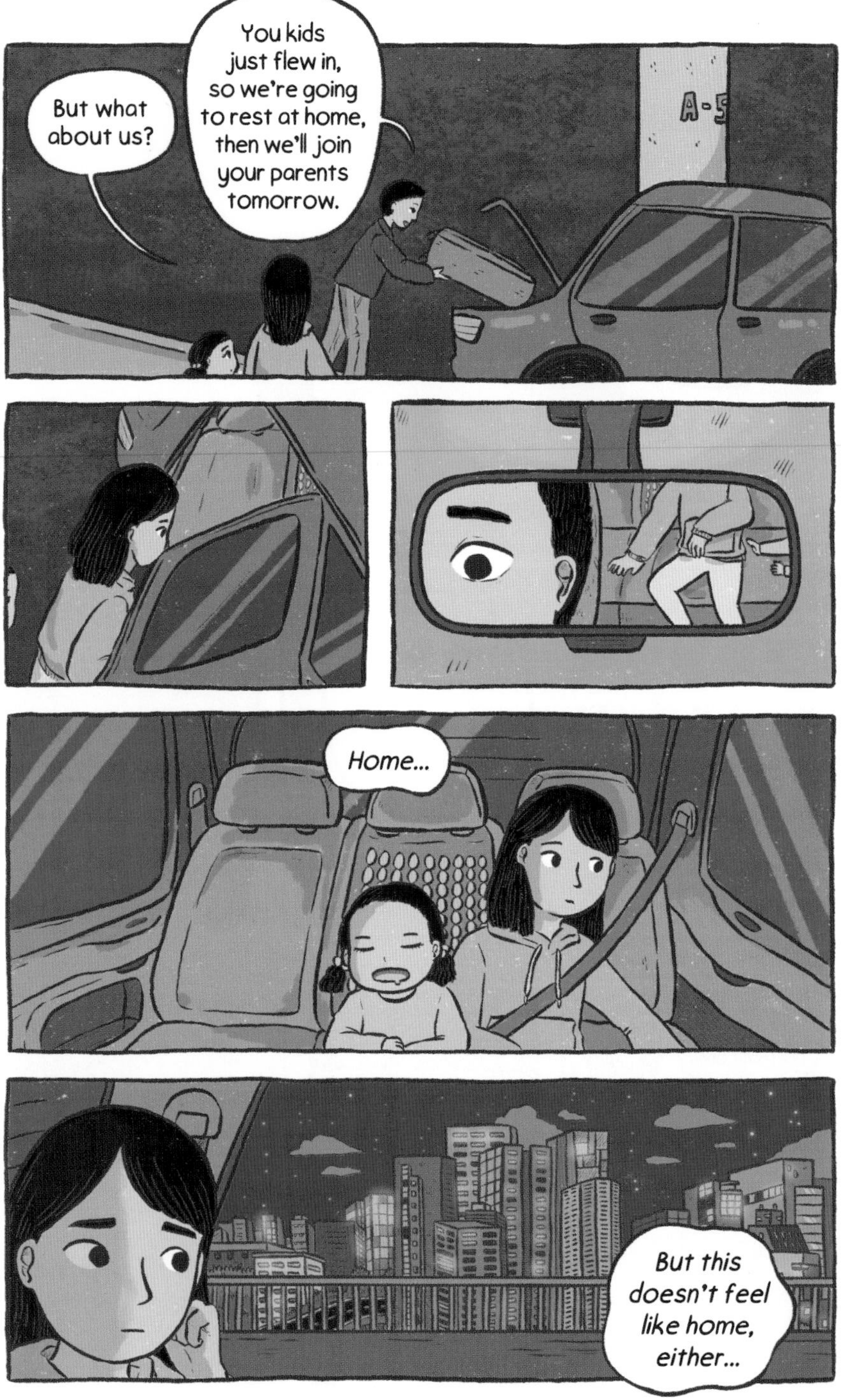
But what about us?
You kids just flew in, so we're going to rest at home, then we'll join your parents tomorrow.
A-5
Home...
But this doesn't feel like home, either...

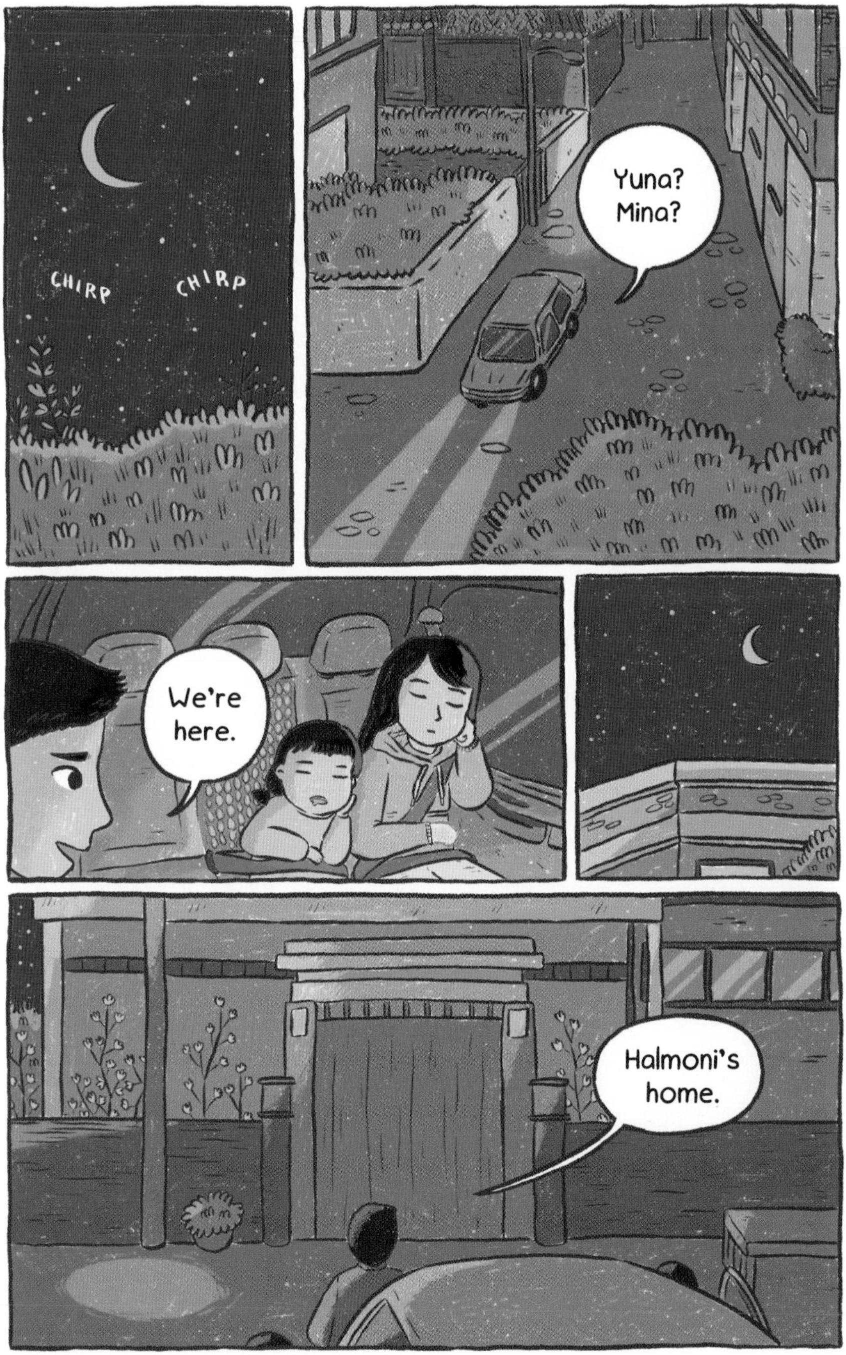
CHIRP CHIRP
Yuna? Mina?
We're here.
Halmoni's home.

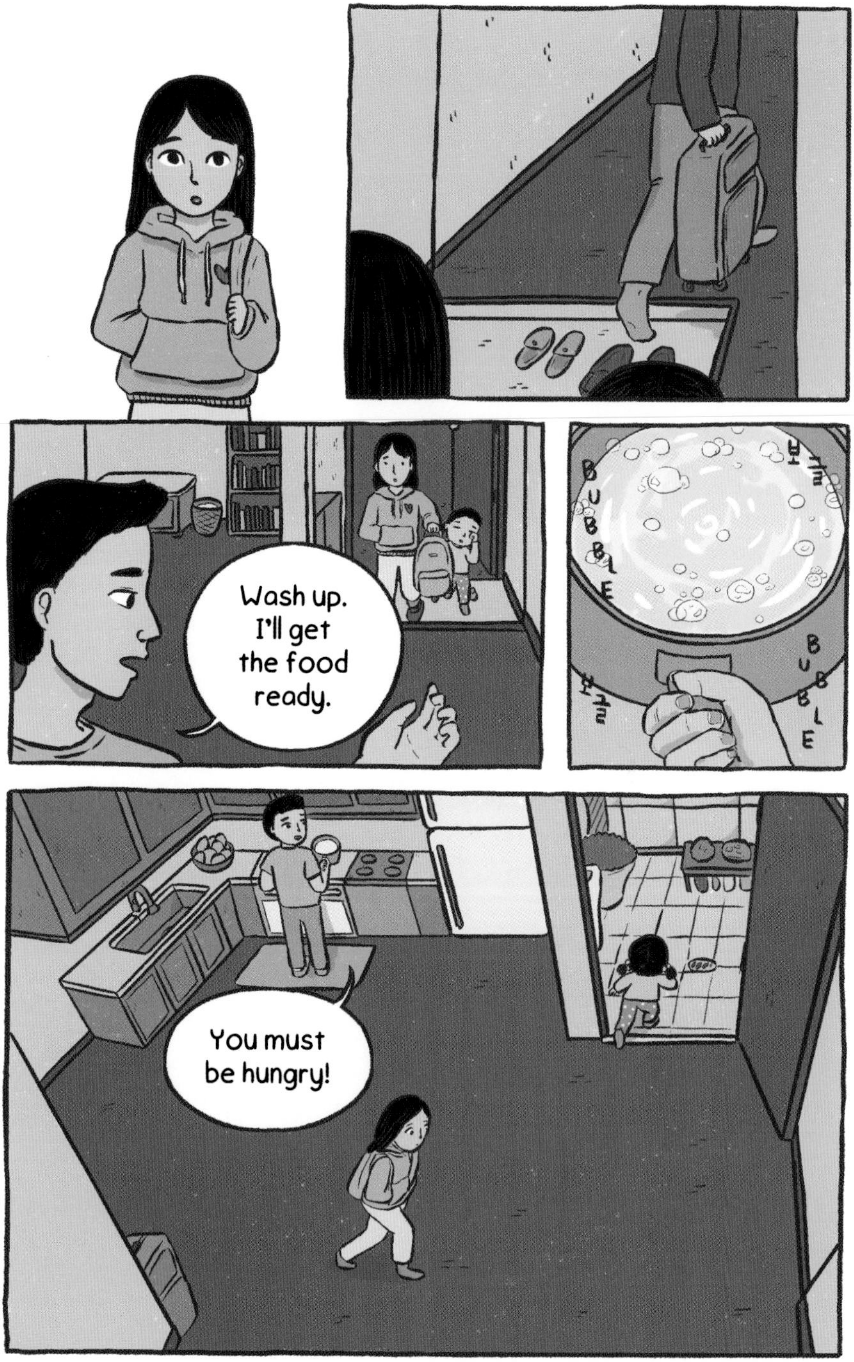

Wash up. I'll get the food ready.
BUBBLE
보글
BUBBLE
보글
You must be hungry!

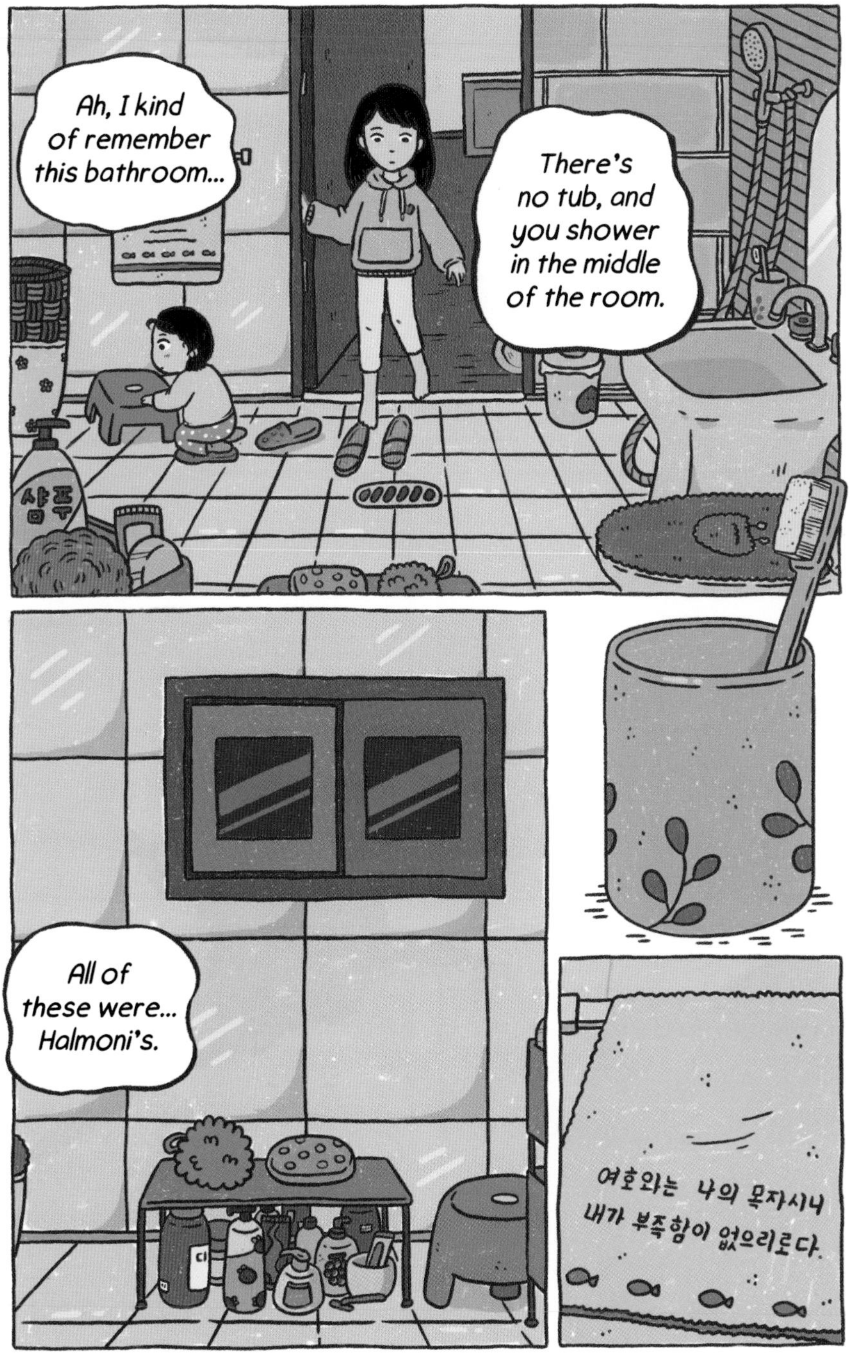
Ah, I kind of remember this bathroom...
There's no tub, and you shower in the middle of the room.
All of these were... Halmoni's.
여호와는 나의 목자시니
내가 부족함이 없으리로다.

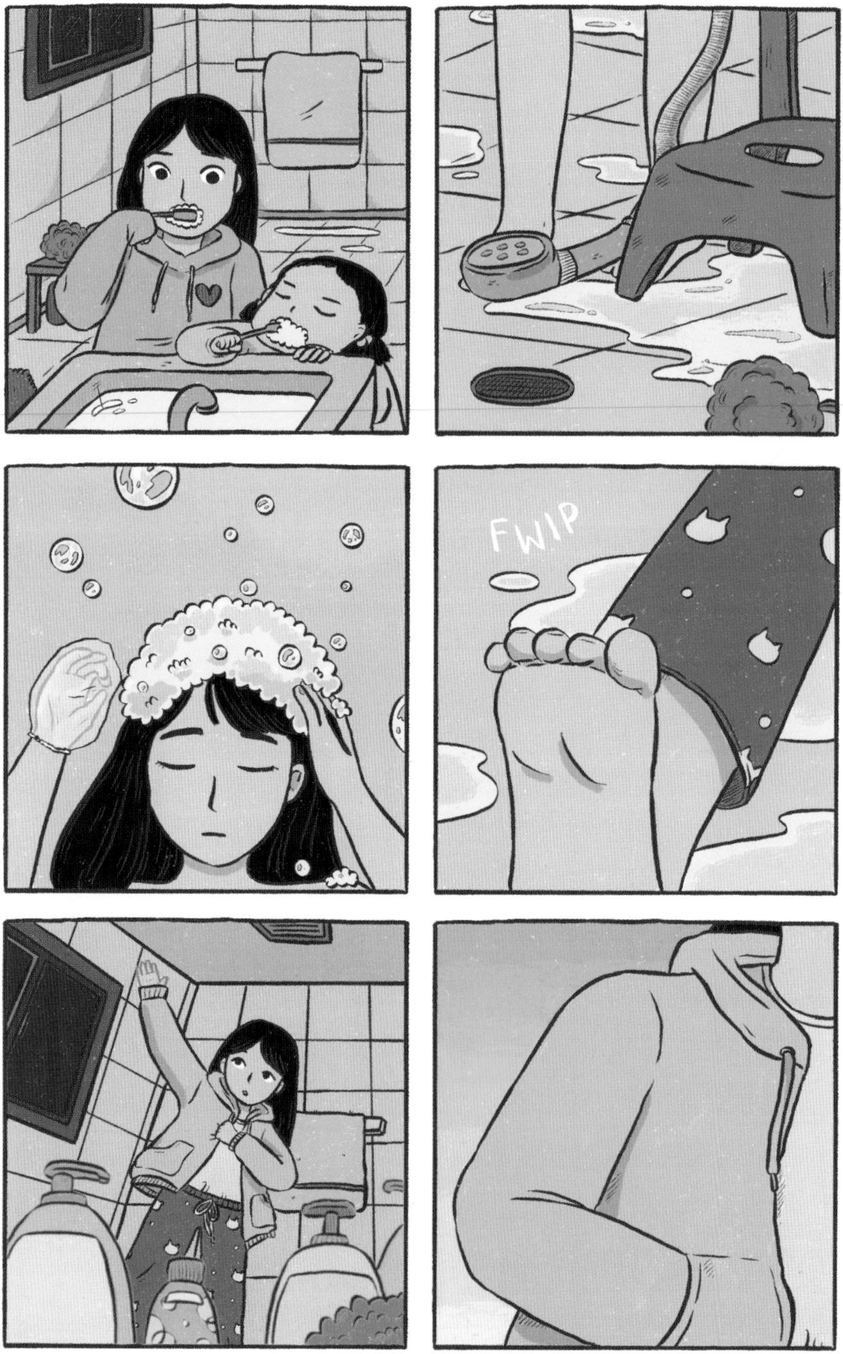
FWIP

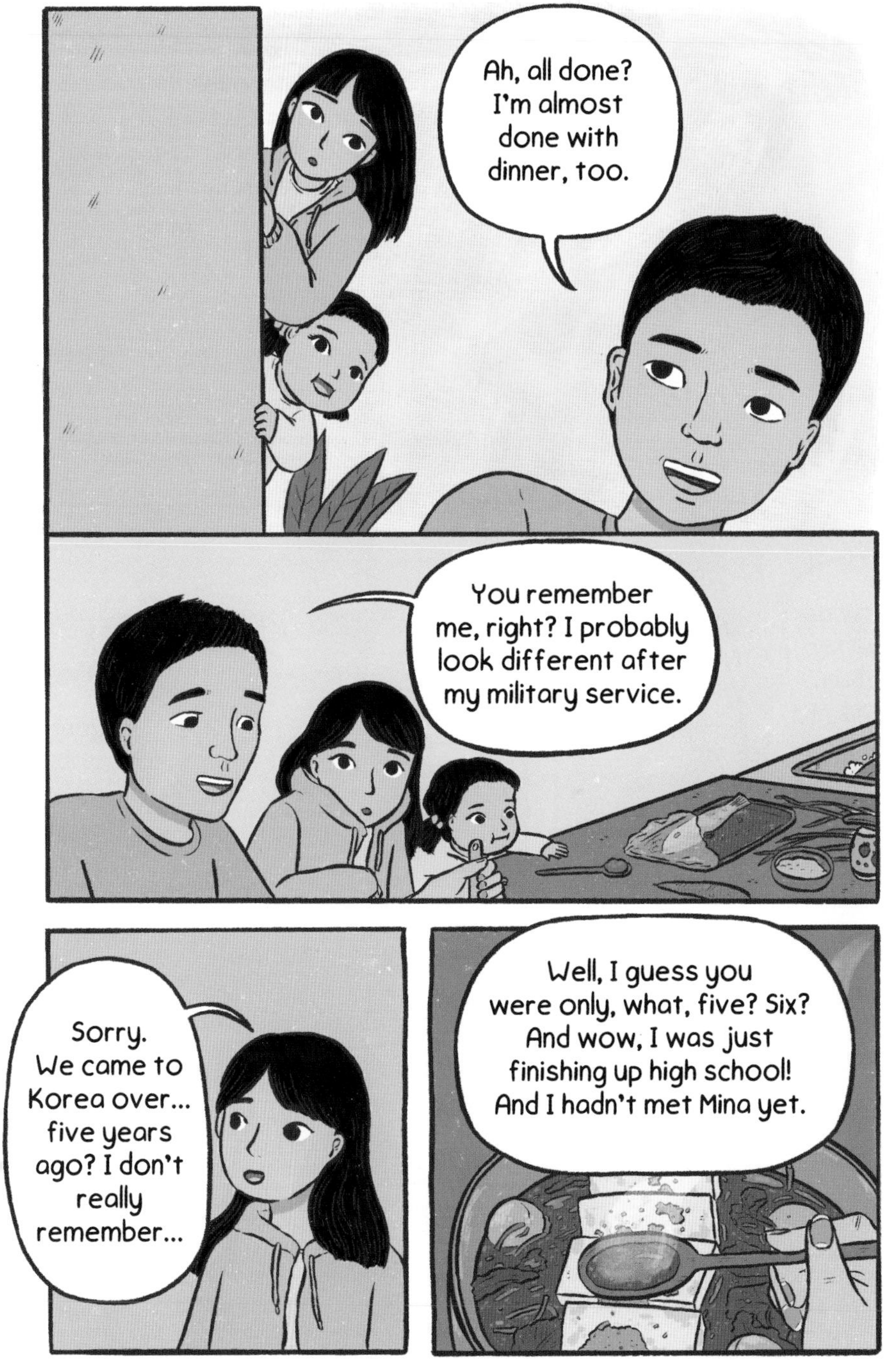
Ah, all done? I'm almost done with dinner, too.
You remember me, right? I probably look different after my military service.
Sorry. We came to Korea over... five years ago? I don't really remember...
Well, I guess you were only, what, five? Six? And wow, I was just finishing up high school! And I hadn't met Mina yet.

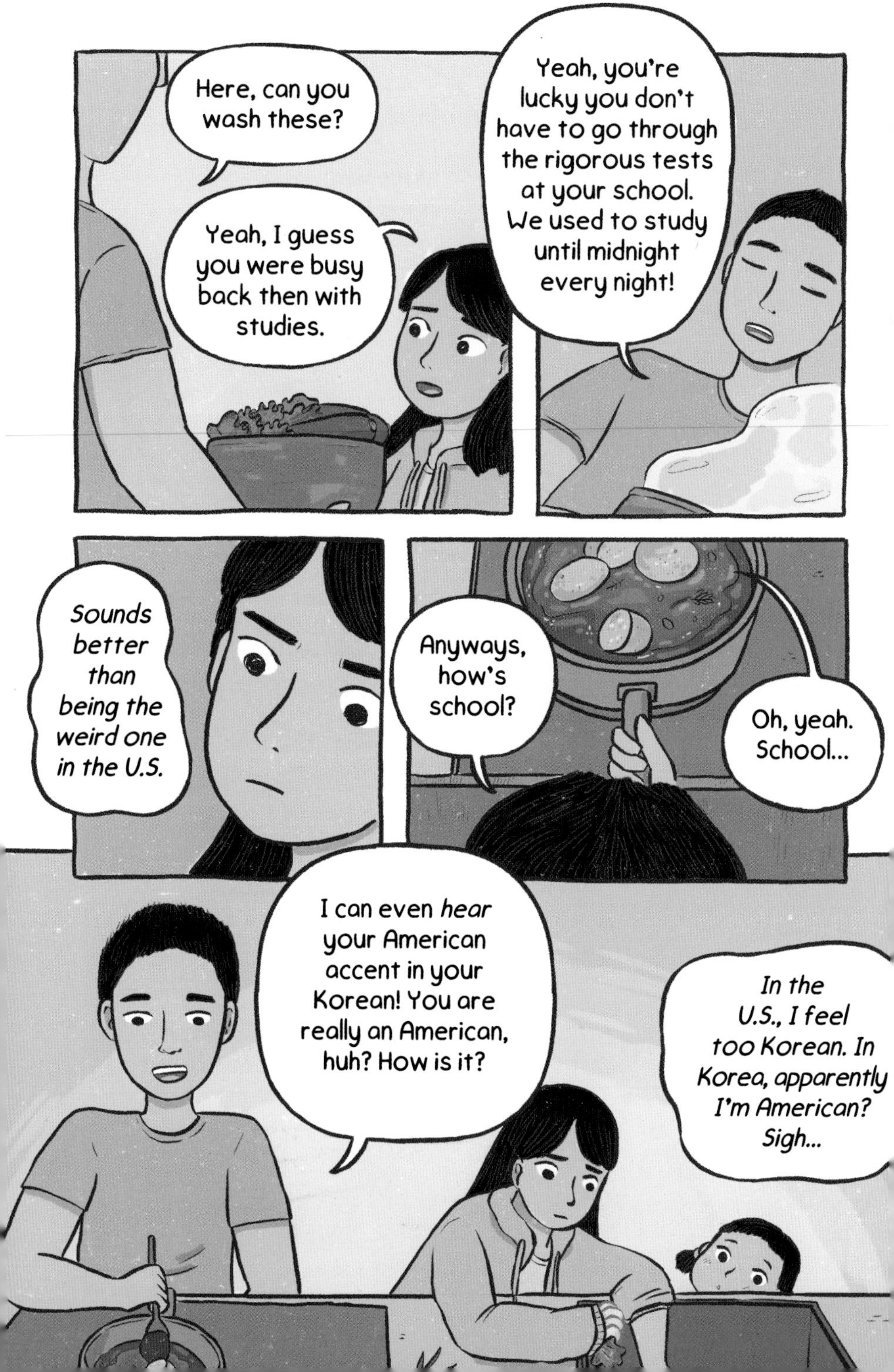
Here, can you wash these?
Yeah, I guess you were busy back then with studies.
Yeah, you're lucky you don't have to go through the rigorous tests at your school. We used to study until midnight every night!
Sounds better than being the weird one in the U.S.
Anyways, how's school?
Oh, yeah. School...
I can even *hear* your American accent in your Korean! You are really an American, huh? How is it?
In the U.S., I feel too Korean. In Korea, apparently I'm American? Sigh...

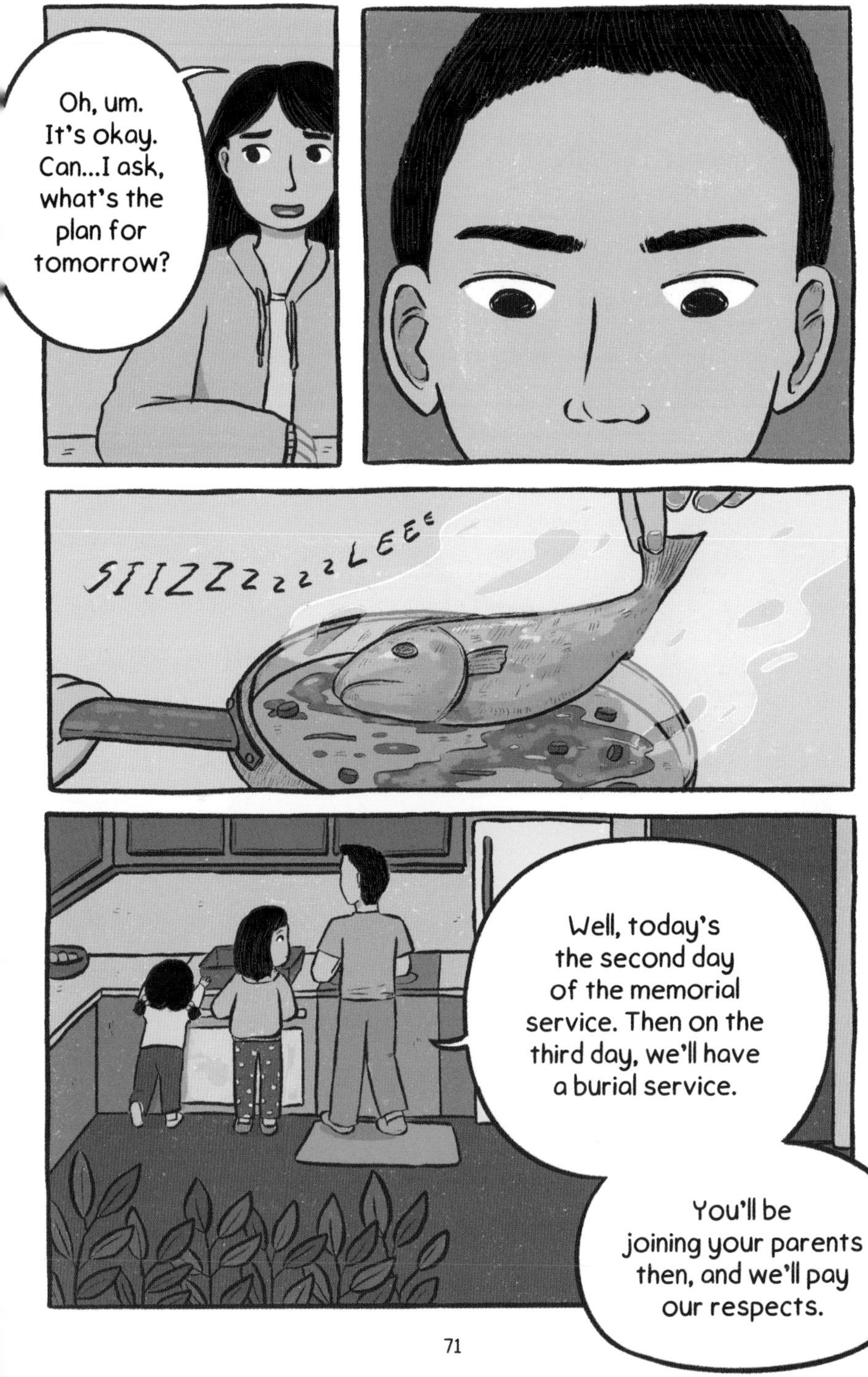
Oh, um. It's okay. Can...I ask, what's the plan for tomorrow?
SIIZZZzzzzLEEE
Well, today's the second day of the memorial service. Then on the third day, we'll have a burial service.
You'll be joining your parents then, and we'll pay our respects.

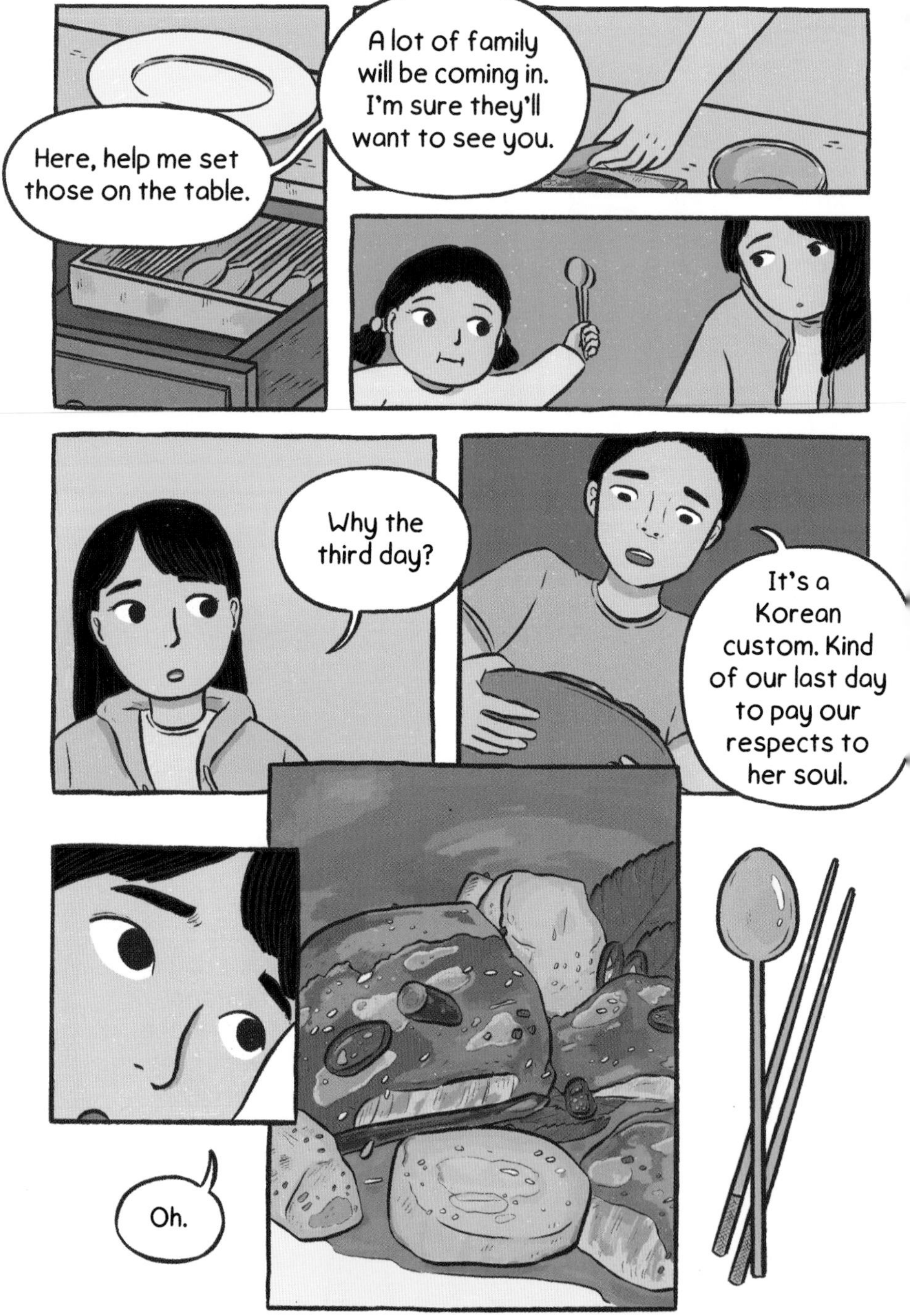
Here, help me set those on the table.
A lot of family will be coming in. I'm sure they'll want to see you.
Why the third day?
It's a Korean custom. Kind of our last day to pay our respects to her soul.
Oh.

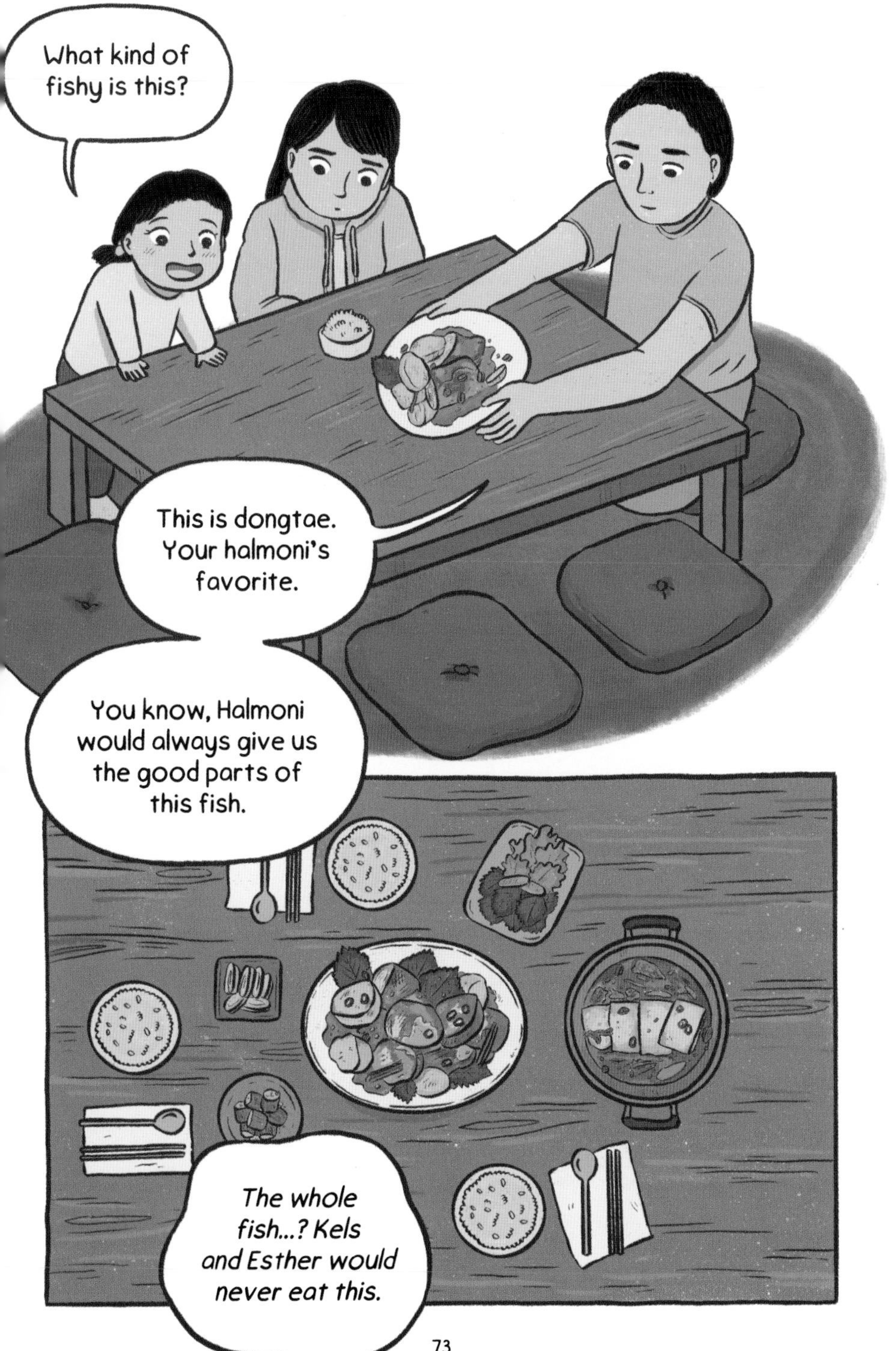
What kind of fishy is this?
This is dongtae. Your halmoni's favorite.
You know, Halmoni would always give us the good parts of this fish.
The whole fish...? Kels and Esther would never eat this.

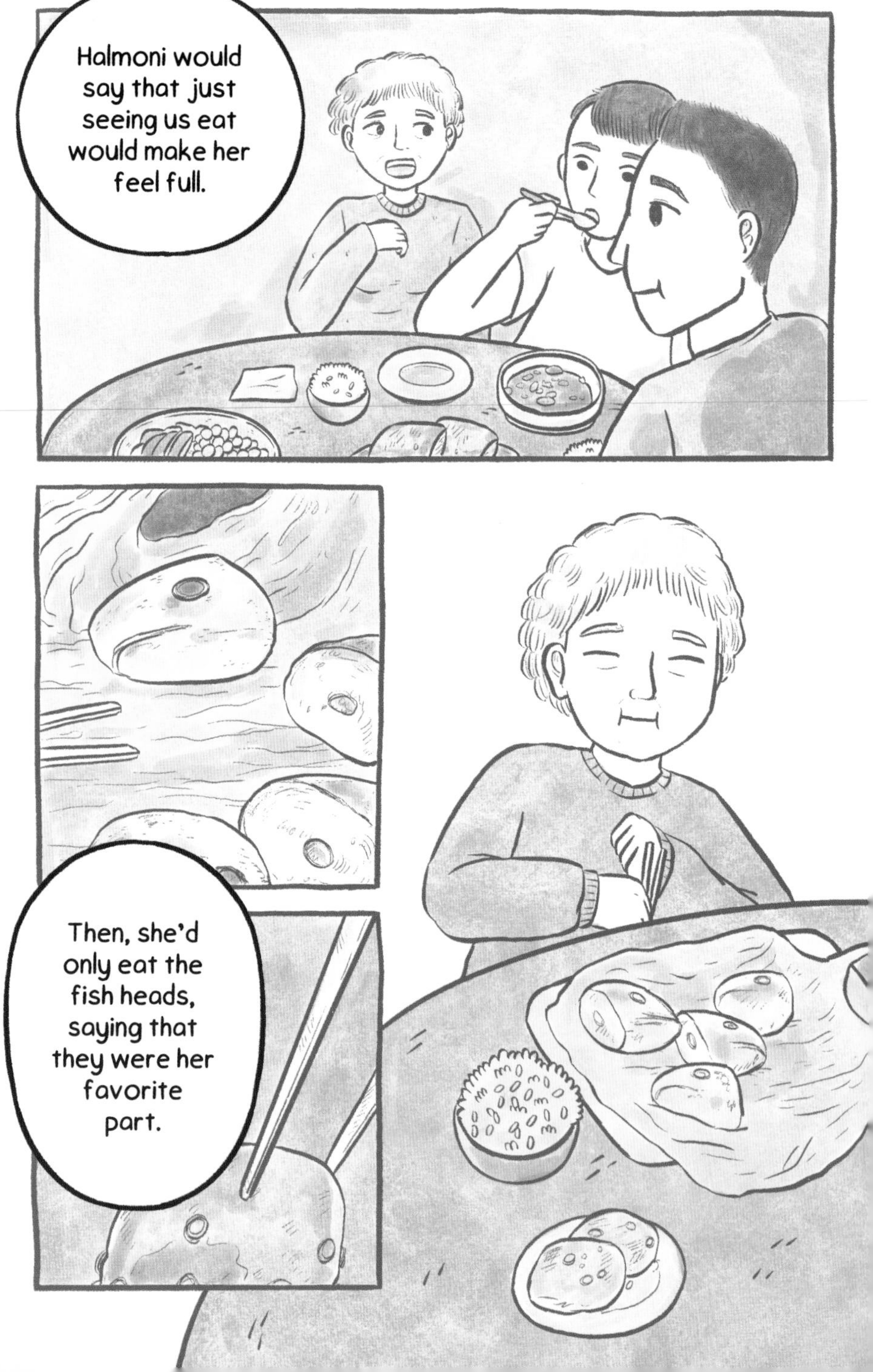
Halmoni would say that just seeing us eat would make her feel full.
Then, she'd only eat the fish heads, saying that they were her favorite part.

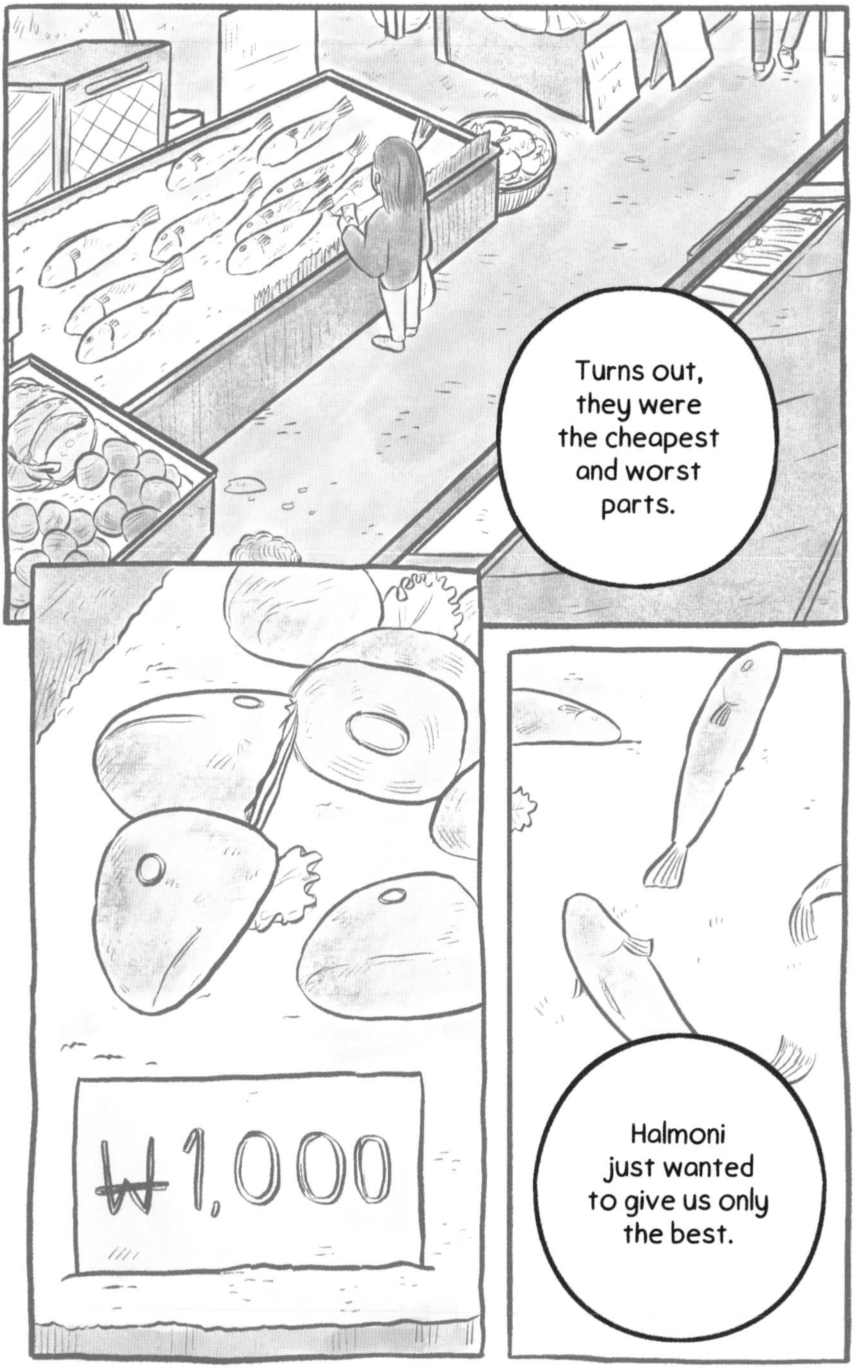
Turns out, they were the cheapest and worst parts.
₩1,000
Halmoni just wanted to give us only the best.

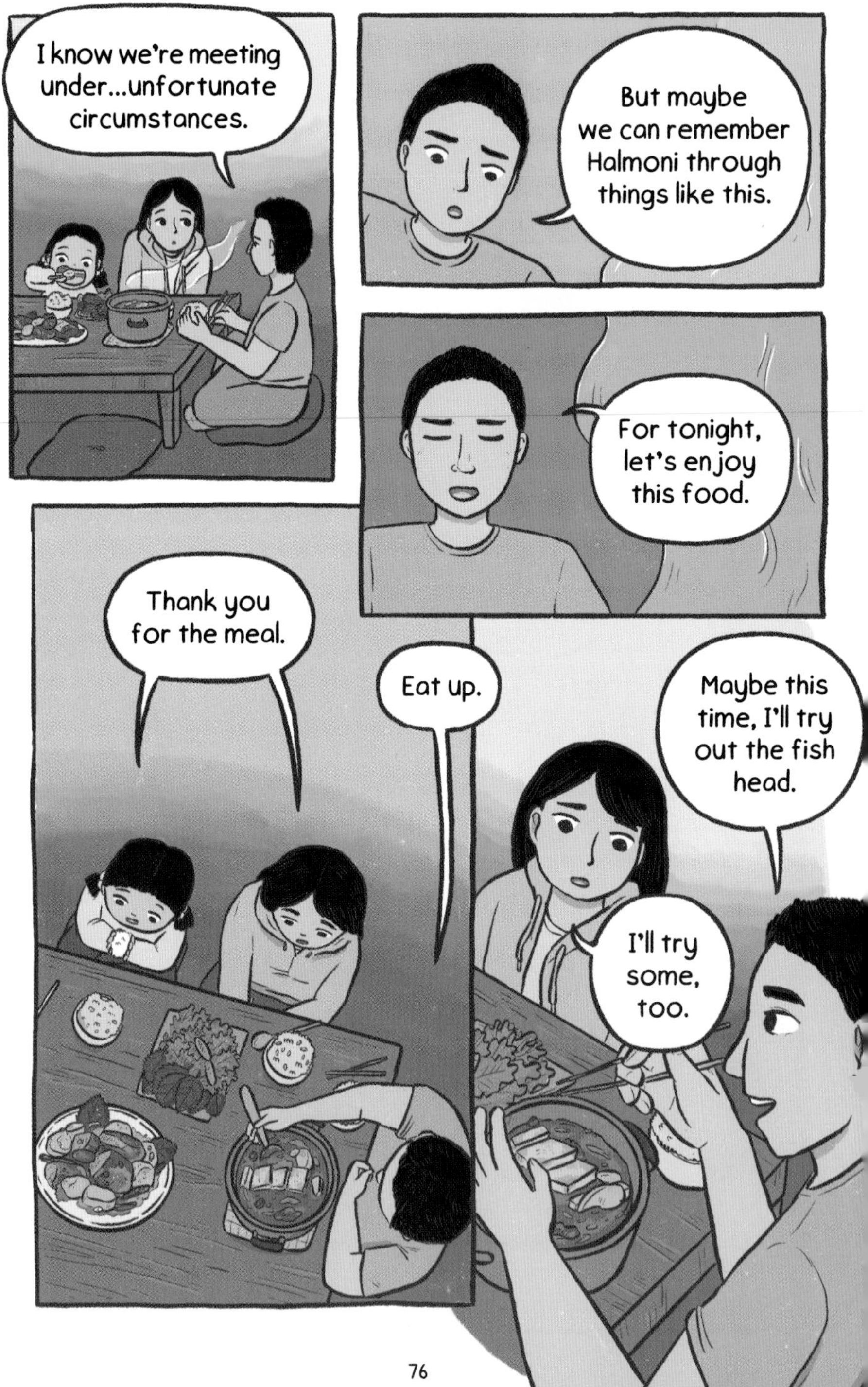
I know we're meeting under...unfortunate circumstances.
But maybe we can remember Halmoni through things like this.
For tonight, let's enjoy this food.
Thank you for the meal.
Eat up.
Maybe this time, I'll try out the fish head.
I'll try some, too.

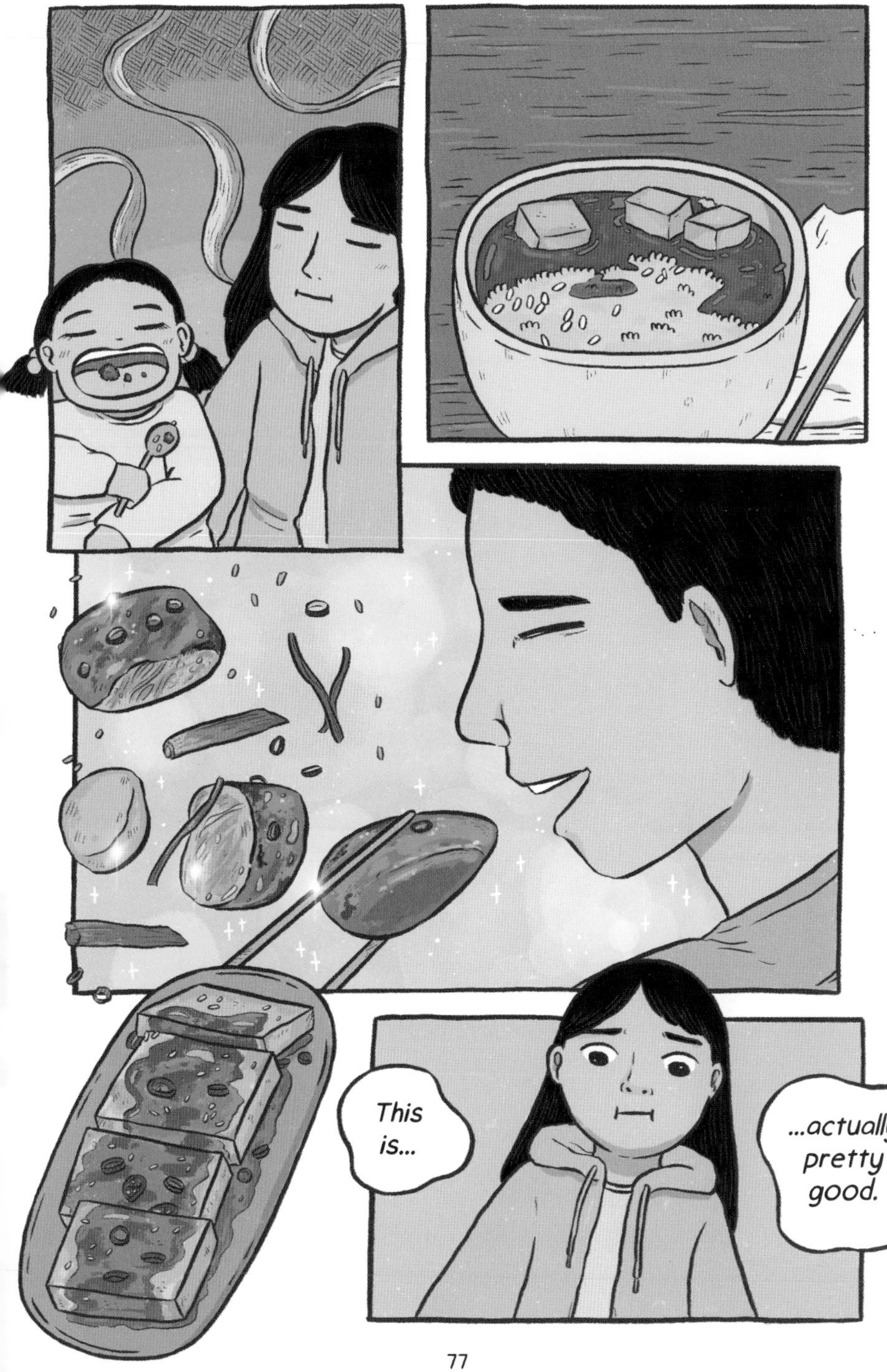
This is...
...actually pretty good.

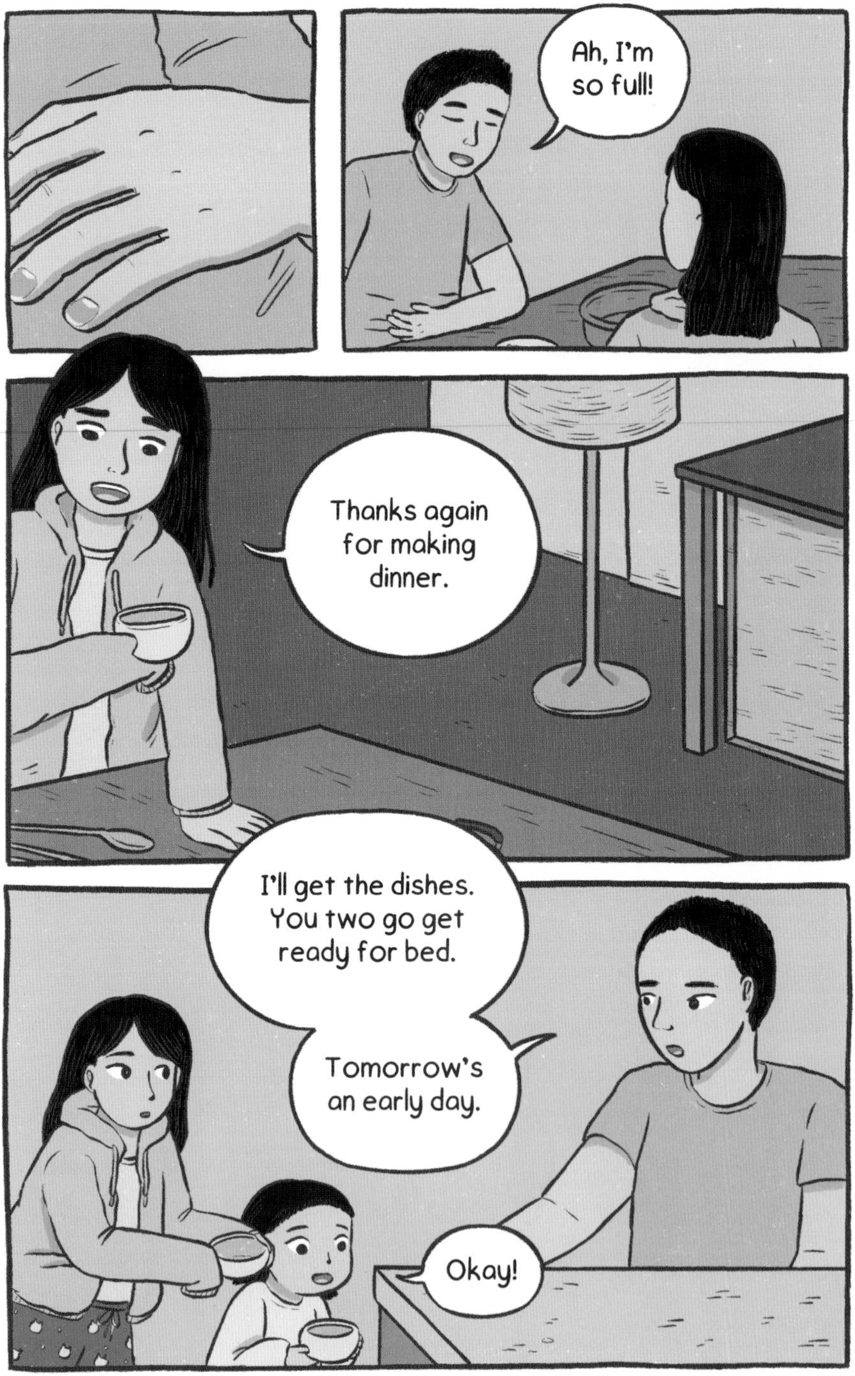
Ah, I'm so full!
Thanks again for making dinner.
I'll get the dishes. You two go get ready for bed.
Tomorrow's an early day.
Okay!

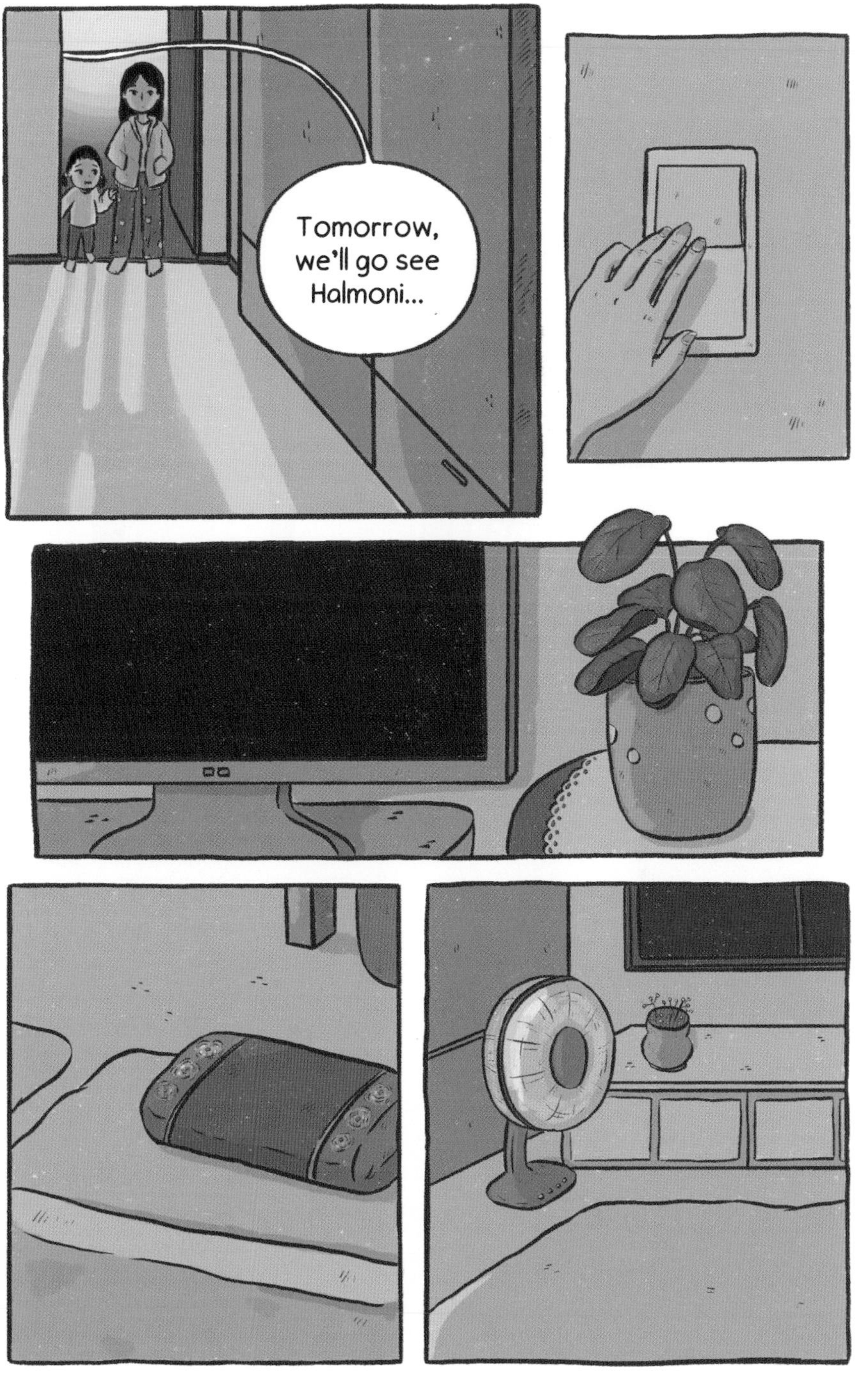
Tomorrow, we'll go see Halmoni...

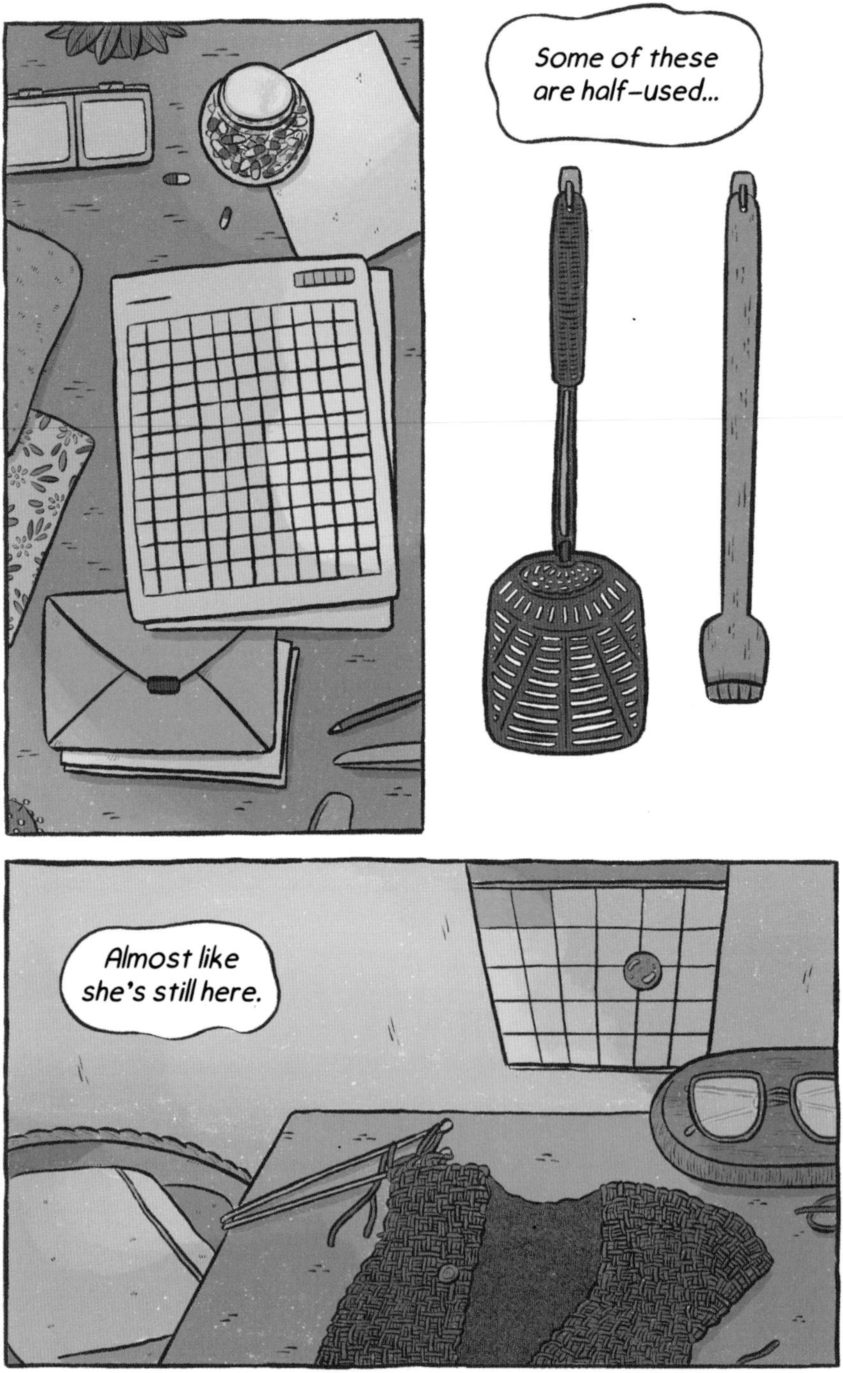
Some of these are half-used...
Almost like she's still here.

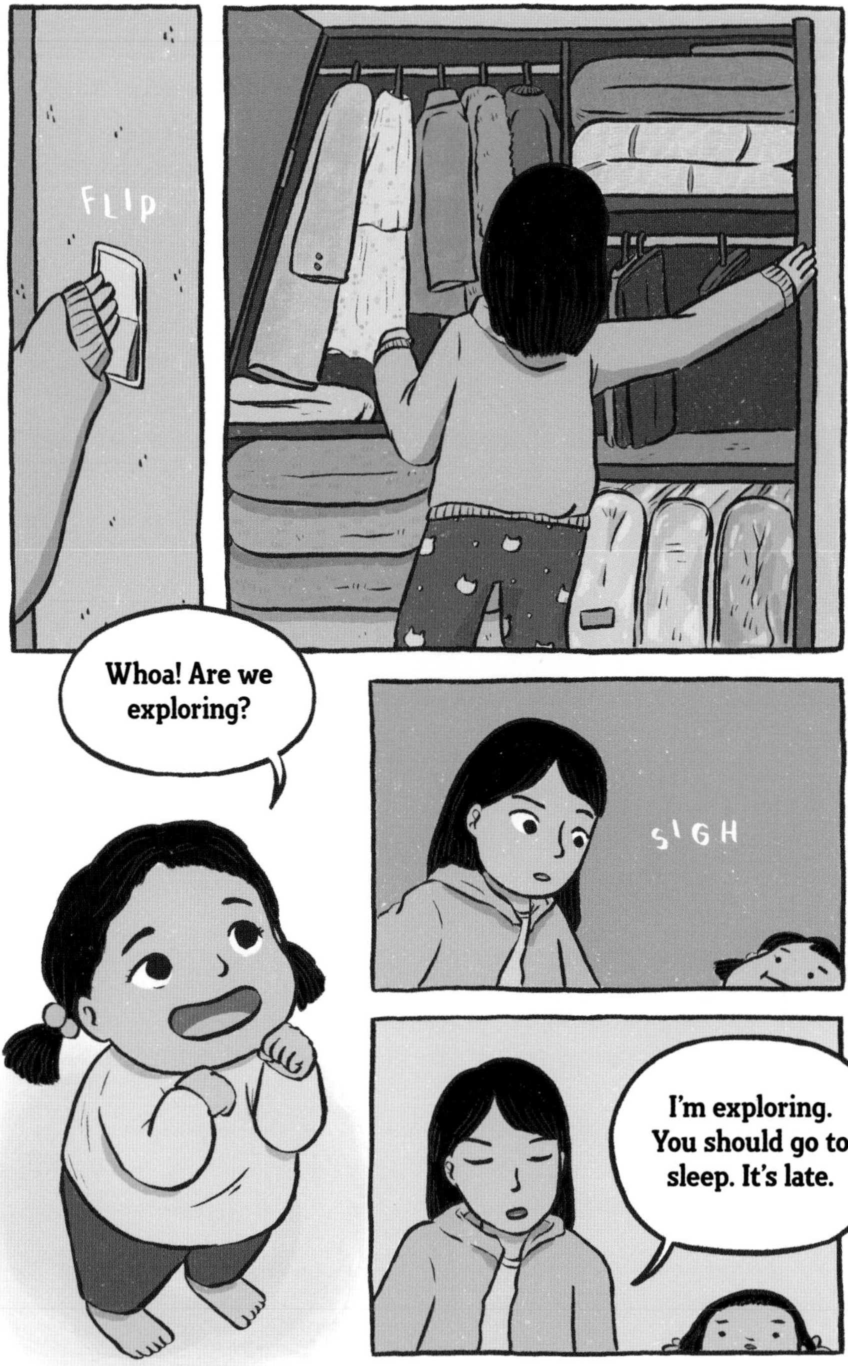
FLIP
Whoa! Are we exploring?
SIGH
I'm exploring. You should go to sleep. It's late.

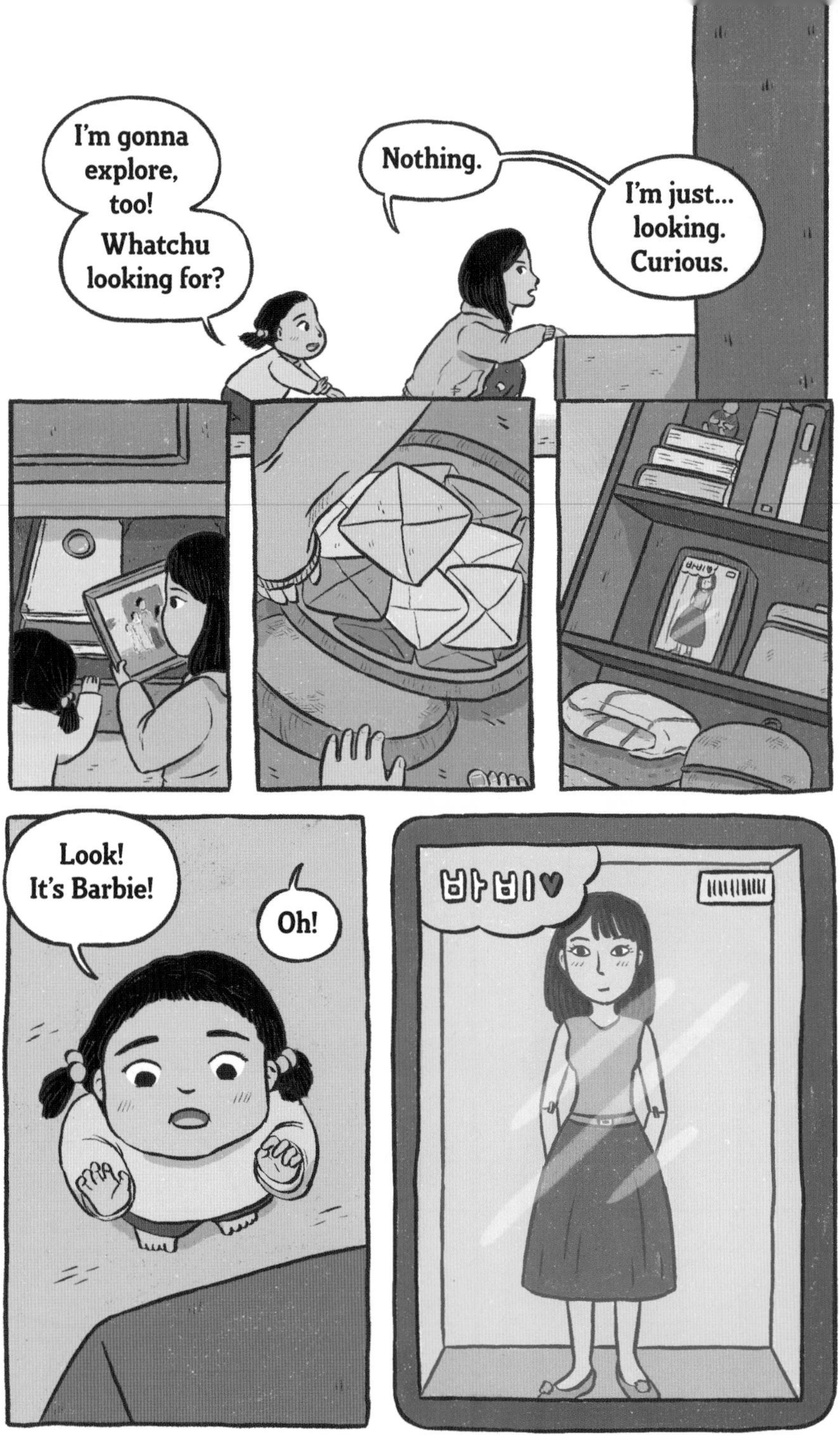

I'm gonna explore, too!
Whatchu looking for?
Nothing.
I'm just... looking. Curious.
Look! It's Barbie!
Oh!
바비♥

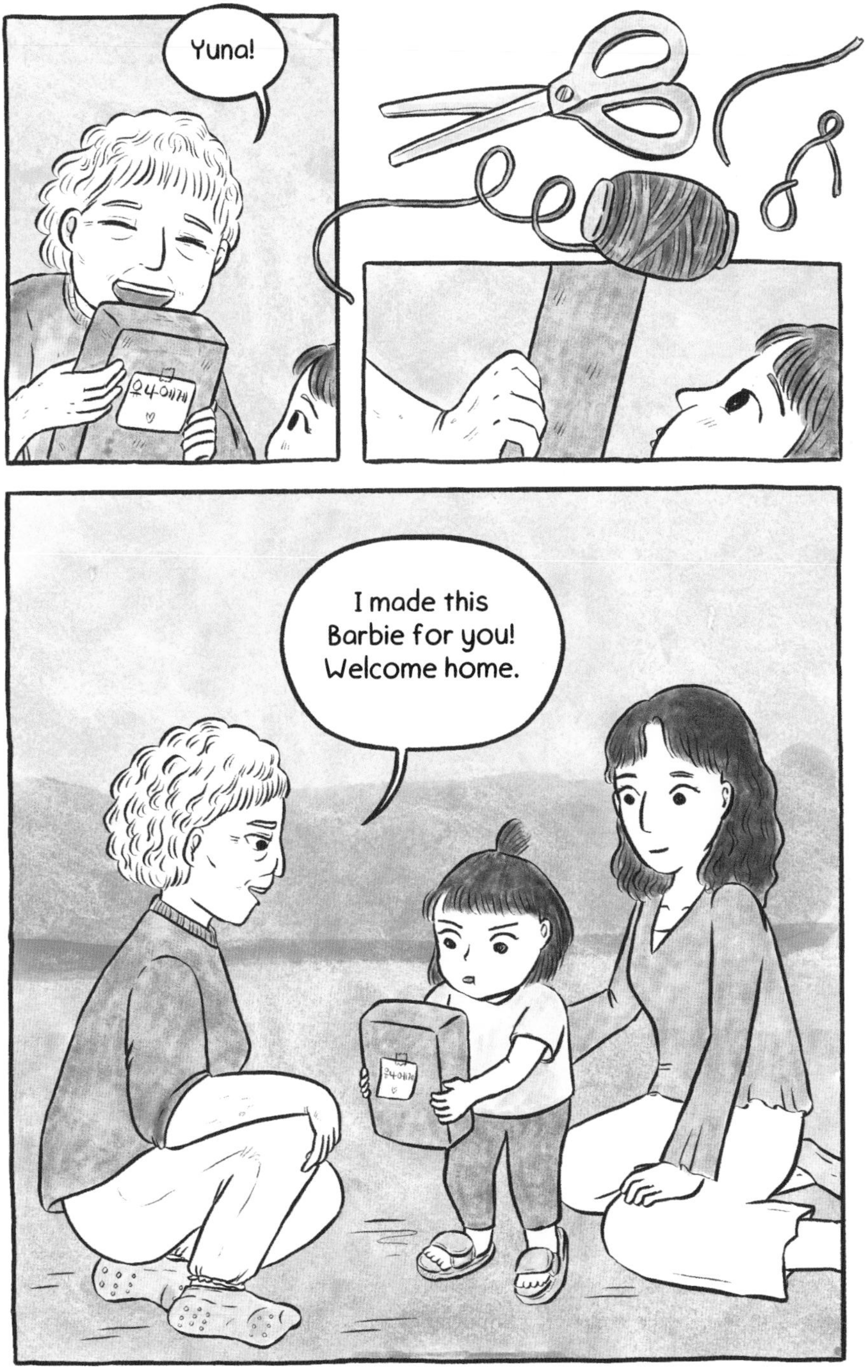
Yuna!
I made this Barbie for you! Welcome home.

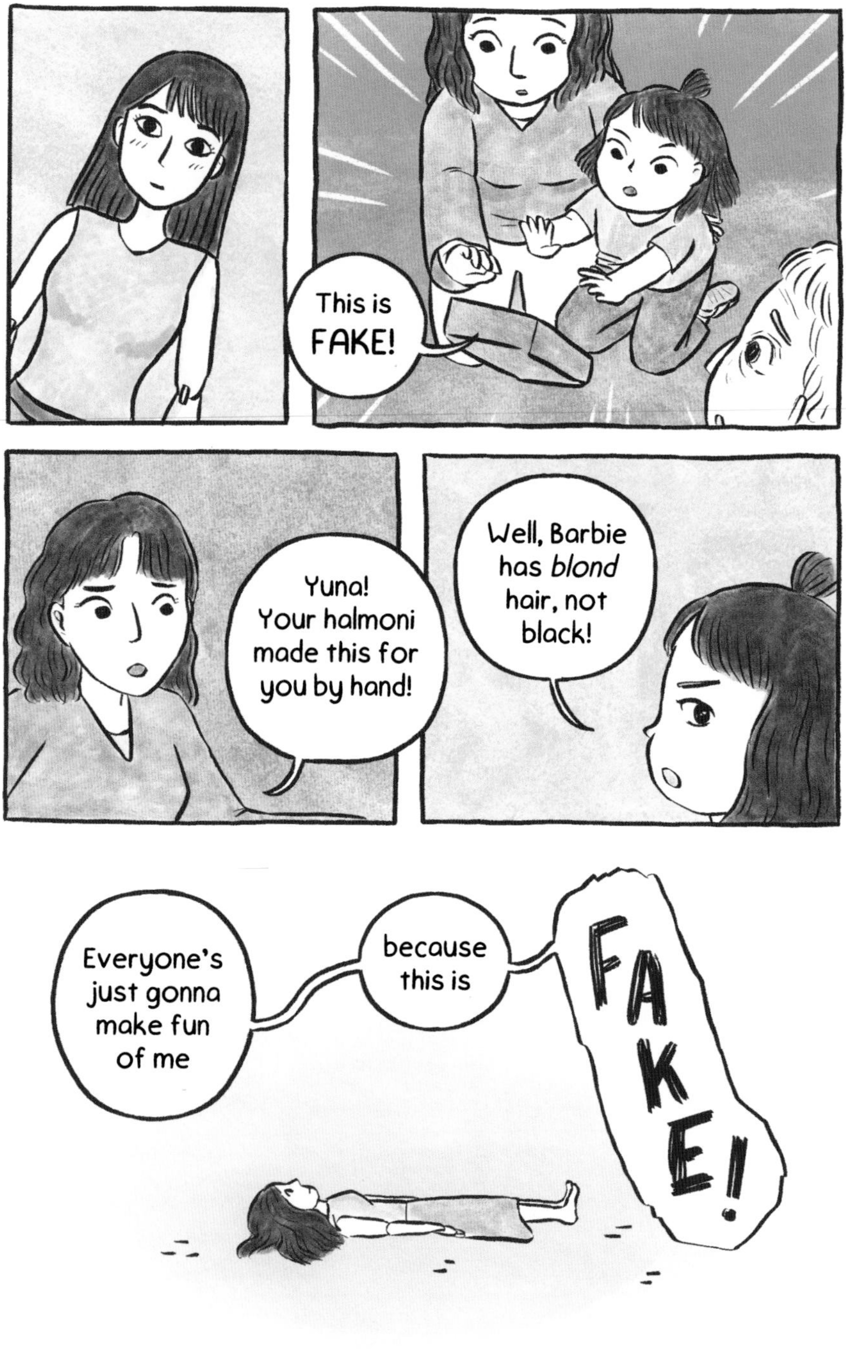
This is FAKE!
Yuna! Your halmoni made this for you by hand!
Well, Barbie has *blond* hair, not black!
Everyone's just gonna make fun of me
because this is
FAKE!

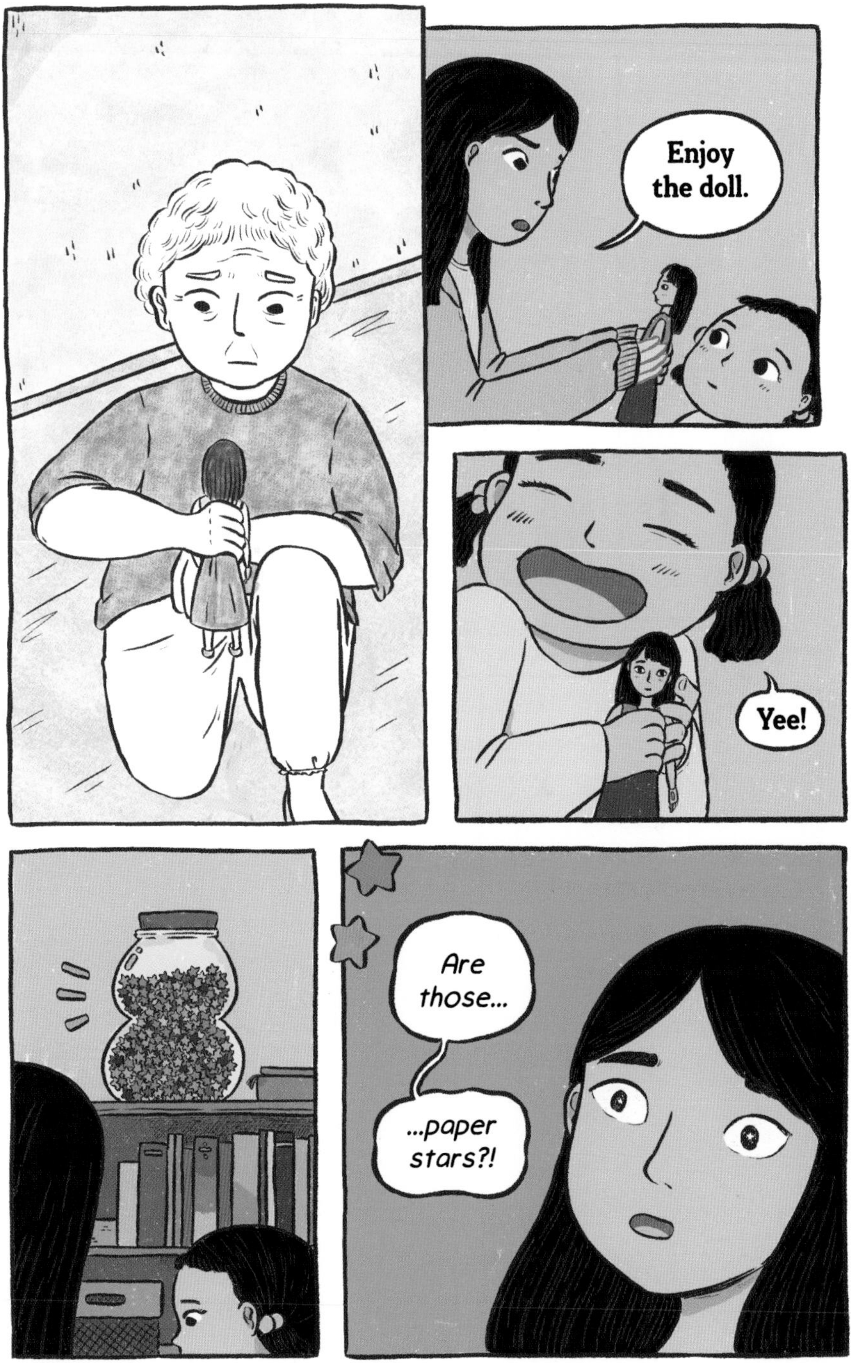
Enjoy the doll.
Yee!
Are those...
...paper stars?!

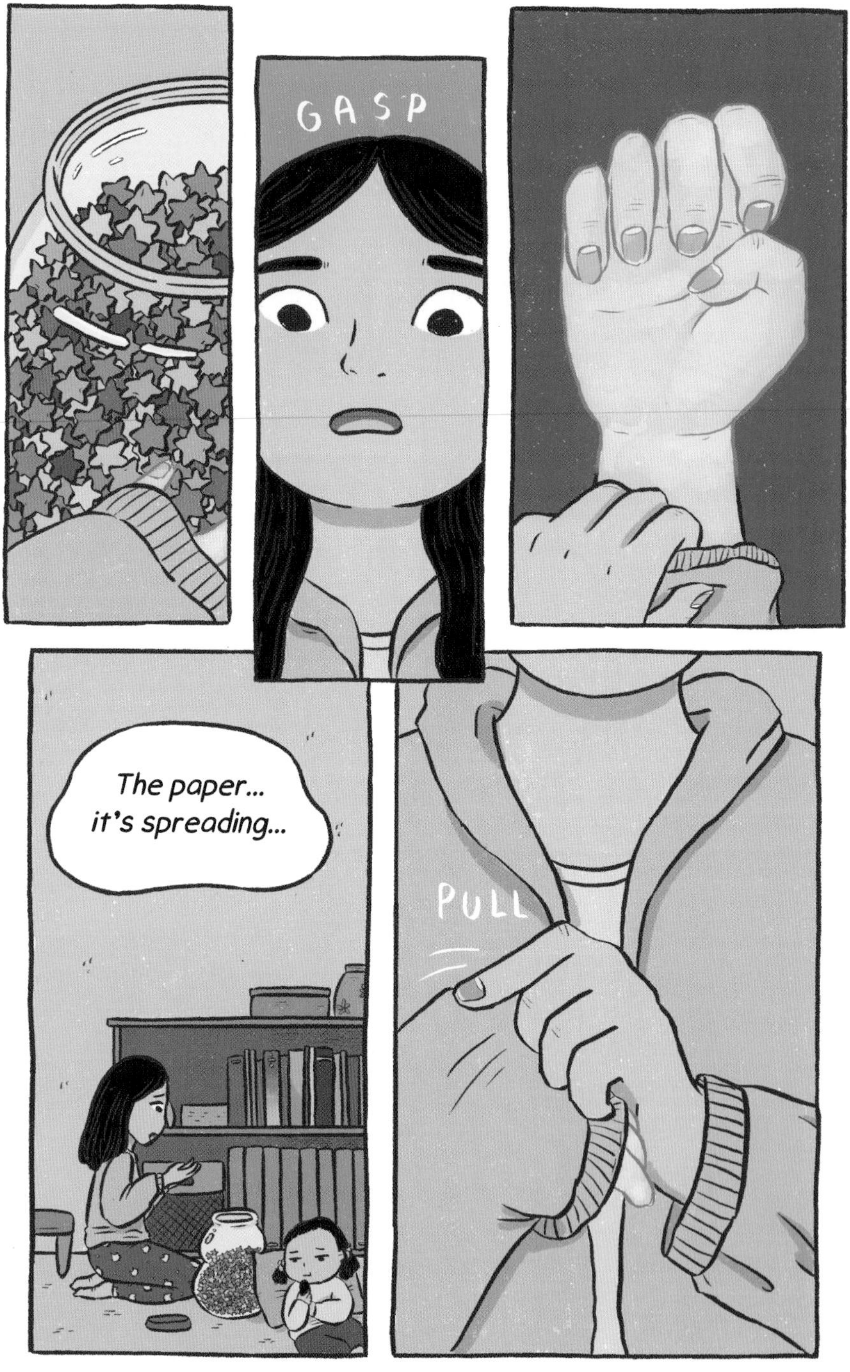
GASP
The paper...
it's spreading...
PULL

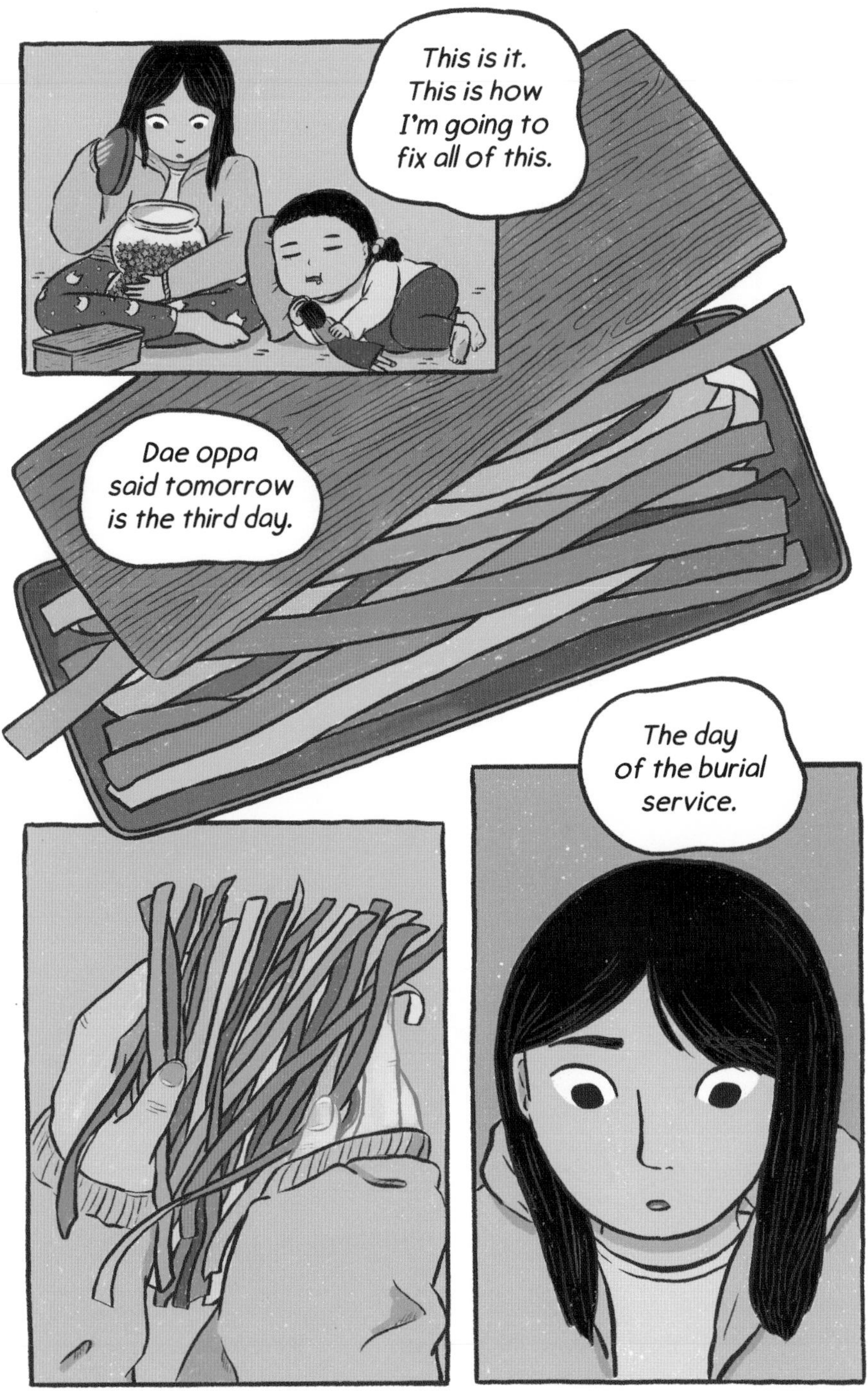
This is it. This is how I'm going to fix all of this.
Dae oppa said tomorrow is the third day.
The day of the burial service.

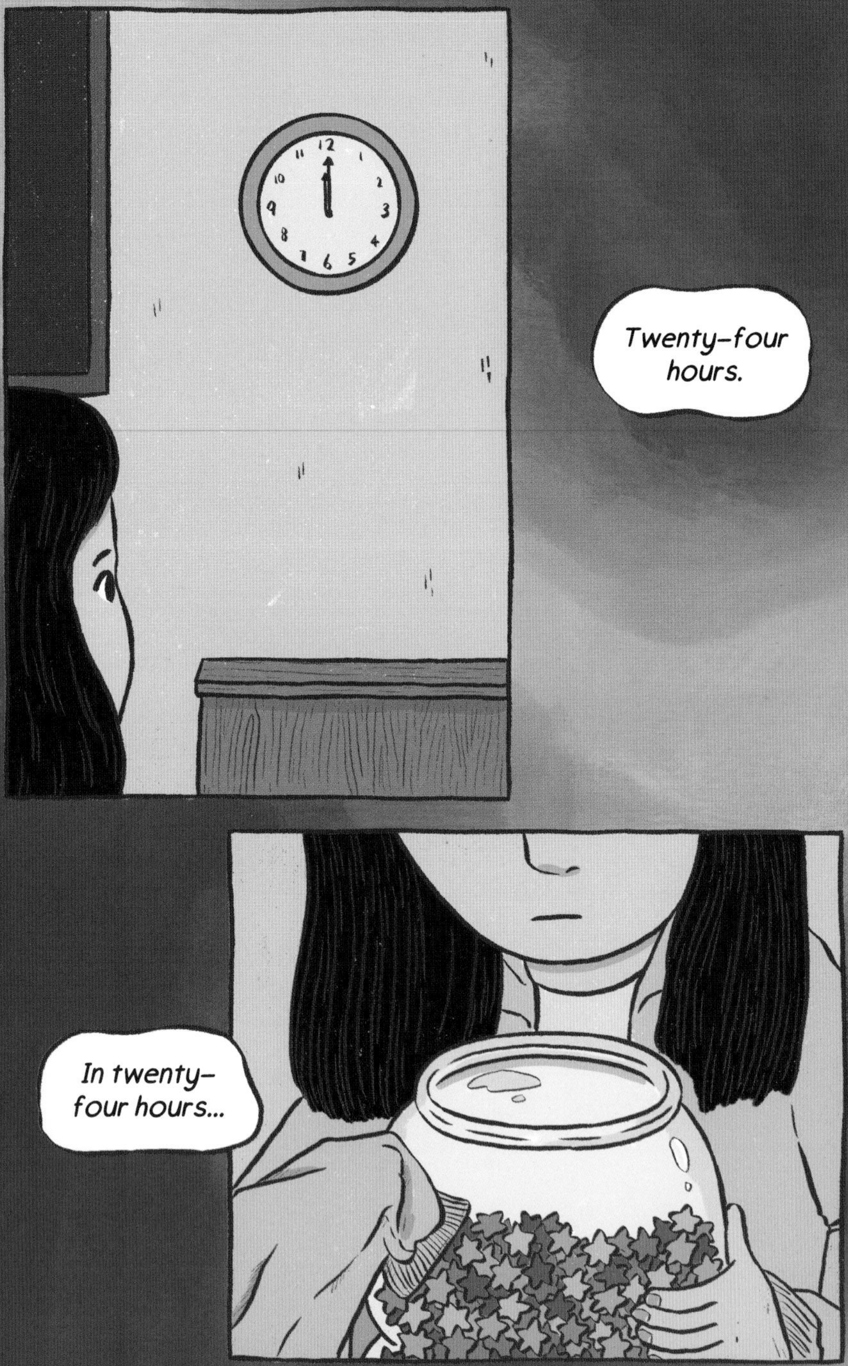
Twenty-four hours.
In twenty-four hours...

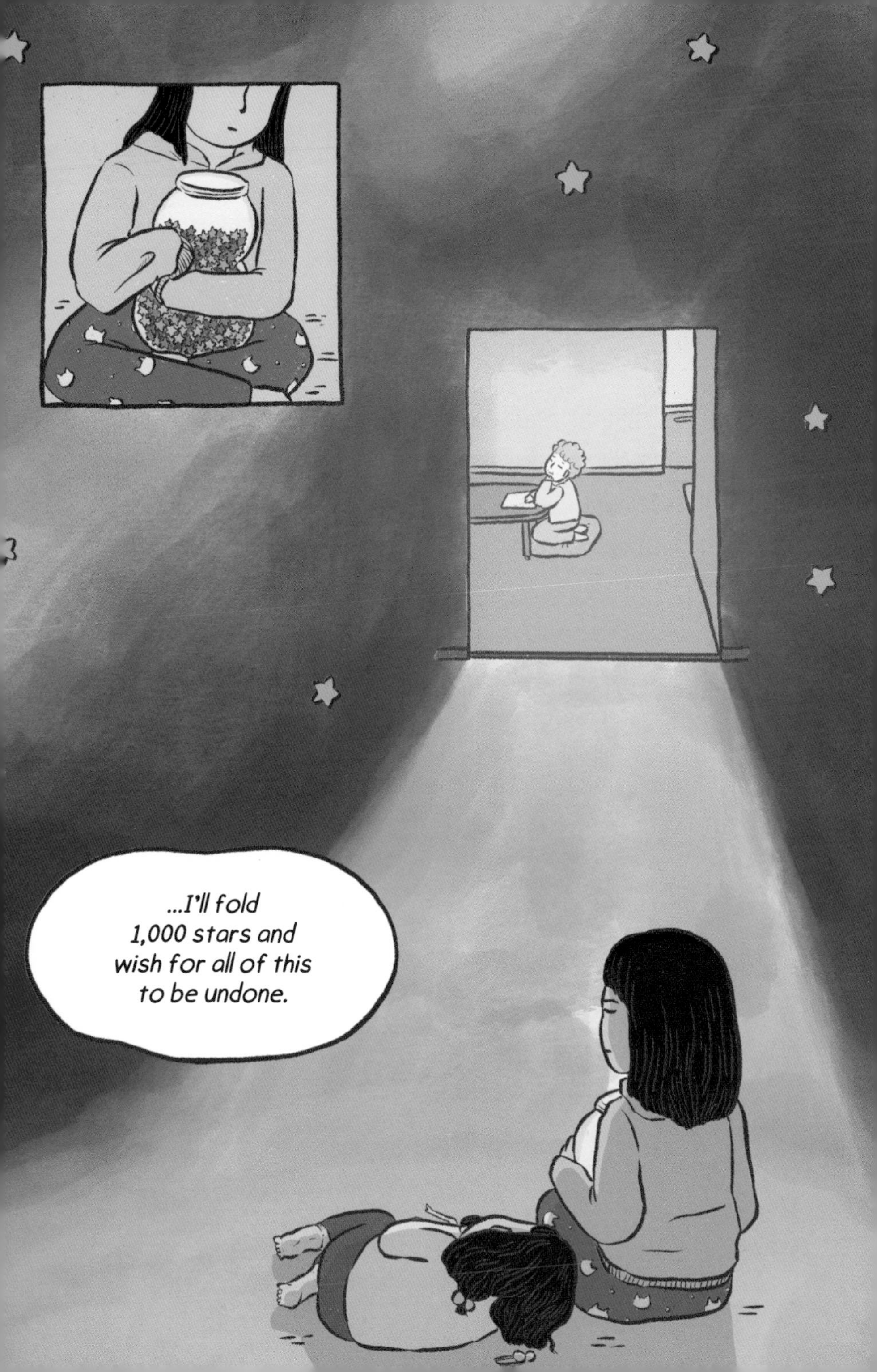
...I'll fold 1,000 stars and wish for all of this to be undone.

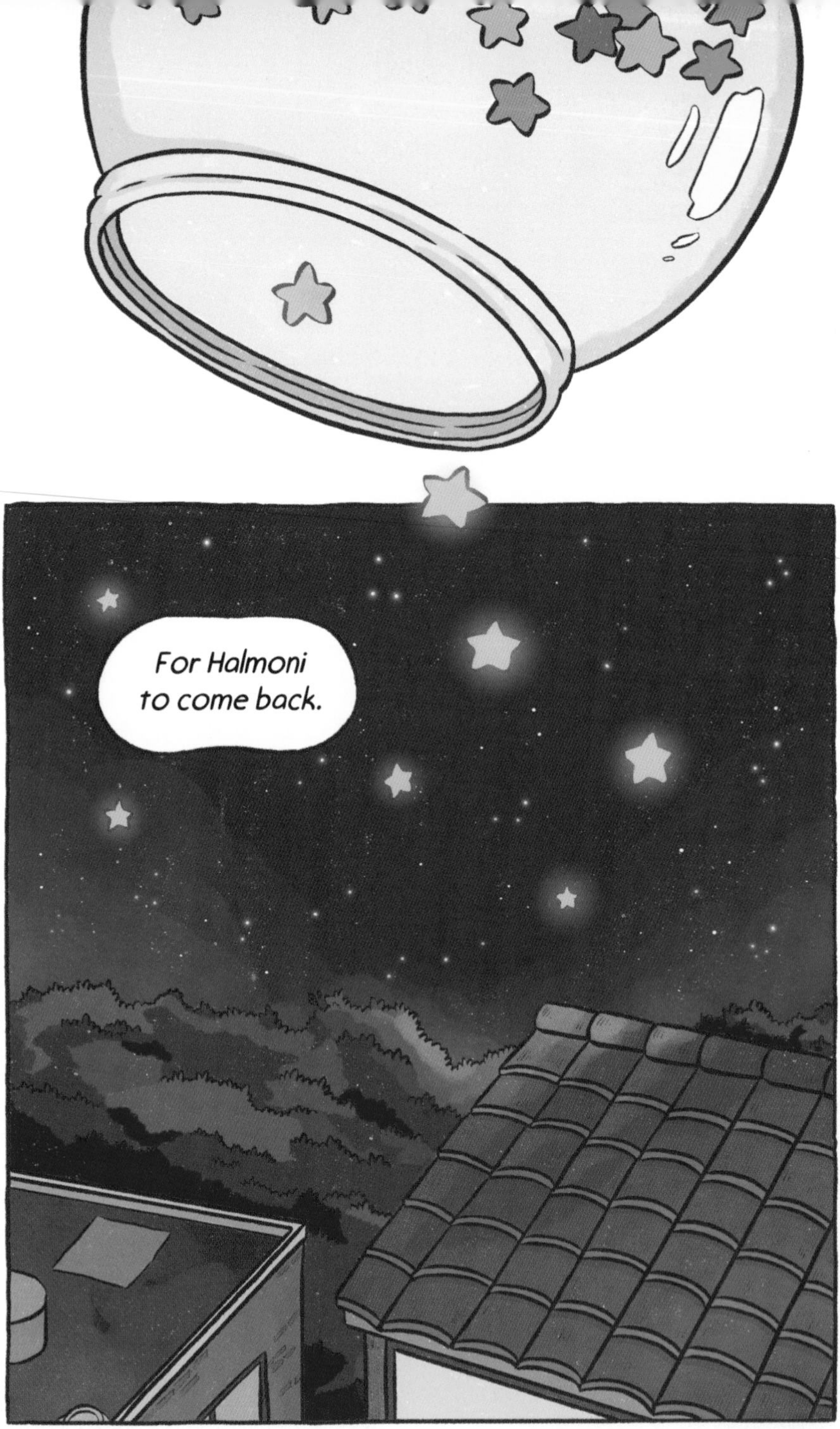
For Halmoni
to come back.

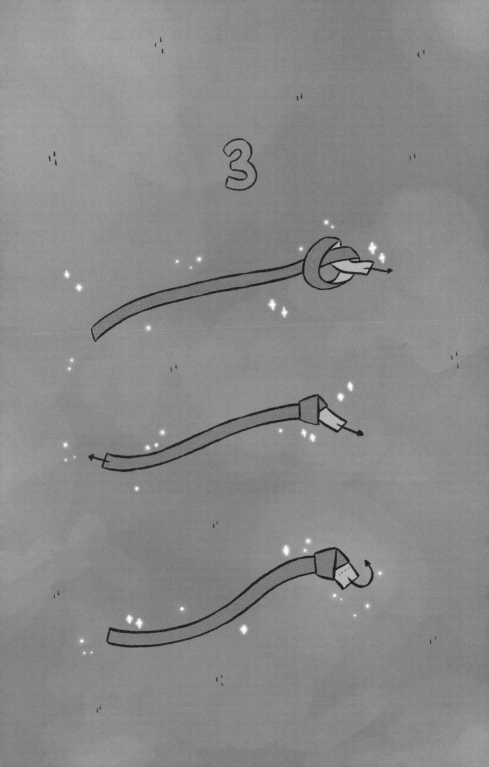

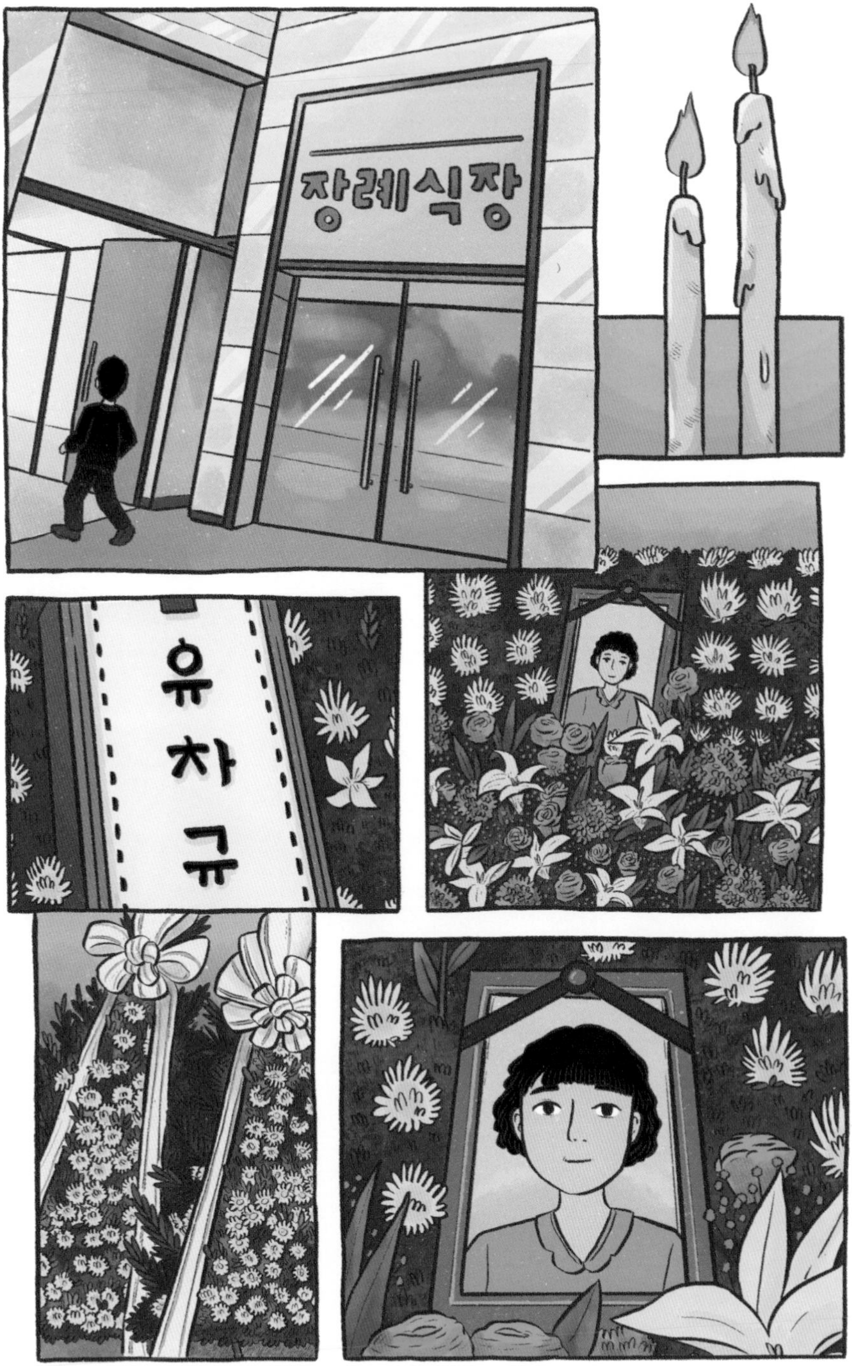
장례식장
유 차 규

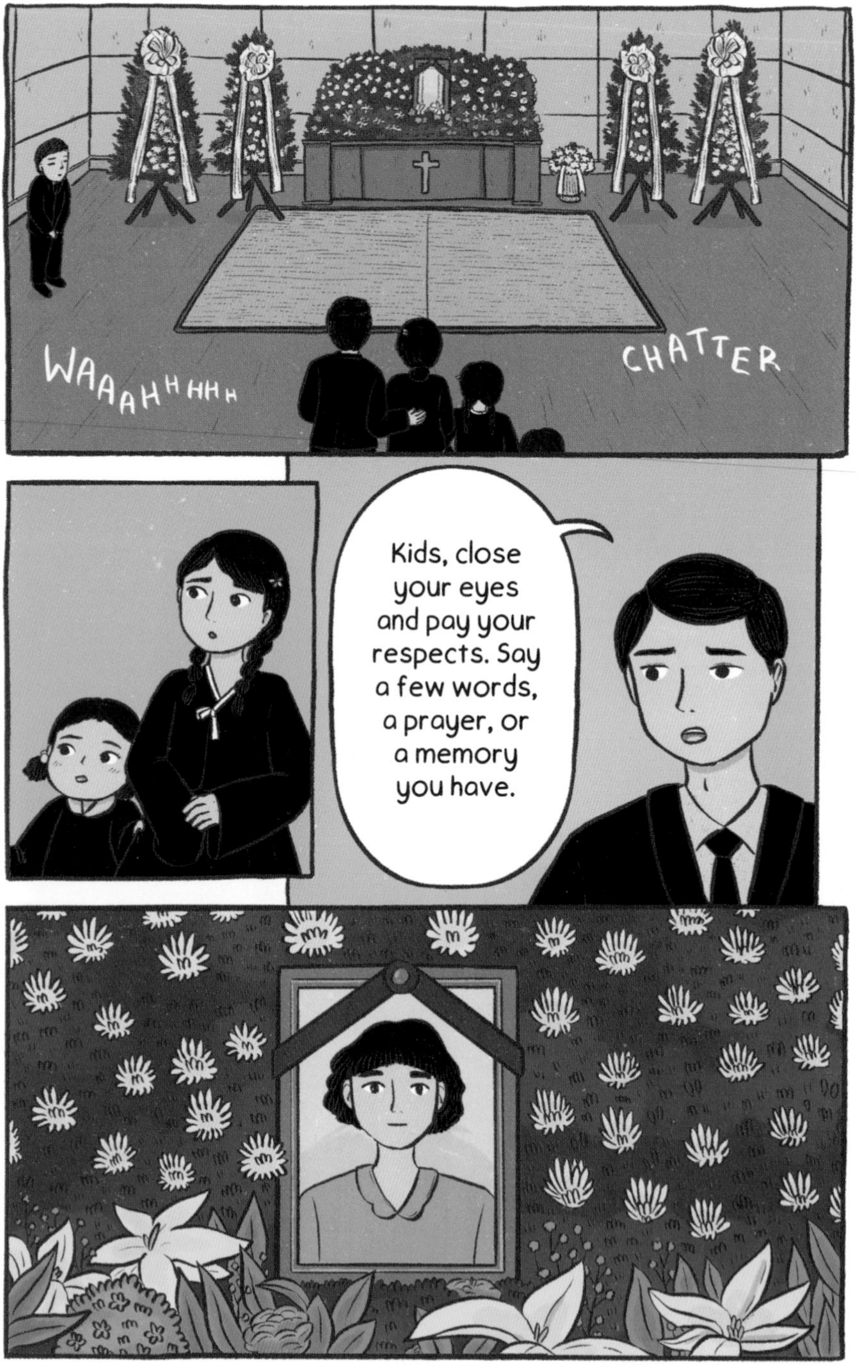
WAAAHHHHH
CHATTER
Kids, close your eyes and pay your respects. Say a few words, a prayer, or a memory you have.

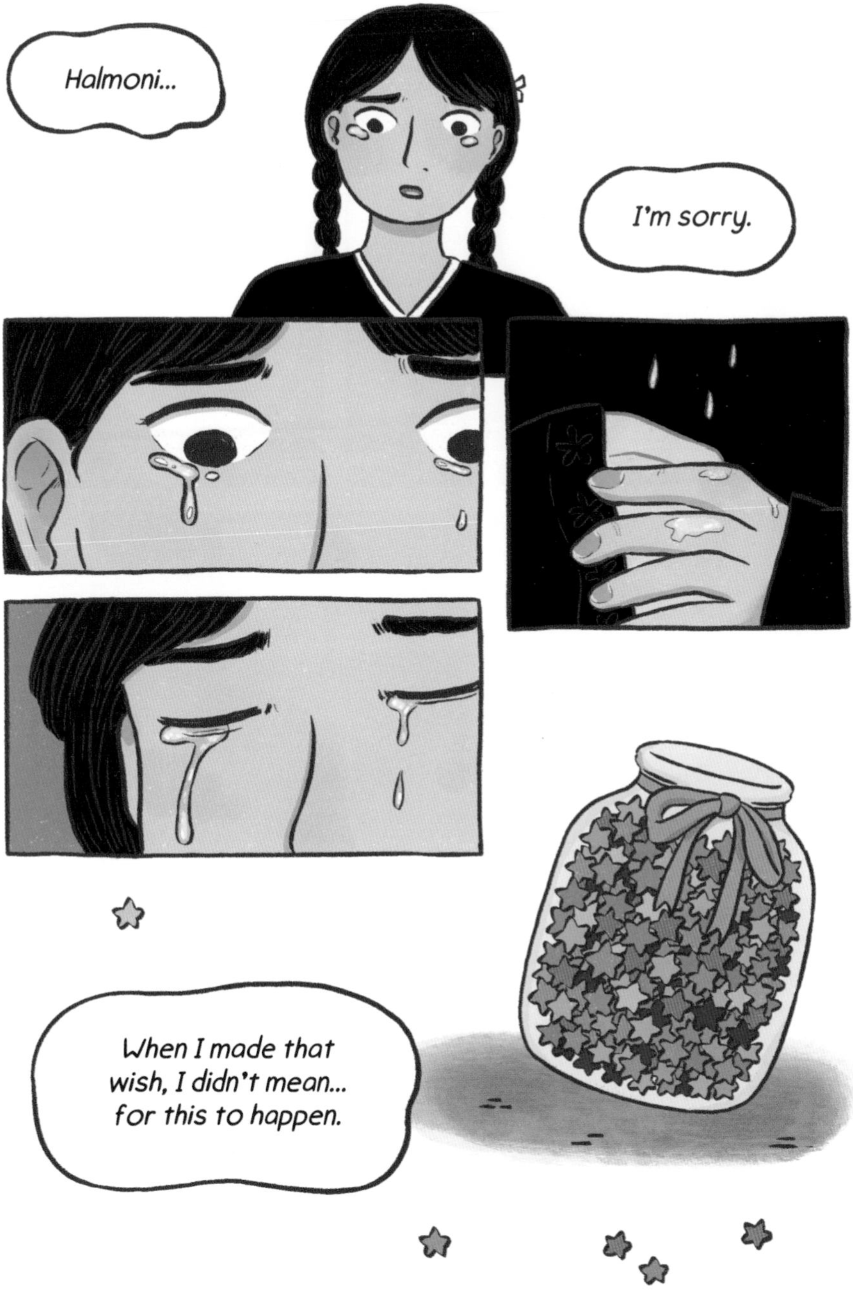
Halmoni...
I'm sorry.
When I made that wish, I didn't mean... for this to happen.

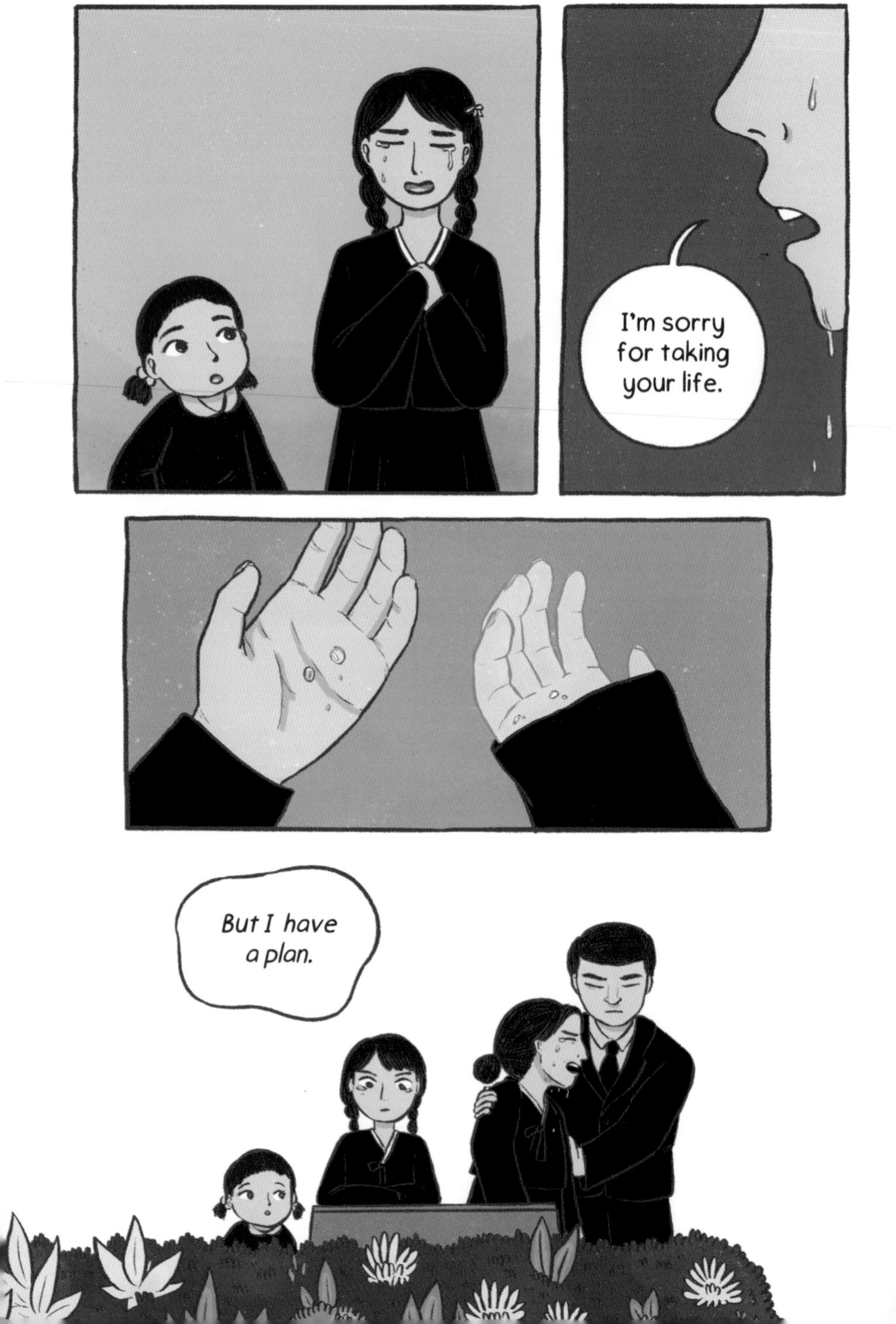

I'm sorry for taking your life.
But I have a plan.

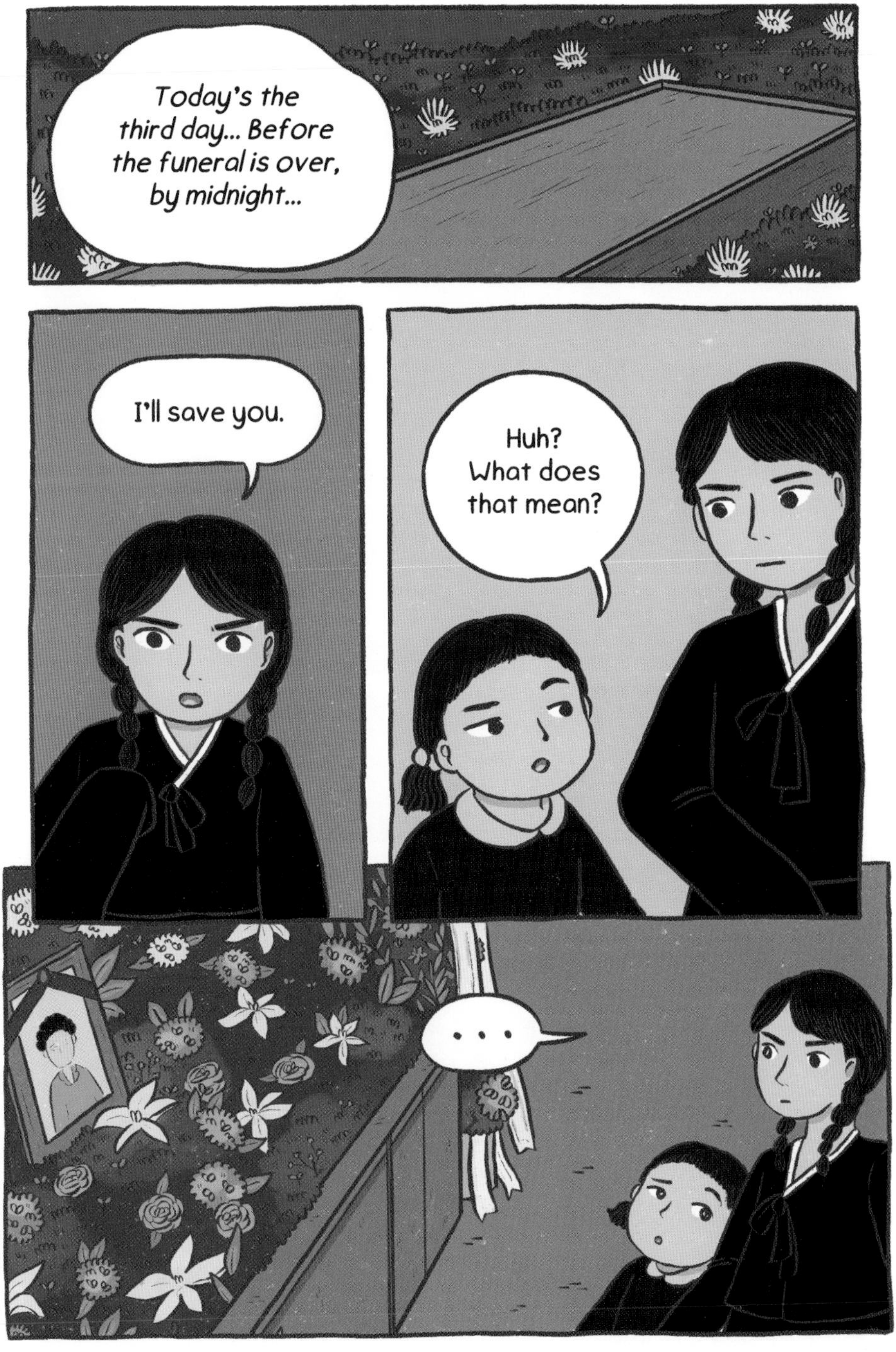
Today's the third day... Before the funeral is over, by midnight...
I'll save you.
Huh? What does that mean?
...

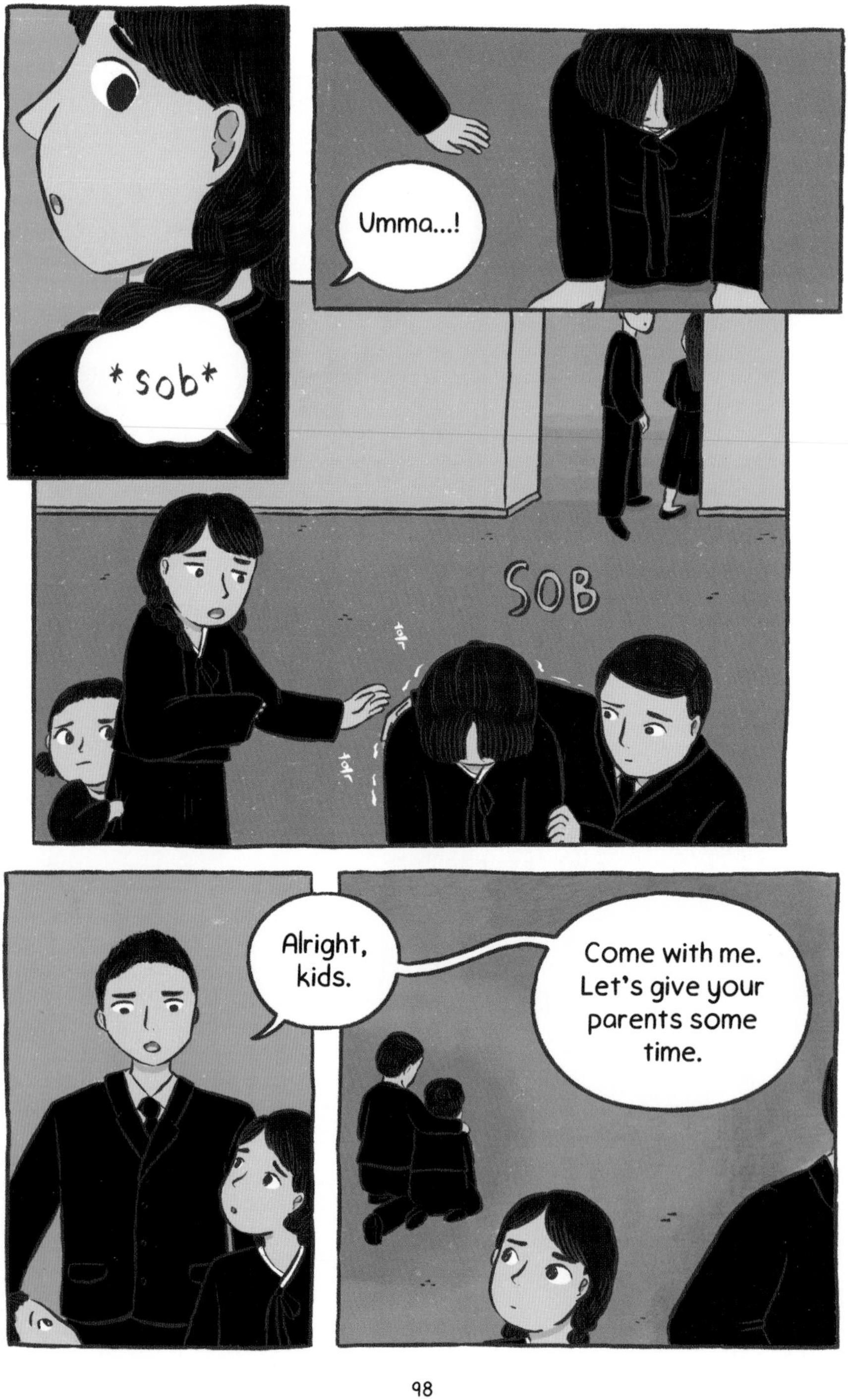
Umma...!
sob
SOB
Alright, kids.
Come with me. Let's give your parents some time.

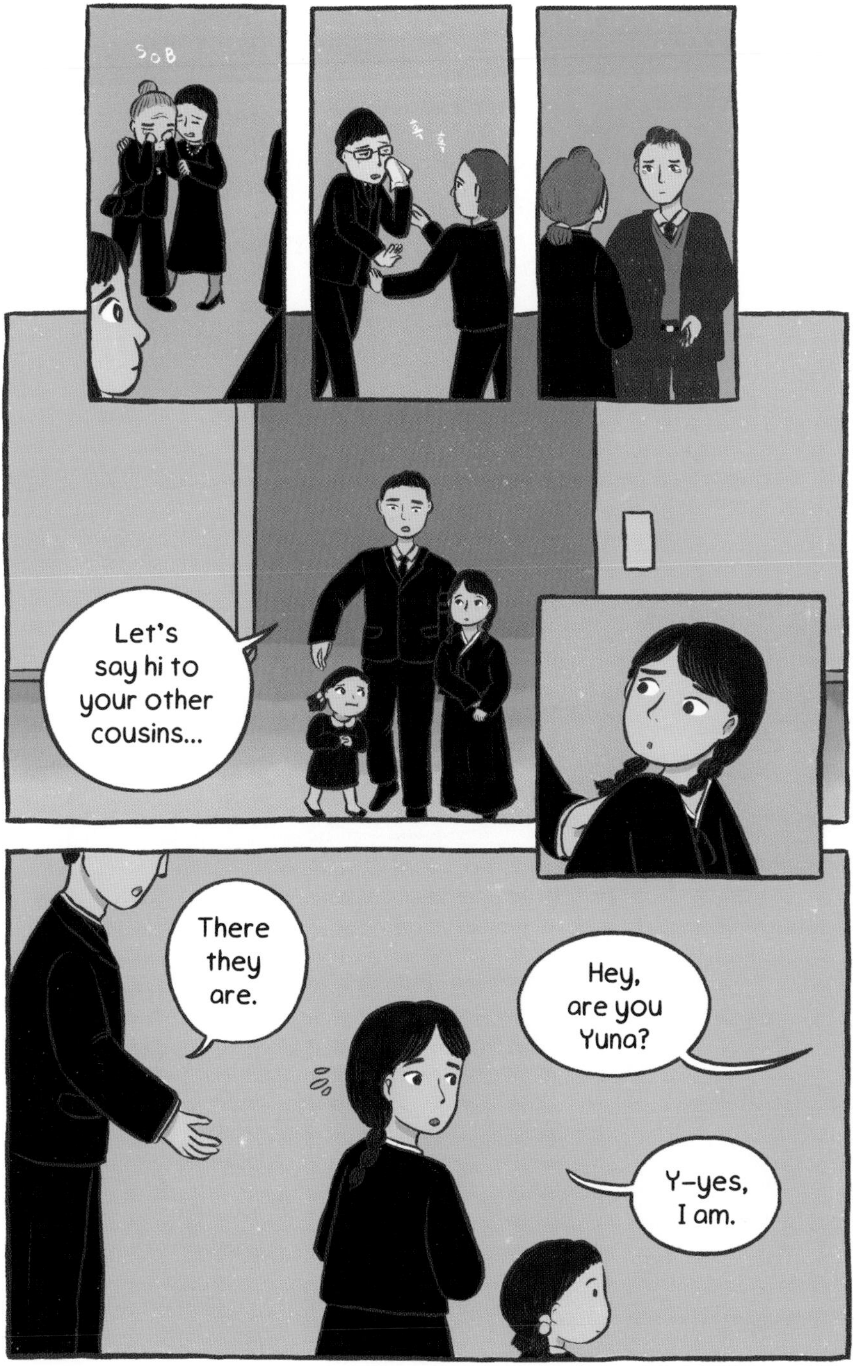
SOB
Let's say hi to your other cousins...
There they are.
Hey, are you Yuna?
Y-yes, I am.

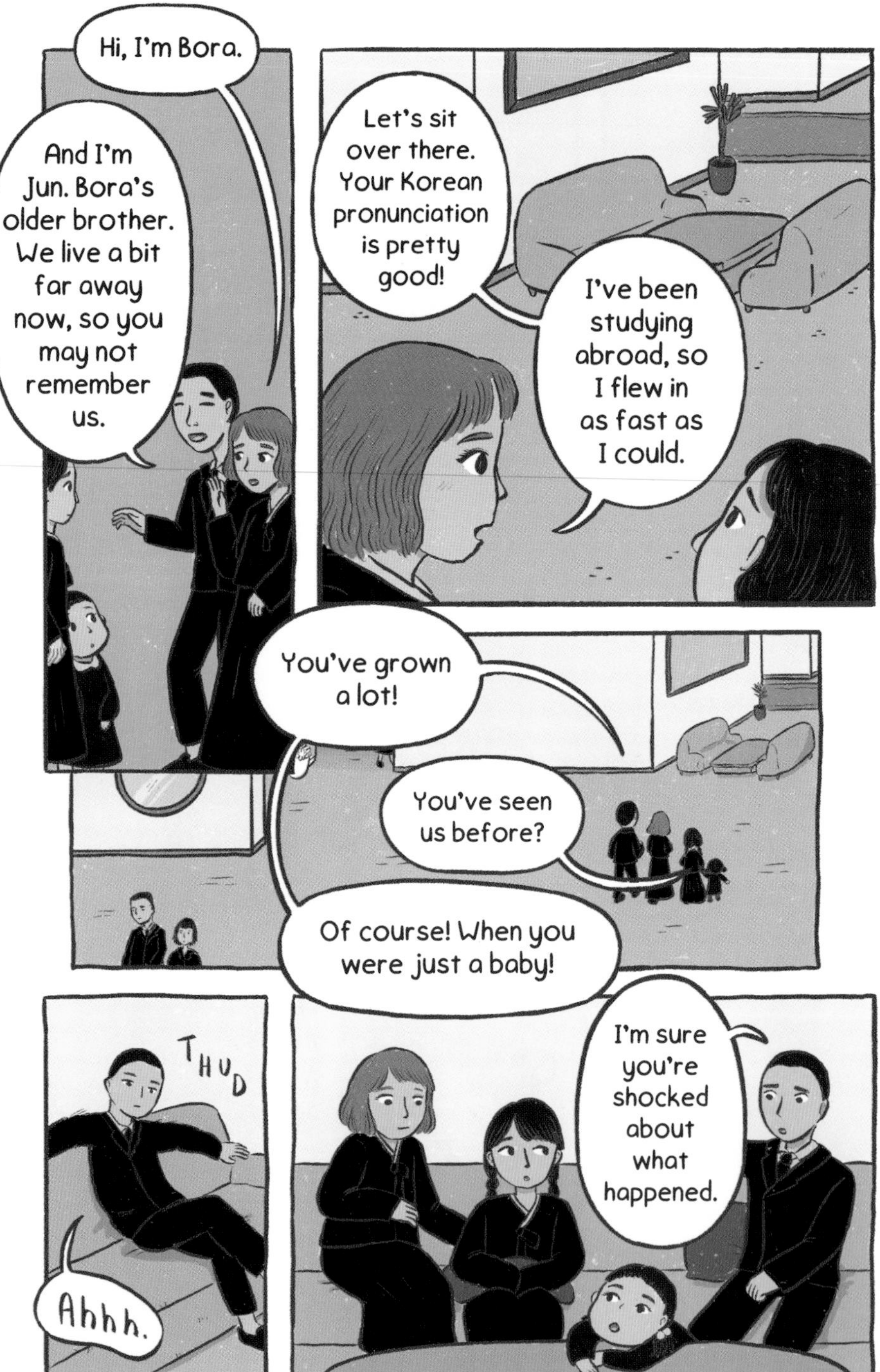
Hi, I'm Bora.
And I'm Jun. Bora's older brother. We live a bit far away now, so you may not remember us.
Let's sit over there. Your Korean pronunciation is pretty good!
I've been studying abroad, so I flew in as fast as I could.
You've grown a lot!
You've seen us before?
Of course! When you were just a baby!
THUD
Ahhh.
I'm sure you're shocked about what happened.

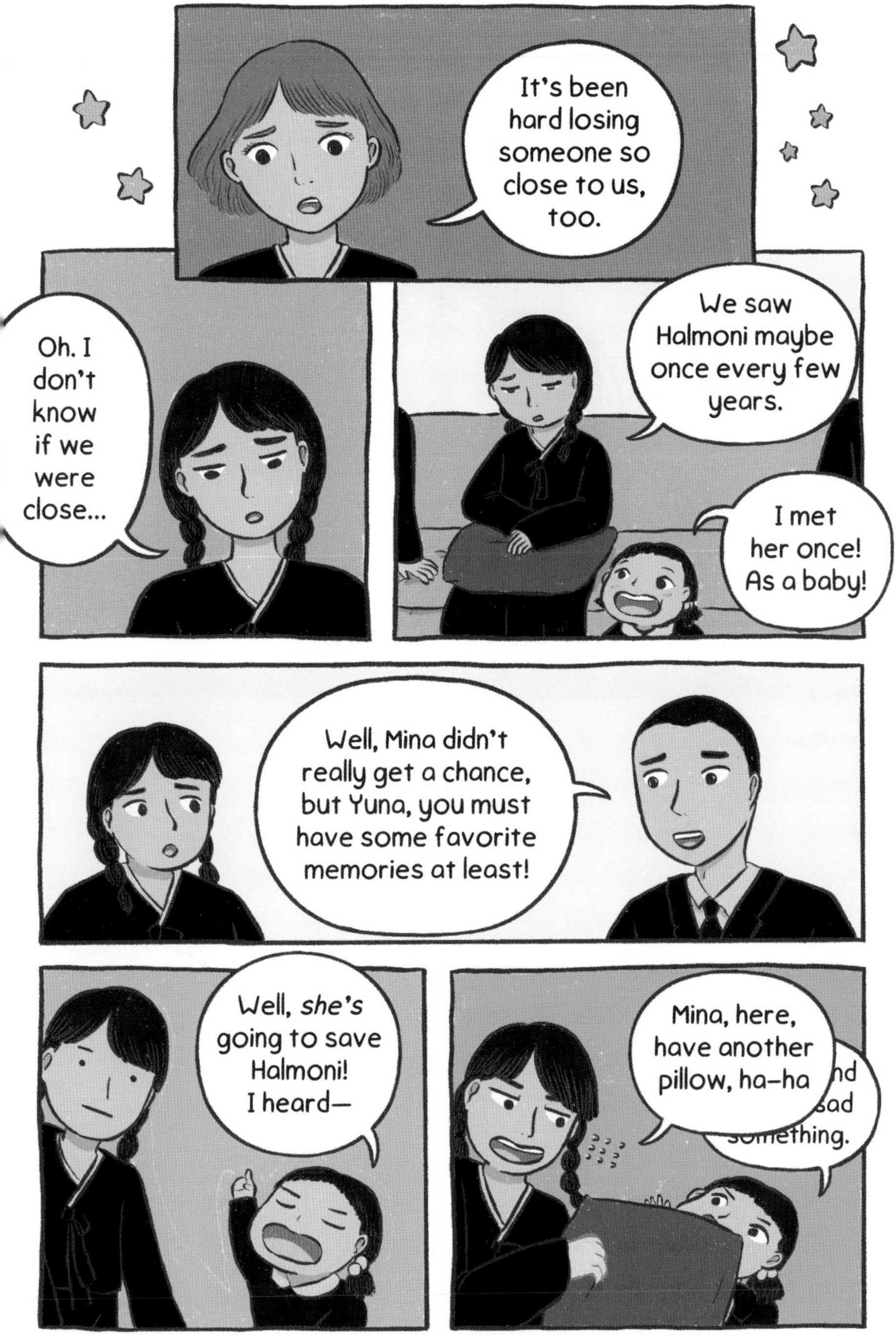
It's been hard losing someone so close to us, too.
Oh. I don't know if we were close...
We saw Halmoni maybe once every few years.
I met her once! As a baby!
Well, Mina didn't really get a chance, but Yuna, you must have some favorite memories at least!
Well, *she's* going to save Halmoni! I heard—
Mina, here, have another pillow, ha-ha

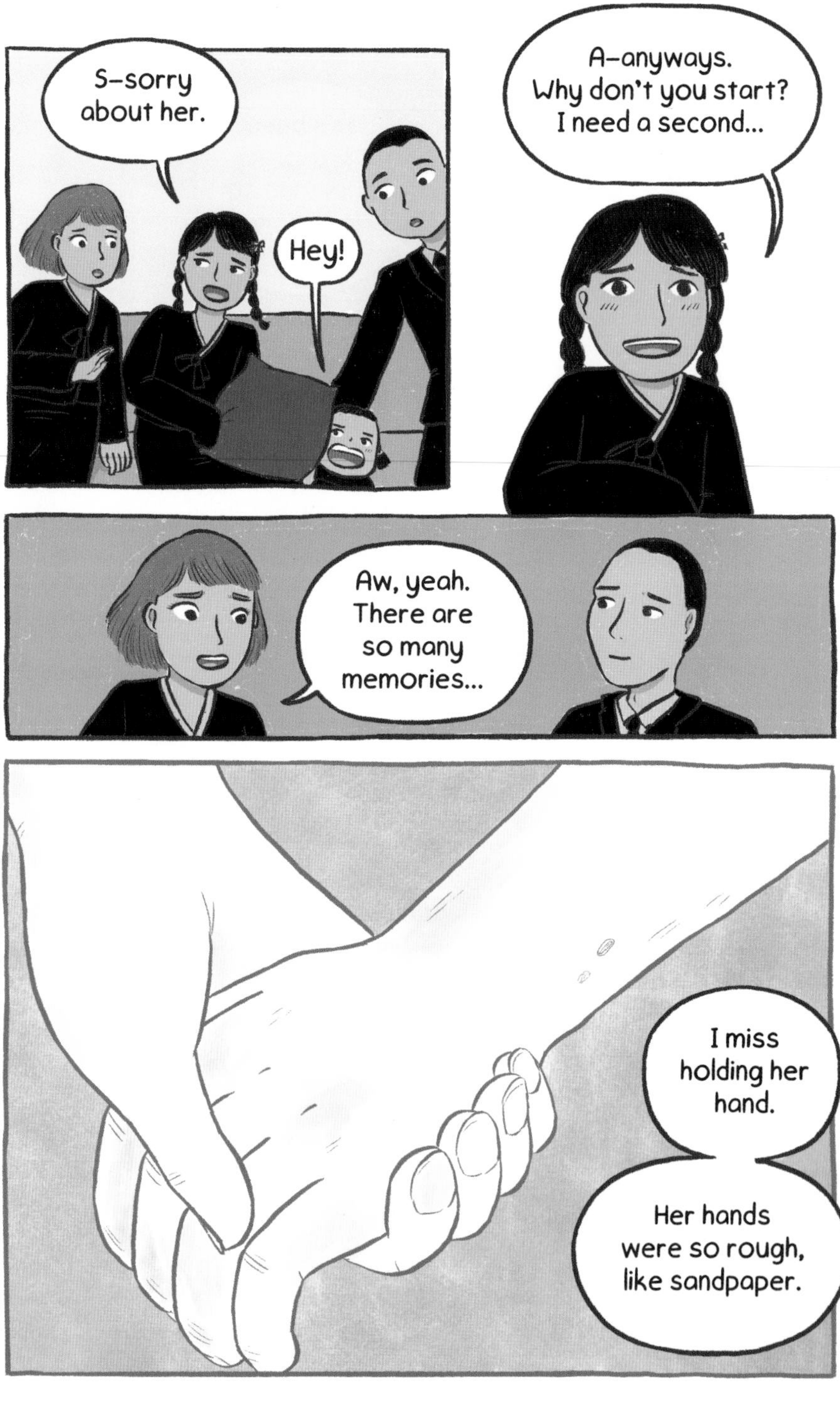
S-sorry about her.
Hey!
A-anyways. Why don't you start? I need a second...
Aw, yeah. There are so many memories...
I miss holding her hand.
Her hands were so rough, like sandpaper.

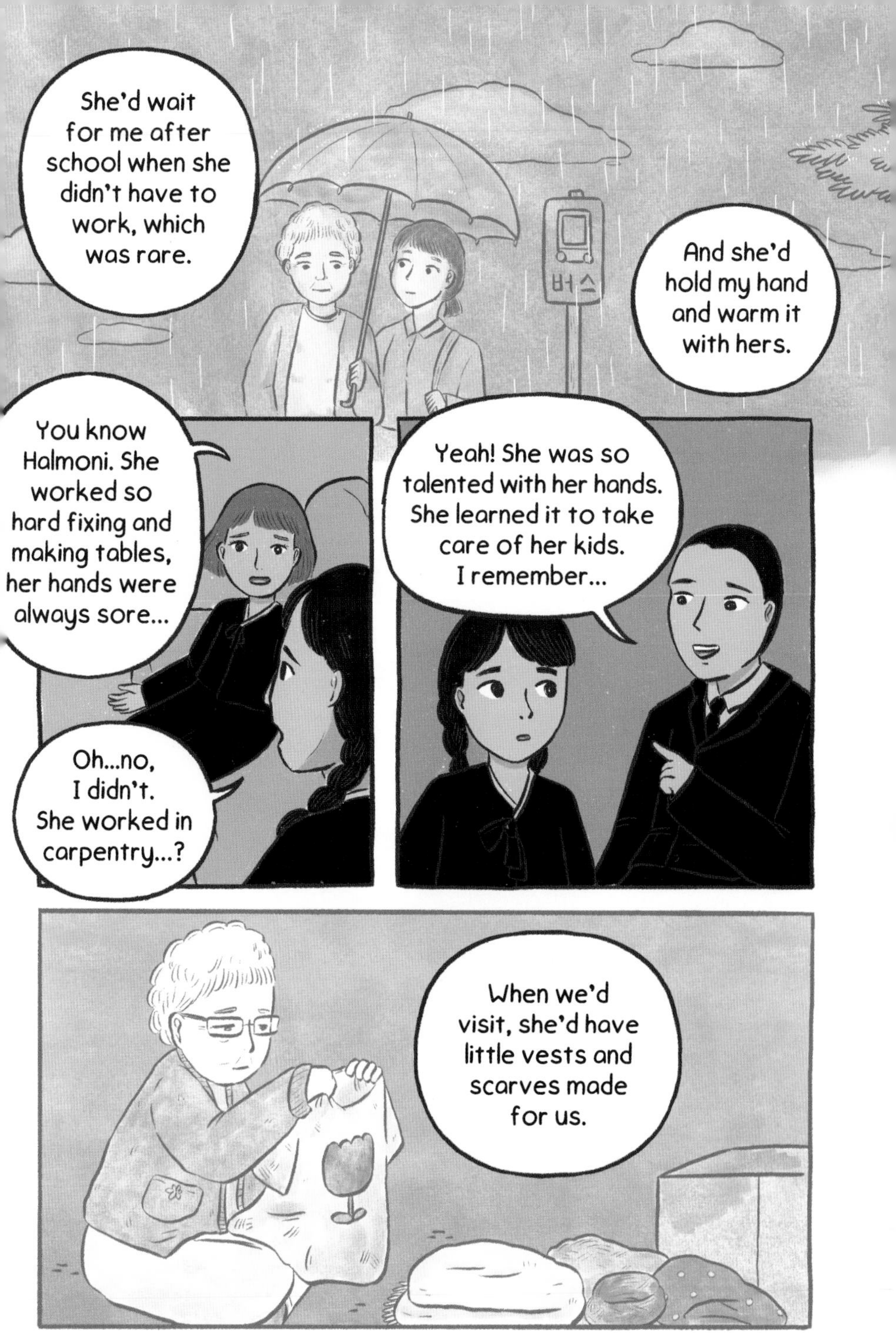
She'd wait for me after school when she didn't have to work, which was rare.
버스
And she'd hold my hand and warm it with hers.
You know Halmoni. She worked so hard fixing and making tables, her hands were always sore...
Oh...no, I didn't. She worked in carpentry...?
Yeah! She was so talented with her hands. She learned it to take care of her kids. I remember...
When we'd visit, she'd have little vests and scarves made for us.

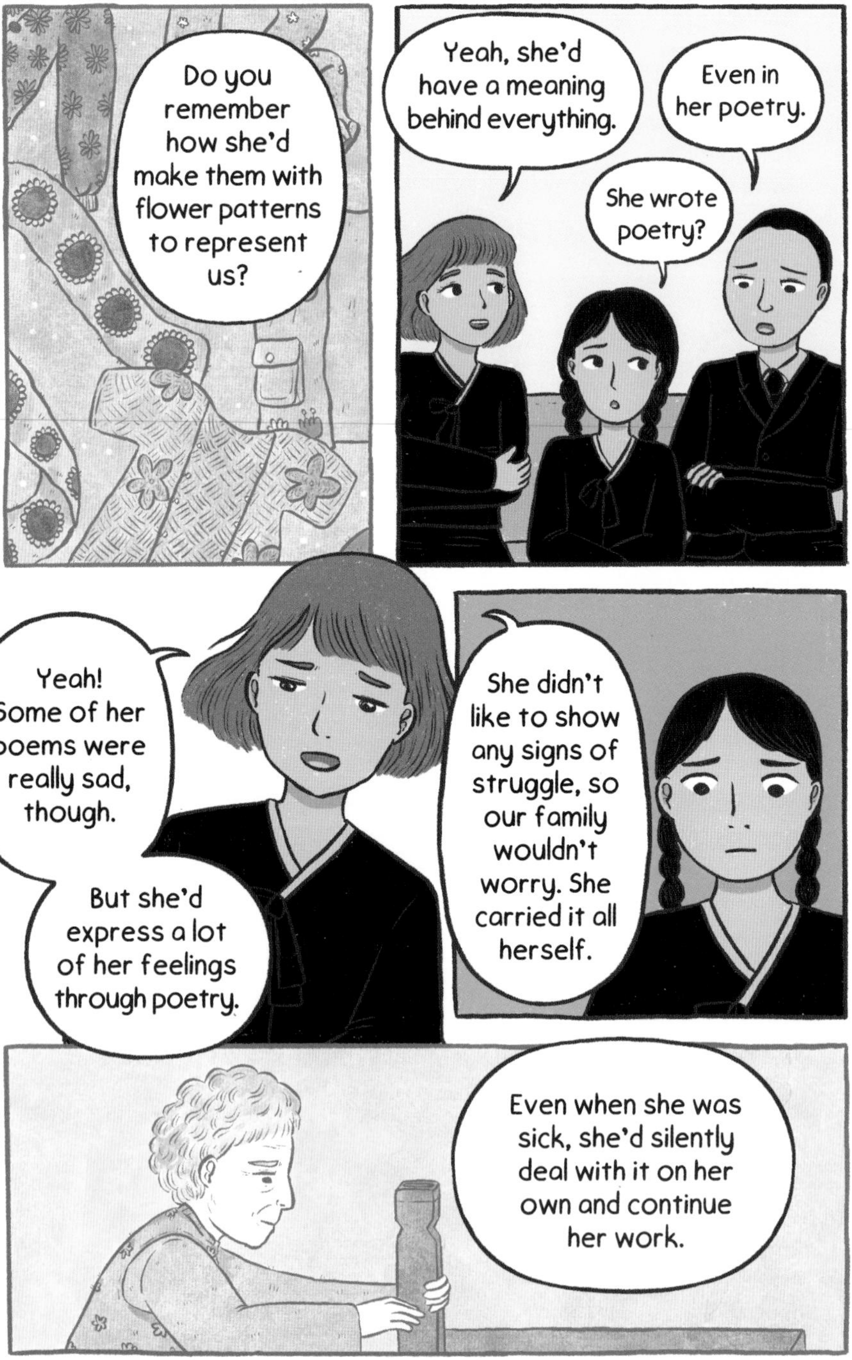
Do you remember how she'd make them with flower patterns to represent us?
Yeah, she'd have a meaning behind everything.
Even in her poetry.
She wrote poetry?
Yeah! Some of her poems were really sad, though.
But she'd express a lot of her feelings through poetry.
She didn't like to show any signs of struggle, so our family wouldn't worry. She carried it all herself.
Even when she was sick, she'd silently deal with it on her own and continue her work.

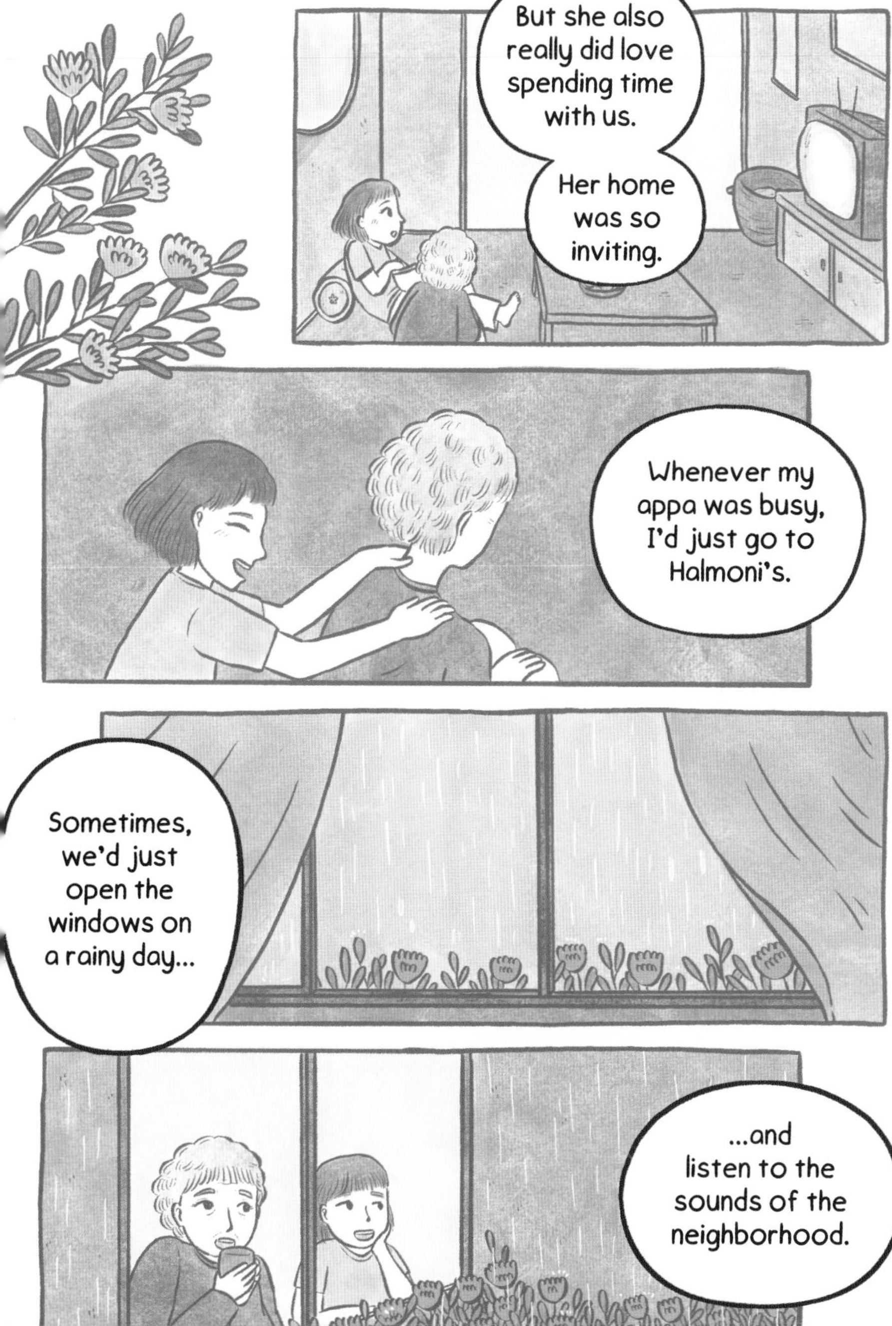
But she also really did love spending time with us.
Her home was so inviting.
Whenever my appa was busy, I'd just go to Halmoni's.
Sometimes, we'd just open the windows on a rainy day...
...and listen to the sounds of the neighborhood.

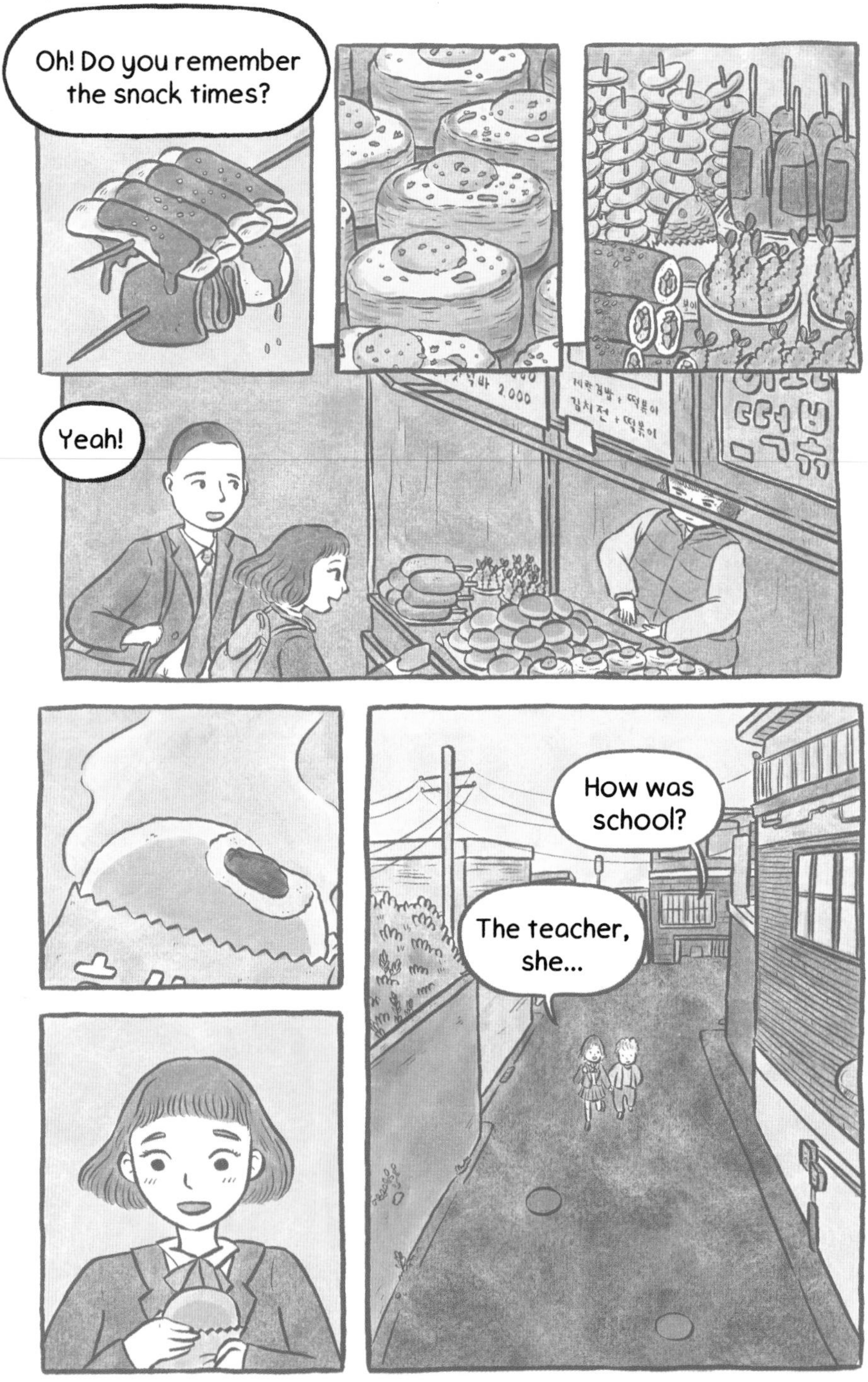
Oh! Do you remember the snack times?
계란김밥 + 떡볶이
김치전 + 떡볶이
Yeah!
How was school?
The teacher, she...

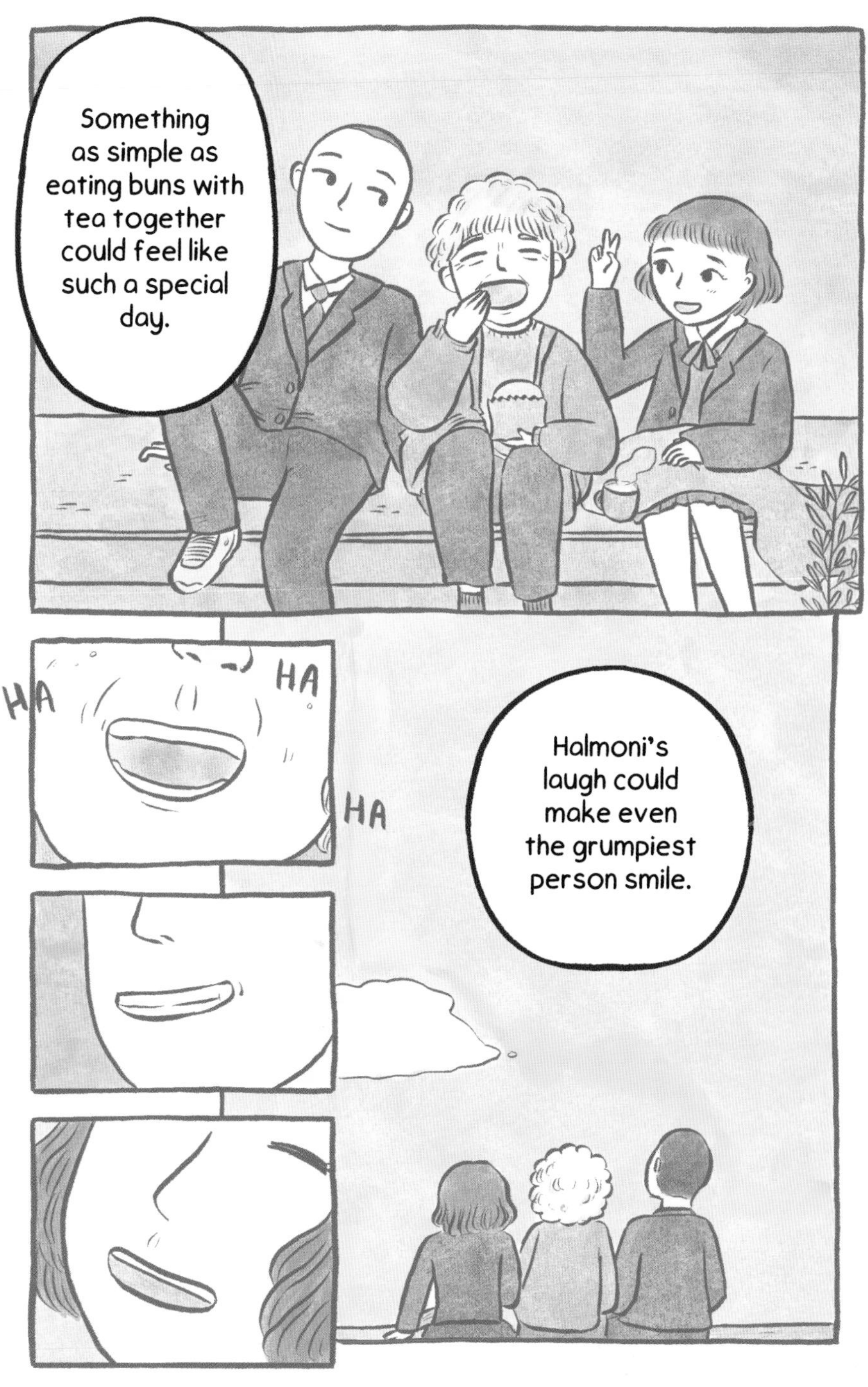

Something as simple as eating buns with tea together could feel like such a special day.
HA HA
HA
Halmoni's laugh could make even the grumpiest person smile.

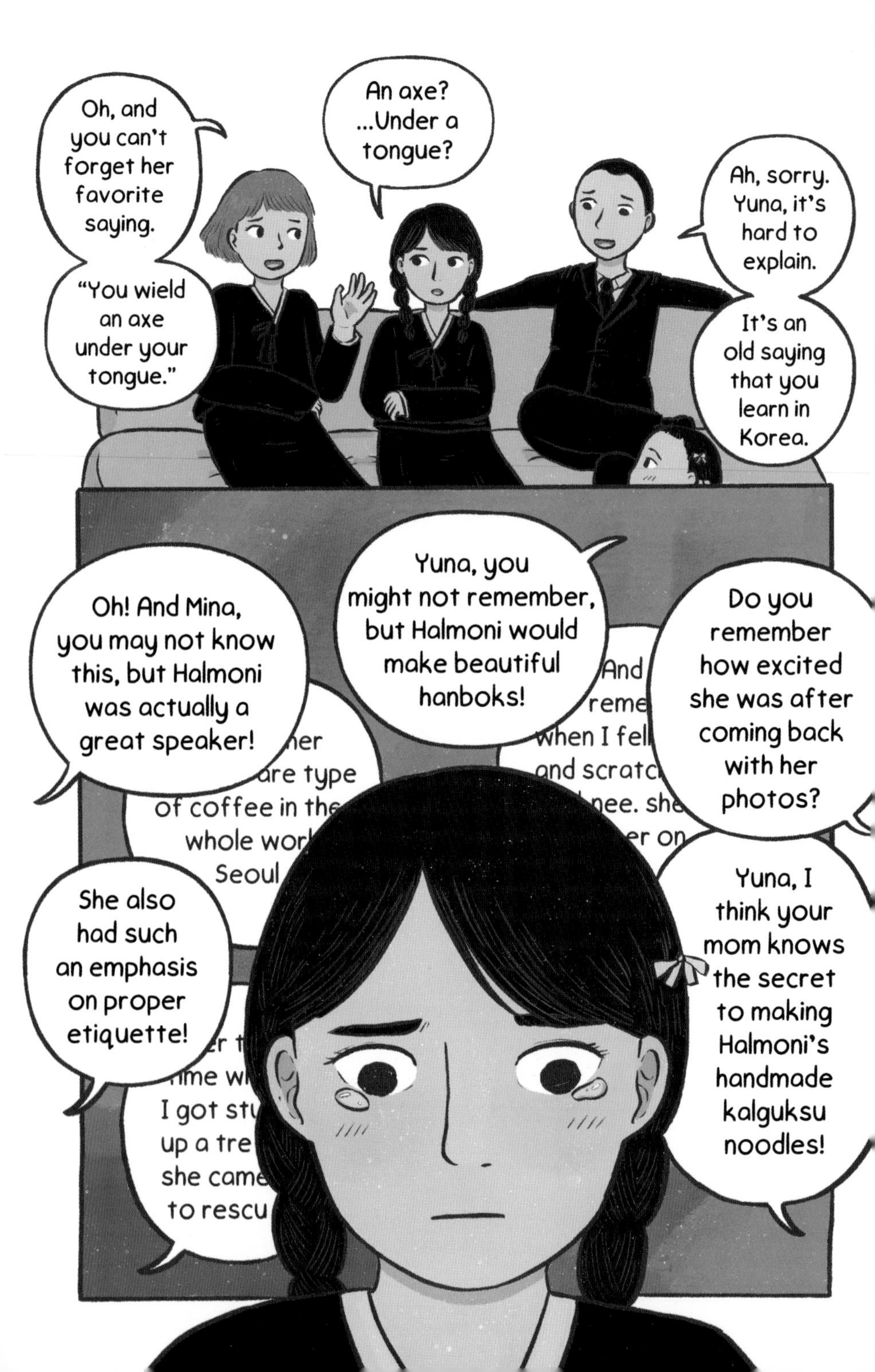
Oh, and you can't forget her favorite saying.
"You wield an axe under your tongue."
An axe? ...Under a tongue?
Ah, sorry. Yuna, it's hard to explain.
It's an old saying that you learn in Korea.
Oh! And Mina, you may not know this, but Halmoni was actually a great speaker!
Yuna, you might not remember, but Halmoni would make beautiful hanboks!
Do you remember how excited she was after coming back with her photos?
She also had such an emphasis on proper etiquette!
Yuna, I think your mom knows the secret to making Halmoni's handmade kalguksu noodles!

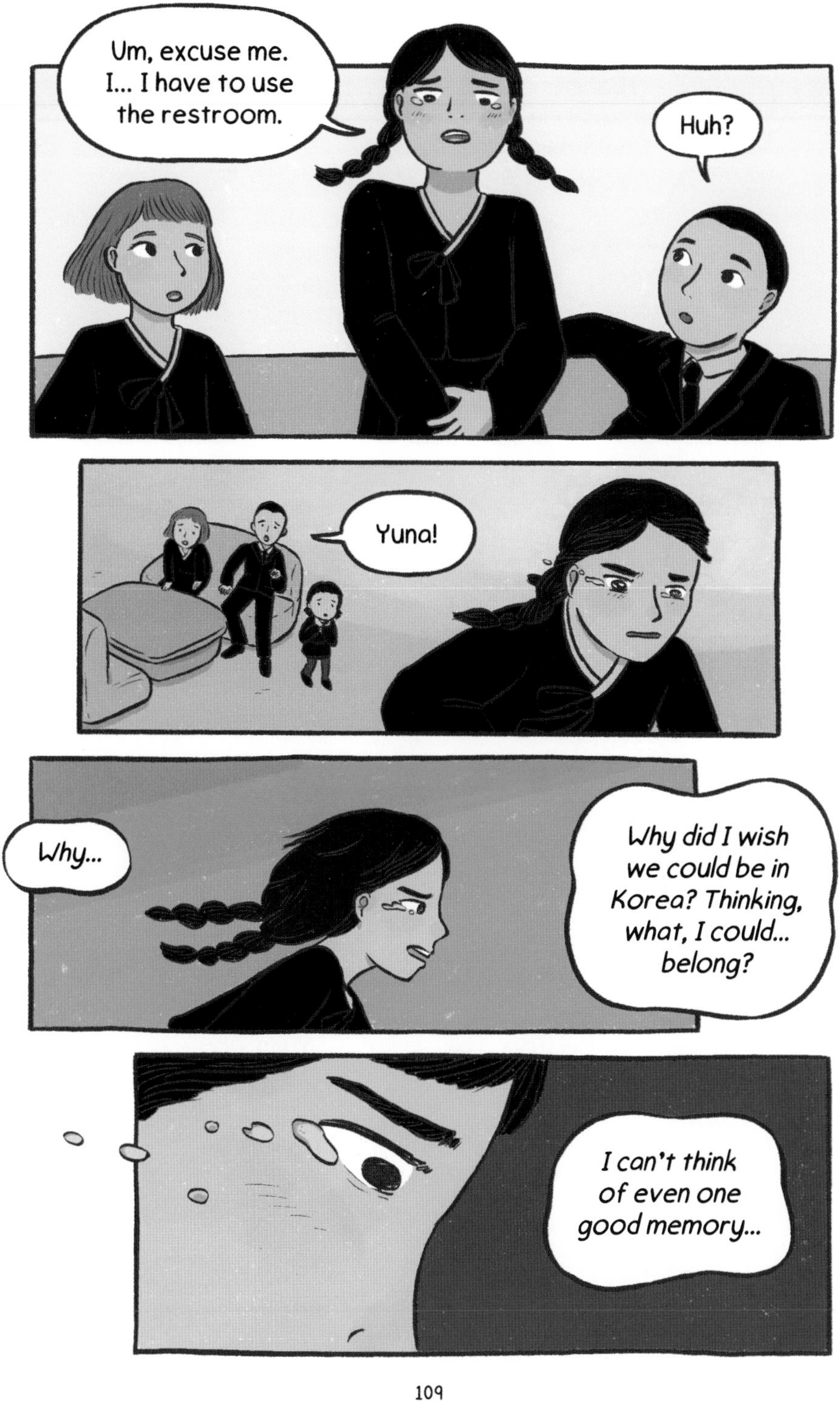
Um, excuse me. I... I have to use the restroom.
Huh?
Yuna!
Why...
Why did I wish we could be in Korea? Thinking, what, I could... belong?
I can't think of even one good memory...

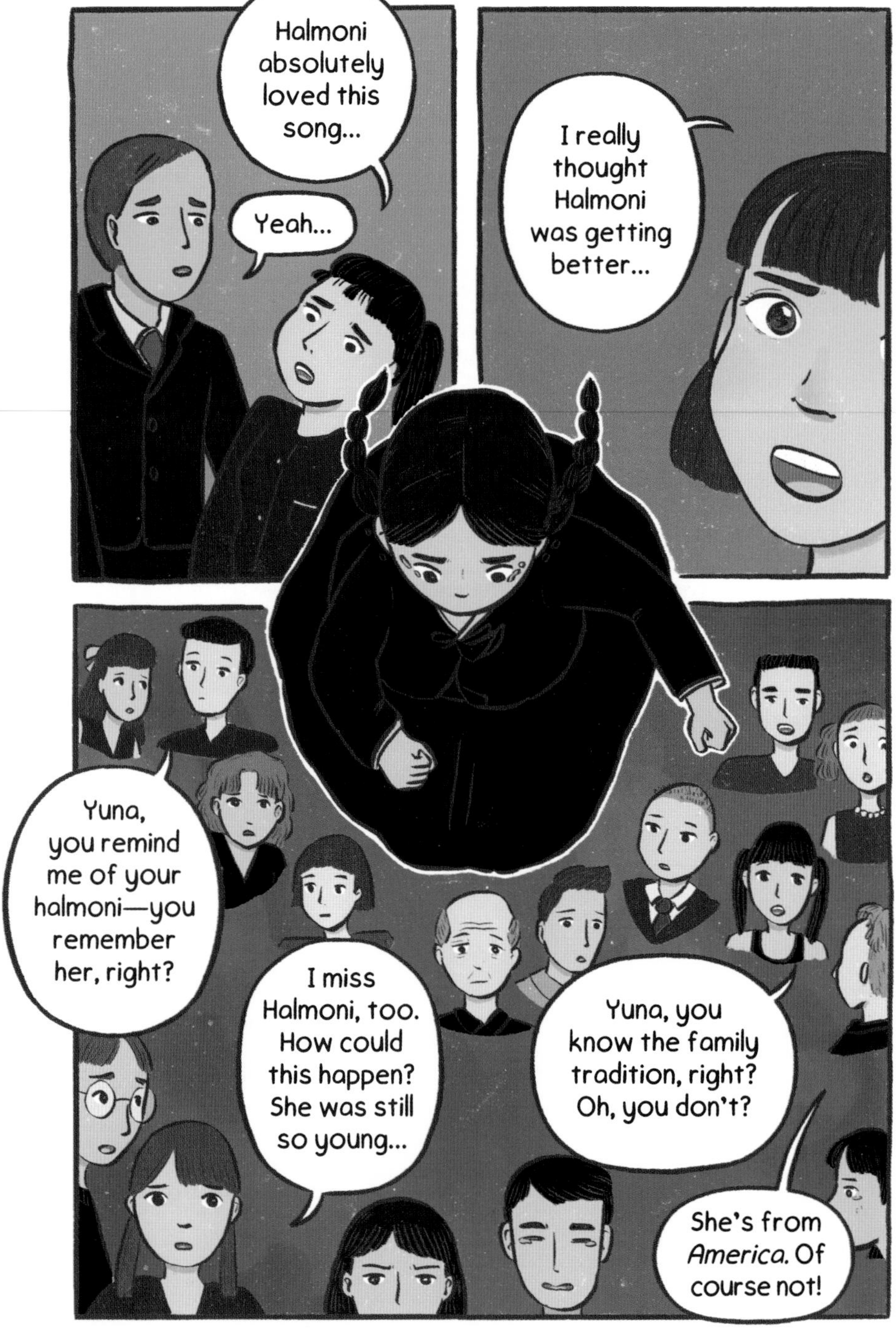
Halmoni absolutely loved this song...
Yeah...
I really thought Halmoni was getting better...
Yuna, you remind me of your halmoni—you remember her, right?
I miss Halmoni, too. How could this happen? She was still so young...
Yuna, you know the family tradition, right? Oh, you don't?
She's from *America*. Of course not!

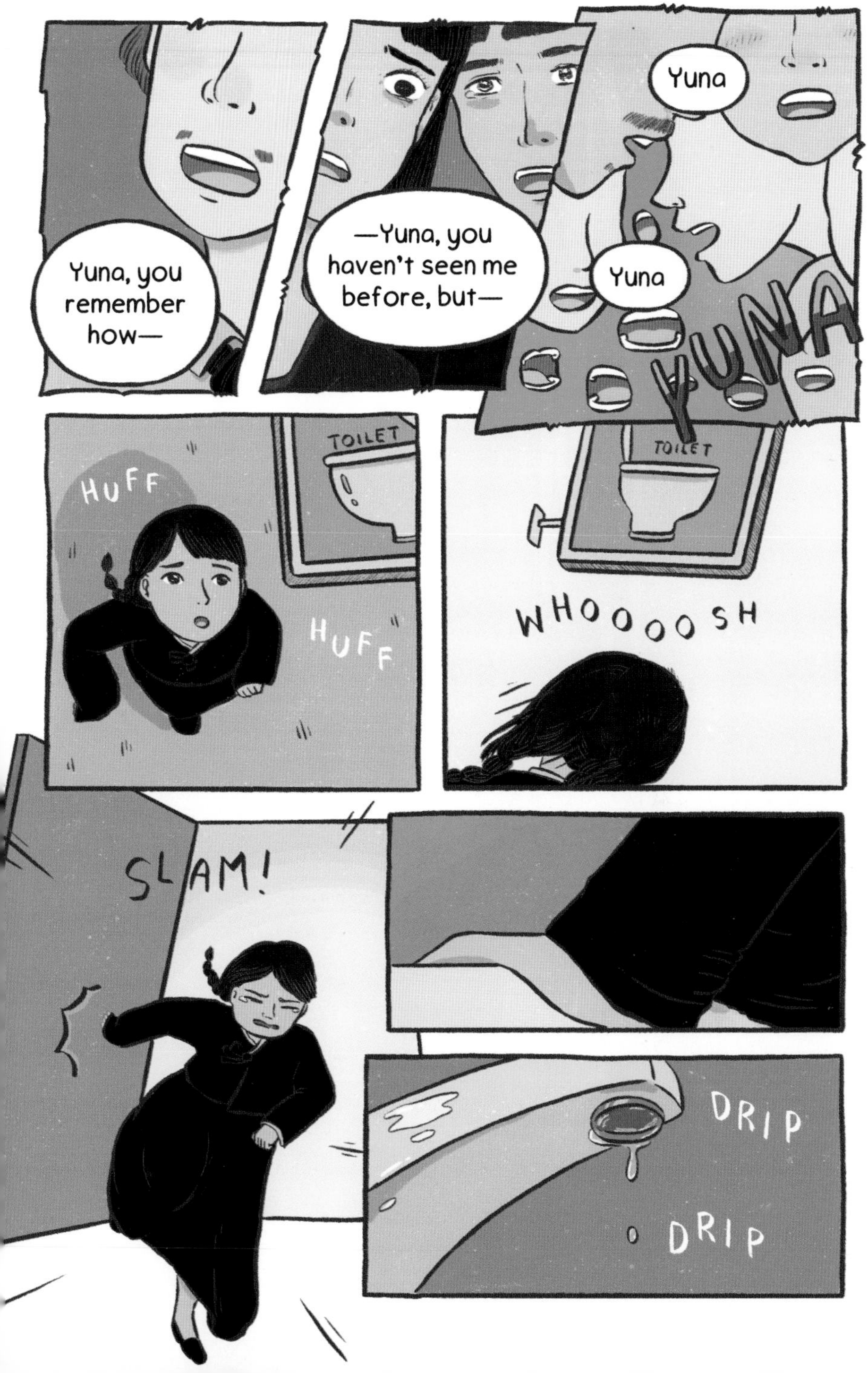
Yuna, you remember how—
—Yuna, you haven't seen me before, but—
Yuna
Yuna
YUNA
TOILET
HUFF
HUFF
TOILET
WHOOOOOSH
SLAM!
DRIP
DRIP

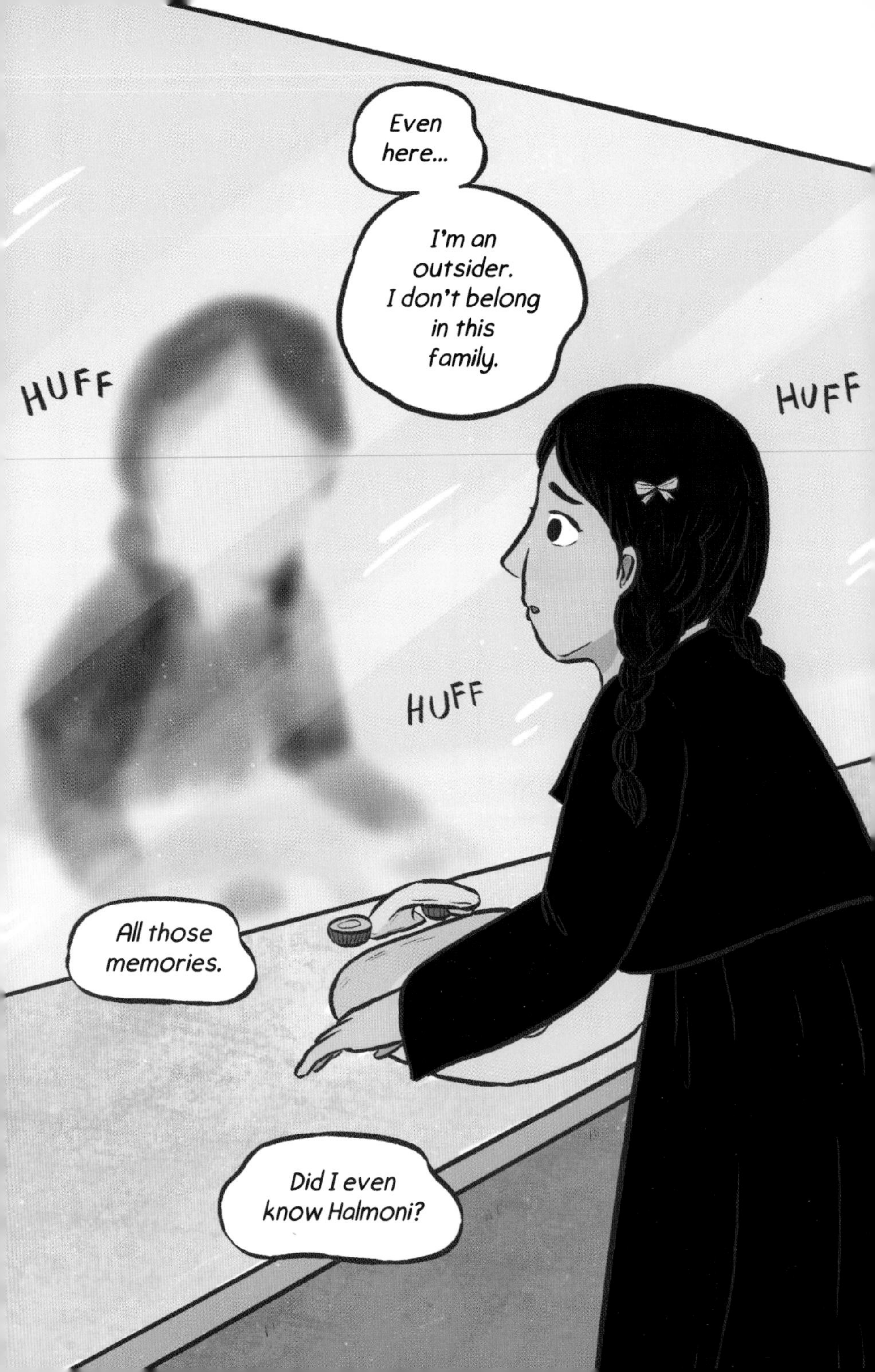
Even here...
I'm an outsider. I don't belong in this family.
HUFF
HUFF
HUFF
All those memories.
Did I even know Halmoni?

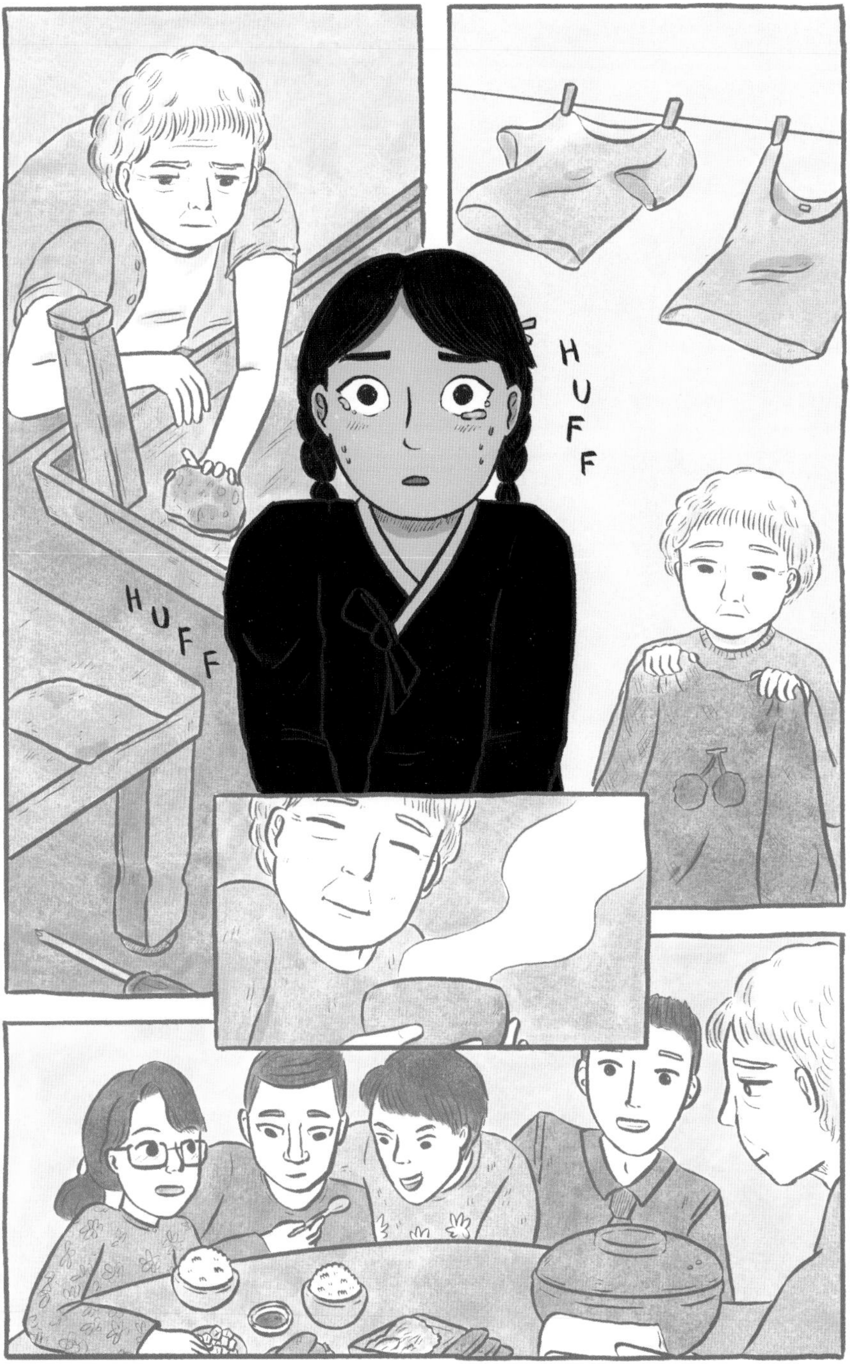
HUFF
HUFF

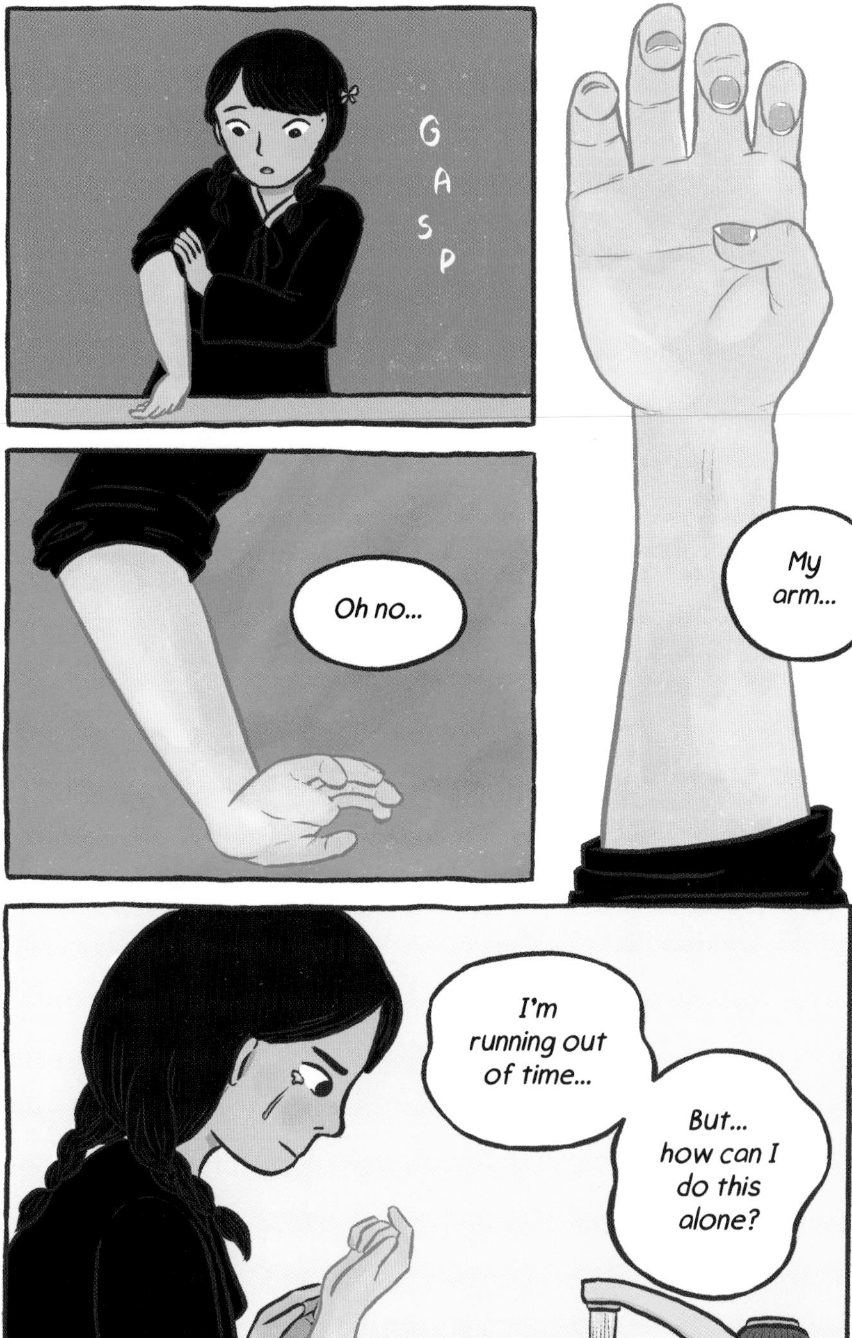
GASP
Oh no...
My arm...
I'm running out of time...
But... how can I do this alone?

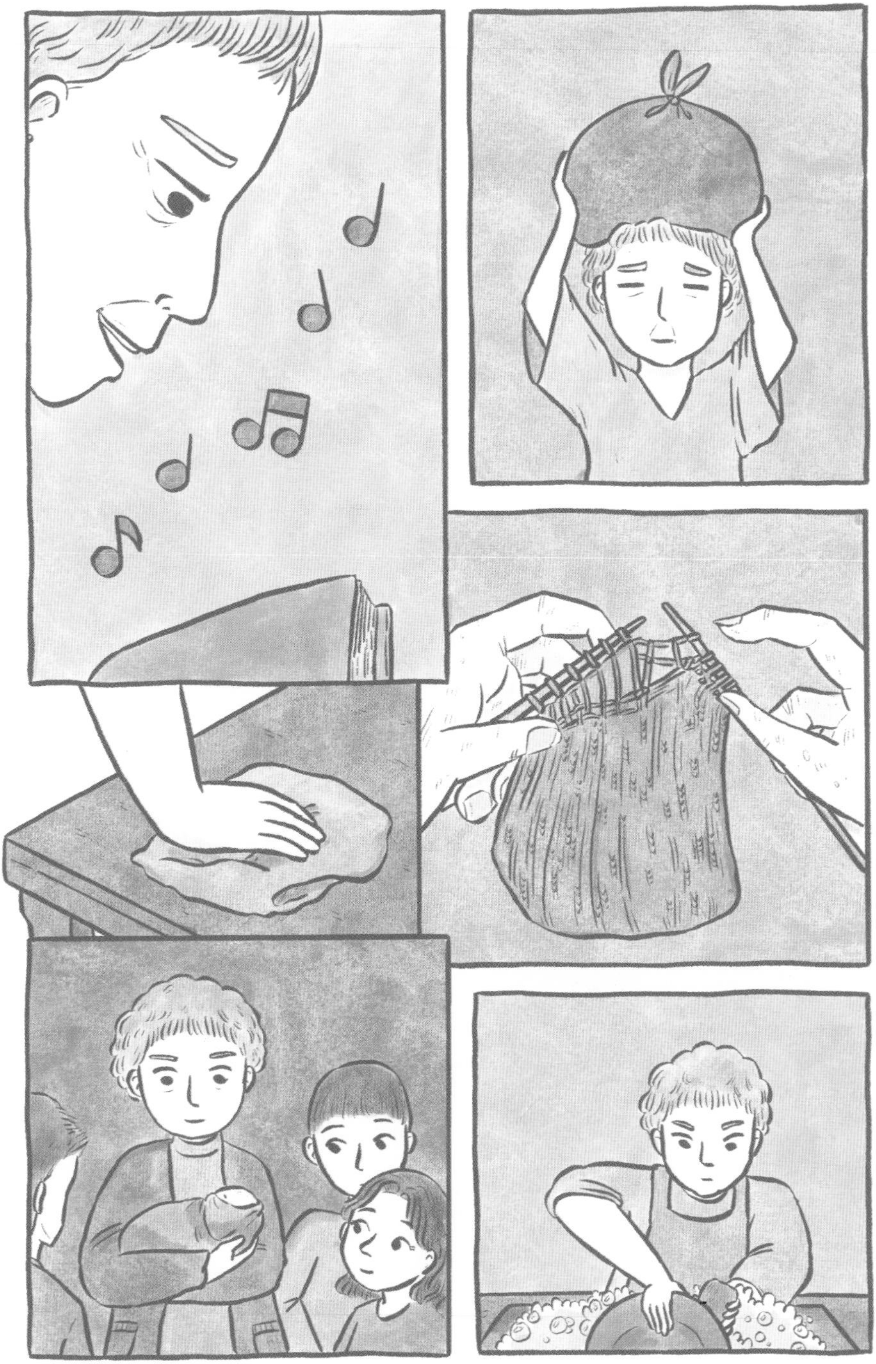

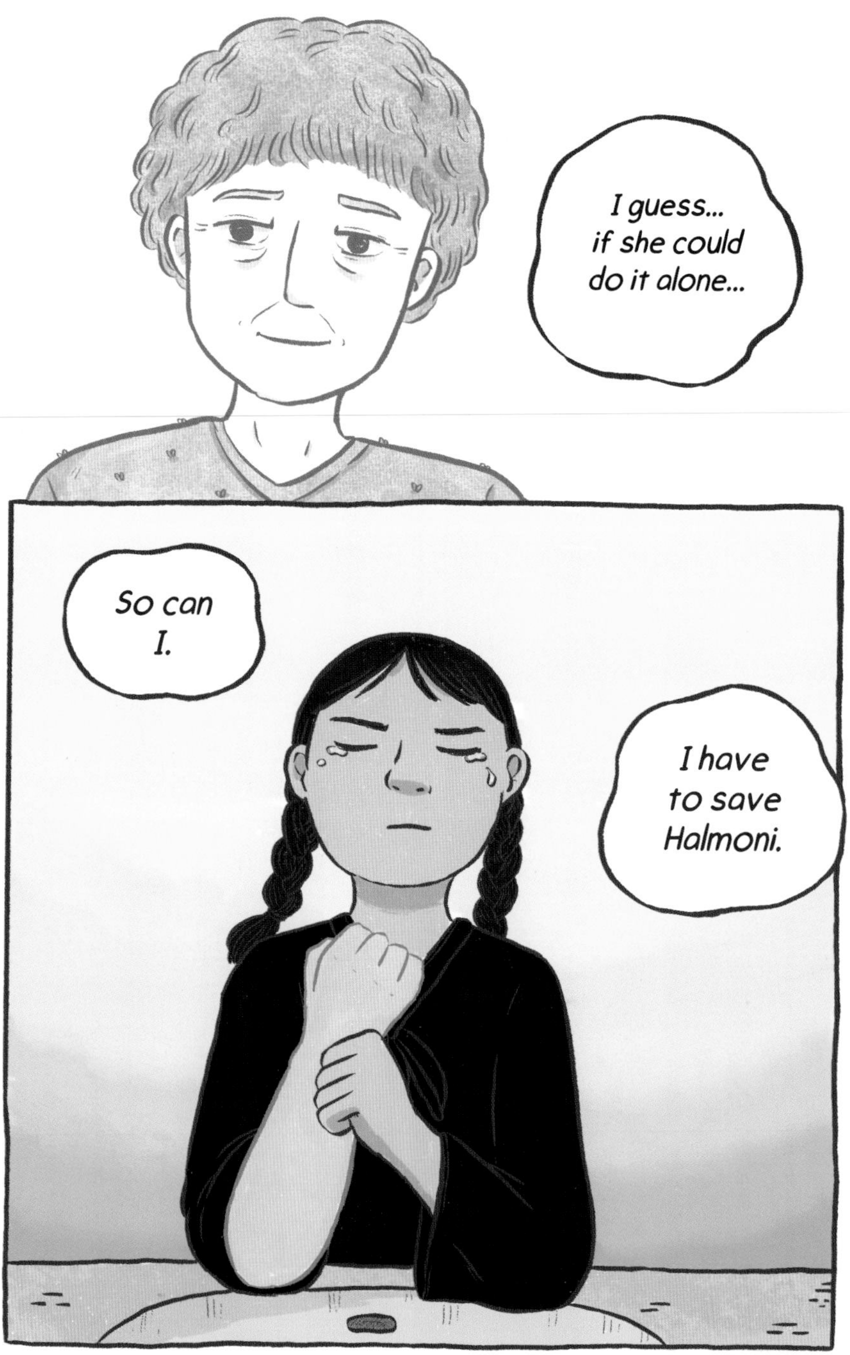
I guess... if she could do it alone...
So can I.
I have to save Halmoni.

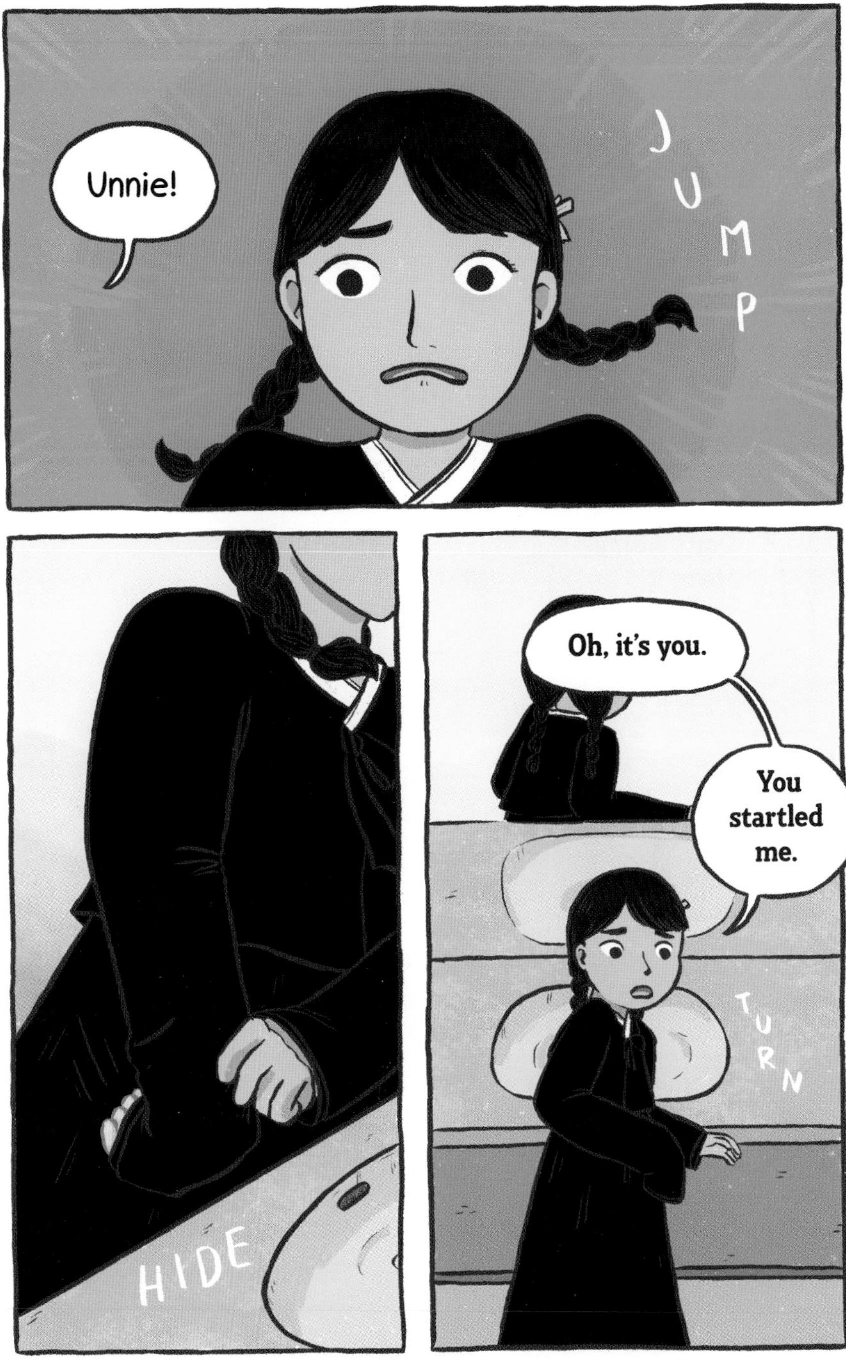
Unnie!
JUMP
HIDE
Oh, it's you.
You startled me.
TURN

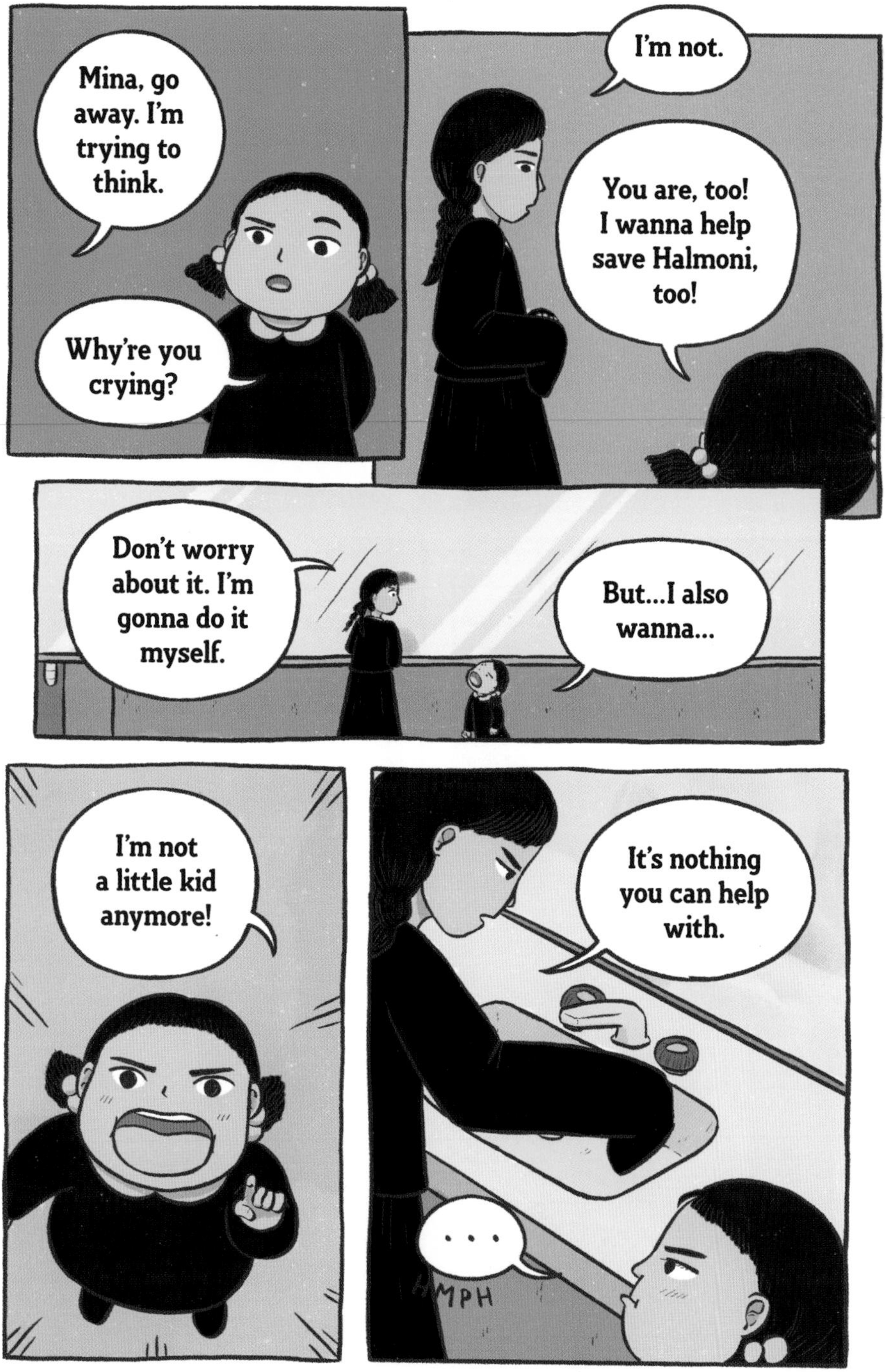

Mina, go away. I'm trying to think.
Why're you crying?
I'm not.
You are, too! I wanna help save Halmoni, too!
Don't worry about it. I'm gonna do it myself.
But...I also wanna...
I'm not a little kid anymore!
It's nothing you can help with.
...
HMPH

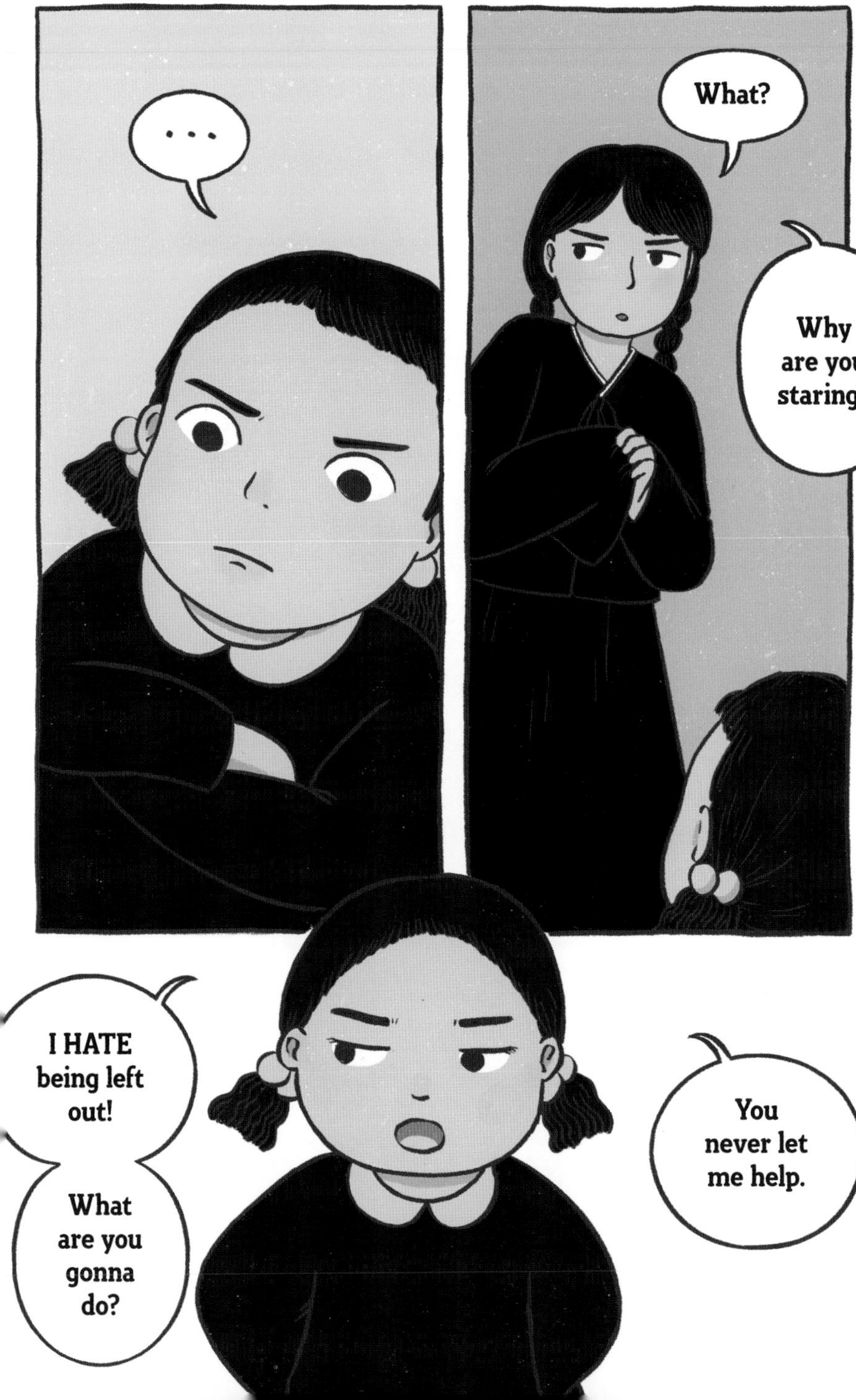
...
What?
Why are you staring?
I HATE being left out!
What are you gonna do?
You never let me help.

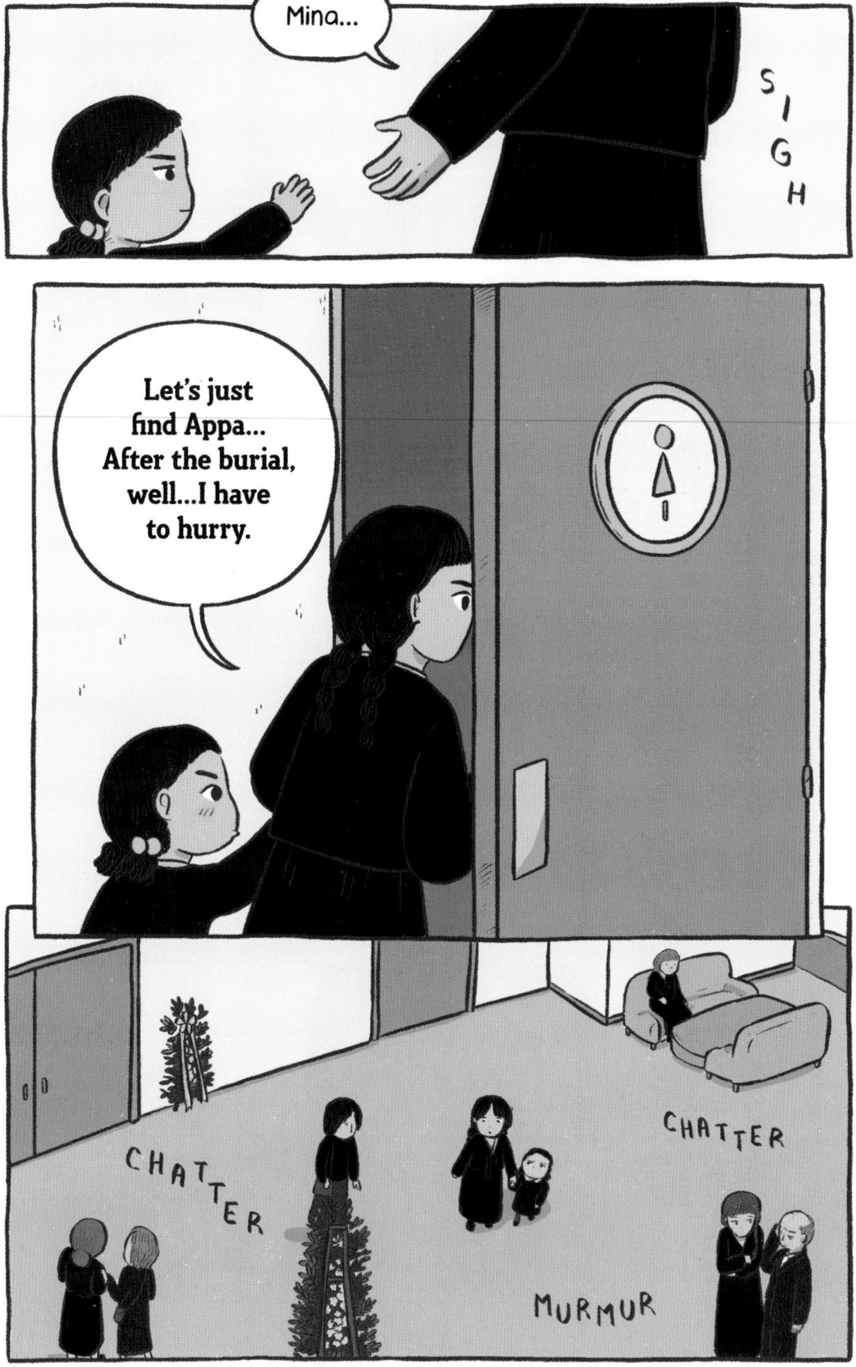
Mina...
SIGH
Let's just find Appa... After the burial, well...I have to hurry.
CHATTER
CHATTER
MURMUR

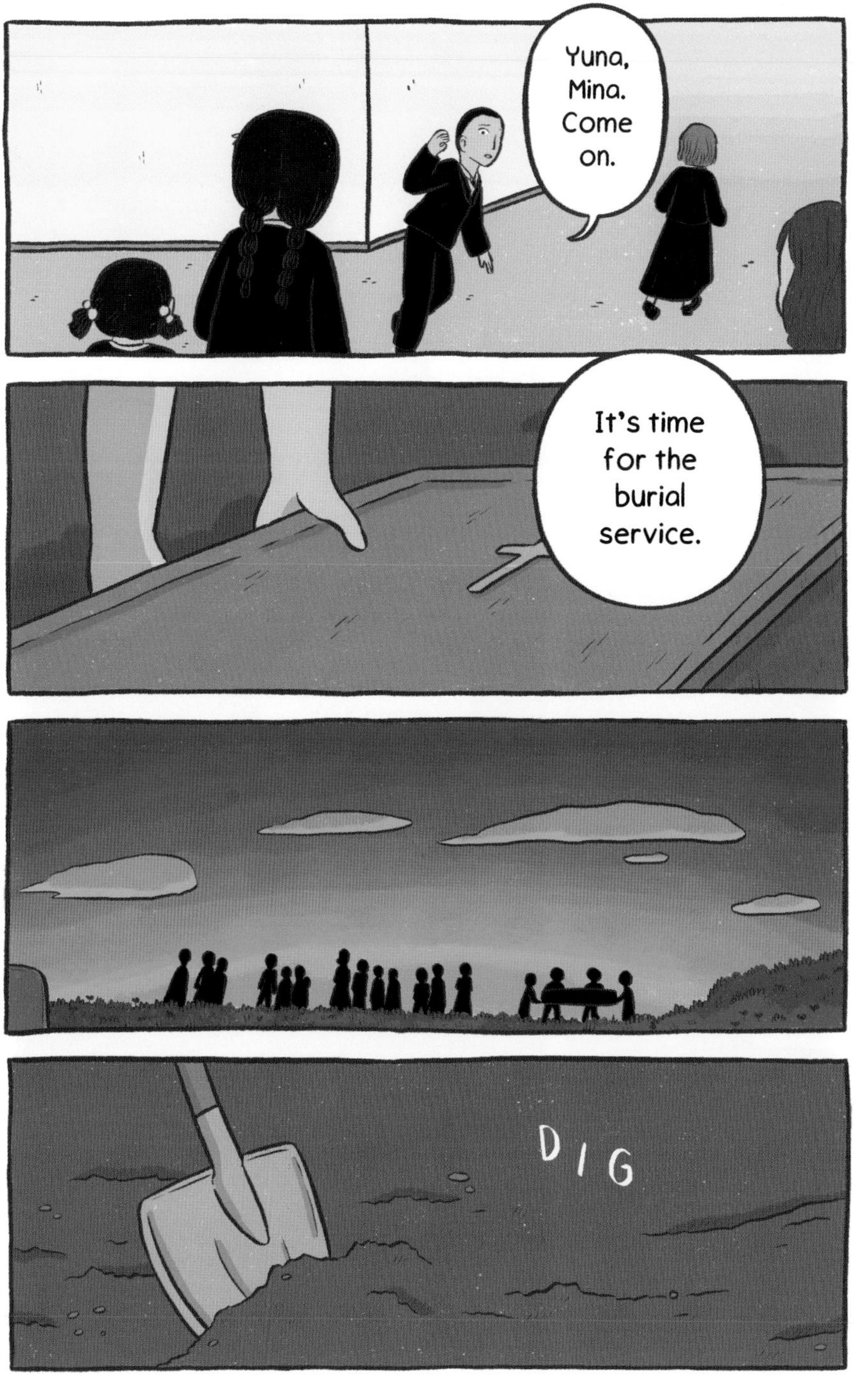
Yuna, Mina. Come on.
It's time for the burial service.
DIG

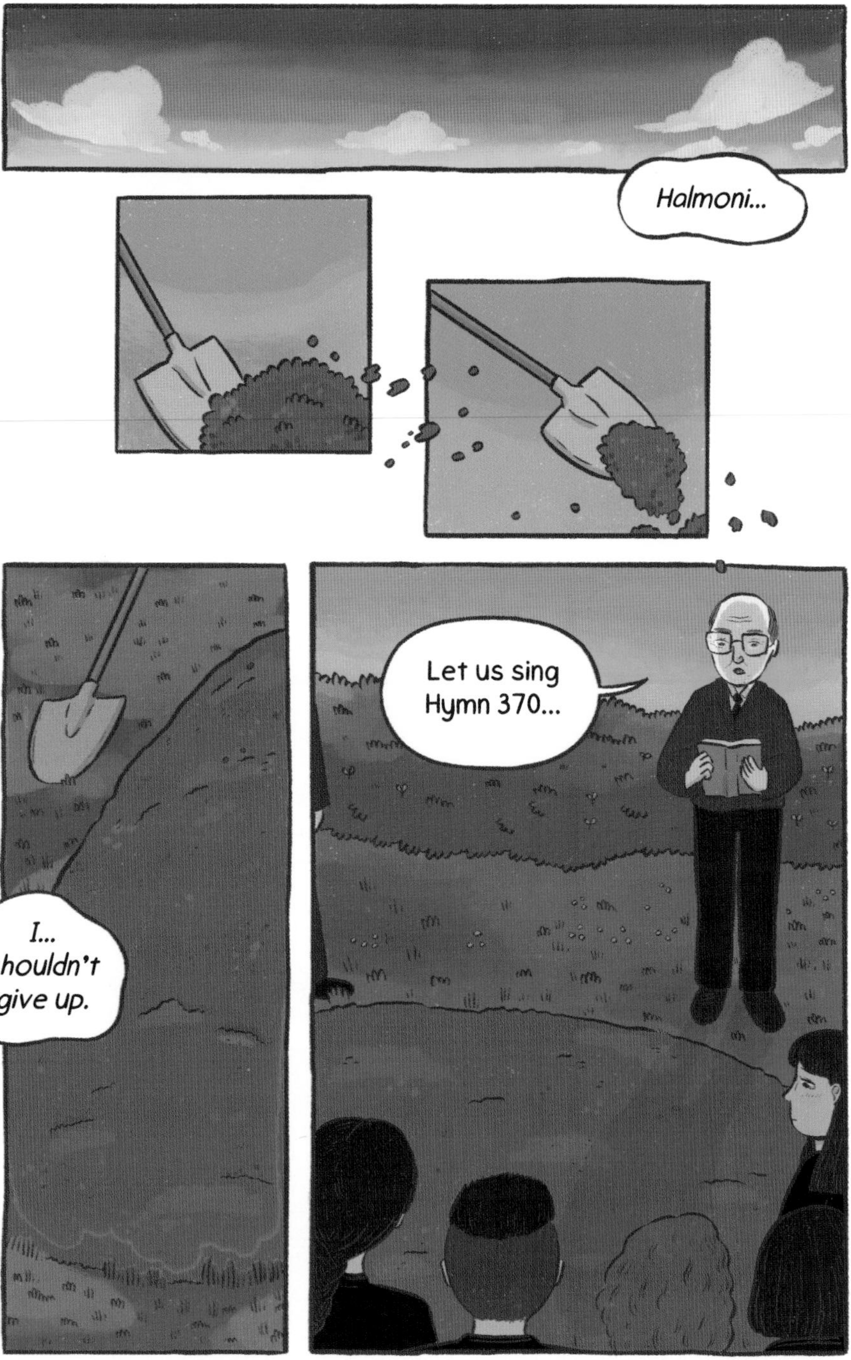
Halmoni...
I... shouldn't give up.
Let us sing Hymn 370...

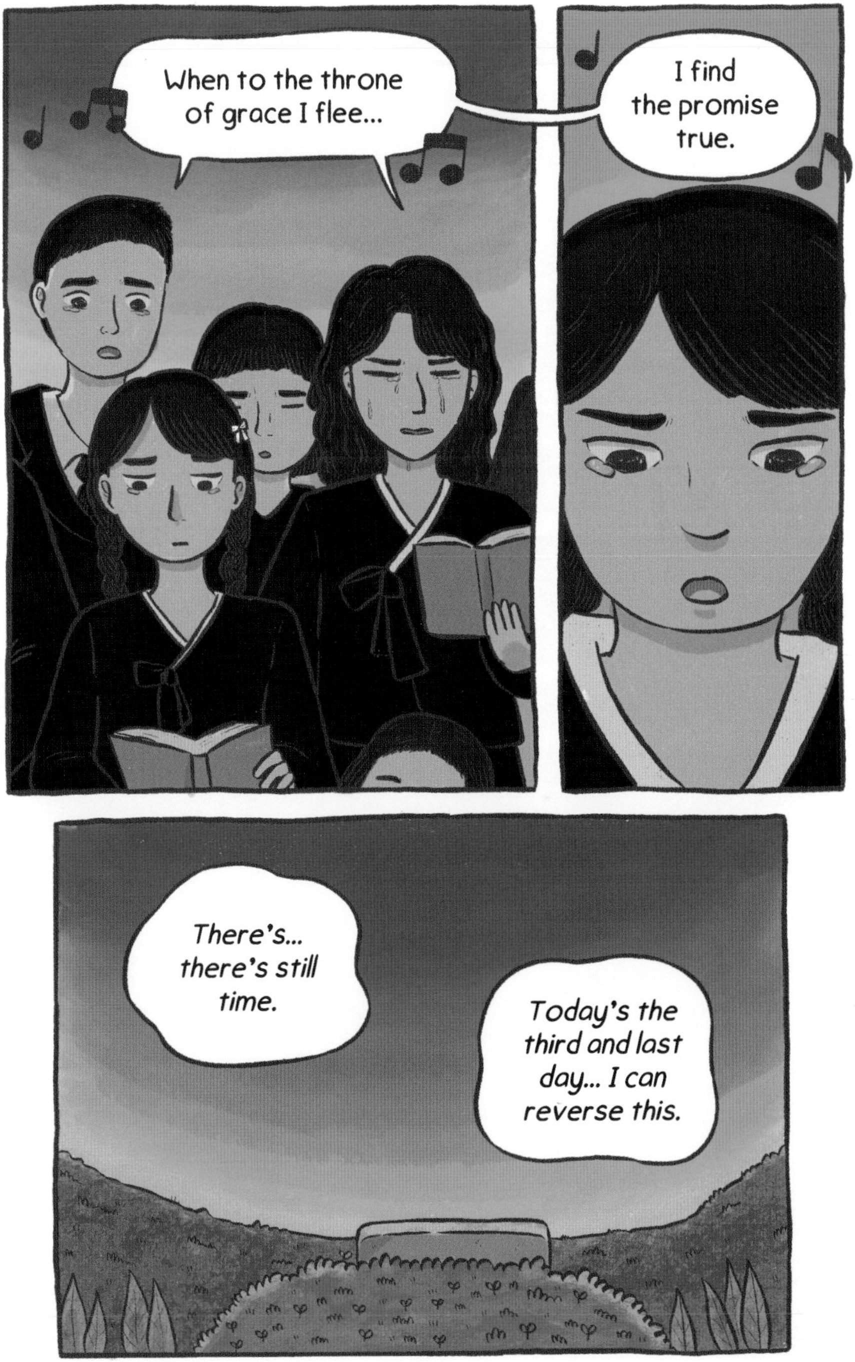
When to the throne of grace I flee...
I find the promise true.
There's... there's still time.
Today's the third and last day... I can reverse this.

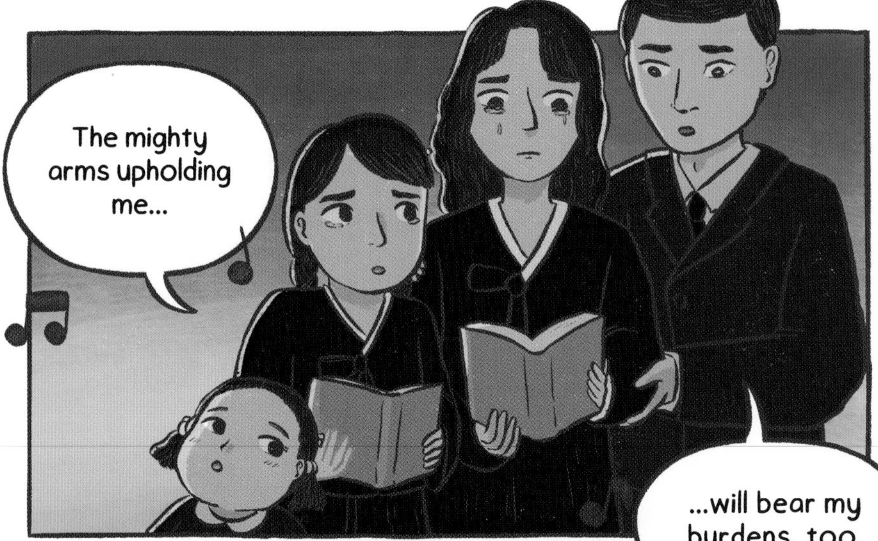
The mighty arms upholding me...
...will bear my burdens, too.

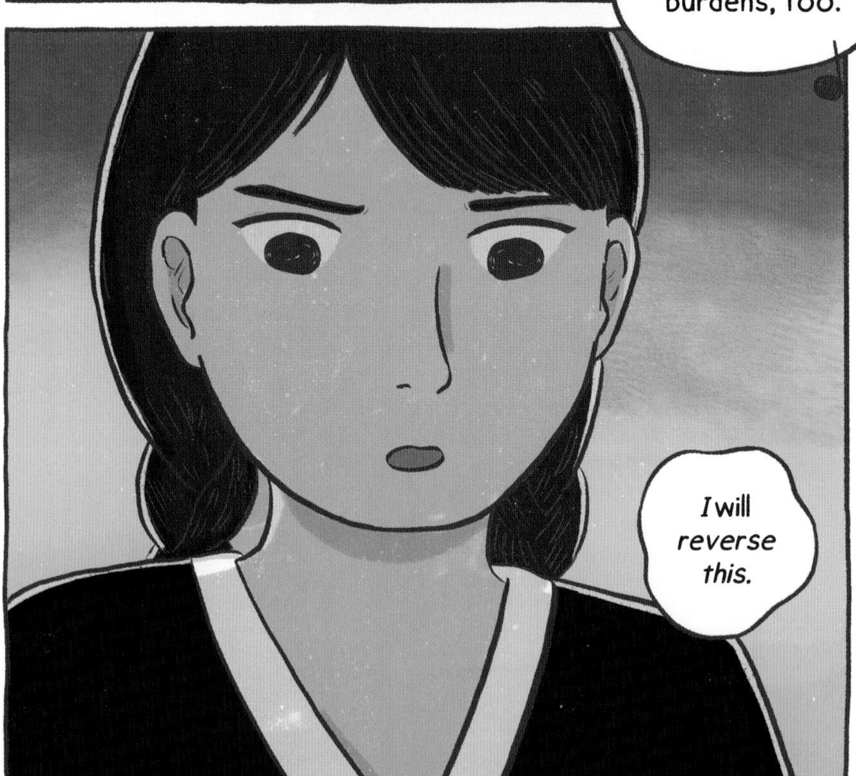
I will reverse this.

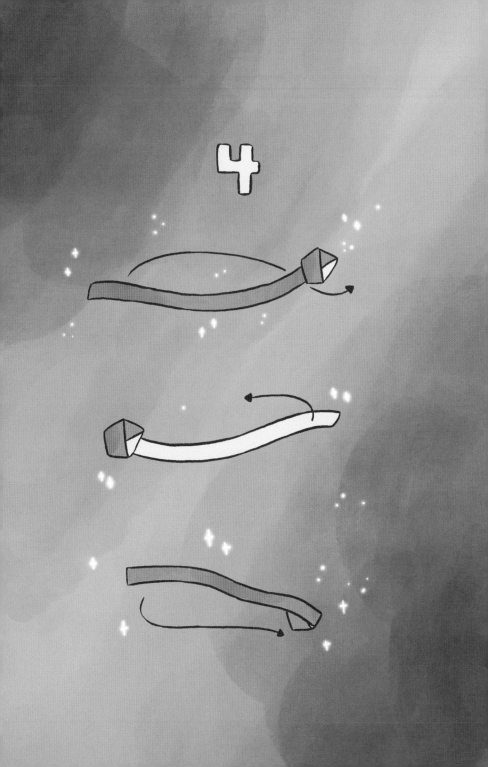

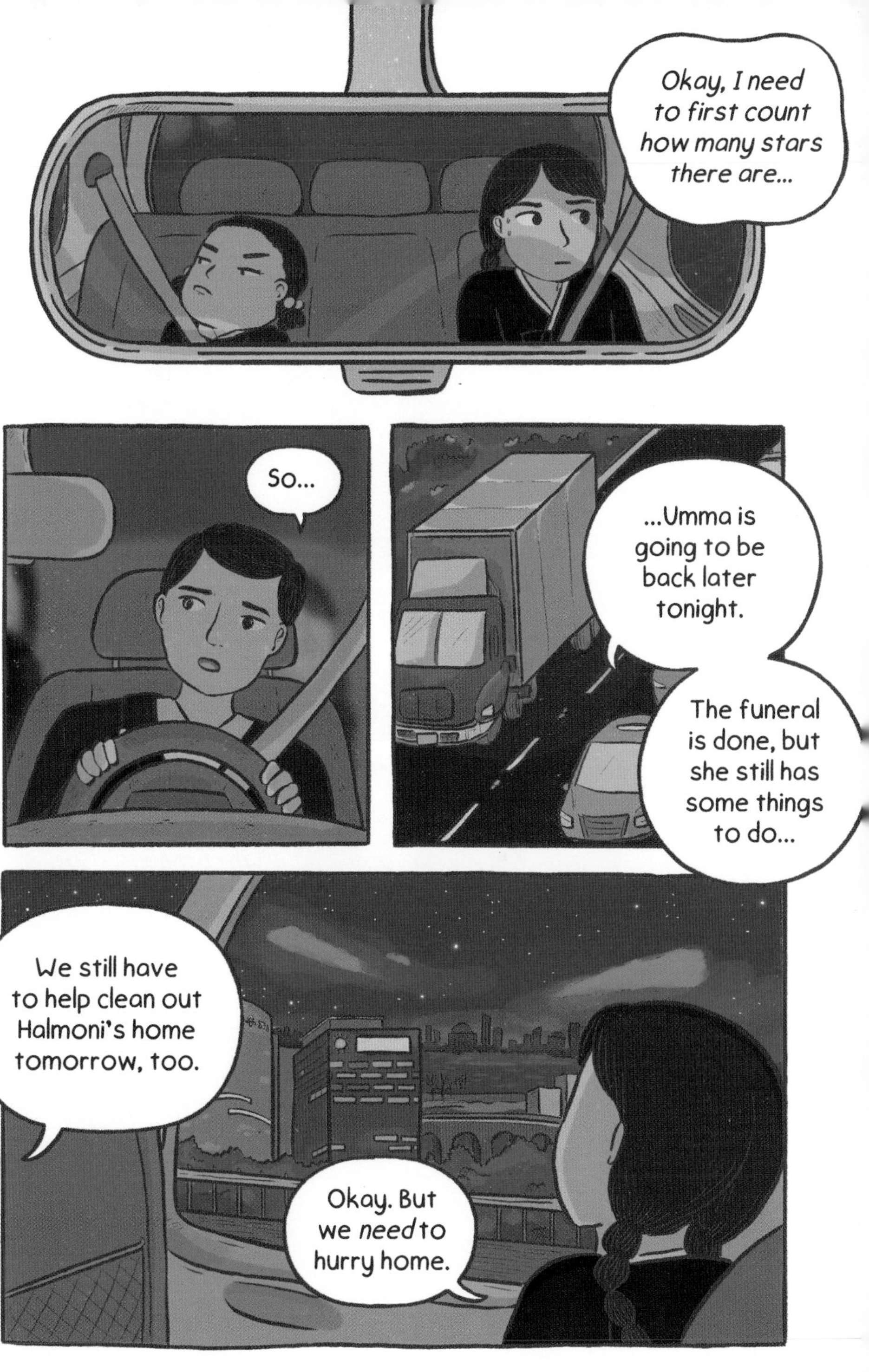
Okay, I need to first count how many stars there are...
So...
...Umma is going to be back later tonight.
The funeral is done, but she still has some things to do...
We still have to help clean out Halmoni's home tomorrow, too.
Okay. But we *need* to hurry home.

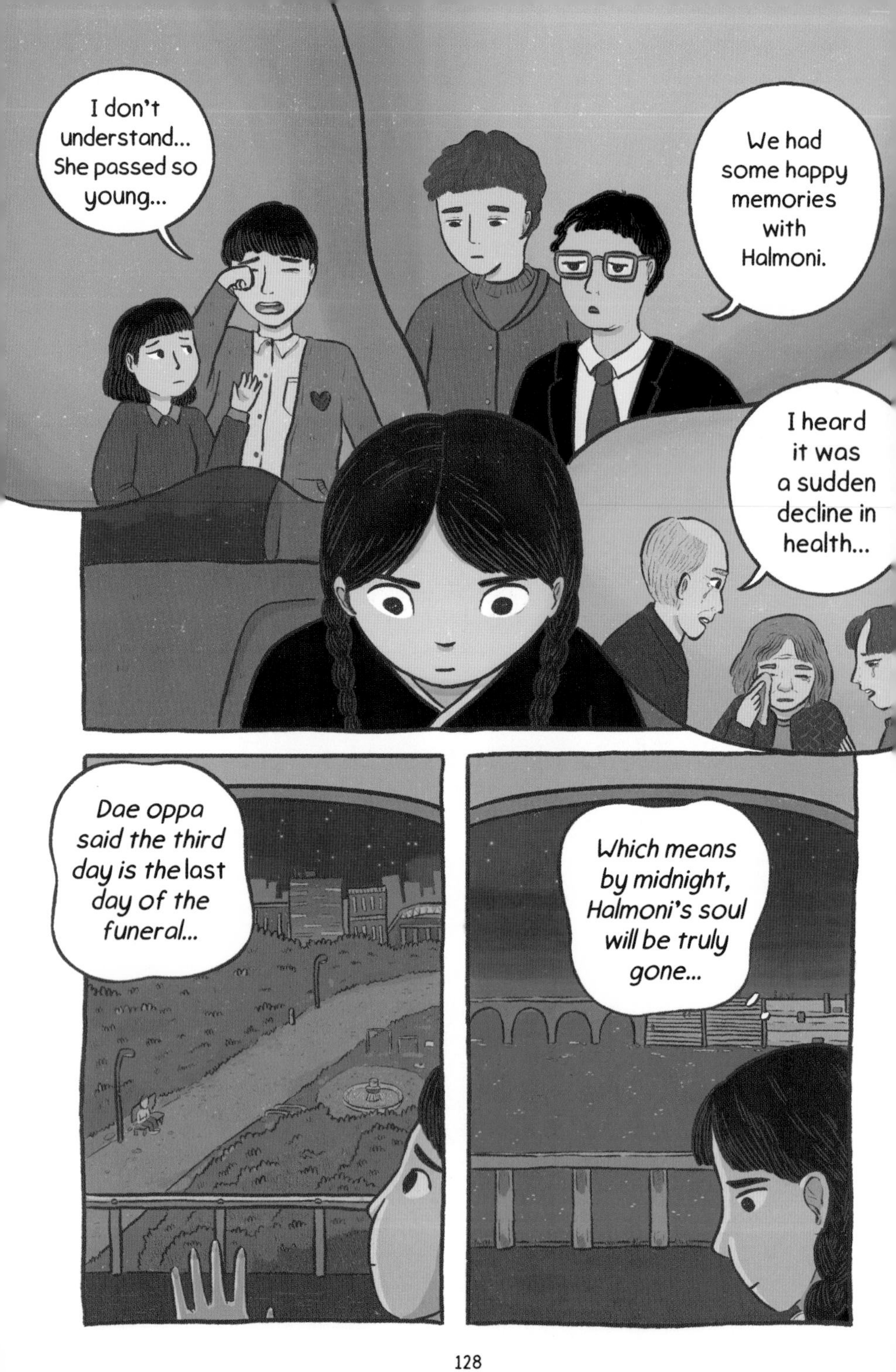
I don't understand... She passed so young...
We had some happy memories with Halmoni.
I heard it was a sudden decline in health...
Dae oppa said the third day is the last day of the funeral...
Which means by midnight, Halmoni's soul will be truly gone...

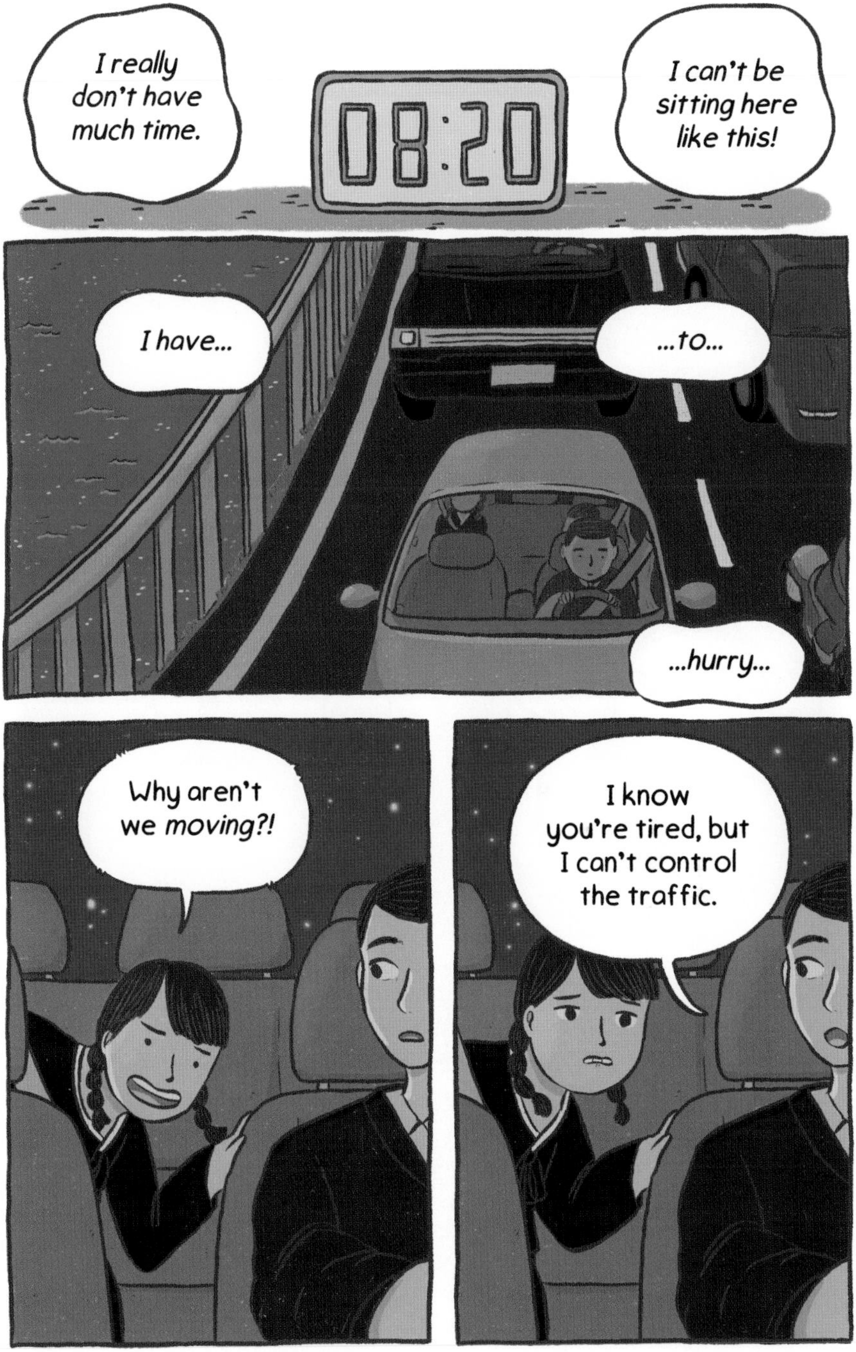
I really don't have much time.
08:20
I can't be sitting here like this!
I have...
...to...
...hurry...
Why aren't we *moving*?!
I know you're tired, but I can't control the traffic.

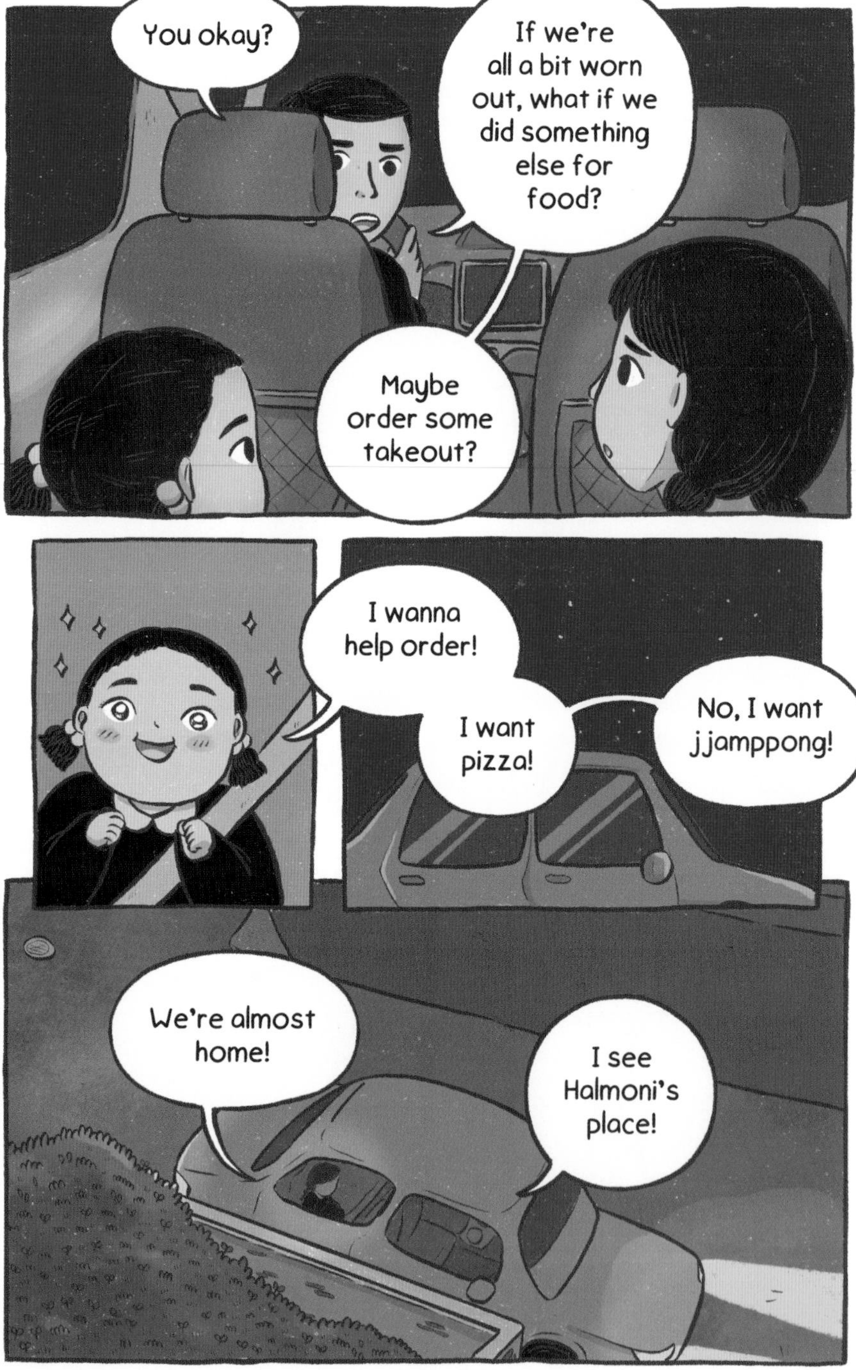
You okay?
If we're all a bit worn out, what if we did something else for food?
Maybe order some takeout?
I wanna help order!
I want pizza!
No, I want jjamppong!
We're almost home!
I see Halmoni's place!

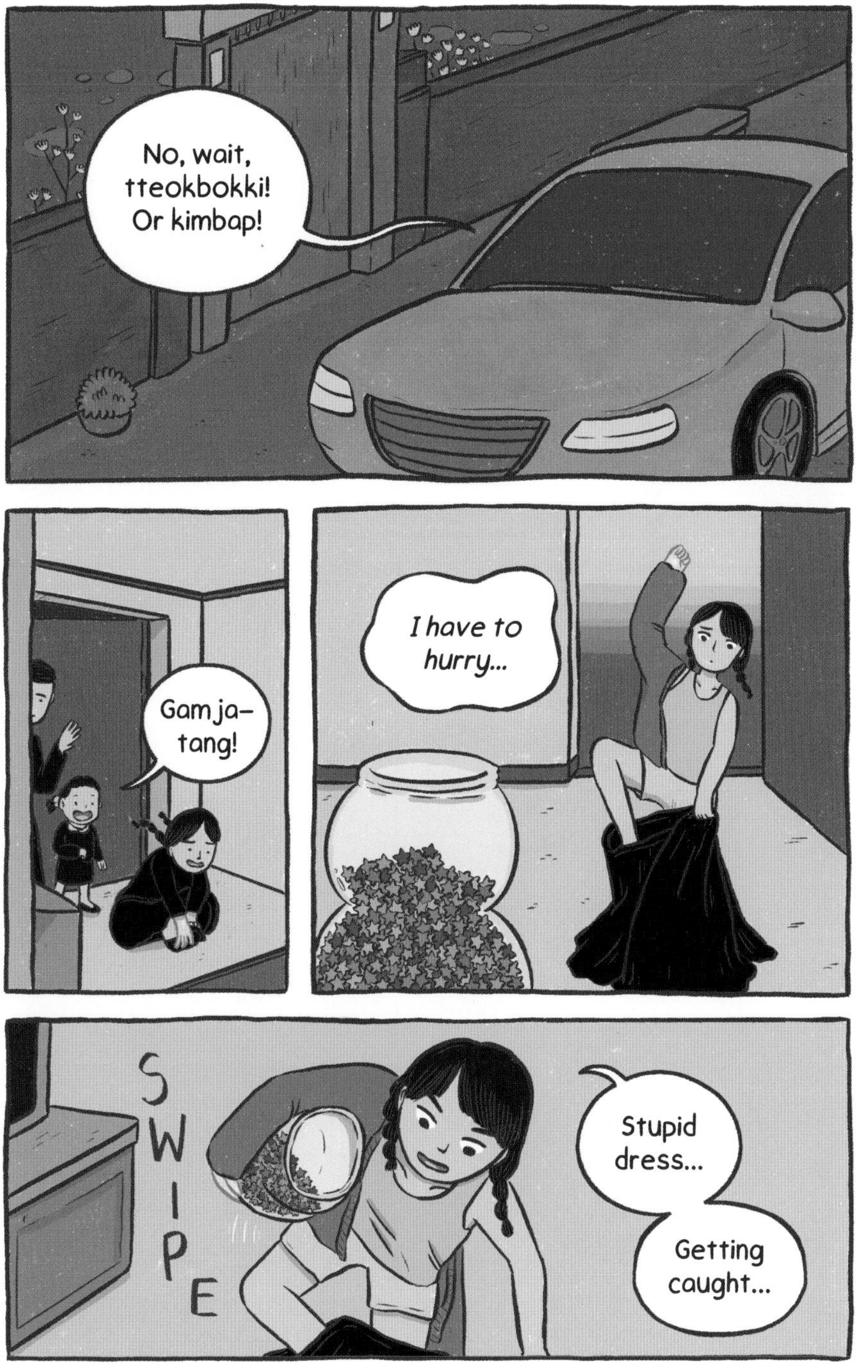
No, wait, tteokbokki! Or kimbap!
Gamja-tang!
I have to hurry...
SWIPE
Stupid dress...
Getting caught...

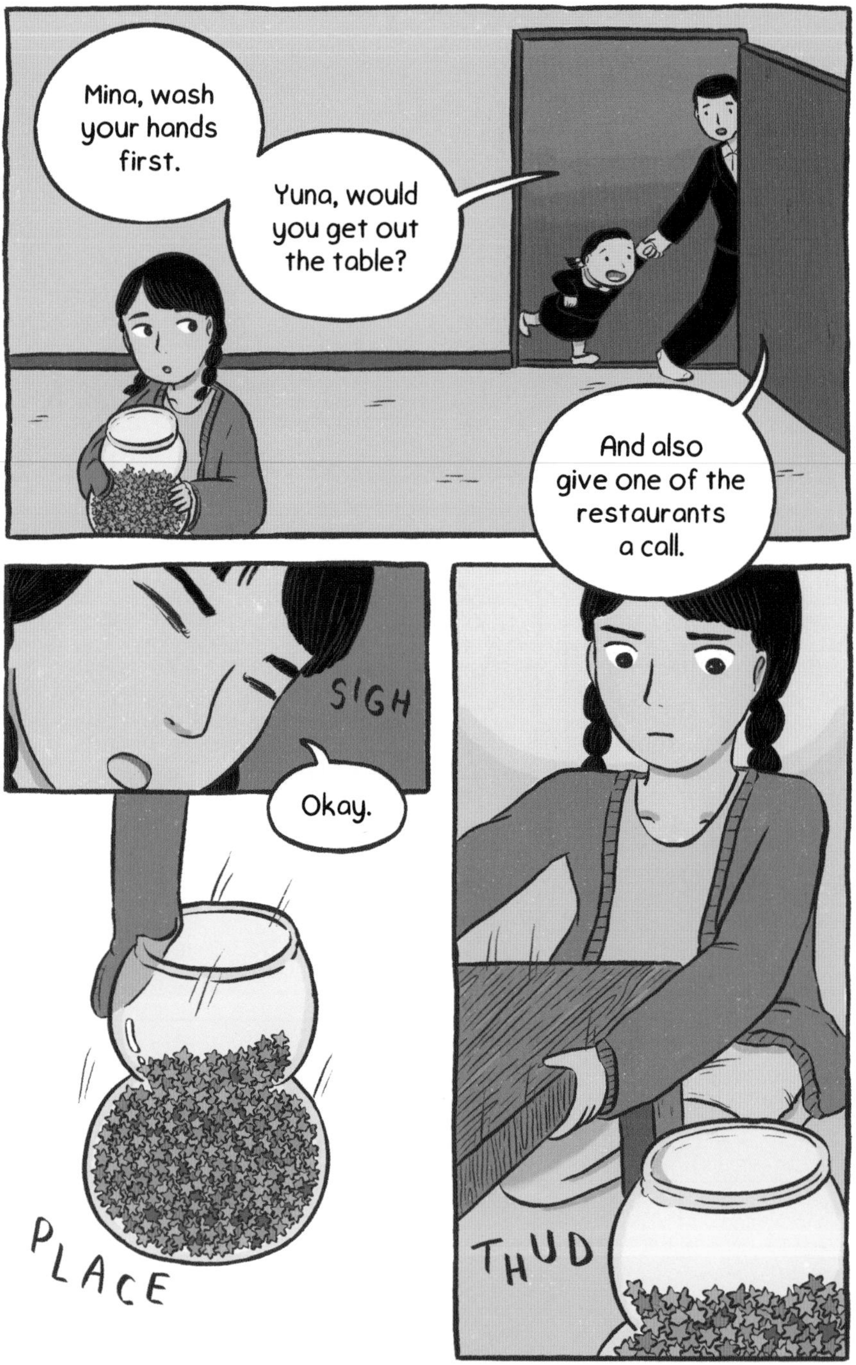
Mina, wash your hands first.
Yuna, would you get out the table?
And also give one of the restaurants a call.
SIGH
Okay.
PLACE
THUD

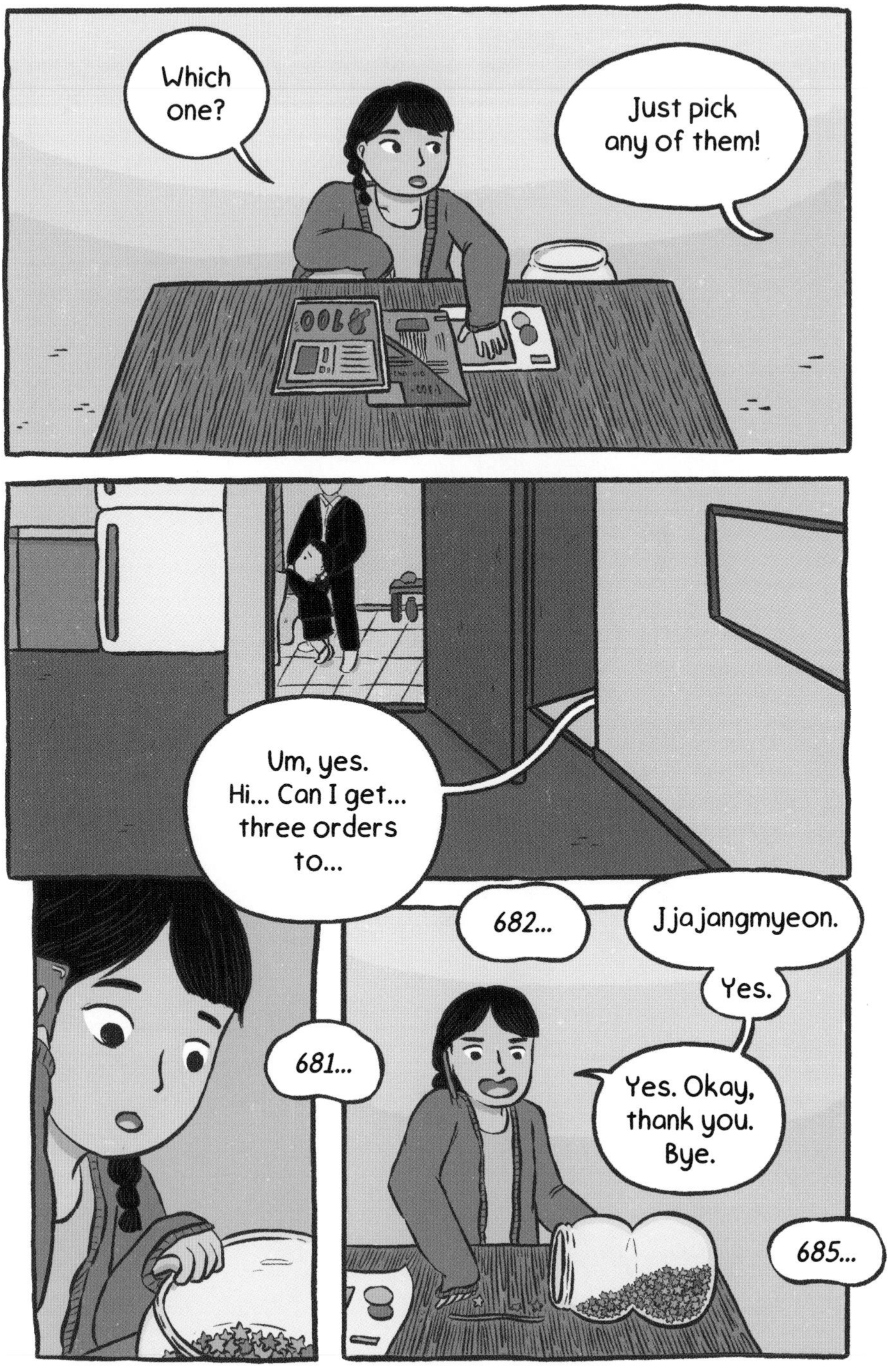
Which one?
Just pick any of them!
Um, yes. Hi... Can I get... three orders to...
681...
682...
Jjajangmyeon.
Yes.
Yes. Okay, thank you. Bye.
685...

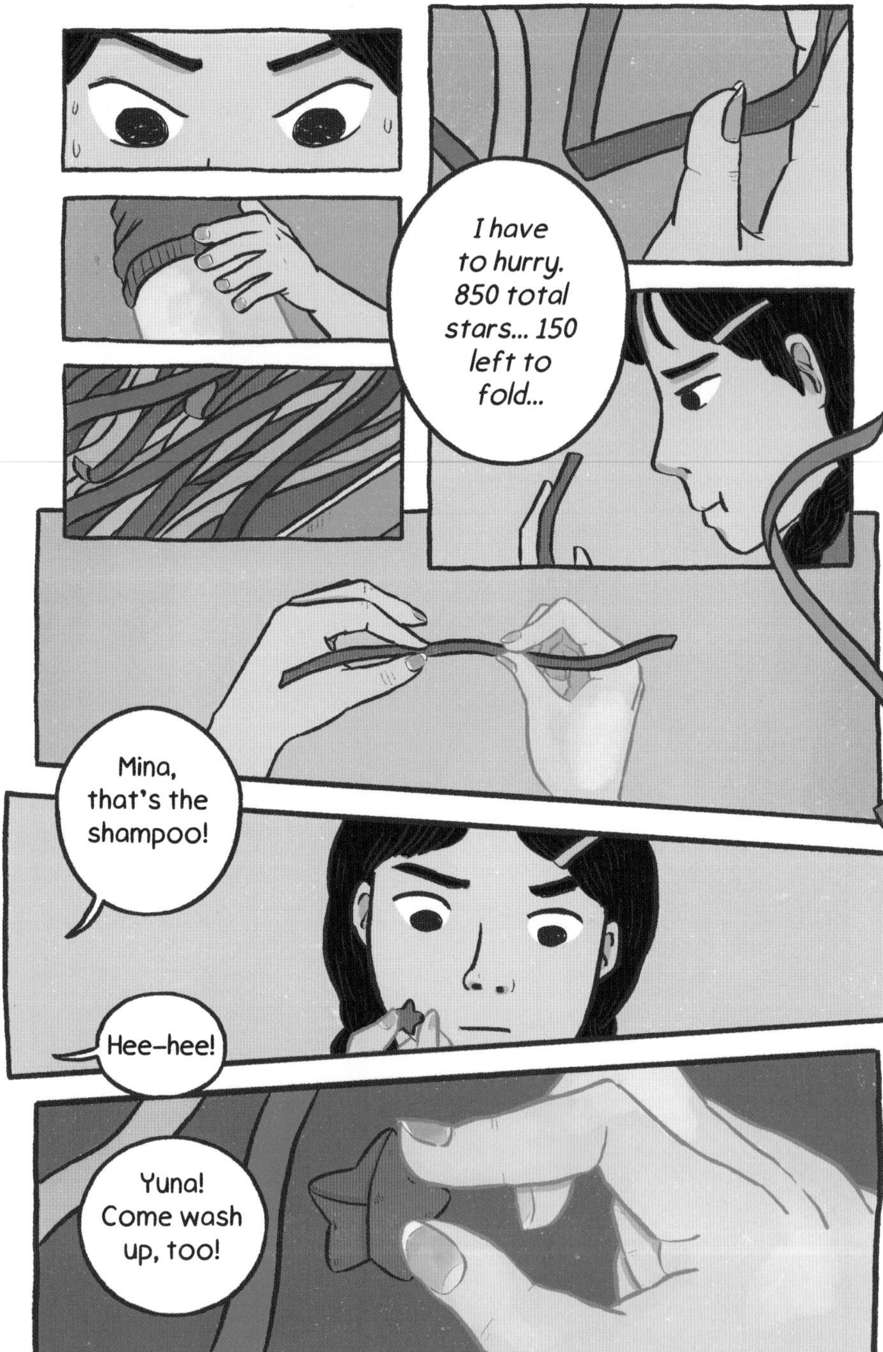
I have to hurry. 850 total stars... 150 left to fold...
Mina, that's the shampoo!
Hee-hee!
Yuna! Come wash up, too!

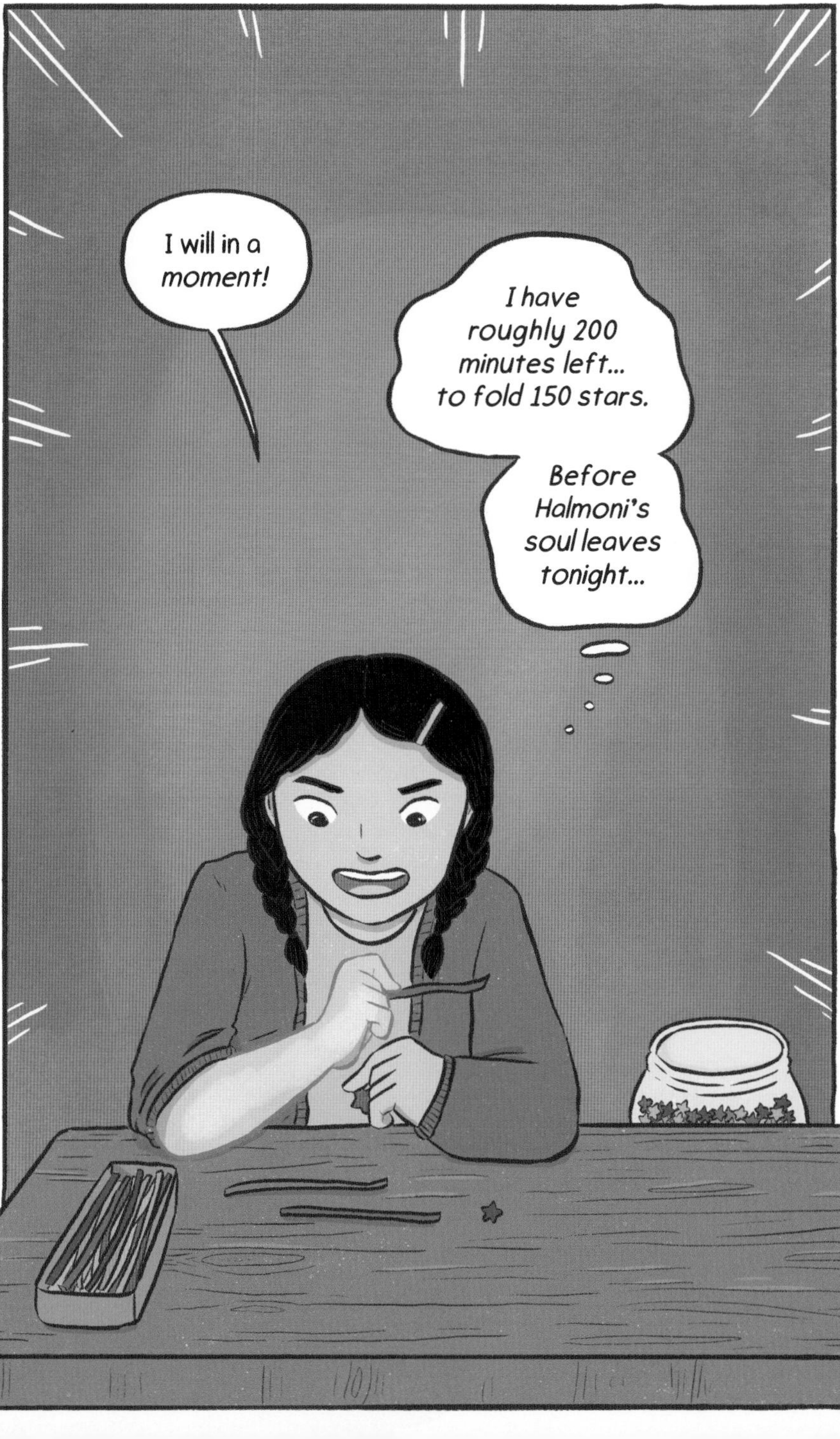
I will in a *moment!*
I have roughly 200 minutes left... to fold 150 stars.
Before Halmoni's soul leaves tonight...

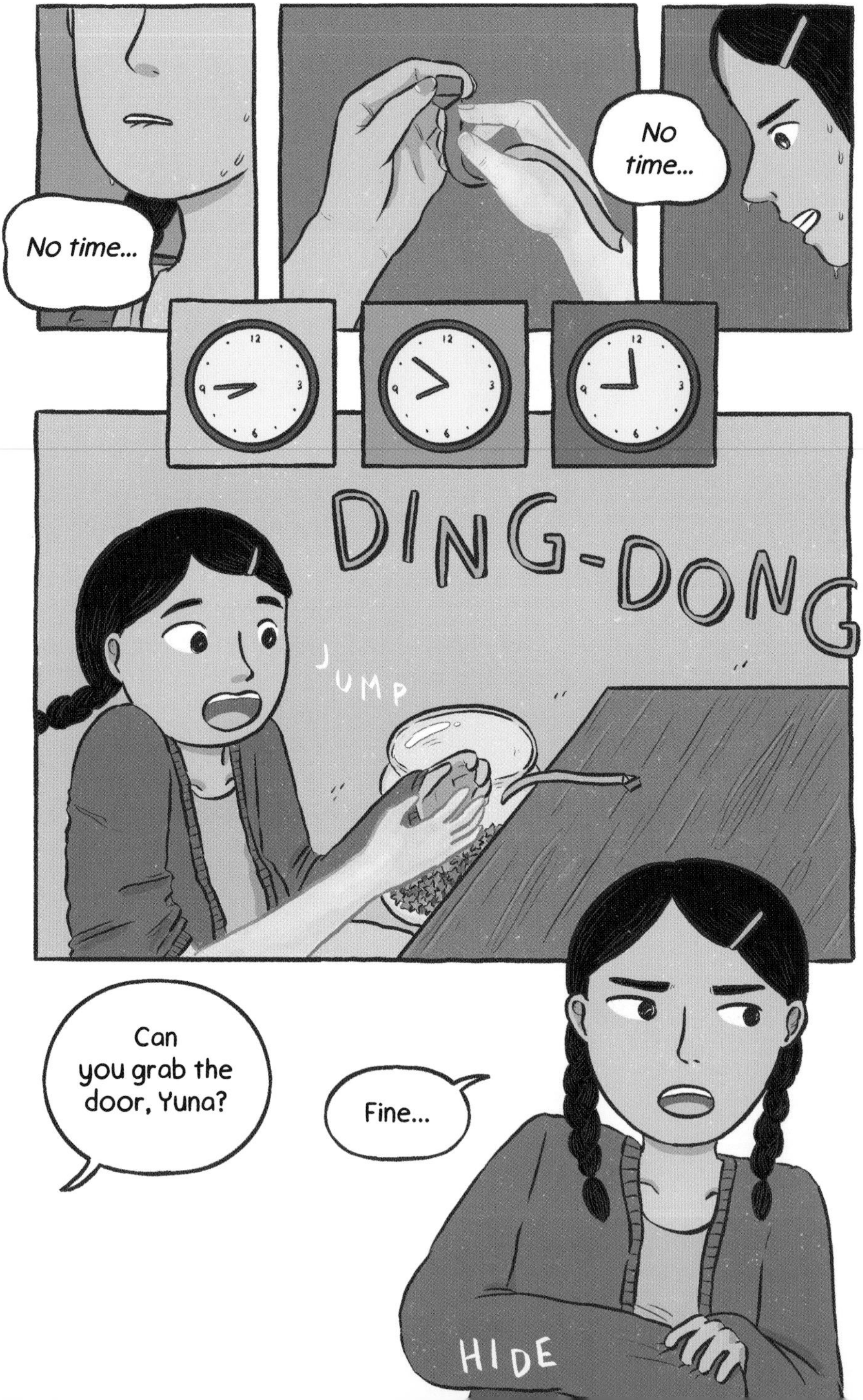
No time...
No time...
DING-DONG
JUMP
Can you grab the door, Yuna?
Fine...
HIDE

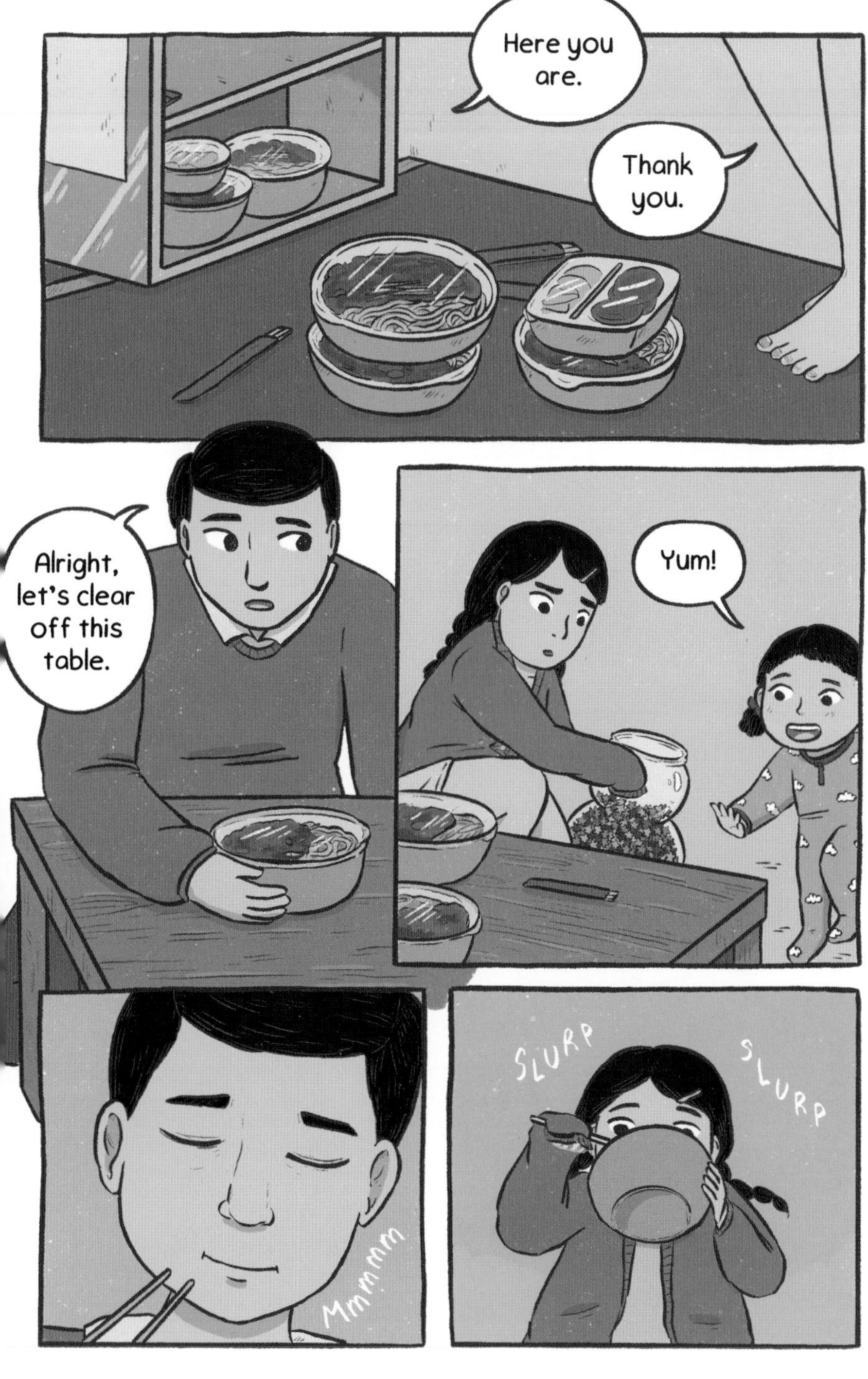
Here you are.
Thank you.
Alright, let's clear off this table.
Yum!
Mmmm
SLURP
SLURP

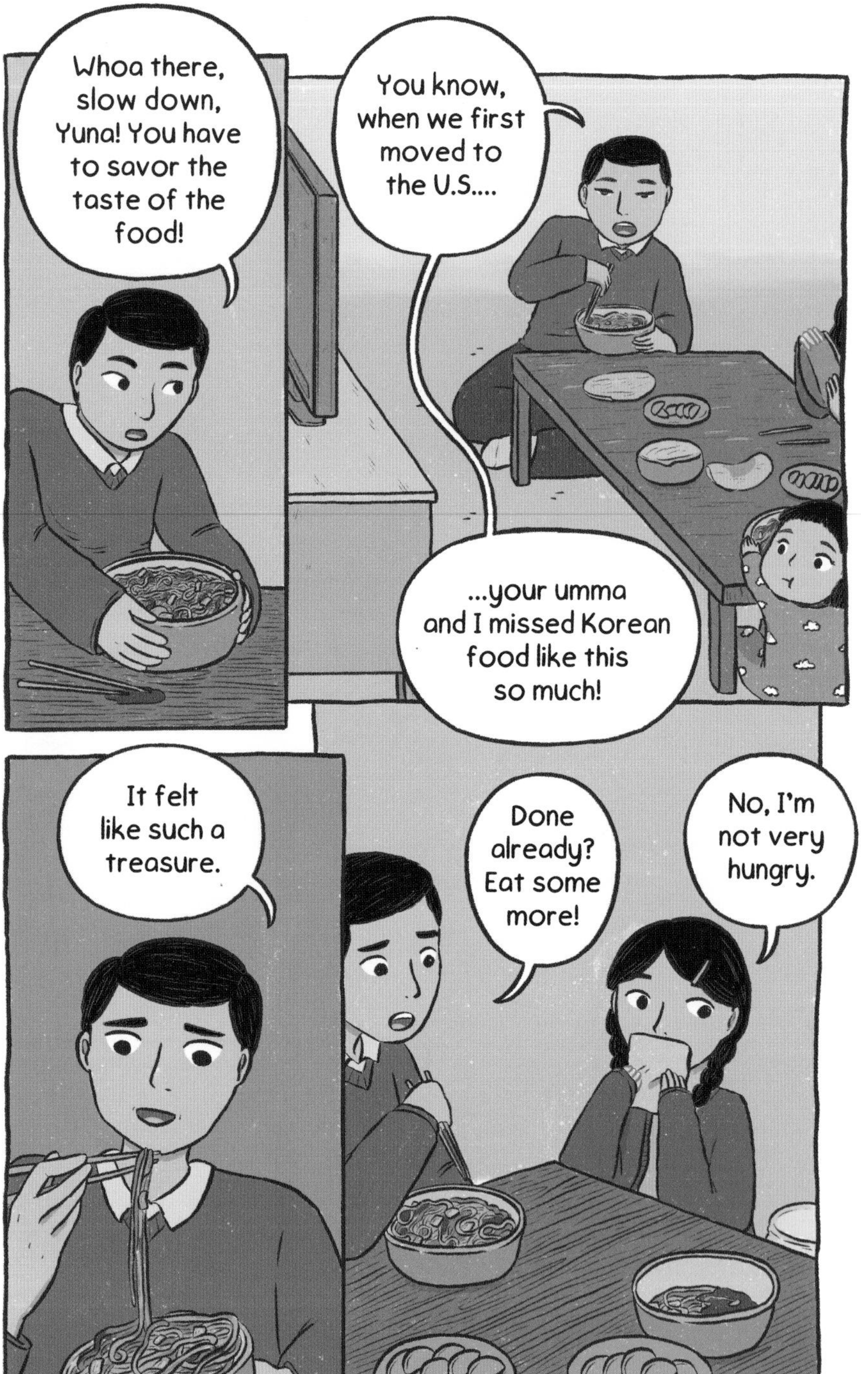
Whoa there, slow down, Yuna! You have to savor the taste of the food!
You know, when we first moved to the U.S....
...your umma and I missed Korean food like this so much!
It felt like such a treasure.
Done already? Eat some more!
No, I'm not very hungry.

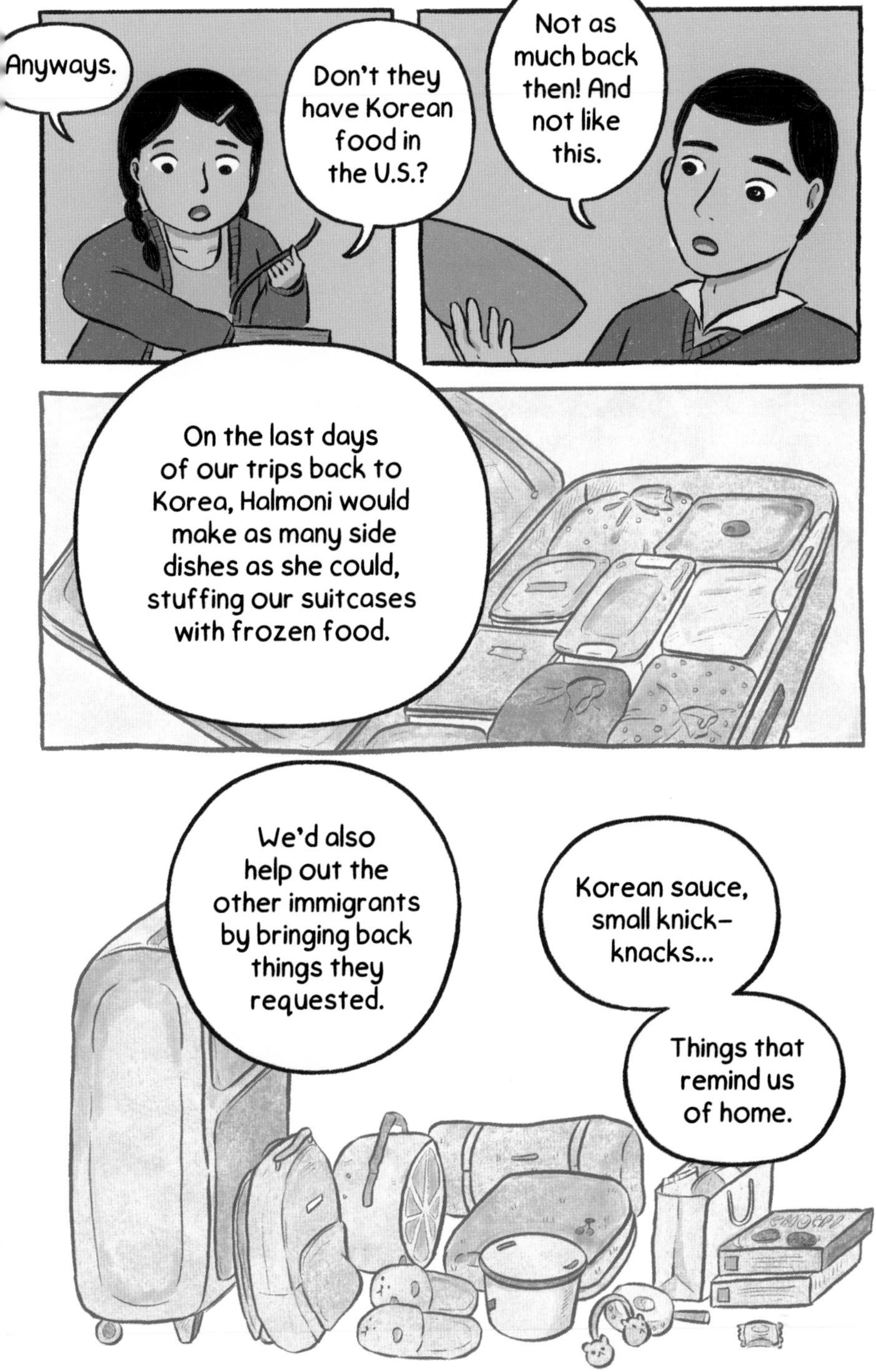
Anyways.
Don't they have Korean food in the U.S.?
Not as much back then! And not like this.
On the last days of our trips back to Korea, Halmoni would make as many side dishes as she could, stuffing our suitcases with frozen food.
We'd also help out the other immigrants by bringing back things they requested.
Korean sauce, small knick-knacks...
Things that remind us of home.

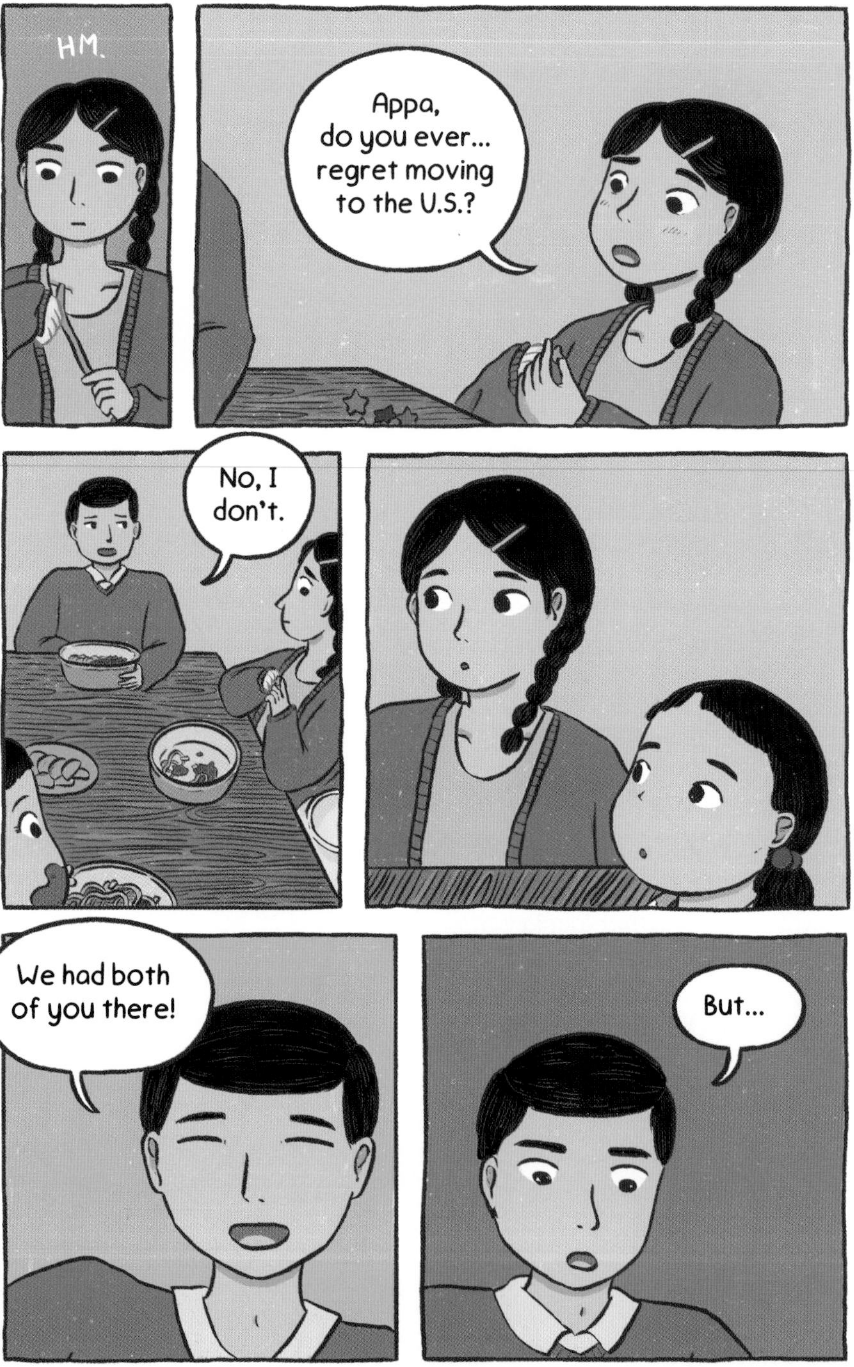
HM.
Appa, do you ever... regret moving to the U.S.?
No, I don't.
We had both of you there!
But...

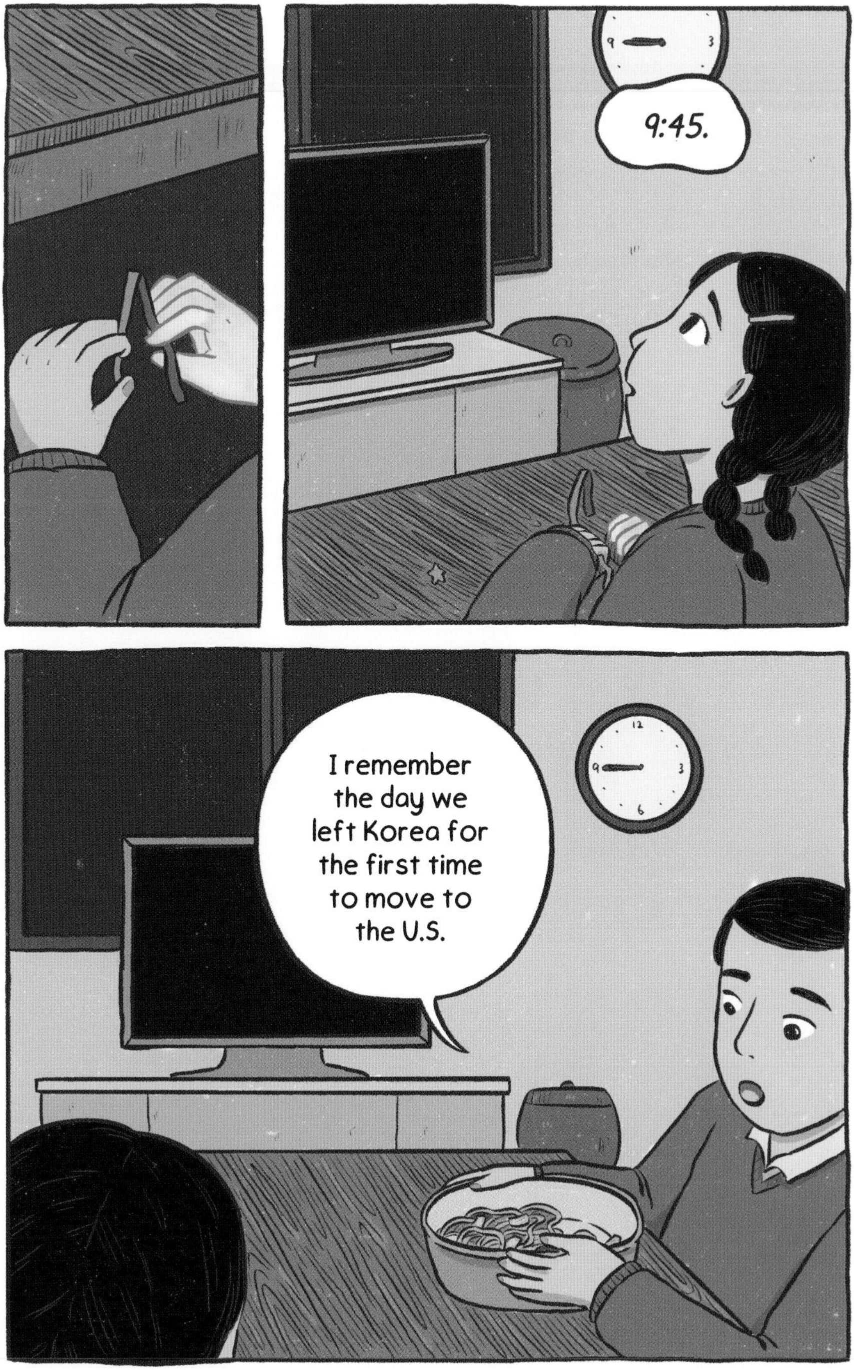
9:45.
I remember the day we left Korea for the first time to move to the U.S.

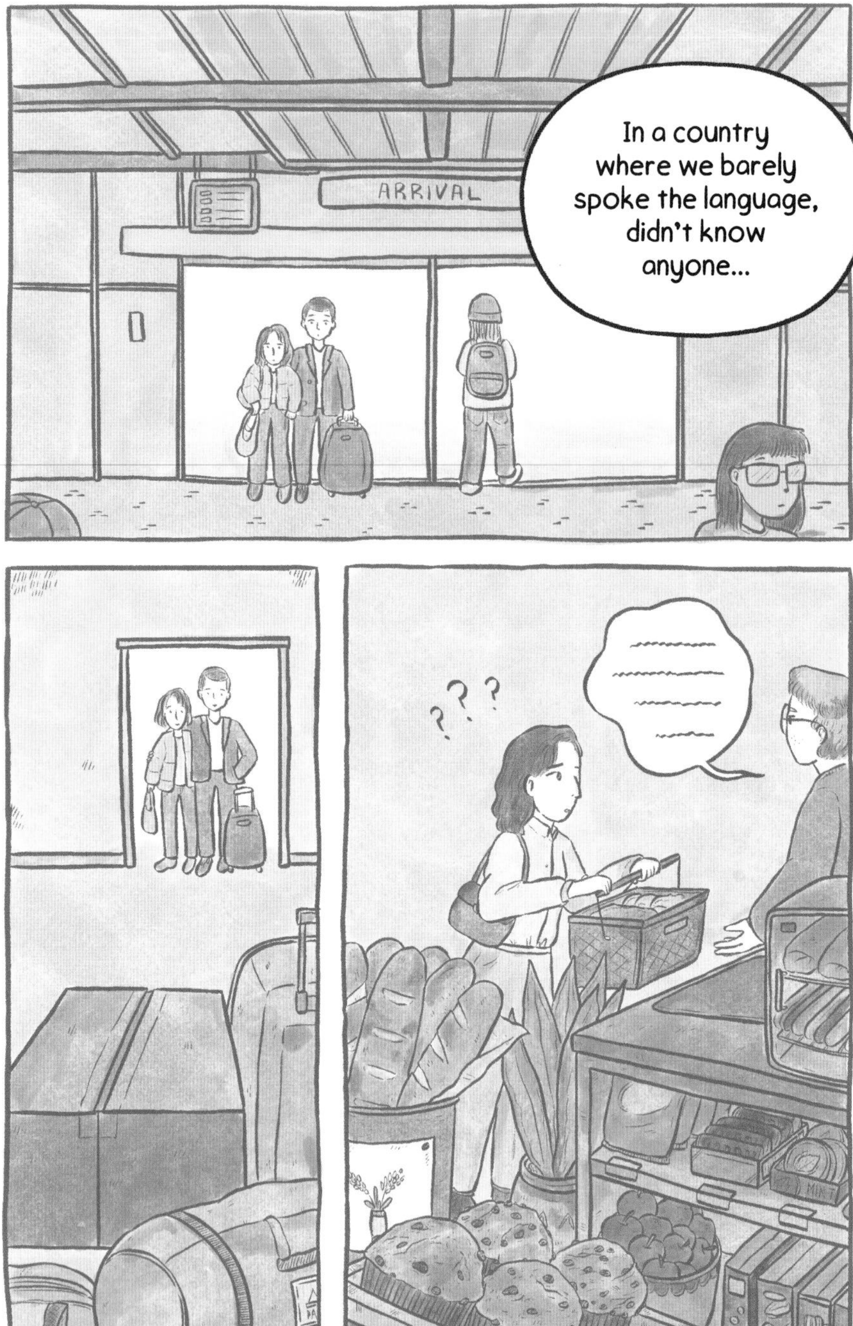
ARRIVAL
In a country where we barely spoke the language, didn't know anyone...
? ? ?
MINT

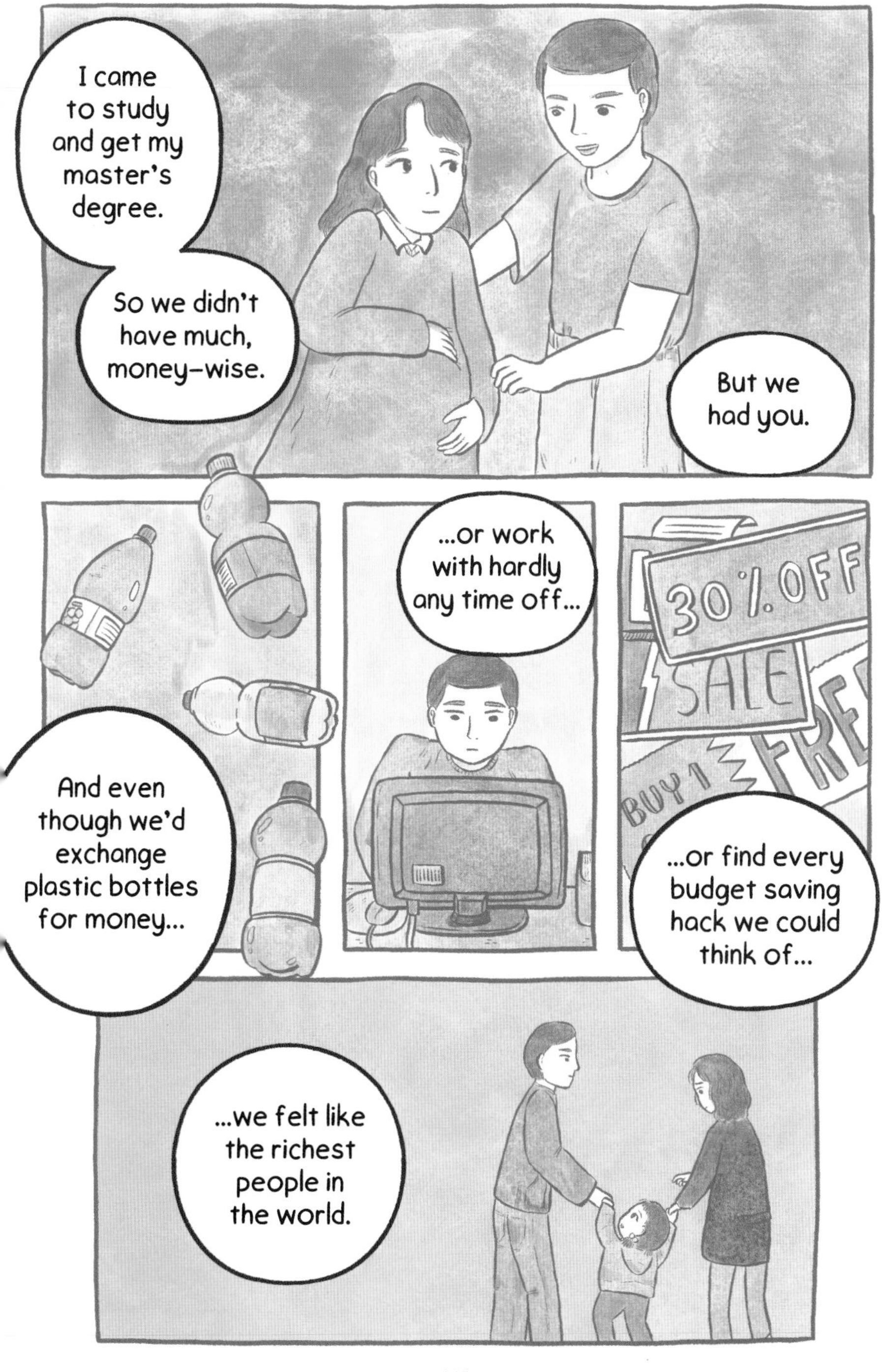
I came to study and get my master's degree.
So we didn't have much, money-wise.
But we had you.
And even though we'd exchange plastic bottles for money...
...or work with hardly any time off...
30% OFF
SALE
BUY 1
...or find every budget saving hack we could think of...
...we felt like the richest people in the world.

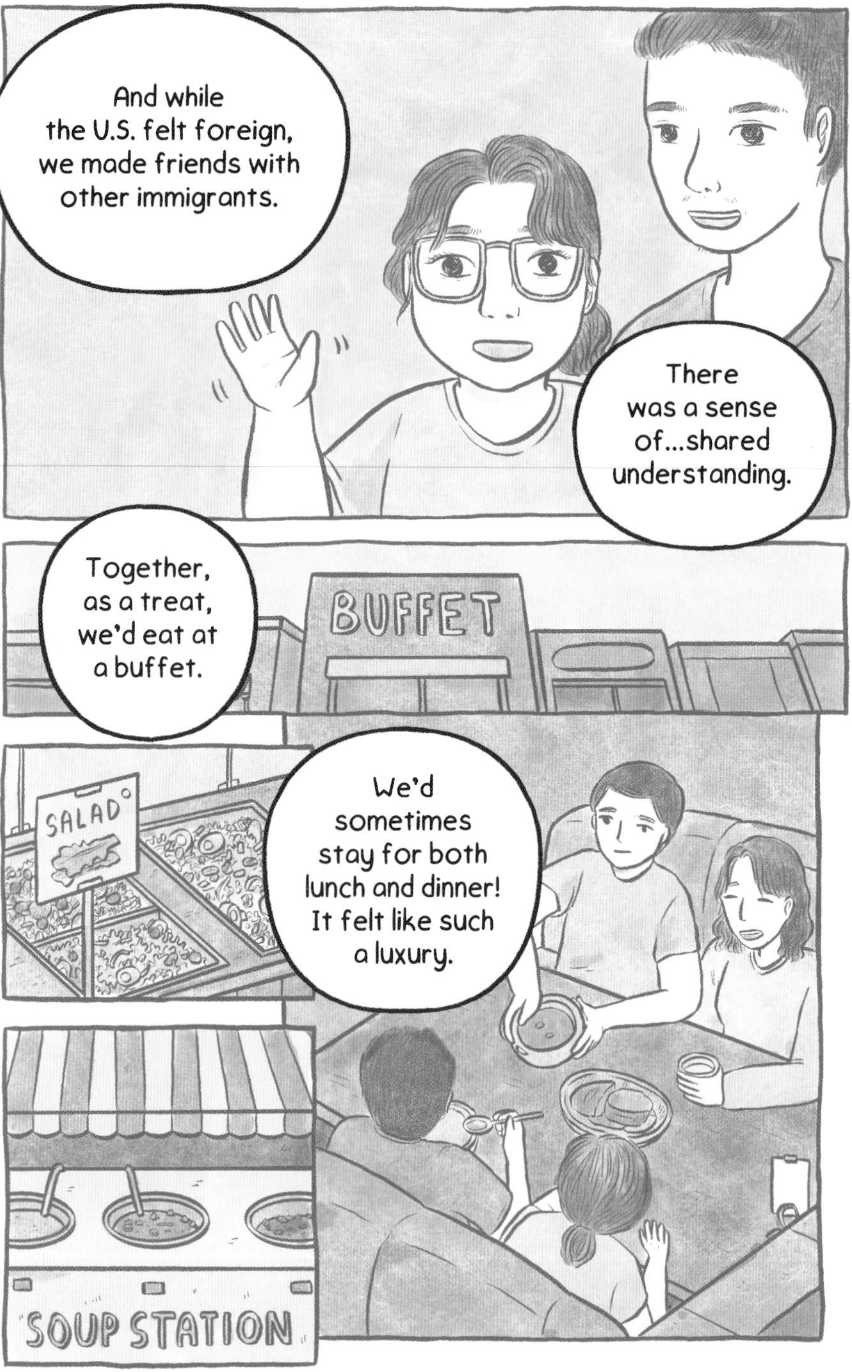
And while the U.S. felt foreign, we made friends with other immigrants.
There was a sense of...shared understanding.
Together, as a treat, we'd eat at a buffet.
BUFFET
SALAD
We'd sometimes stay for both lunch and dinner! It felt like such a luxury.
SOUP STATION

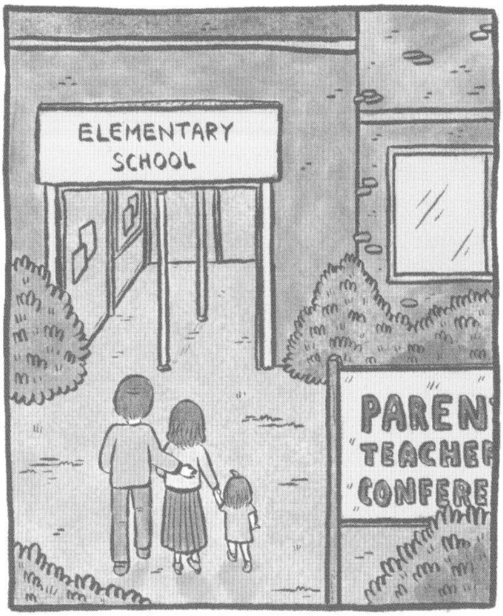
ELEMENTARY SCHOOL
PAREN
"TEACHE
"CONFERE

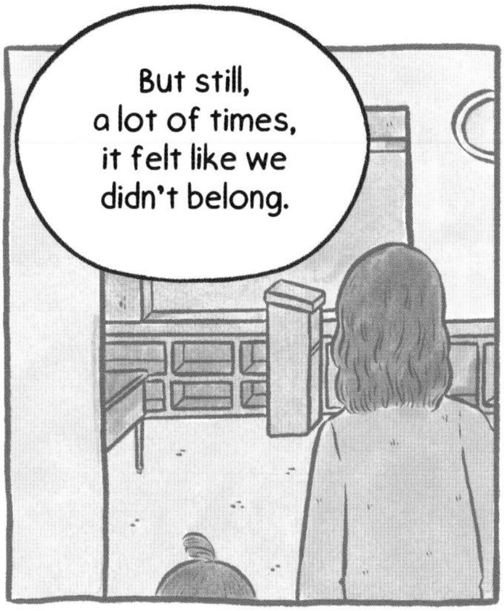
But still, a lot of times, it felt like we didn't belong.

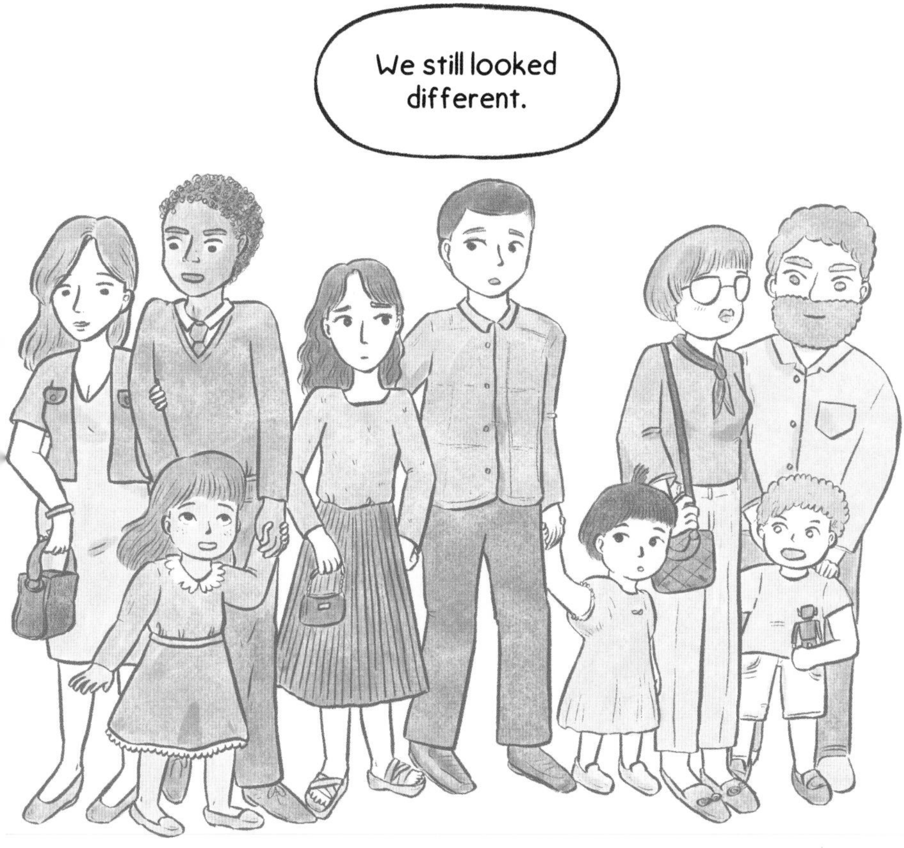
We still looked different.

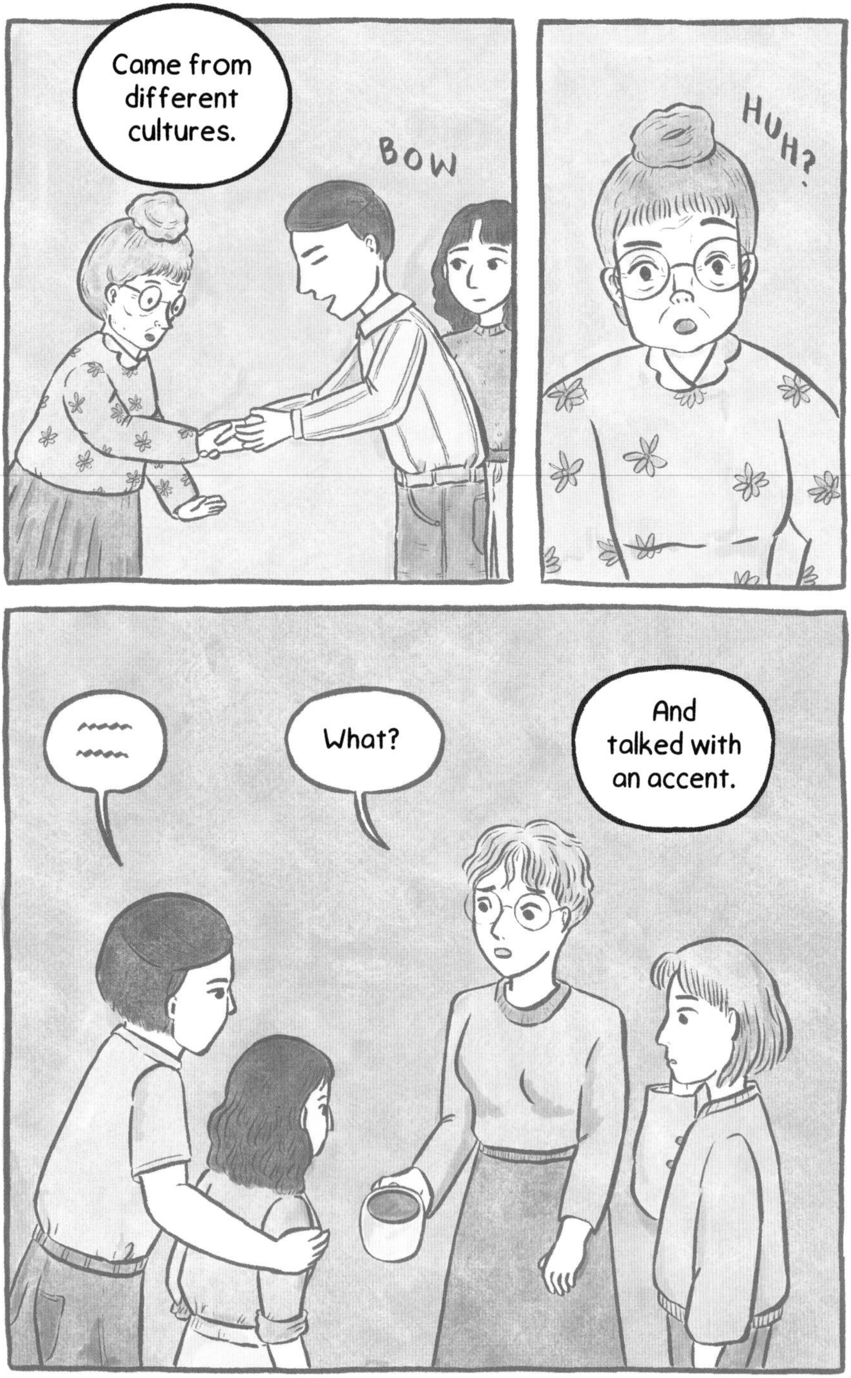
Came from different cultures.
BOW
HUH?
What?
And talked with an accent.

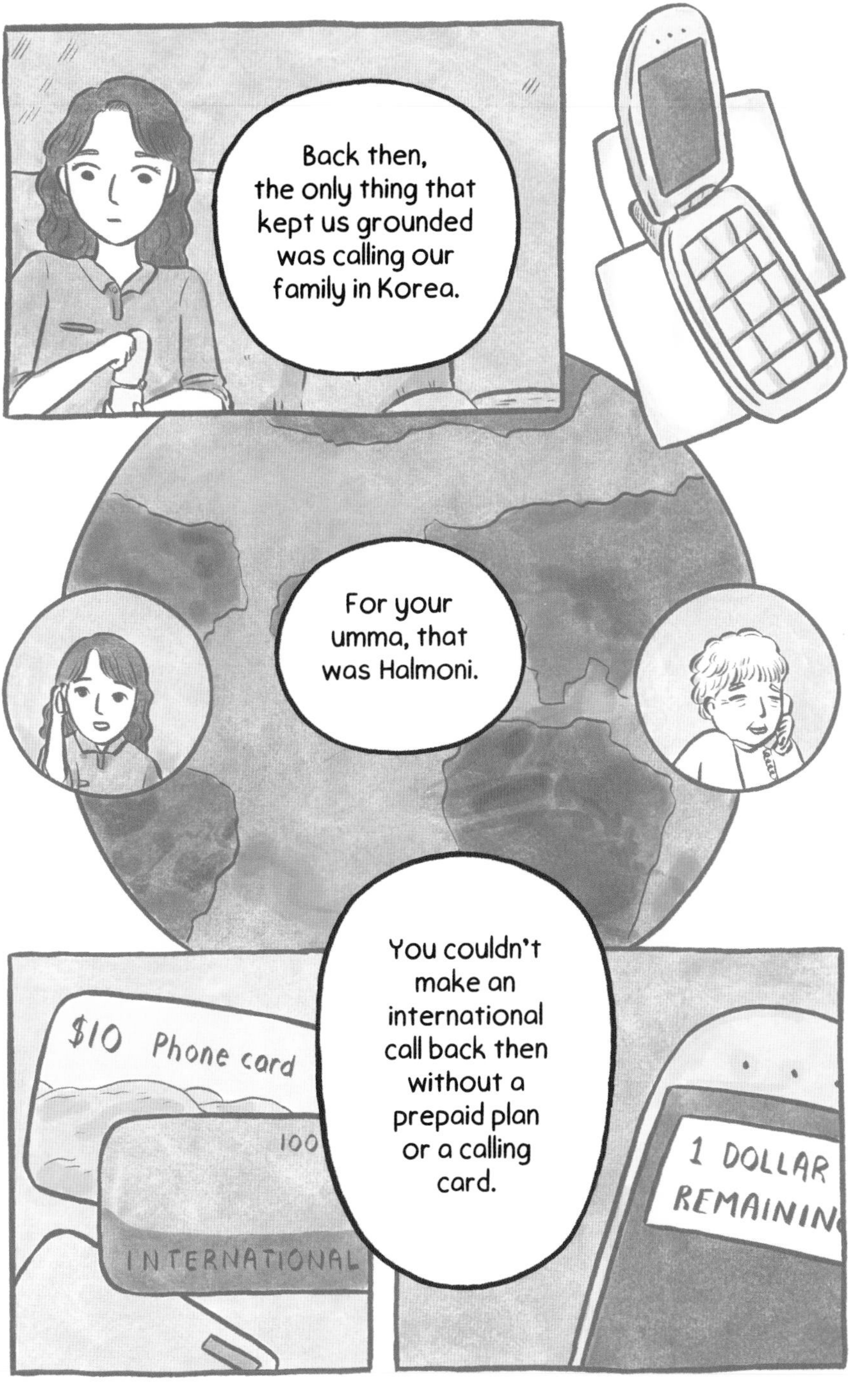
Back then, the only thing that kept us grounded was calling our family in Korea.
For your umma, that was Halmoni.
You couldn't make an international call back then without a prepaid plan or a calling card.
$10 Phone card
100
INTERNATIONAL
1 DOLLAR REMAININ

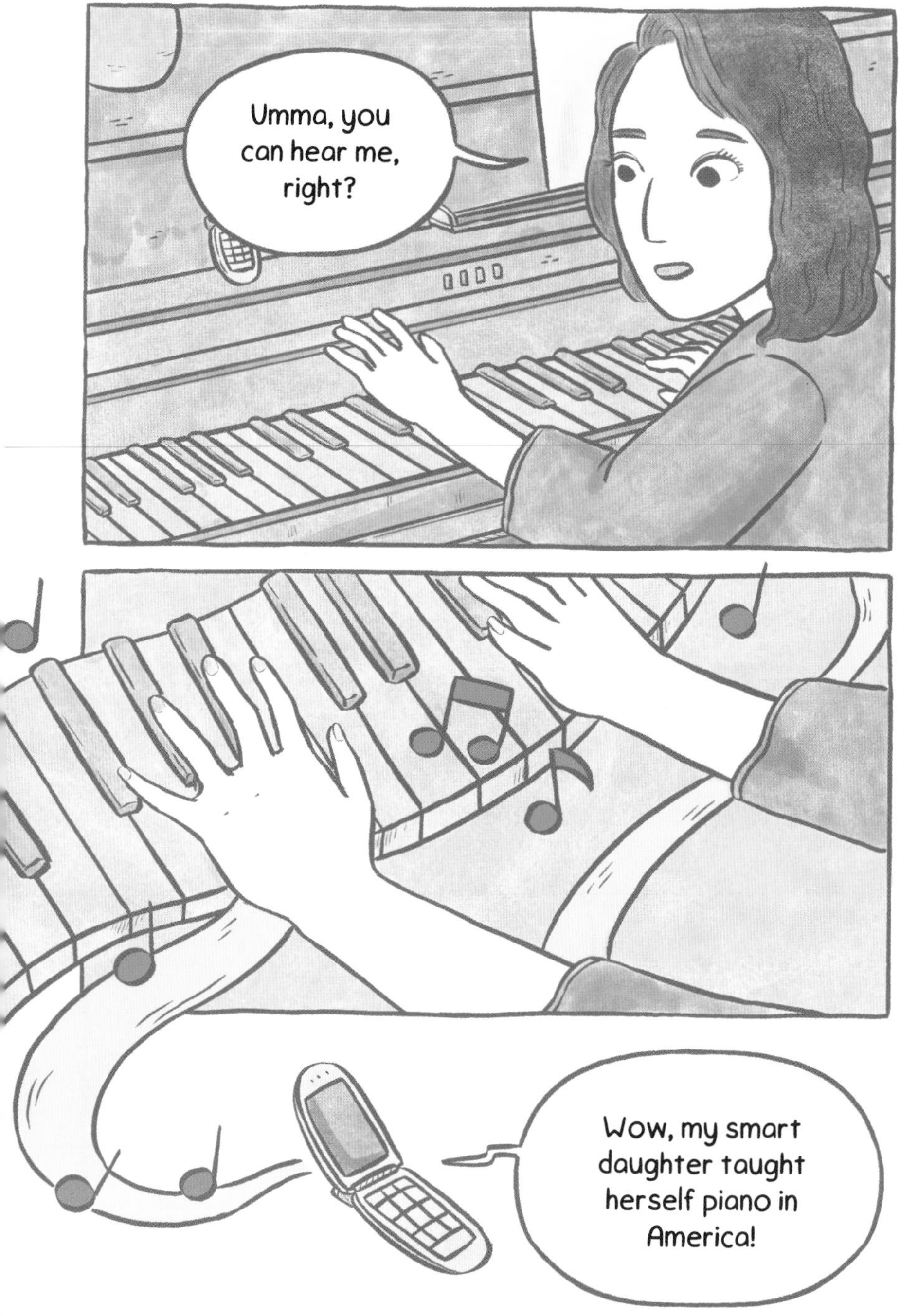
Umma, you can hear me, right?
Wow, my smart daughter taught herself piano in America!

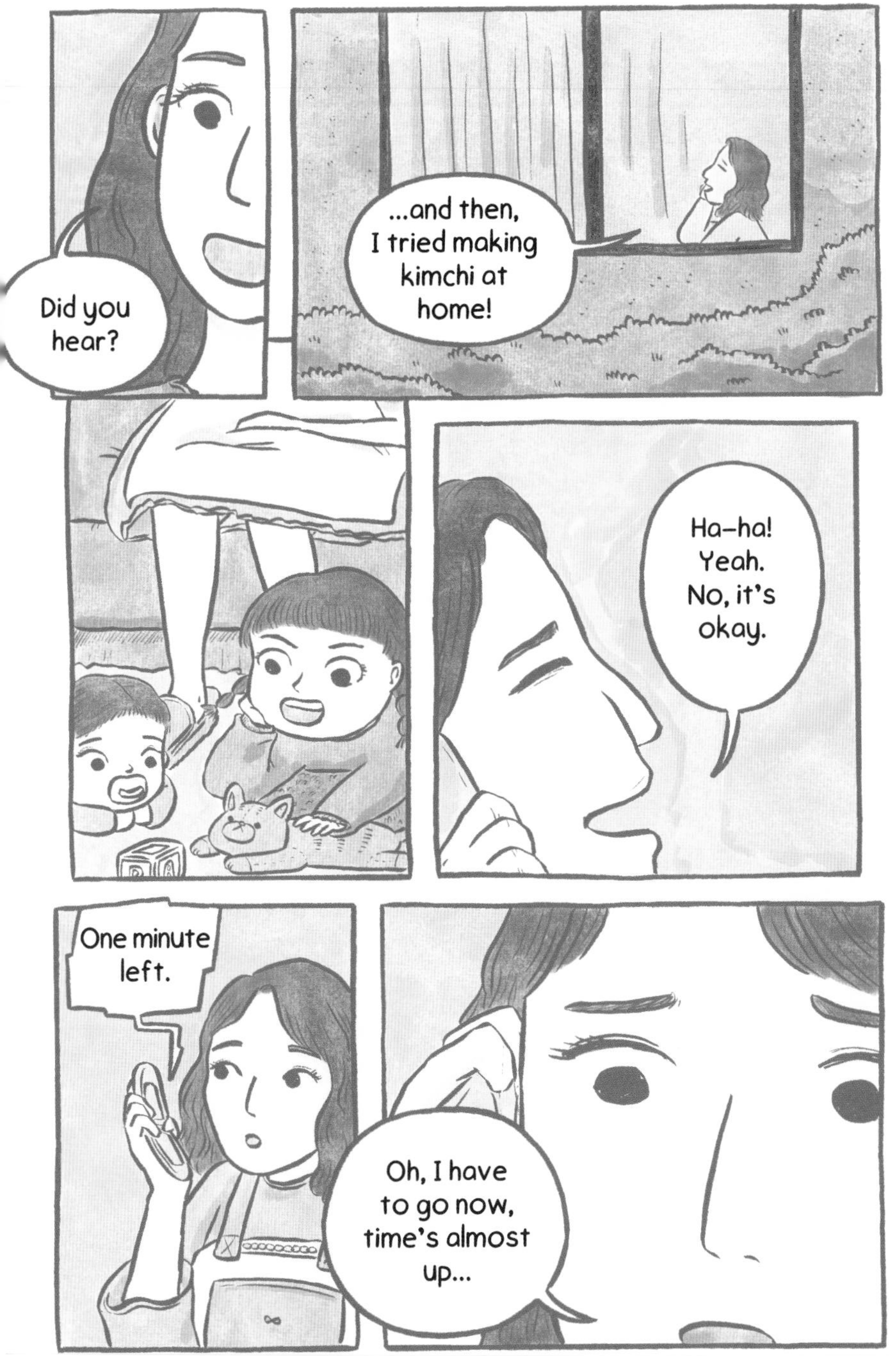
Did you hear?
...and then, I tried making kimchi at home!
Ha-ha! Yeah. No, it's okay.
One minute left.
Oh, I have to go now, time's almost up...

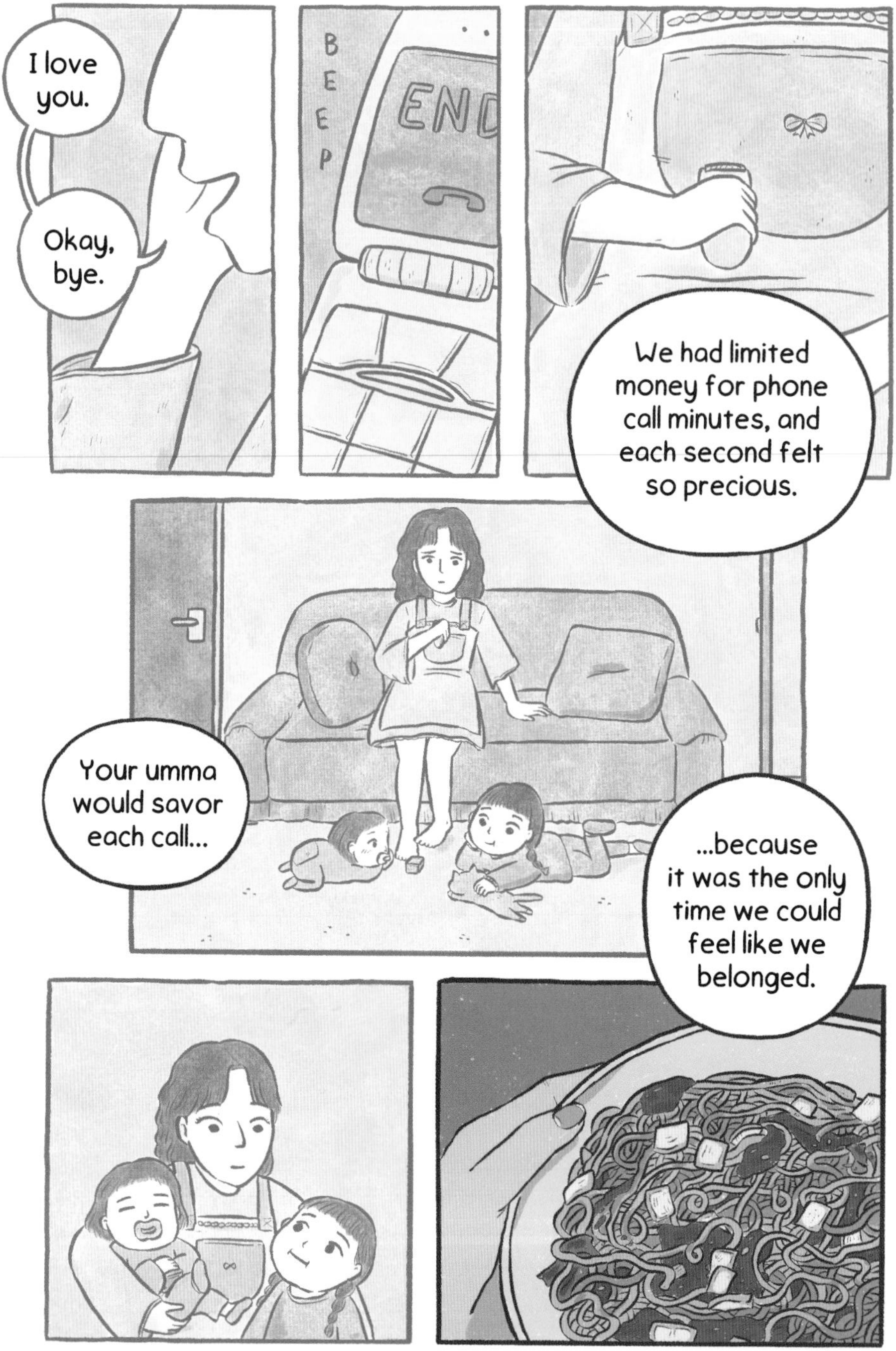
I love you.
Okay, bye.
BEEP
END
We had limited money for phone call minutes, and each second felt so precious.
Your umma would savor each call...
...because it was the only time we could feel like we belonged.

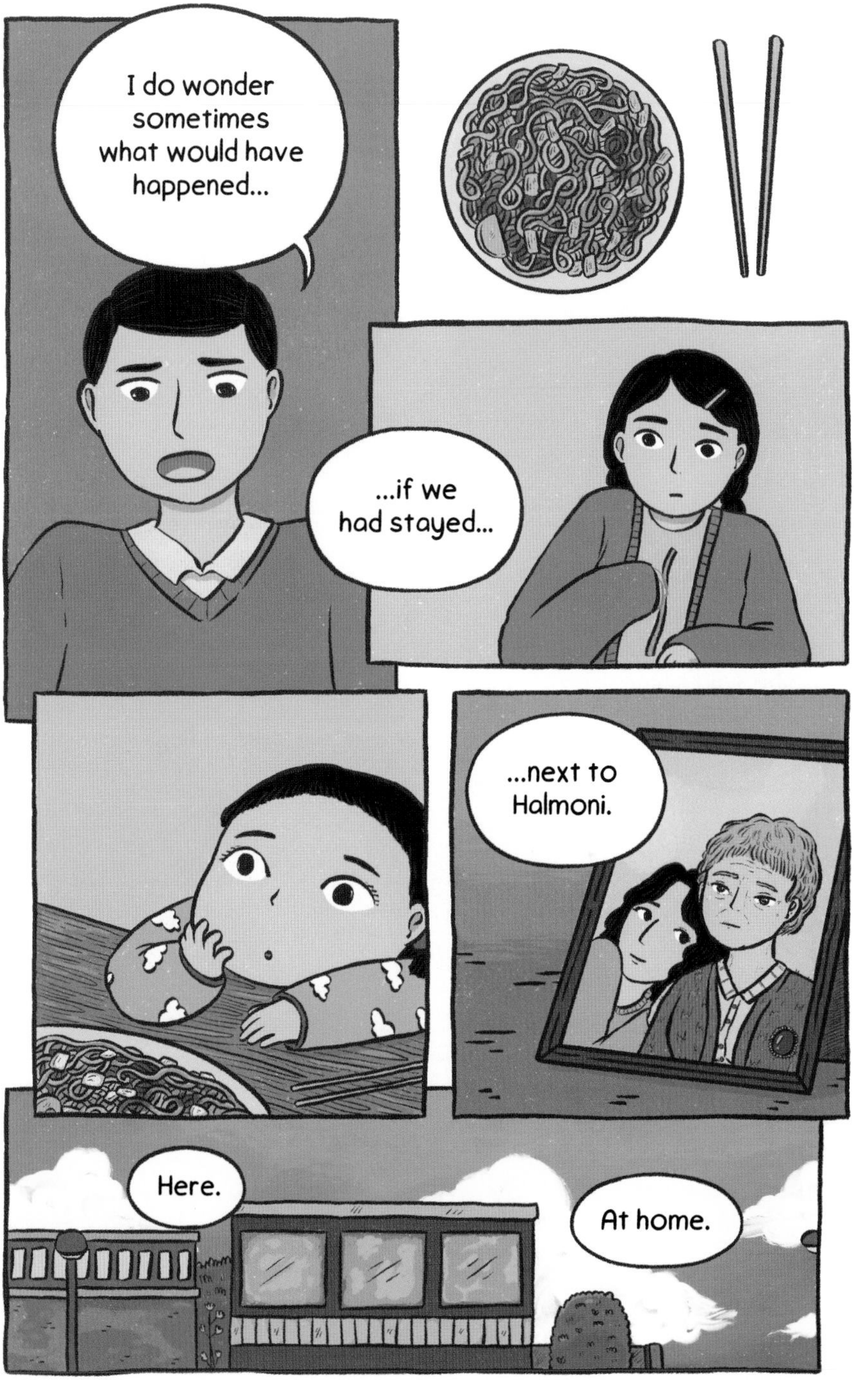
I do wonder sometimes what would have happened...
...if we had stayed...
...next to Halmoni.
Here.
At home.

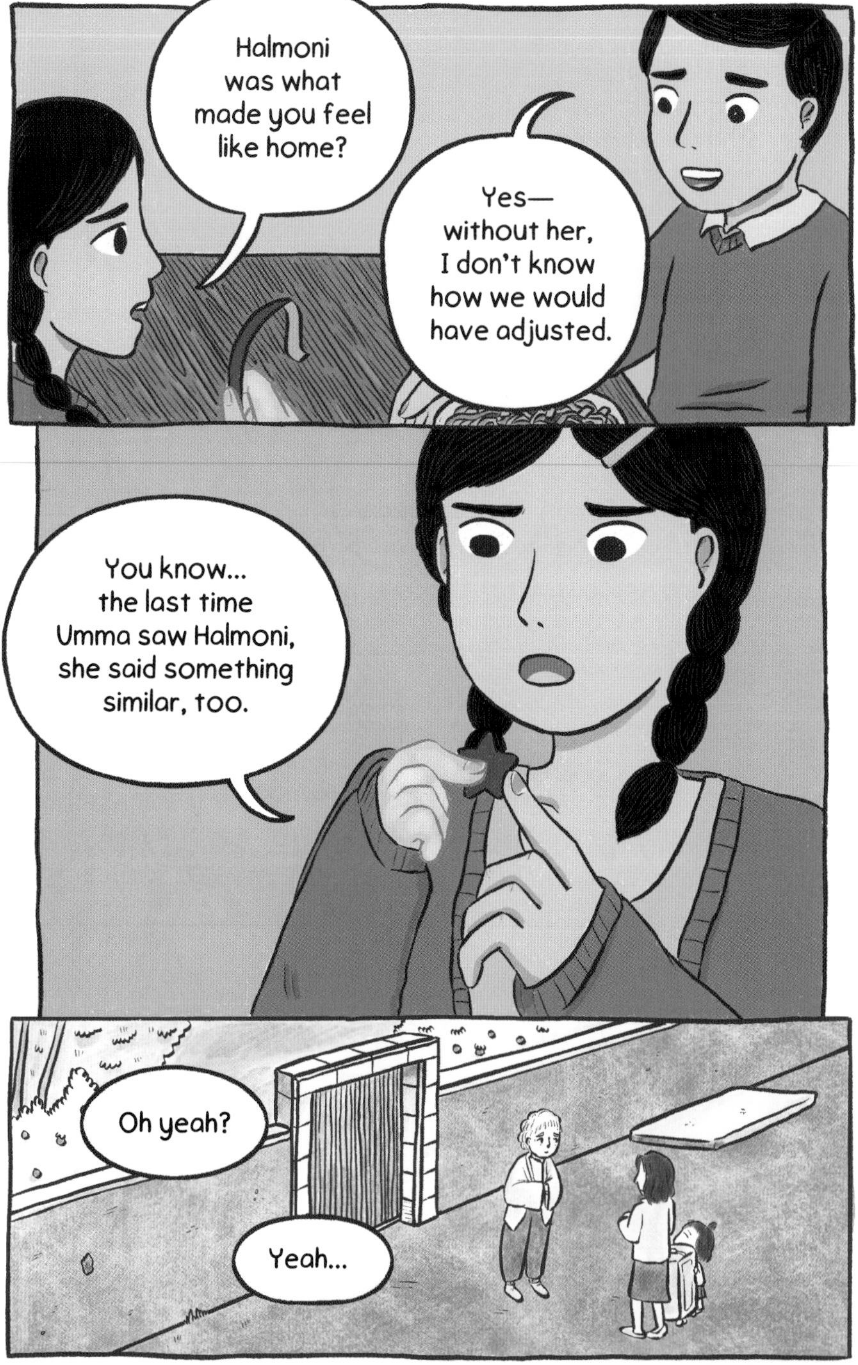
Halmoni was what made you feel like home?
Yes— without her, I don't know how we would have adjusted.
You know... the last time Umma saw Halmoni, she said something similar, too.
Oh yeah?
Yeah...

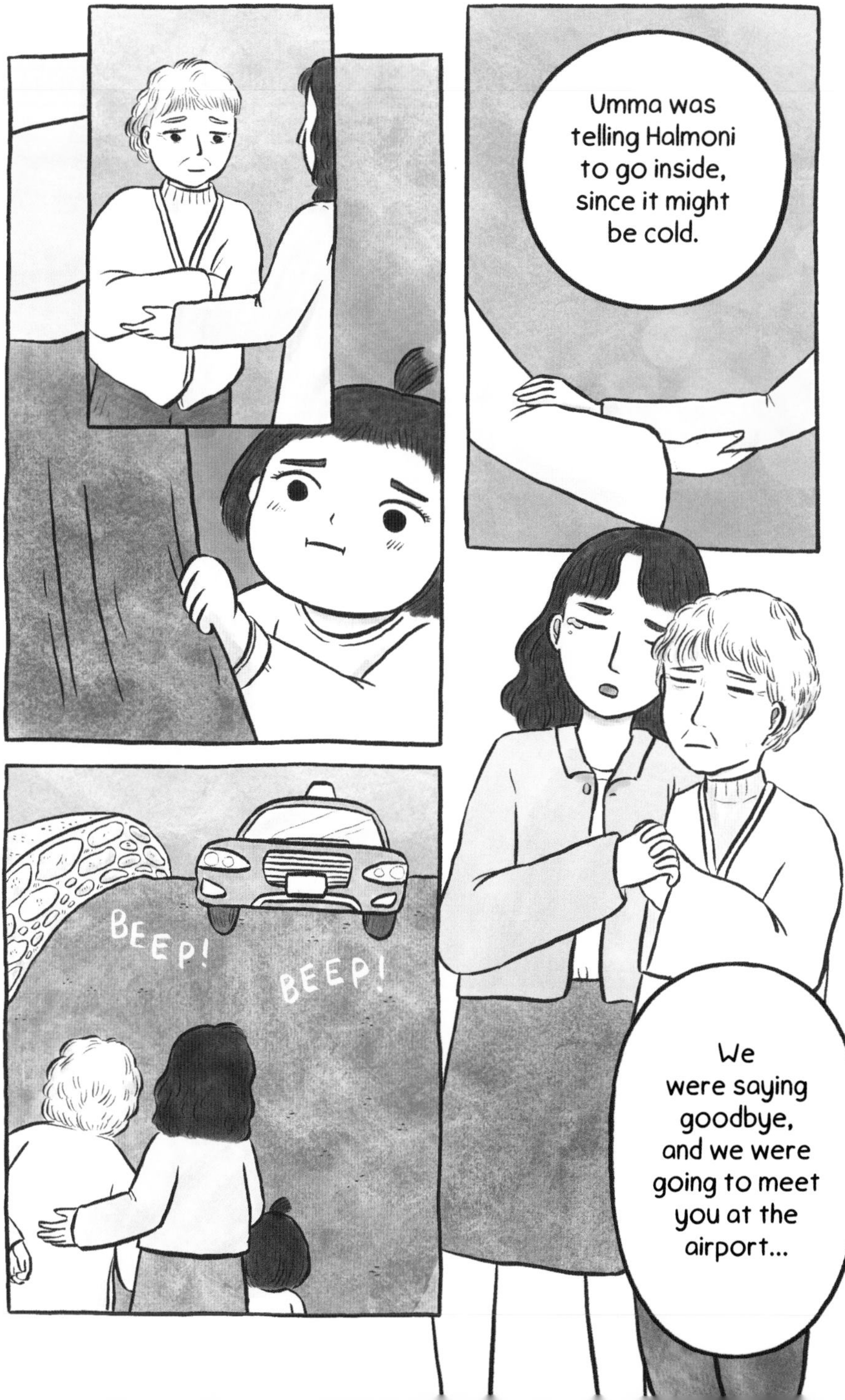
Umma was telling Halmoni to go inside, since it might be cold.
BEEP!
BEEP!
We were saying goodbye, and we were going to meet you at the airport...

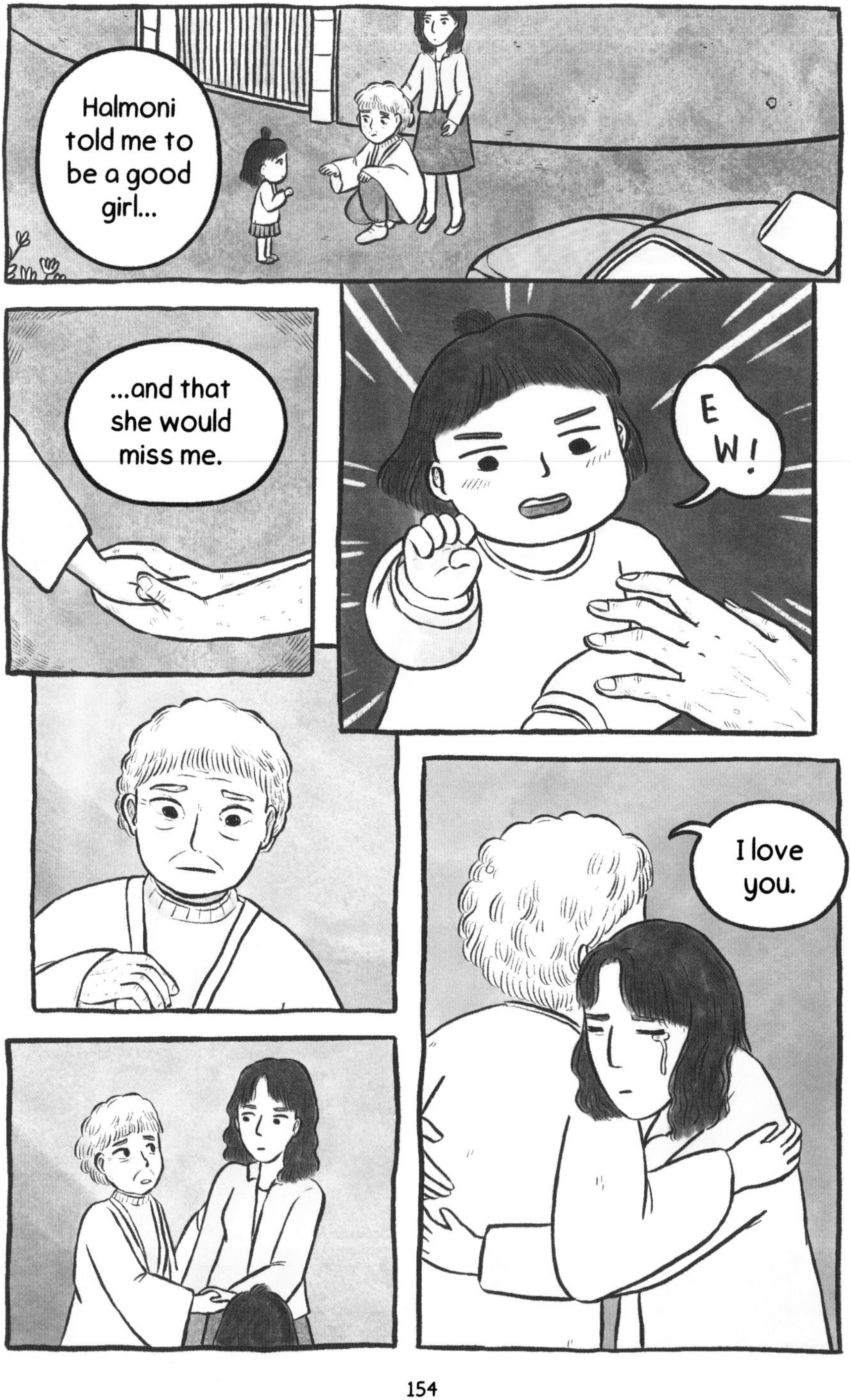
Halmoni told me to be a good girl...
...and that she would miss me.
EW!
I love you.

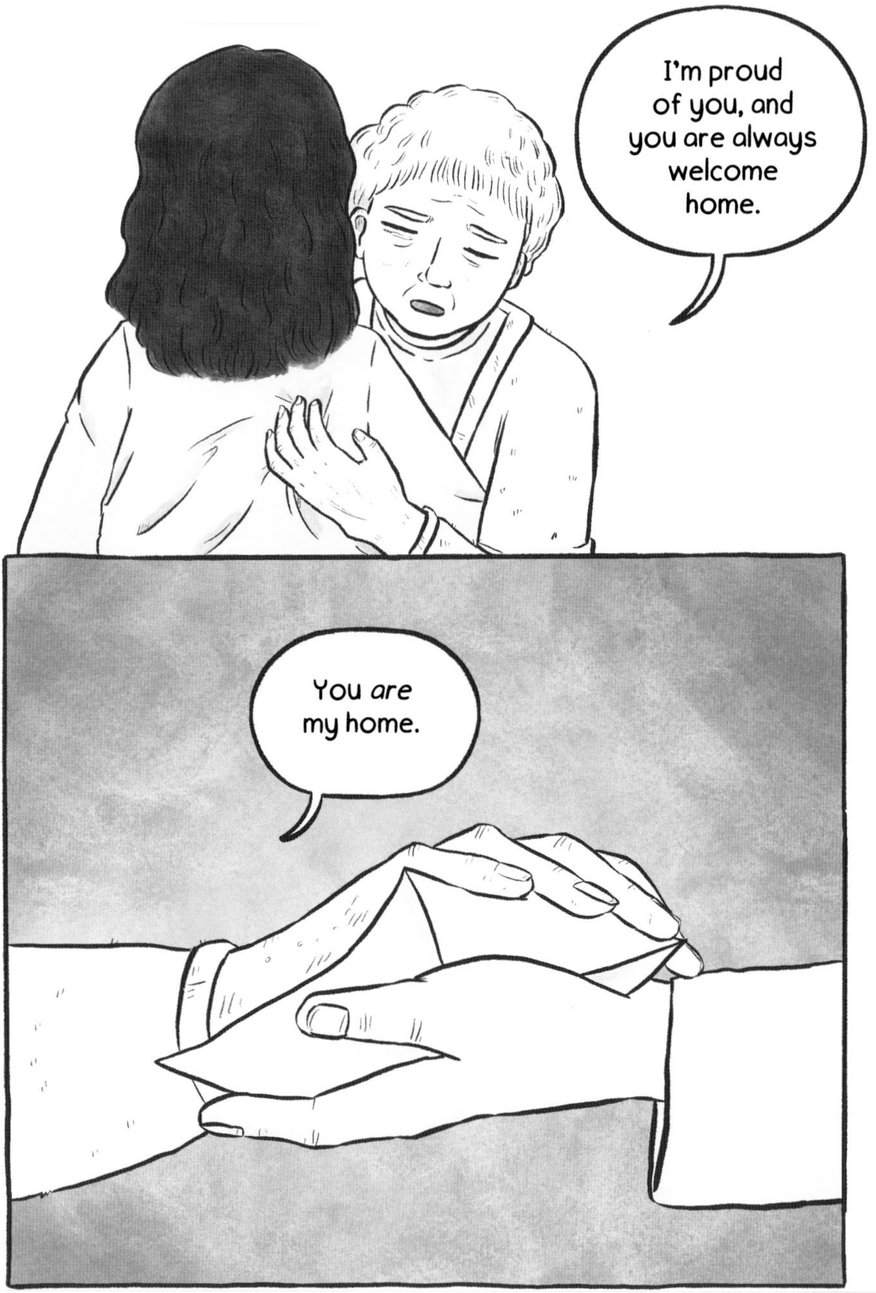
I'm proud
of you, and
you are always
welcome
home.
You *are*
my home.

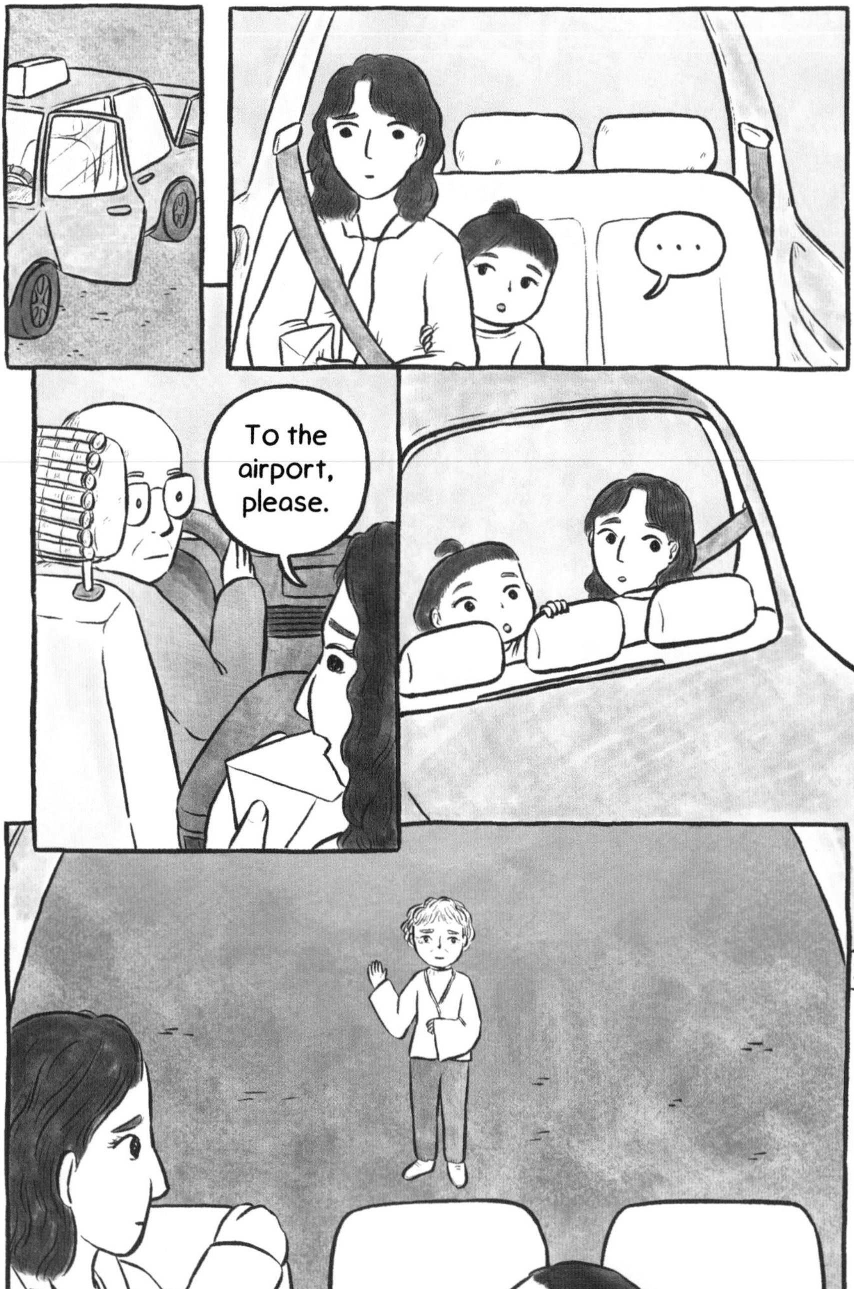
...
To the airport, please.

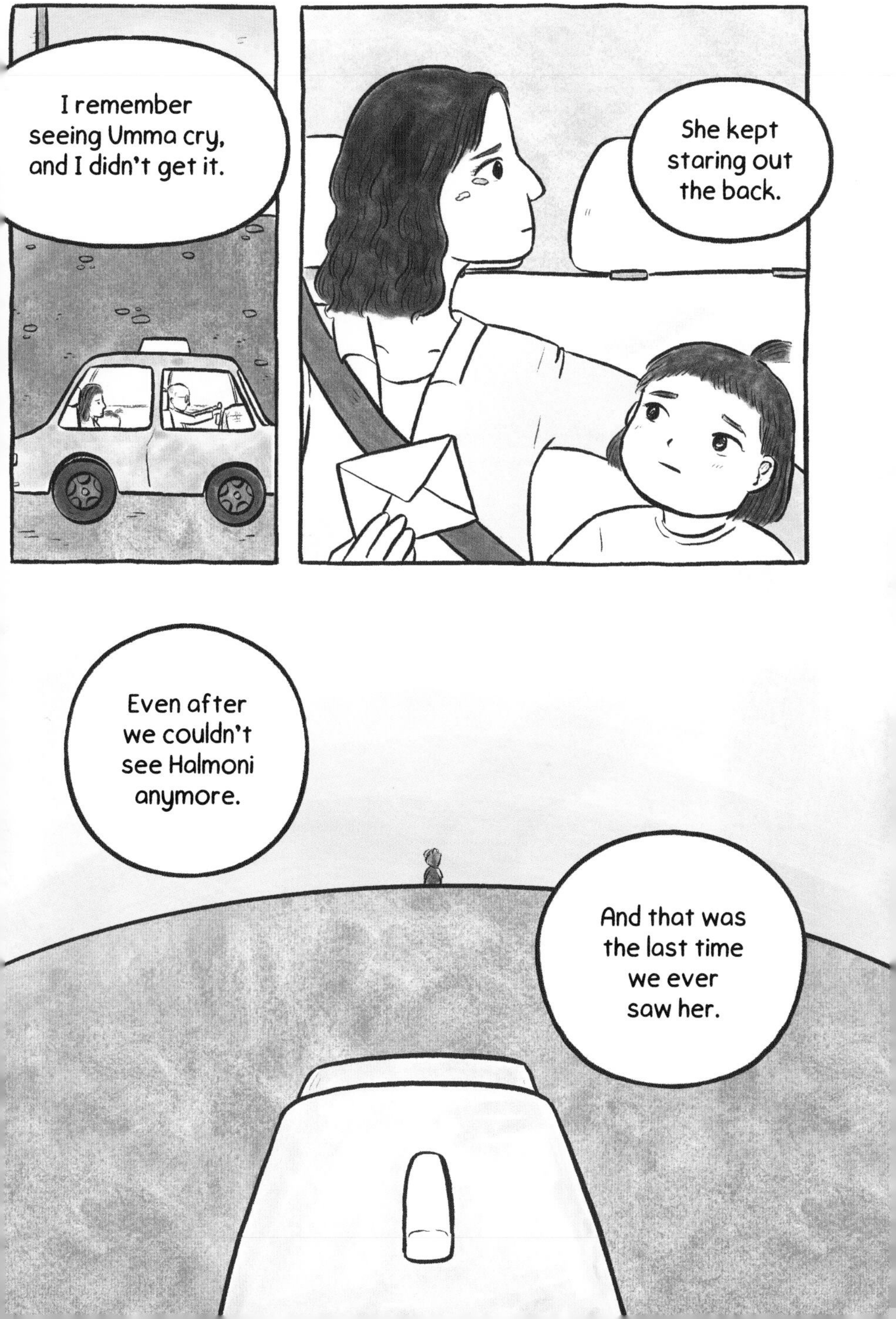
I remember seeing Umma cry, and I didn't get it.
She kept staring out the back.
Even after we couldn't see Halmoni anymore.
And that was the last time we ever saw her.

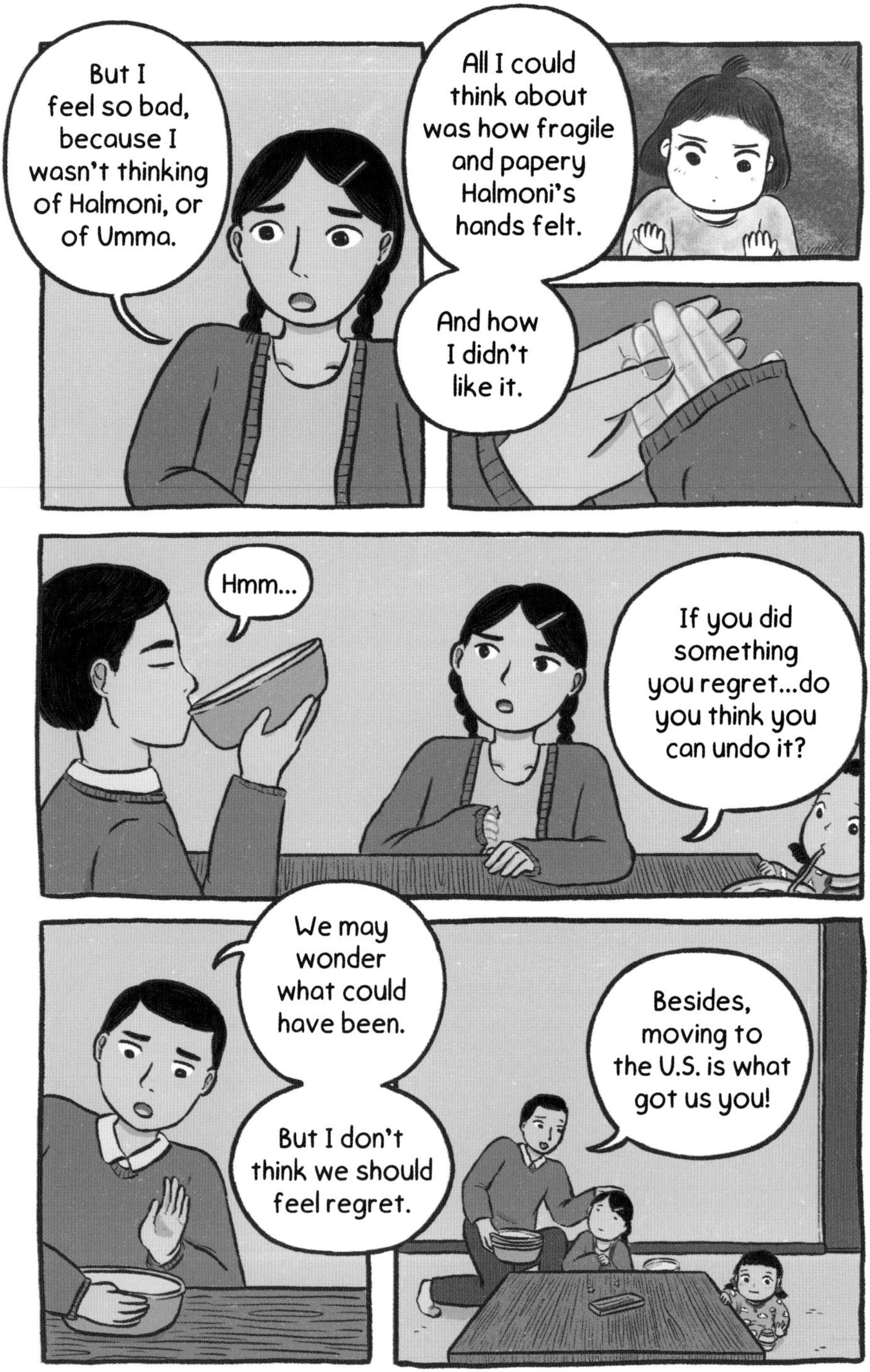
But I feel so bad, because I wasn't thinking of Halmoni, or of Umma.
All I could think about was how fragile and papery Halmoni's hands felt.
And how I didn't like it.
Hmm...
If you did something you regret...do you think you can undo it?
We may wonder what could have been.
But I don't think we should feel regret.
Besides, moving to the U.S. is what got us you!

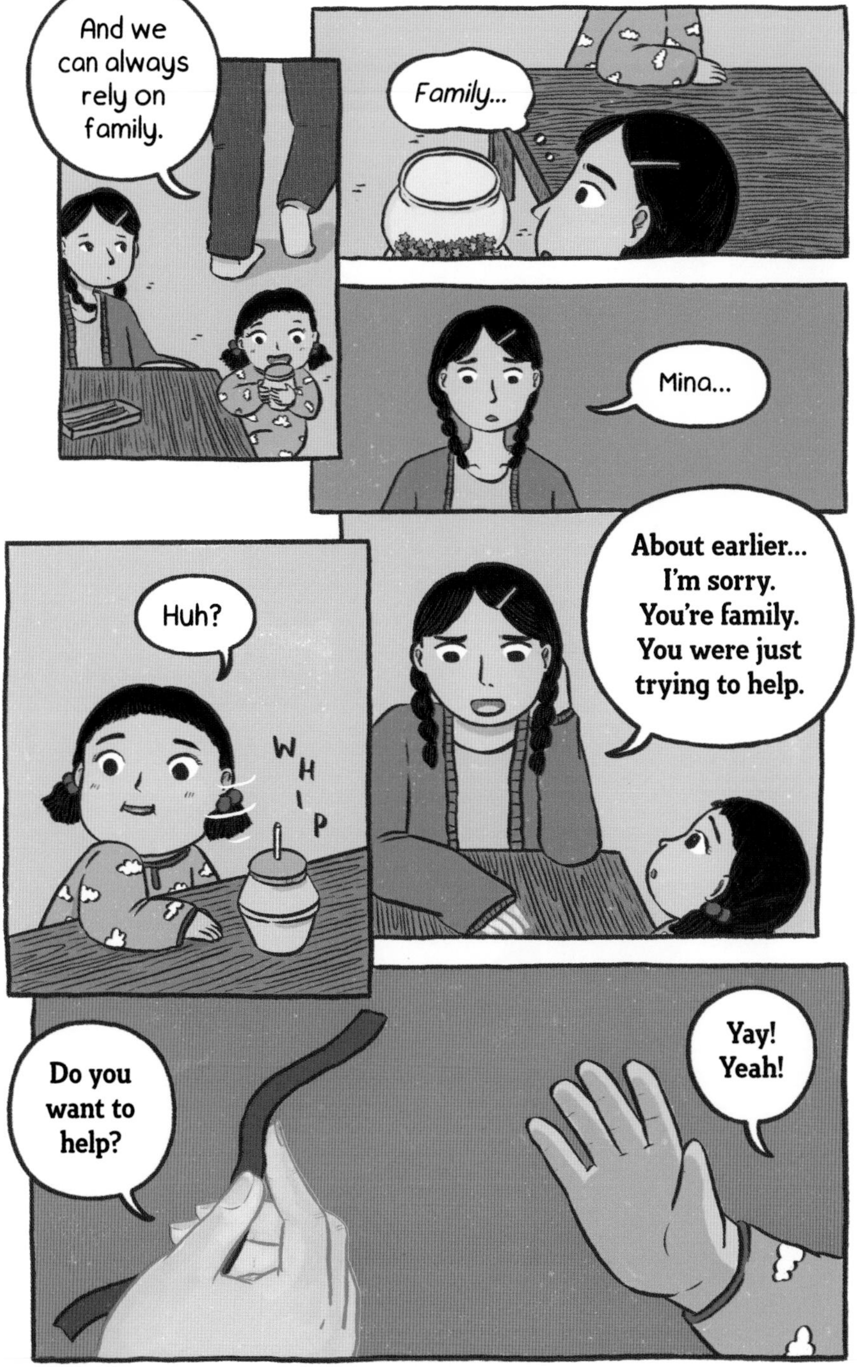
And we can always rely on family.
Family...
Mina...
Huh?
WHIP
About earlier... I'm sorry. You're family. You were just trying to help.
Do you want to help?
Yay! Yeah!

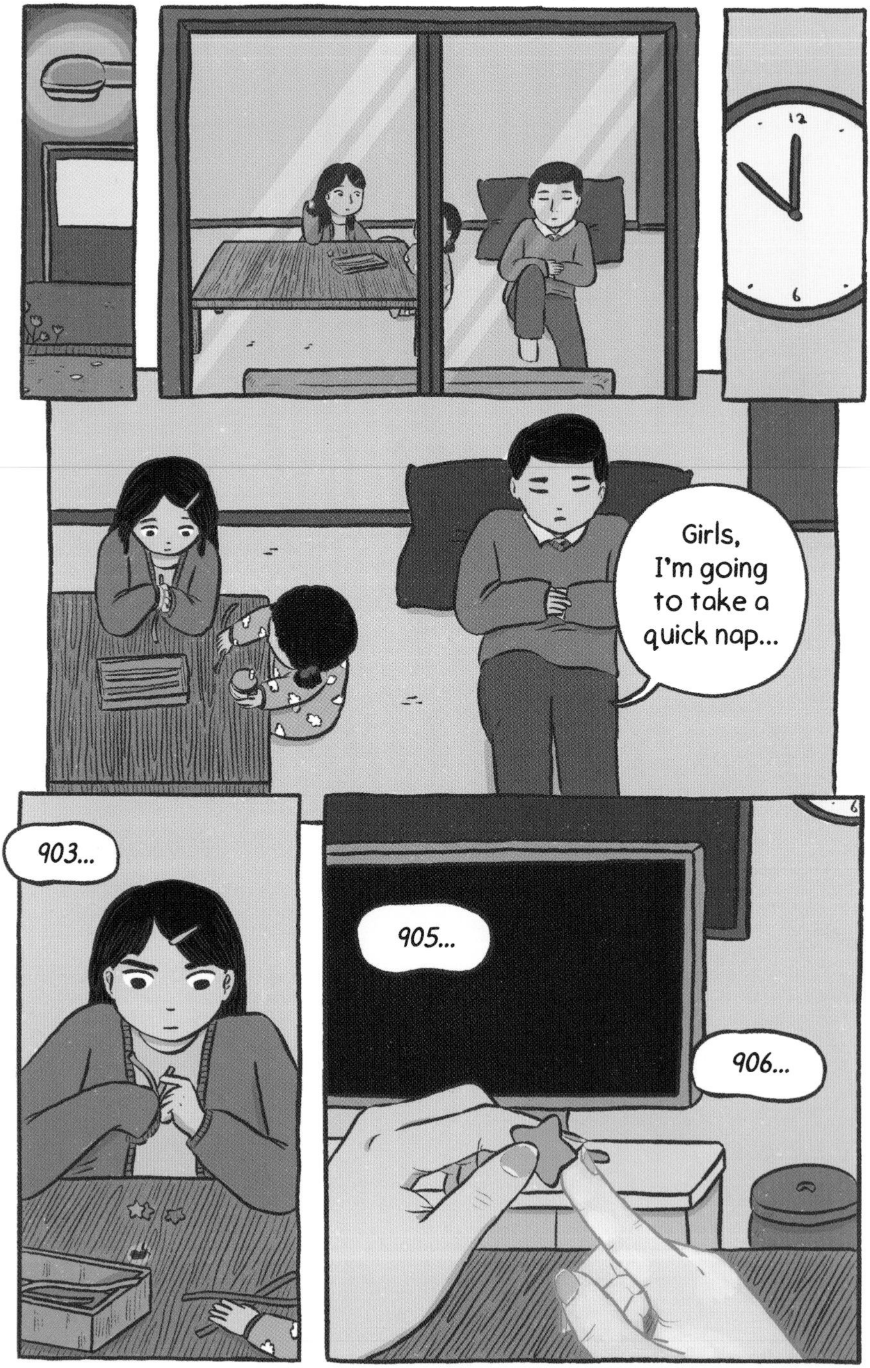
Girls, I'm going to take a quick nap...
903...
905...
906...

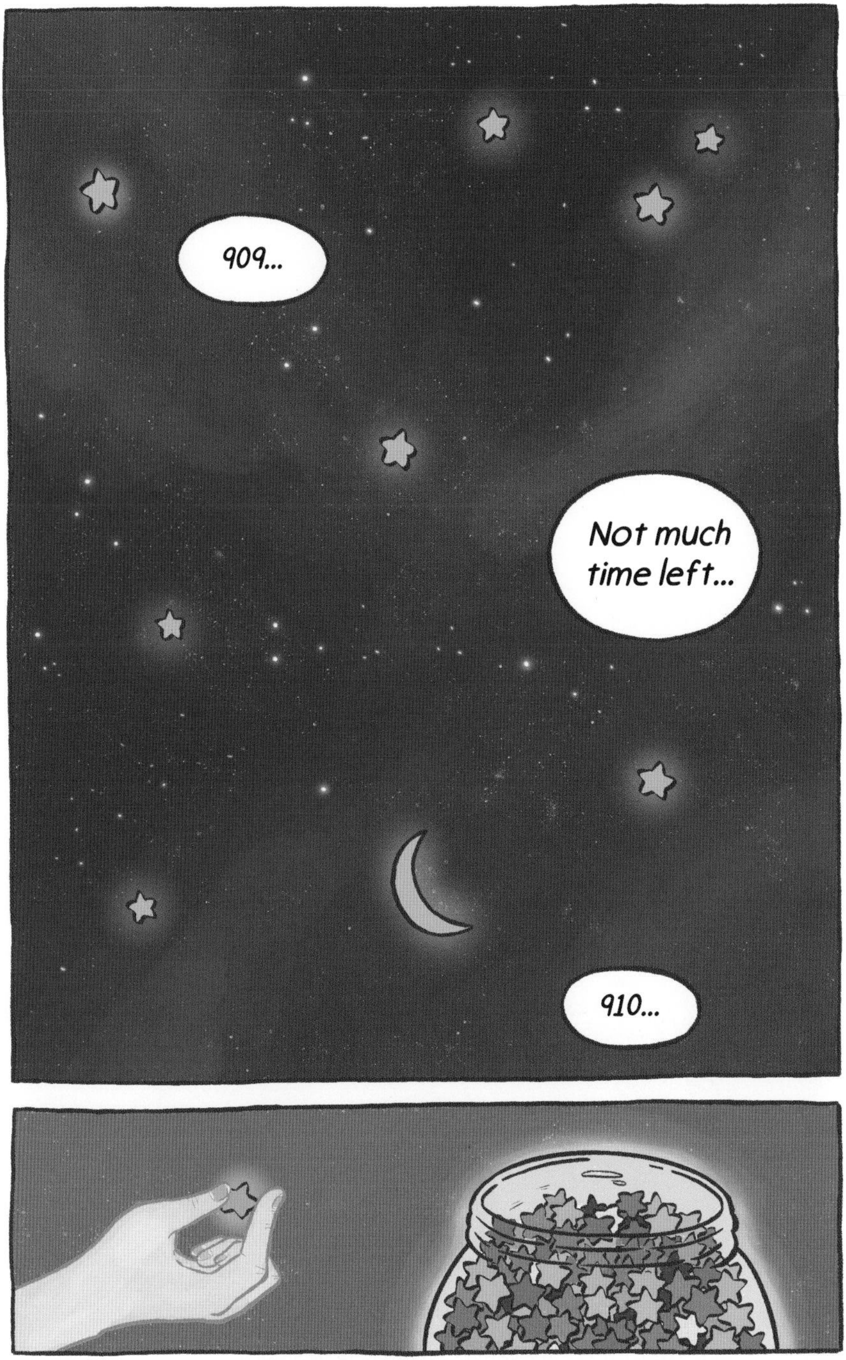
909...
Not much time left...
910...

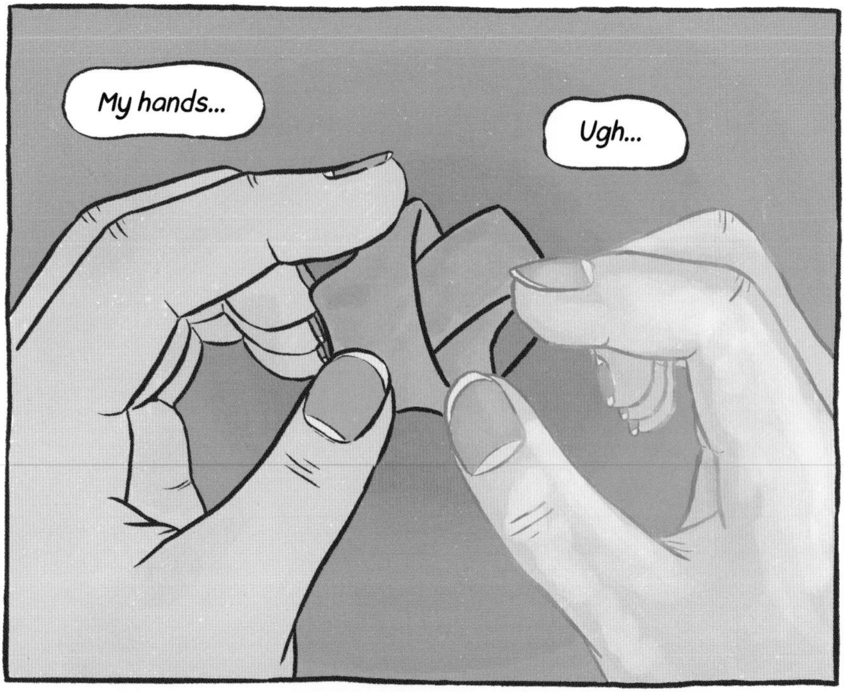
My hands...
Ugh...

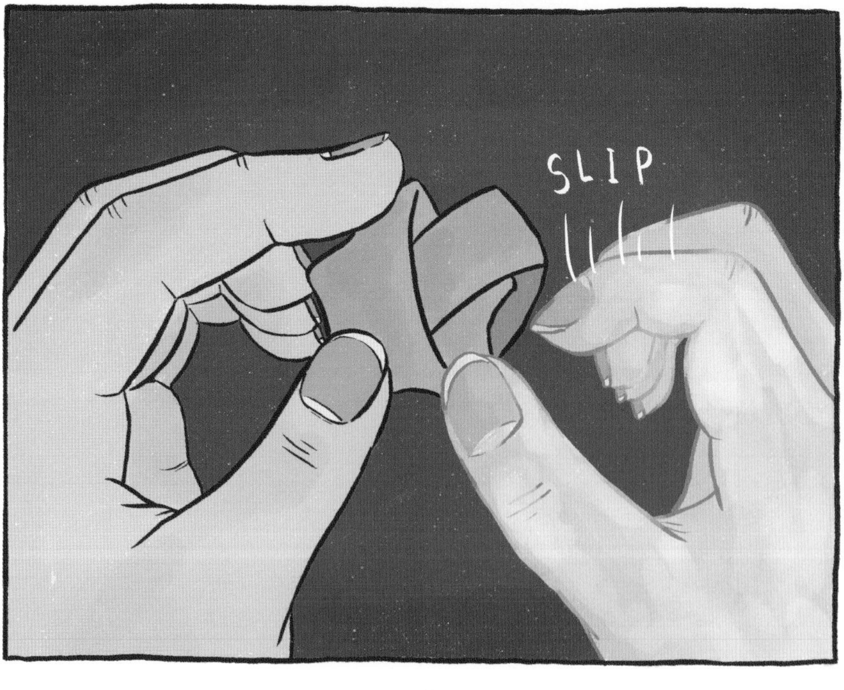
SLIP

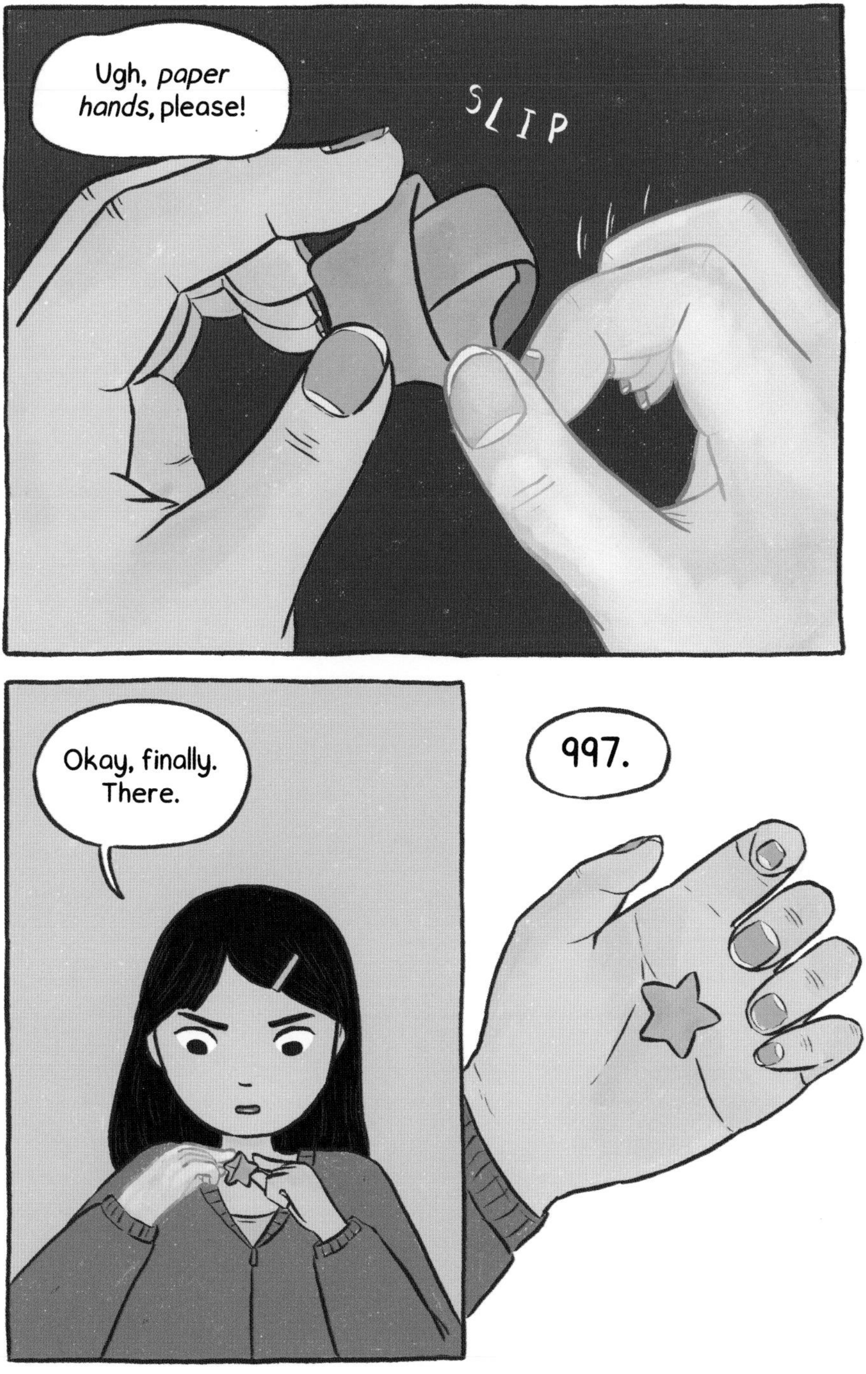
Ugh, *paper hands,* please!
SLIP
Okay, finally. There.
997.

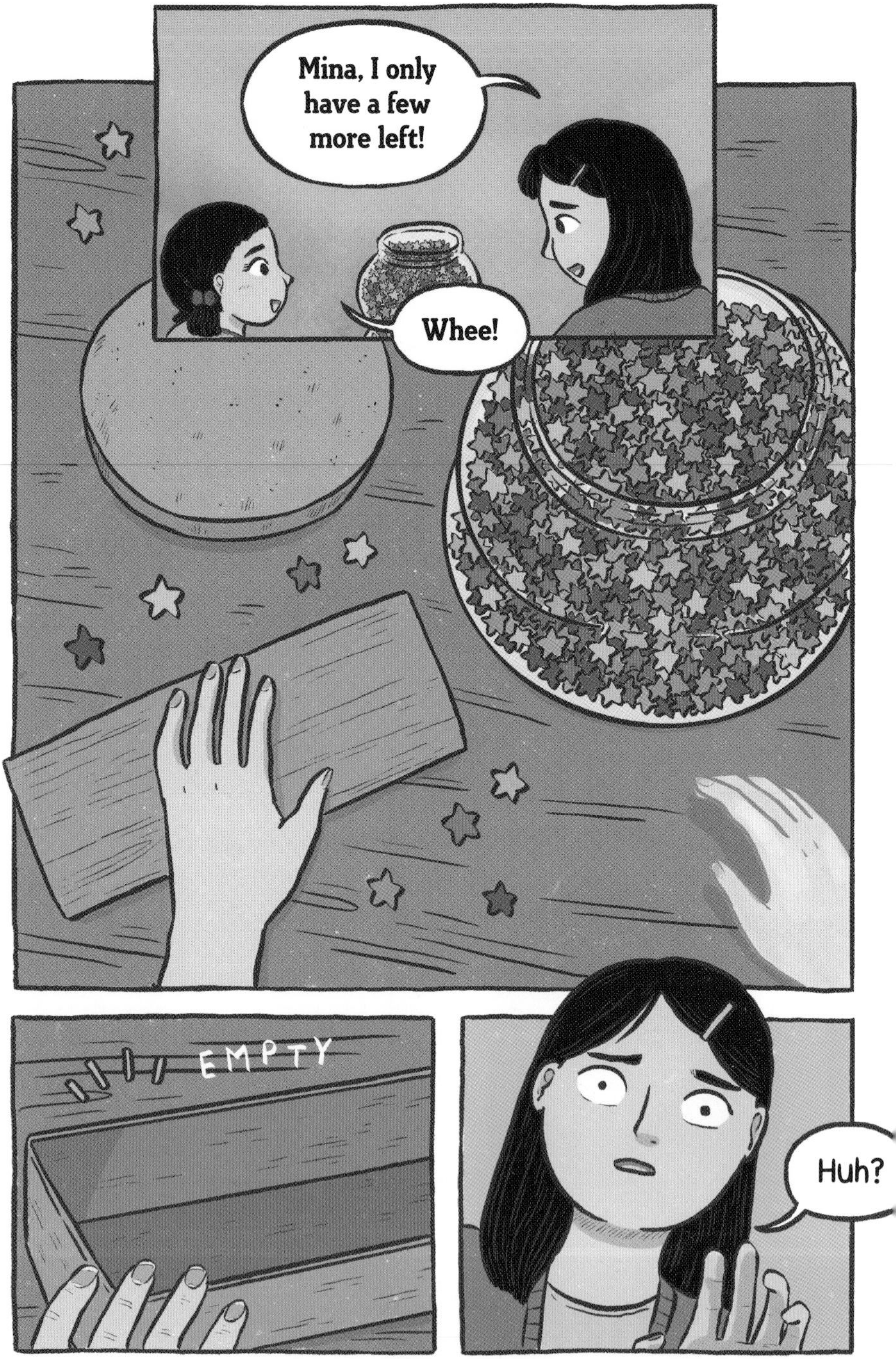
Mina, I only have a few more left!
Whee!
EMPTY
Huh?

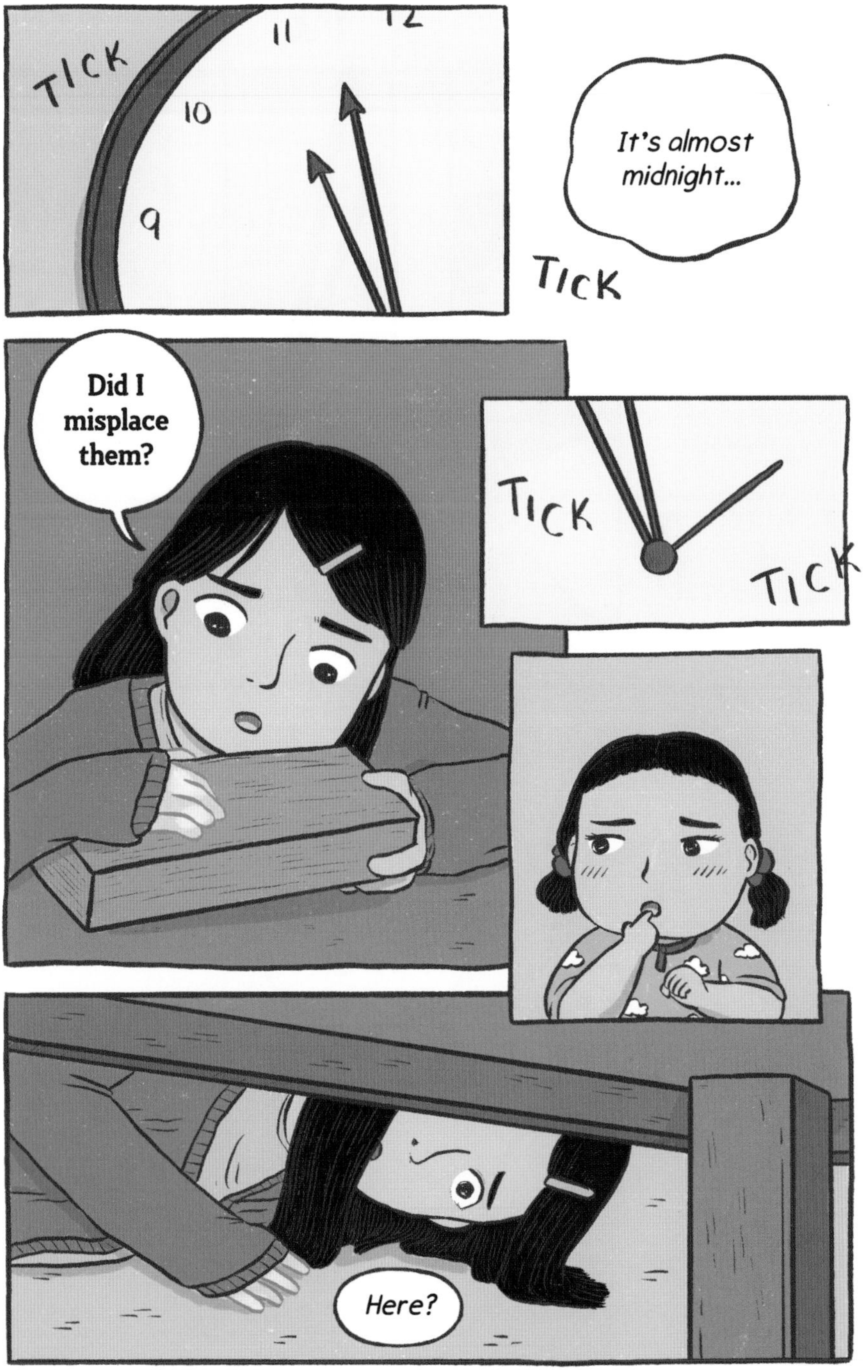
TICK
It's almost midnight...
TICK
Did I misplace them?
TICK
TICK
Here?

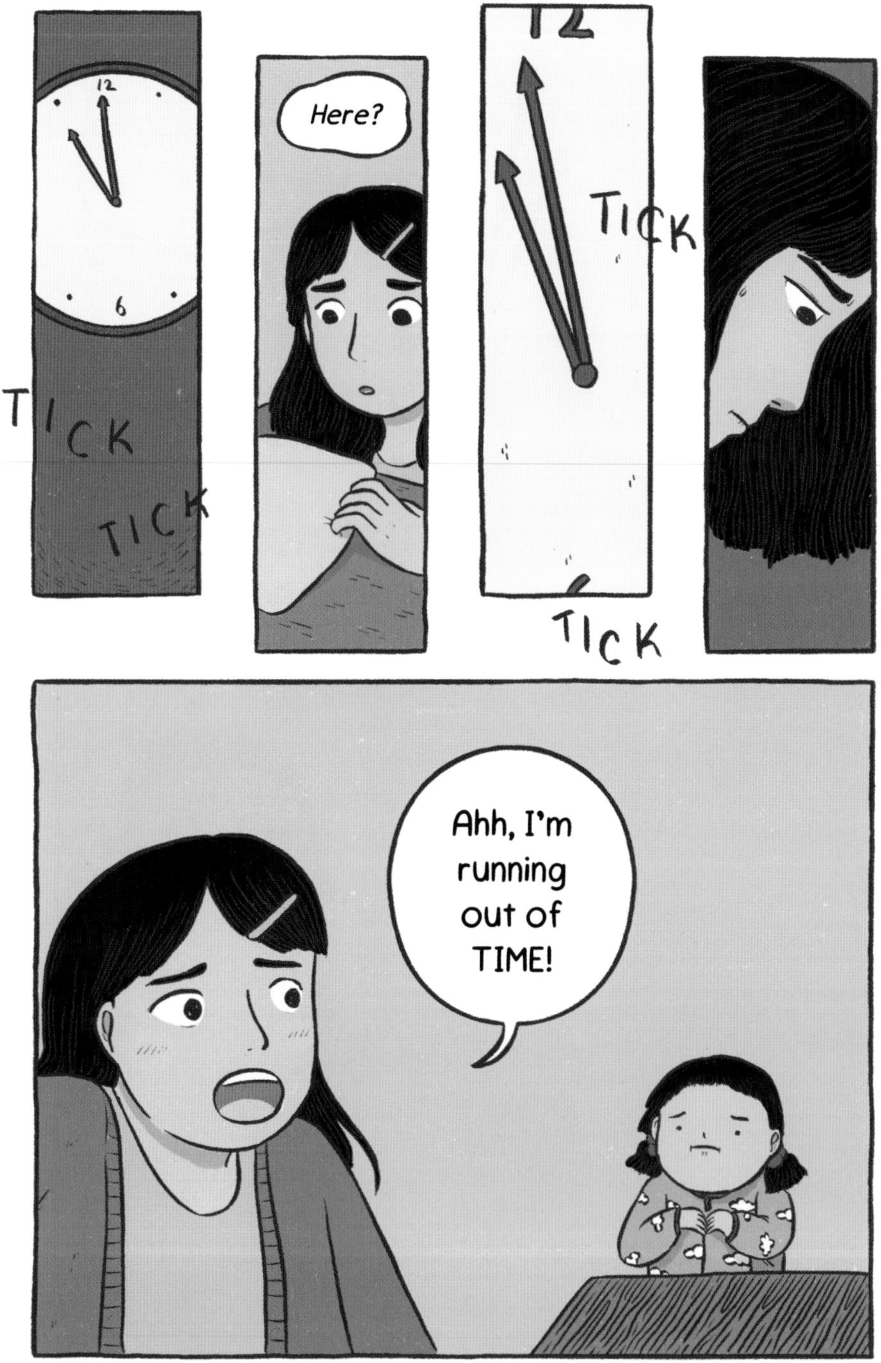
TICK
TICK
Here?
TICK
TICK
Ahh, I'm running out of TIME!

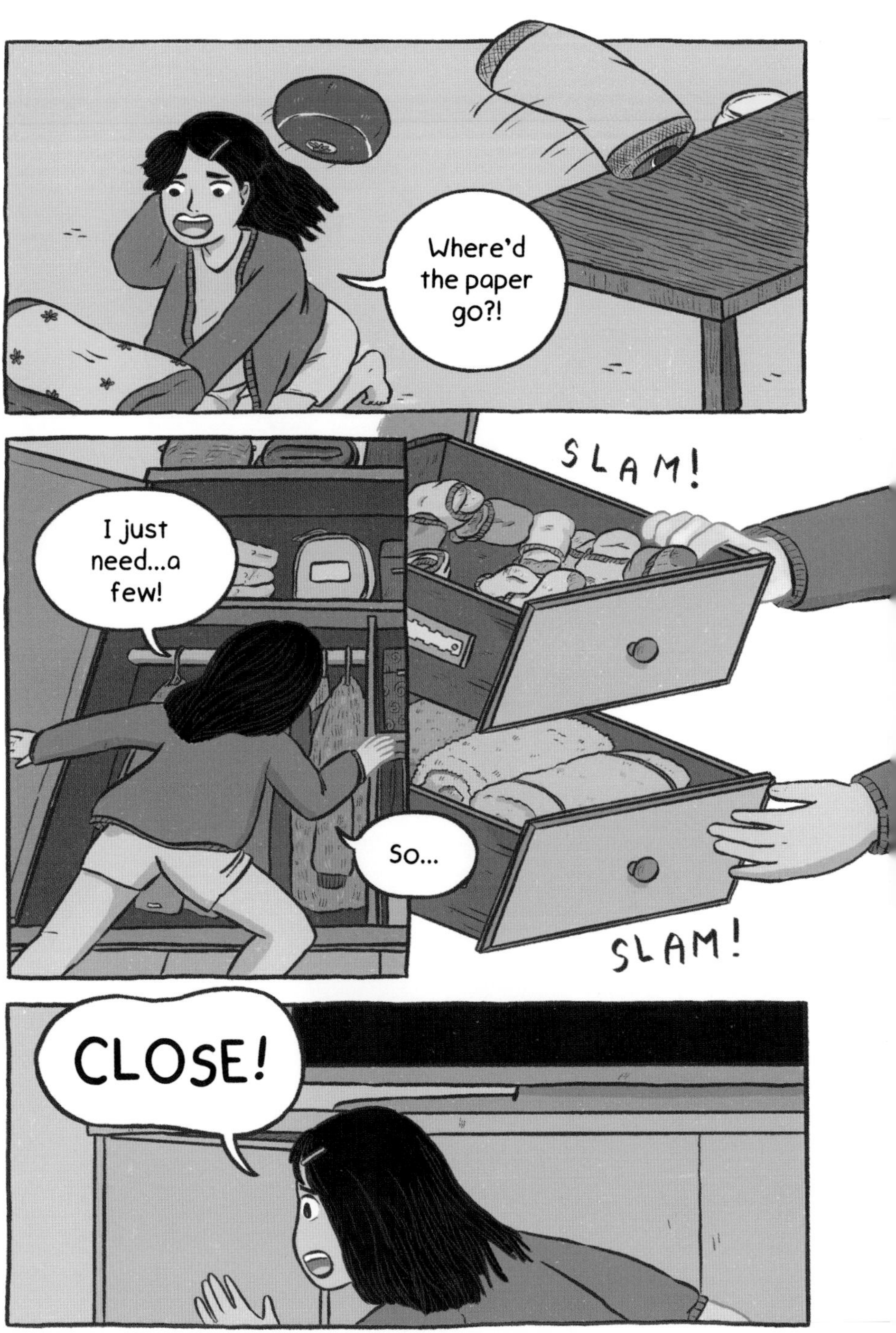
Where'd the paper go?!
SLAM!
I just need...a few!
So...
SLAM!
CLOSE!

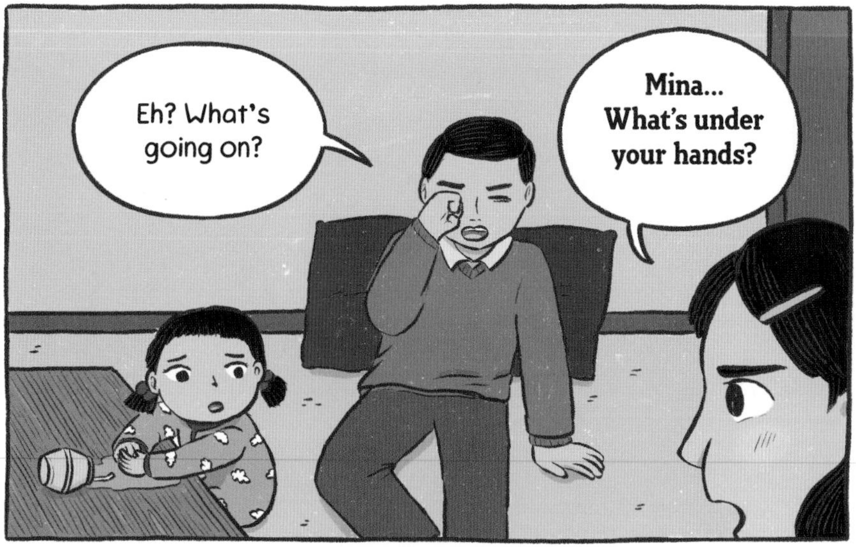
Eh? What's
going on?
Mina...
What's under
your hands?

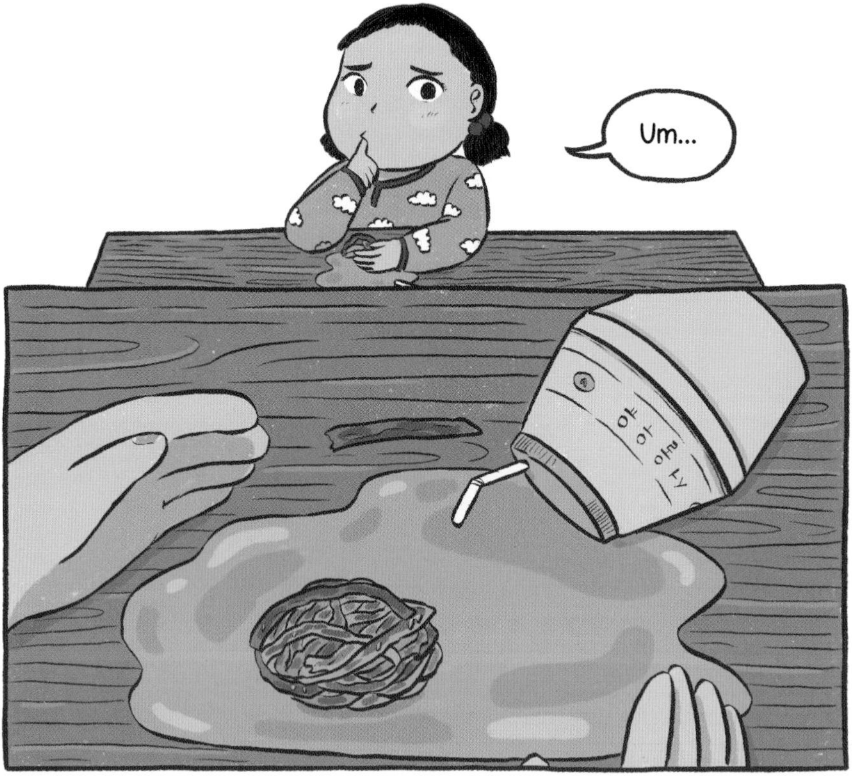
Um...

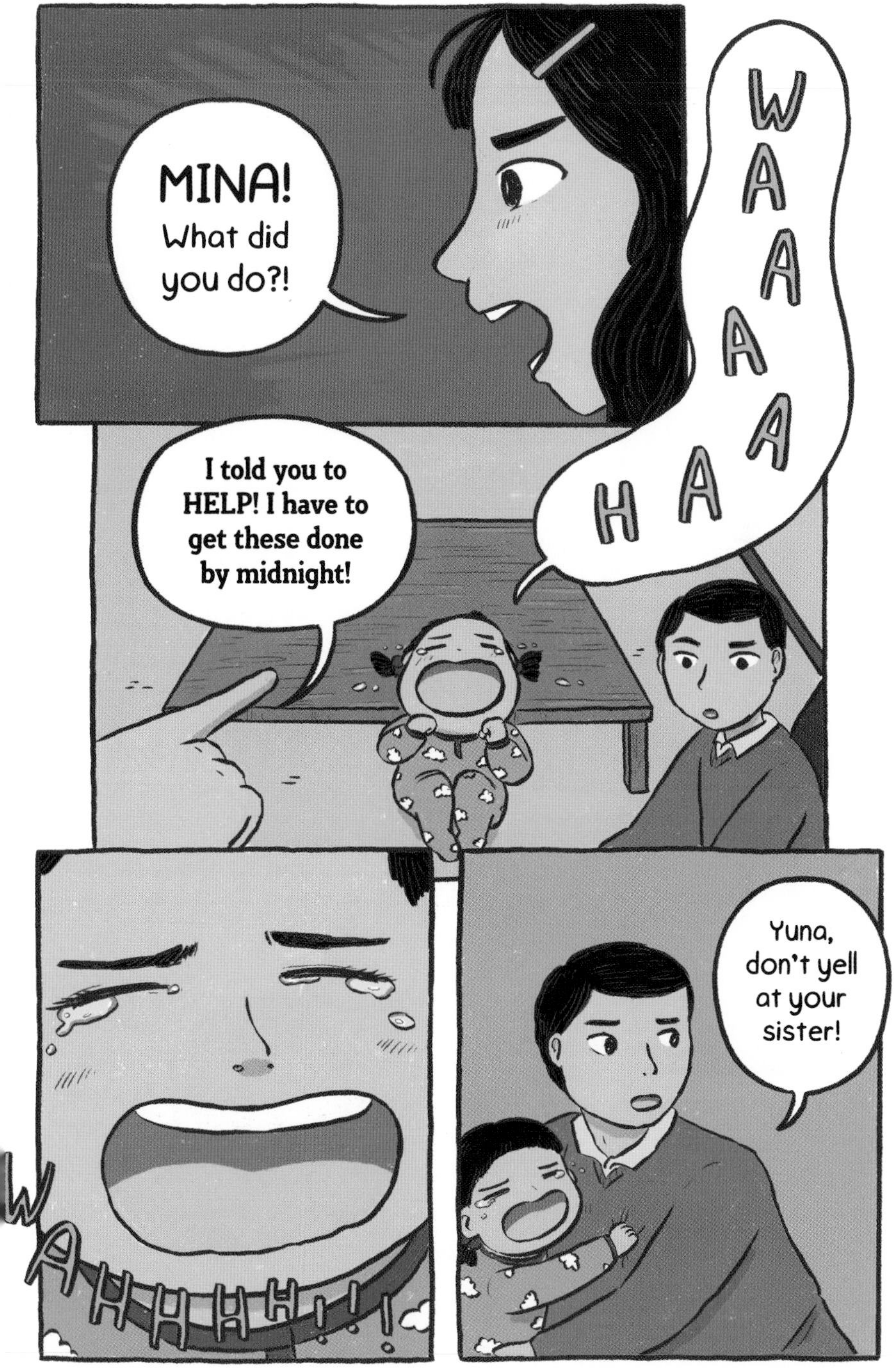
MINA!
What did you do?!
WAAAAAHHA
I told you to HELP! I have to get these done by midnight!
WAAHHHHH!!!
Yuna, don't yell at your sister!

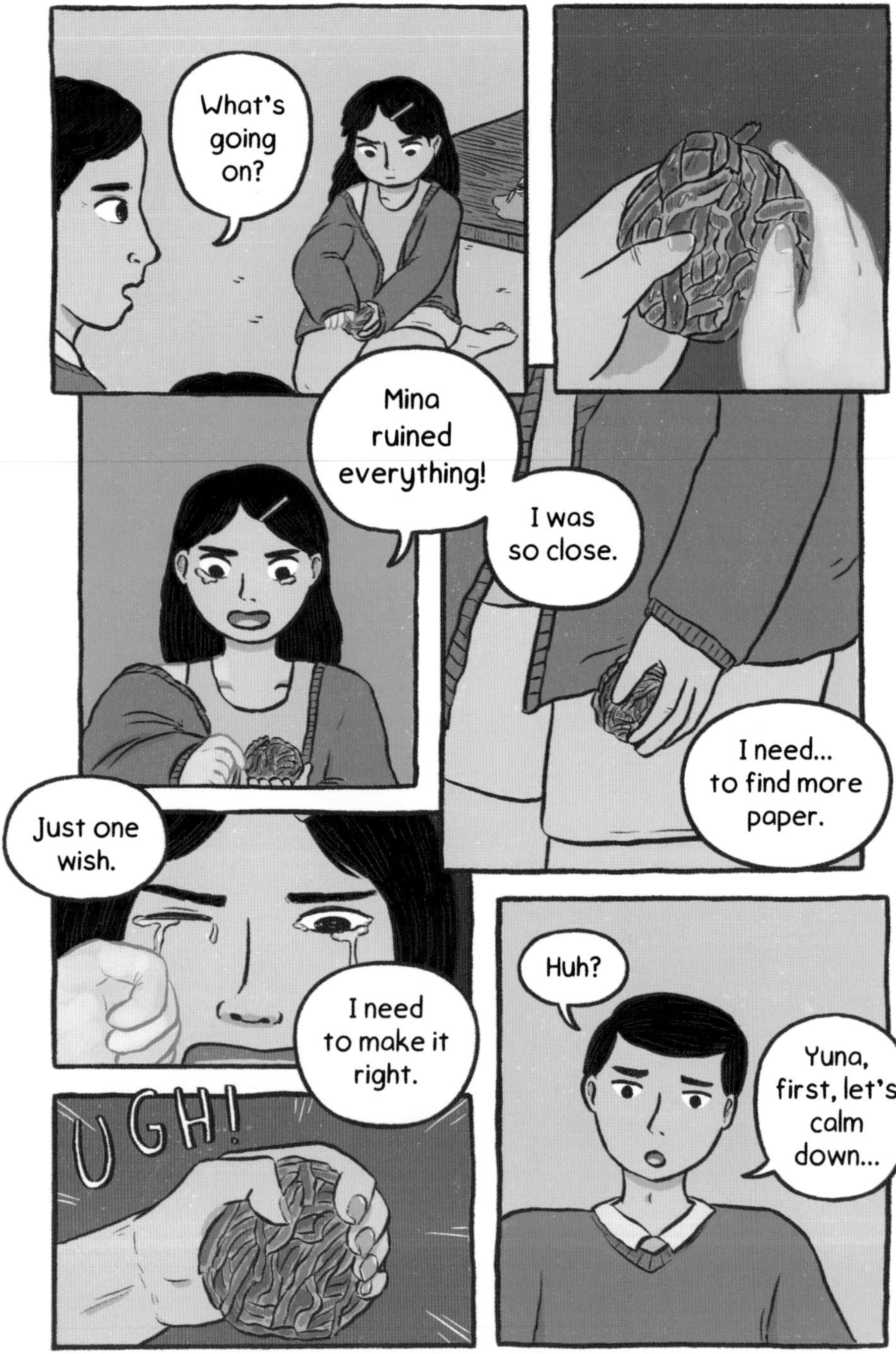
What's going on?
Mina ruined everything!
I was so close.
I need... to find more paper.
Just one wish.
I need to make it right.
UGH!
Huh?
Yuna, first, let's calm down...

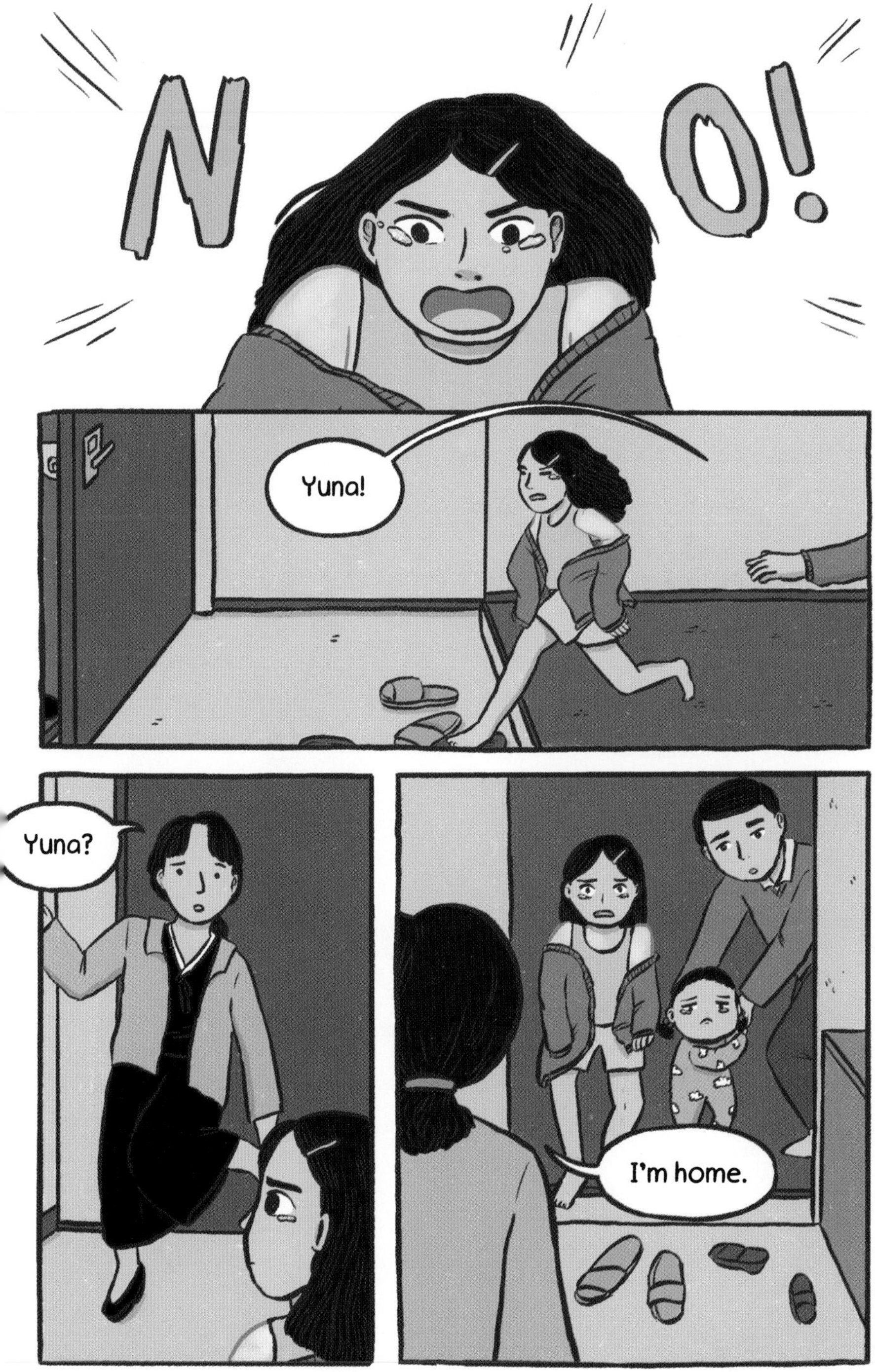
NO!
Yuna!
Yuna?
I'm home.

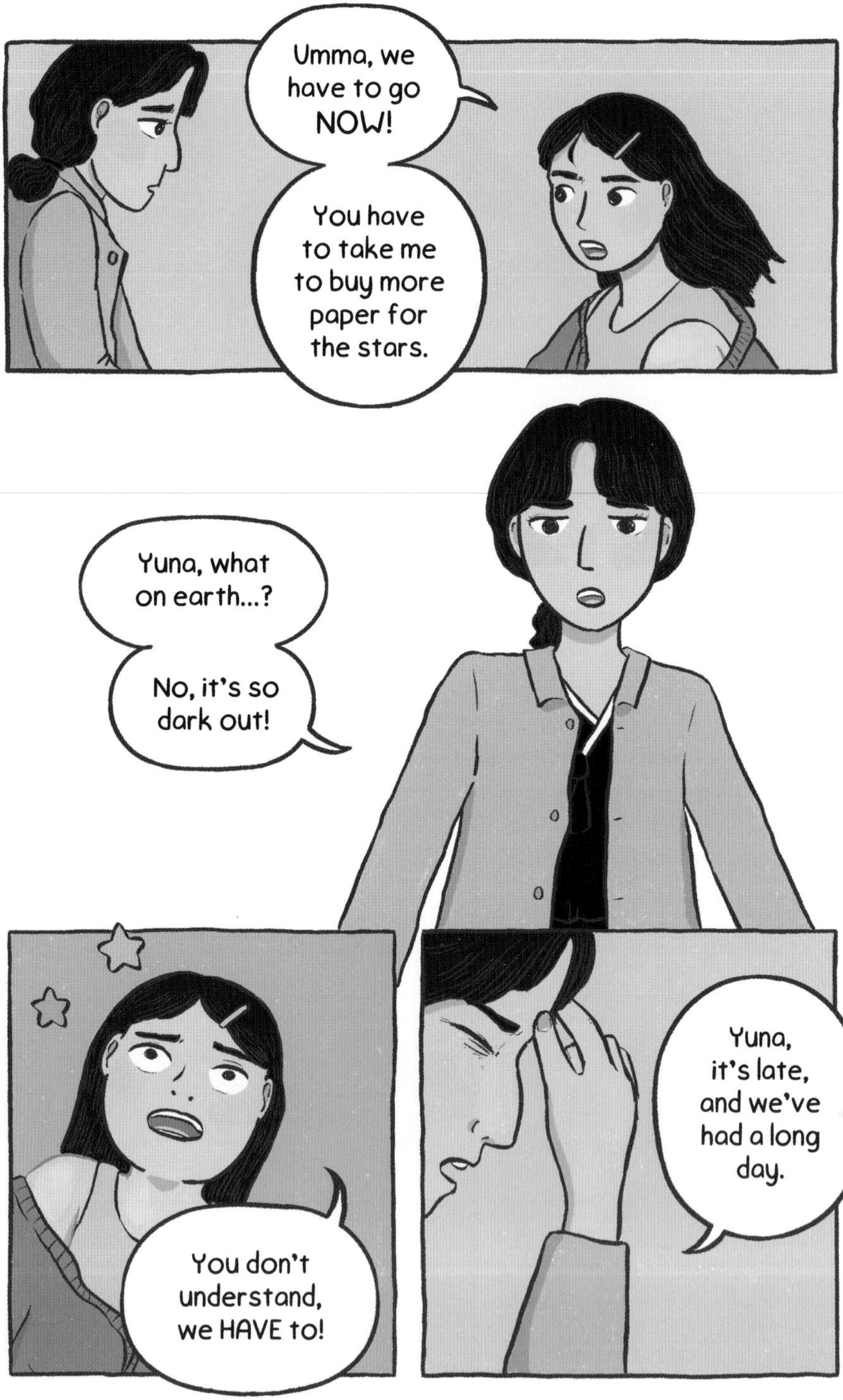
Umma, we have to go NOW!
You have to take me to buy more paper for the stars.
Yuna, what on earth...?
No, it's so dark out!
You don't understand, we HAVE to!
Yuna, it's late, and we've had a long day.

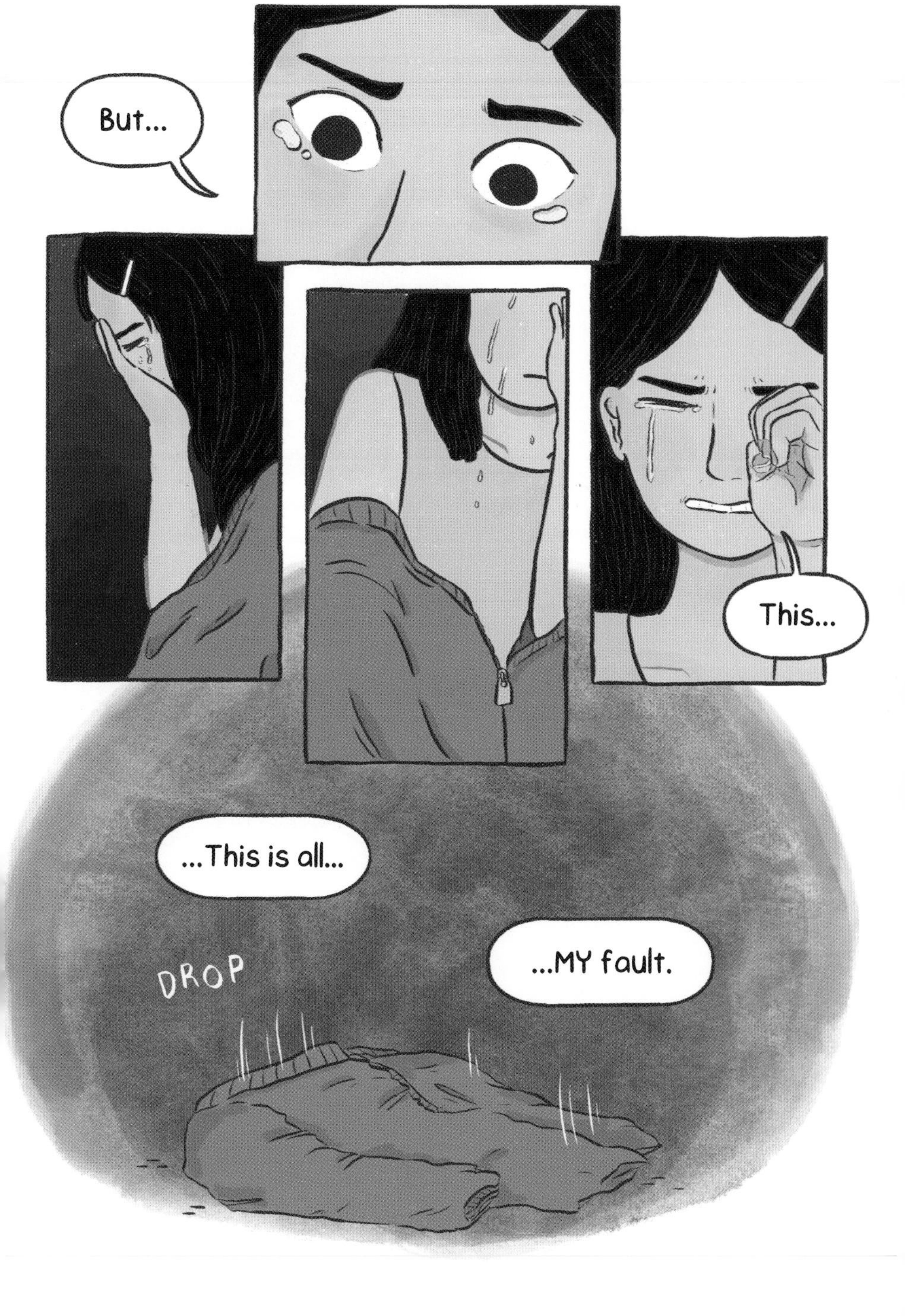
But...
This...
...This is all...
...MY fault.
DROP

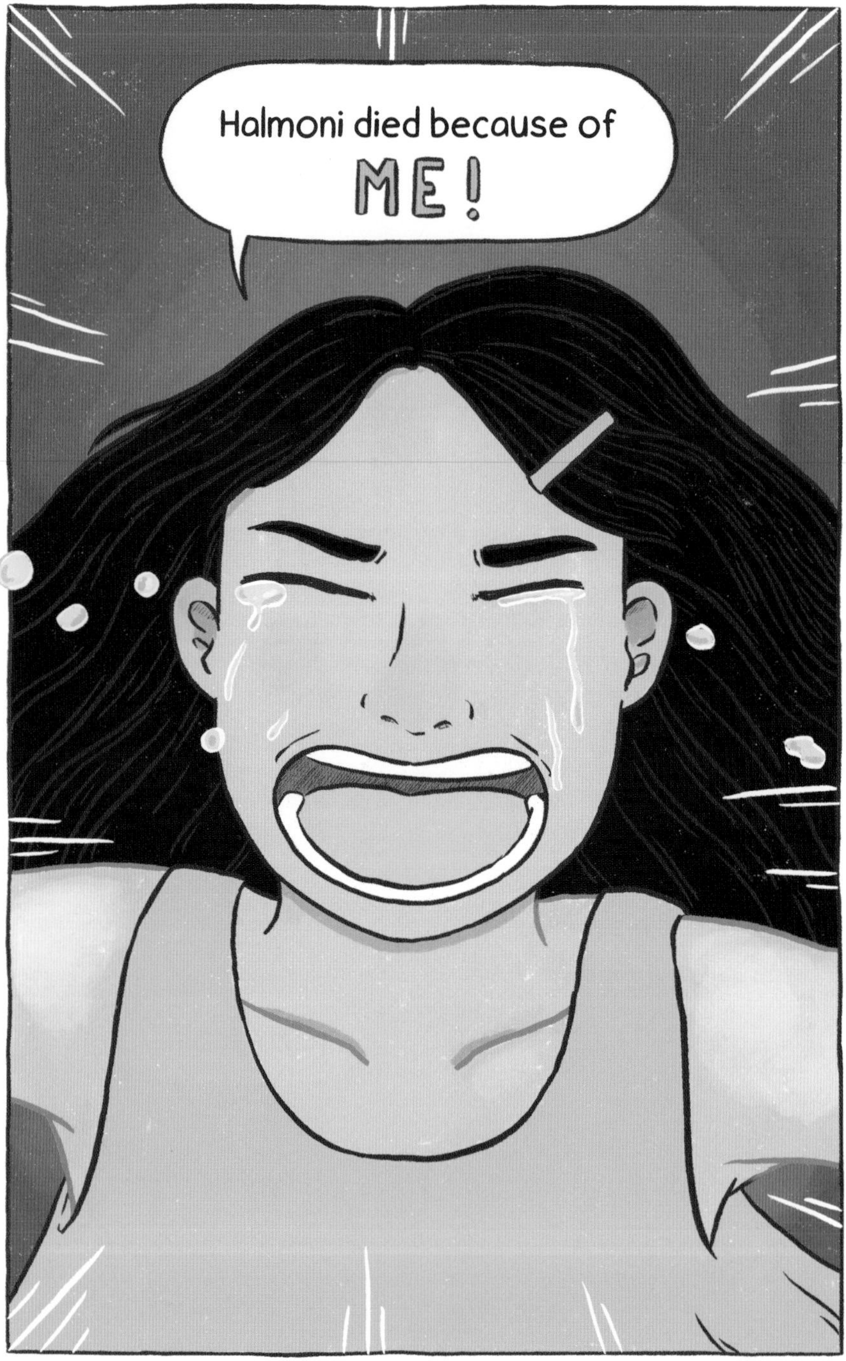
Halmoni died because of
ME!

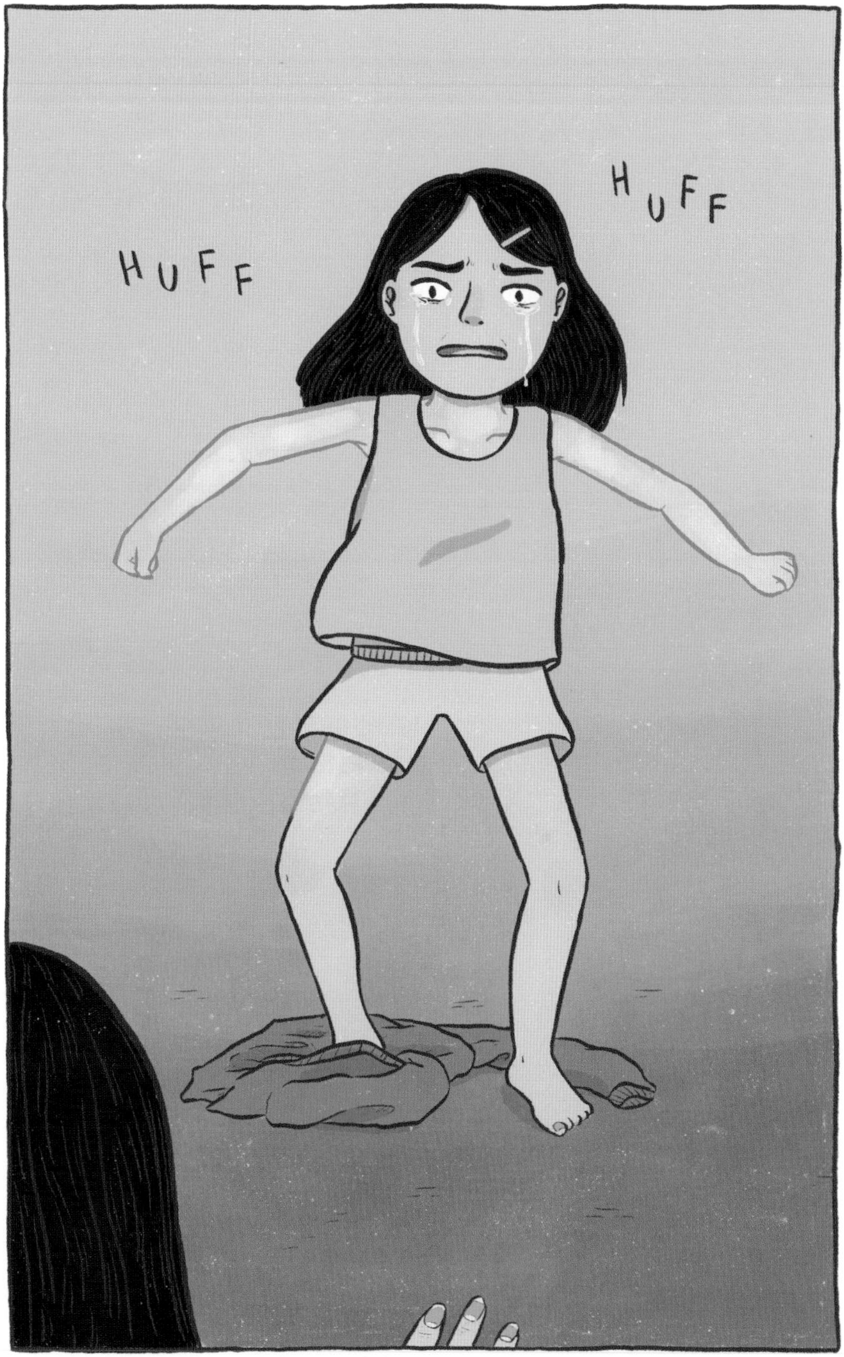
HUFF
HUFF

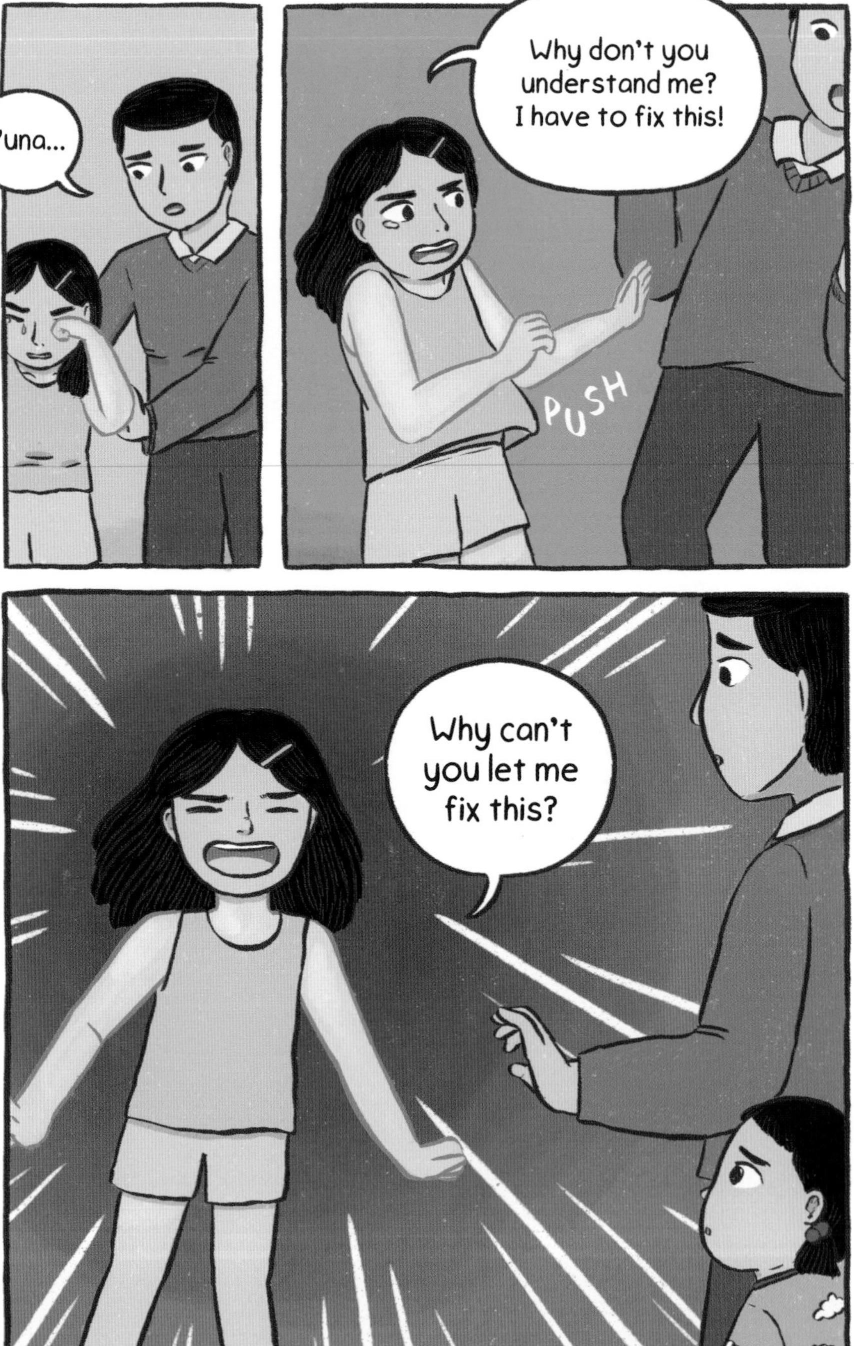
Yuna...
Why don't you understand me? I have to fix this!
PUSH
Why can't you let me fix this?

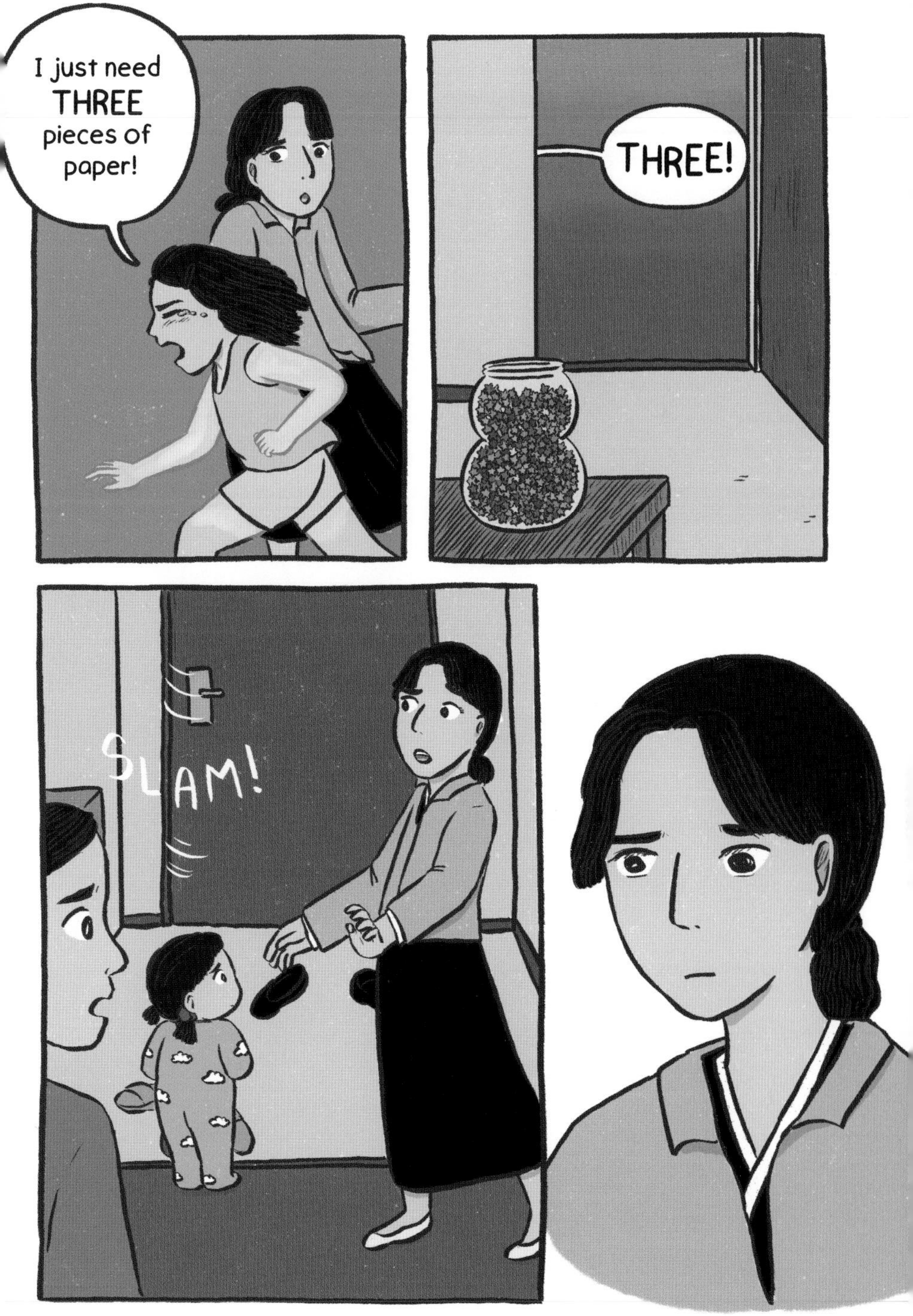
I just need THREE pieces of paper!
THREE!
SLAM!

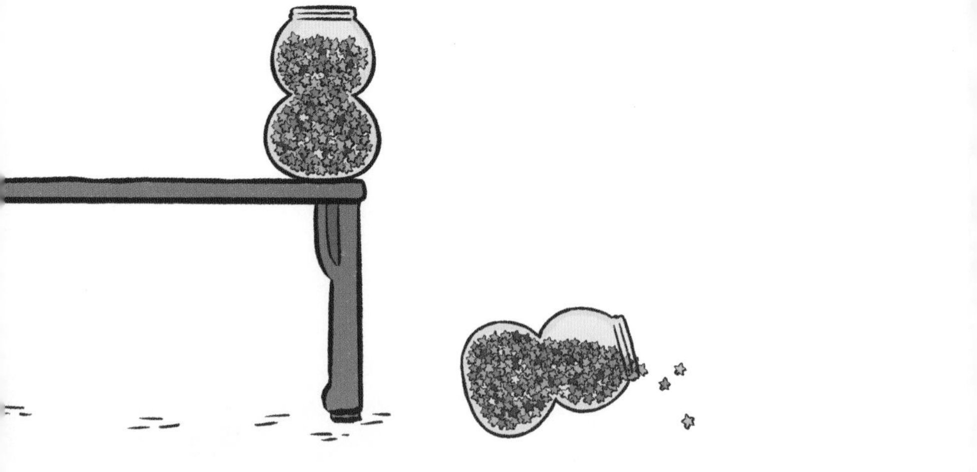
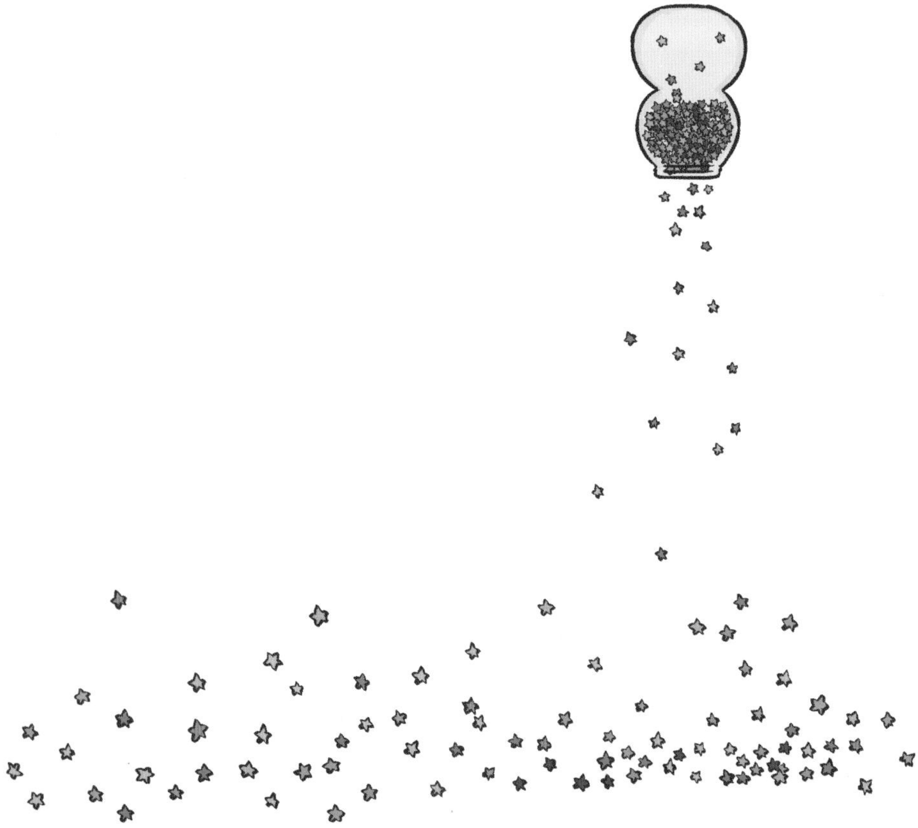

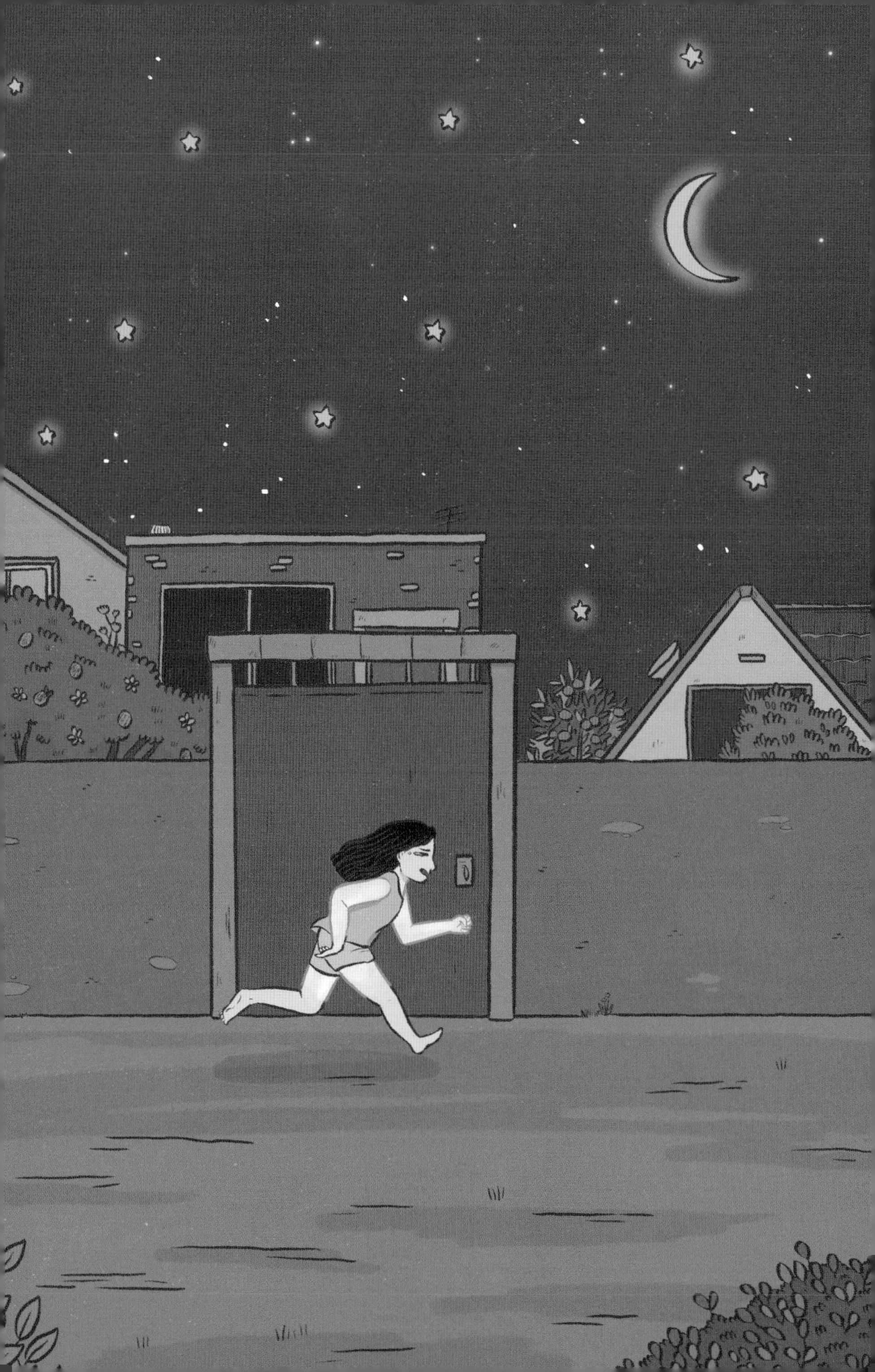

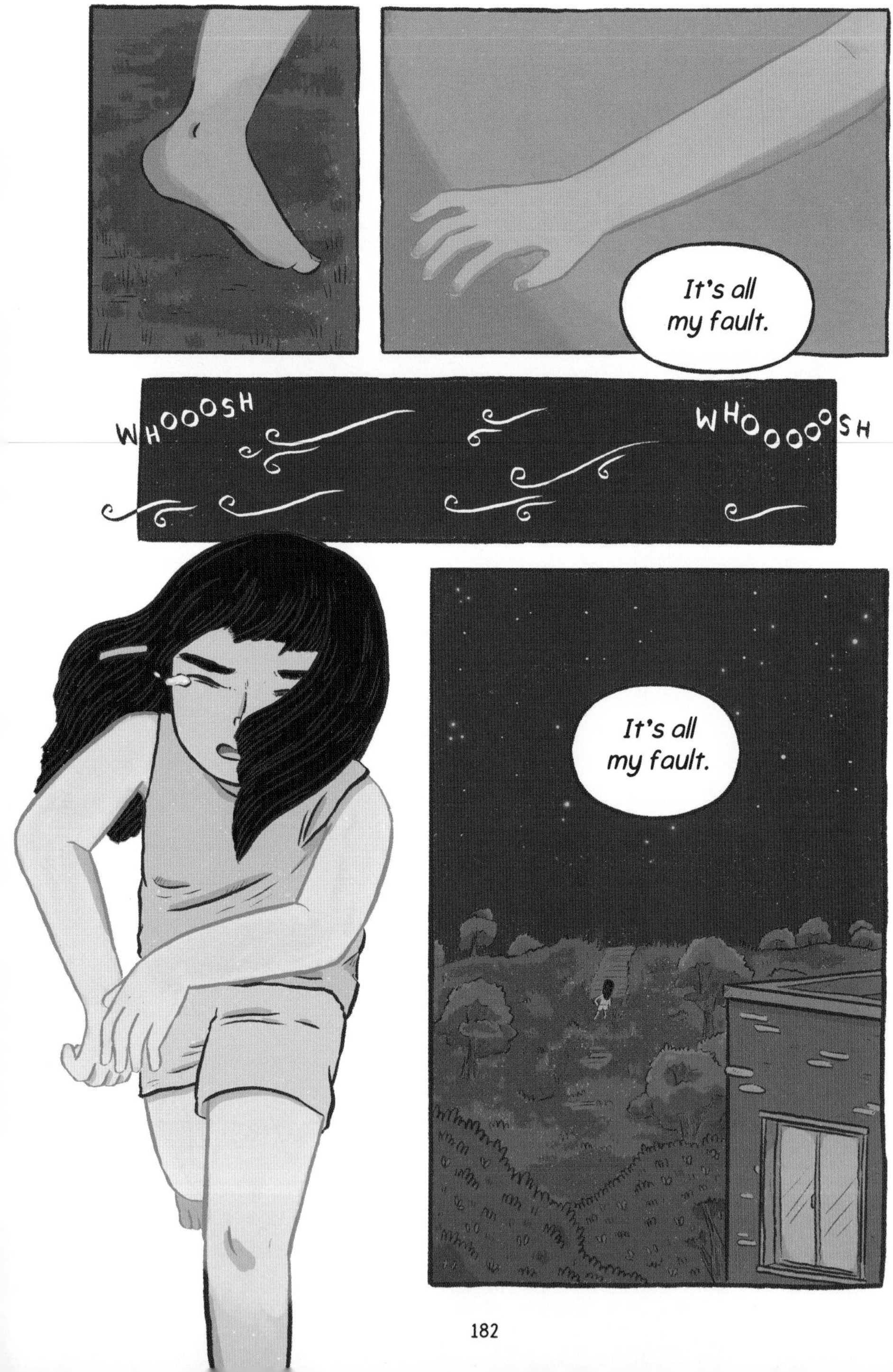
It's all my fault.
WHOOOSH
WHOOOOOOSH
It's all my fault.

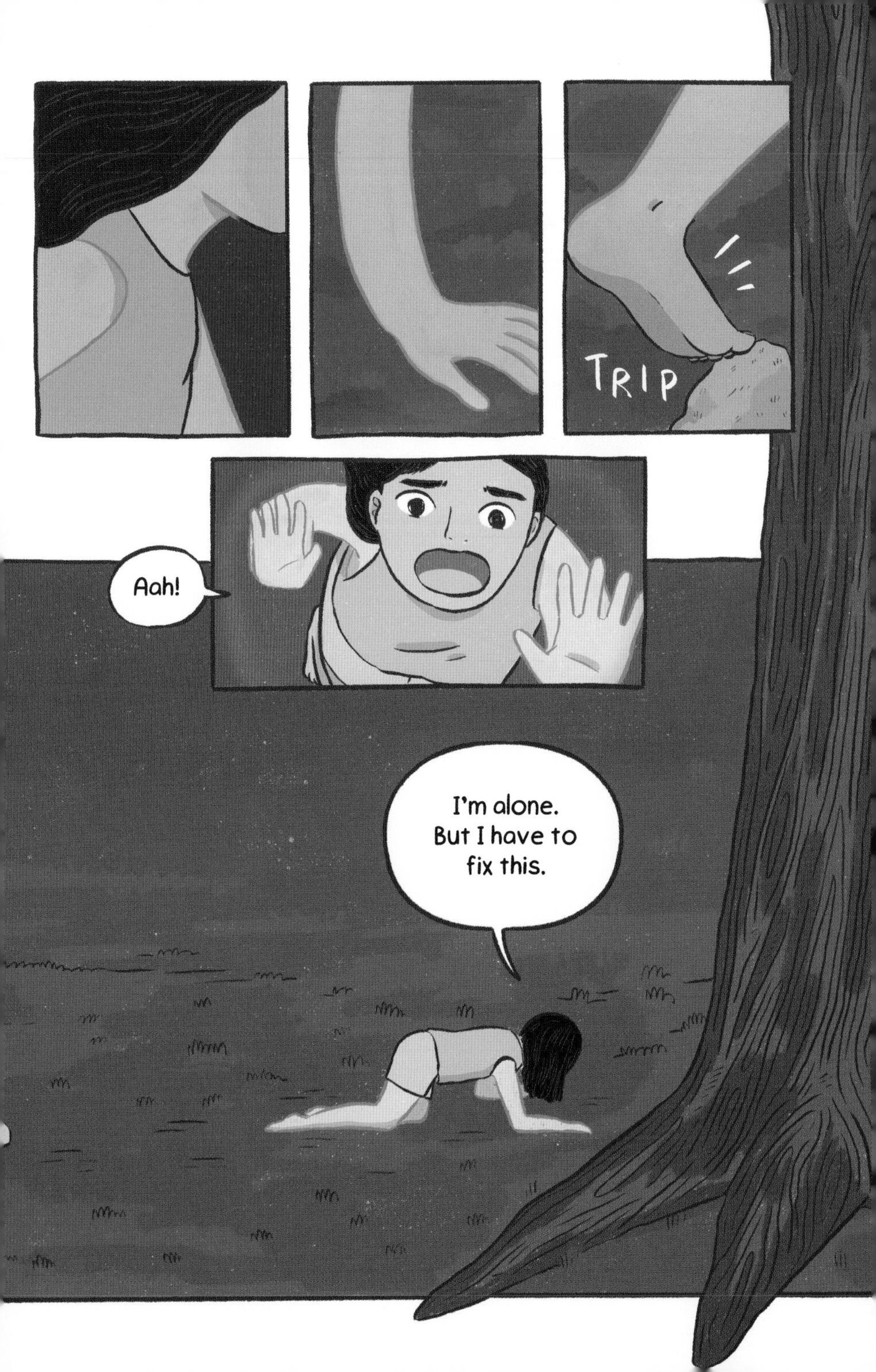
TRIP
Aah!
I'm alone.
But I have to
fix this.

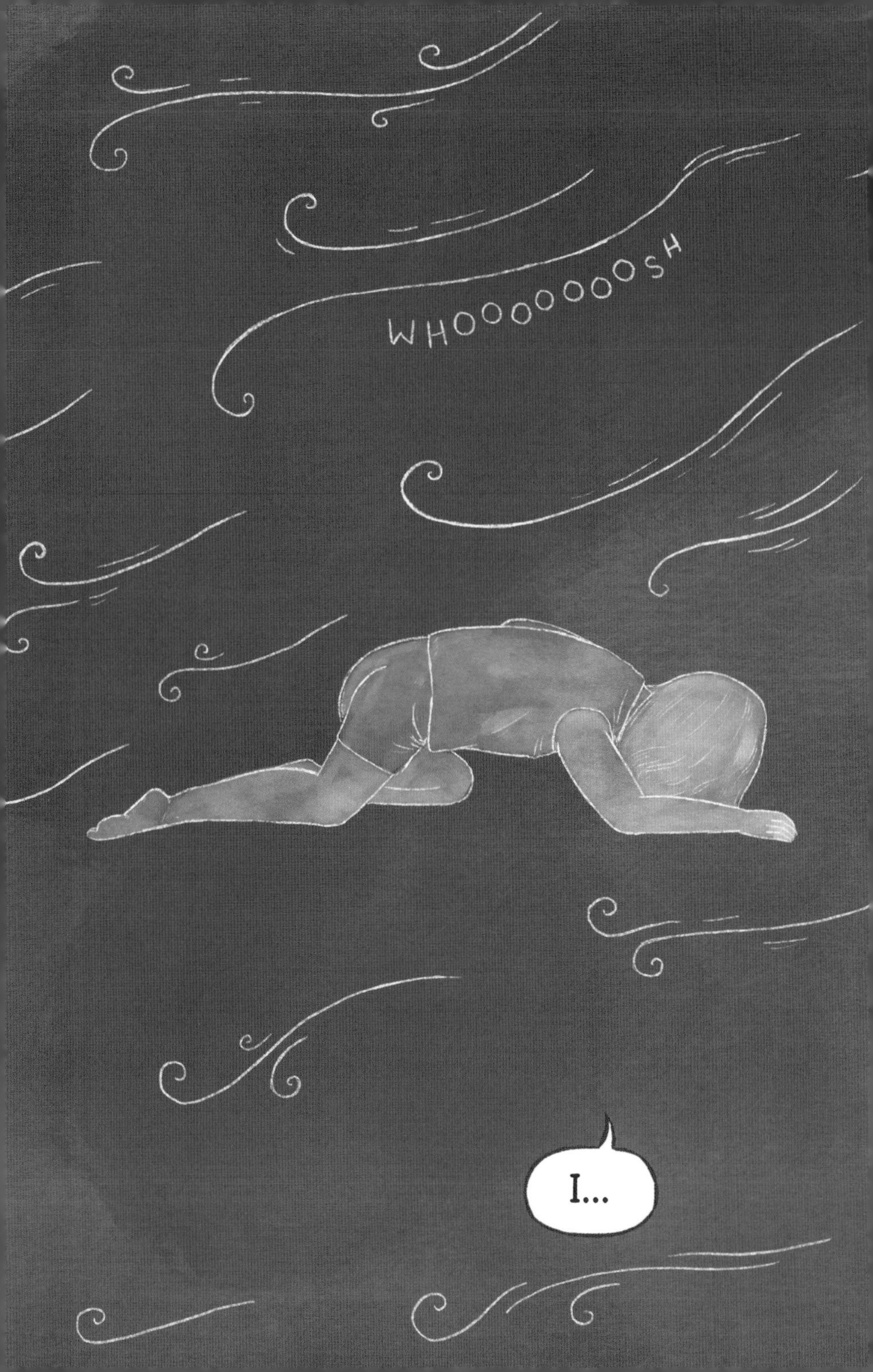
WHOOOOOOOOSH
I...

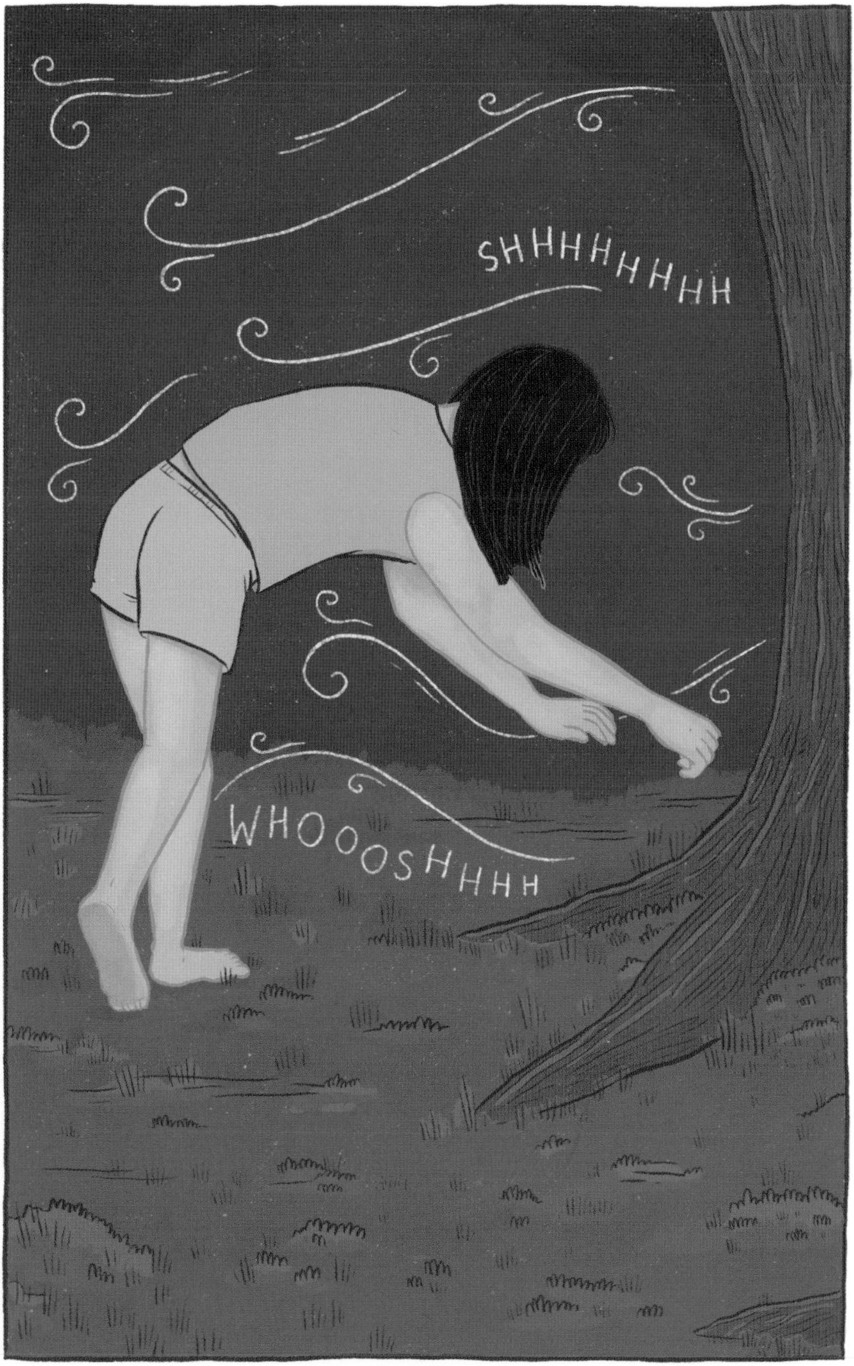
SHHHHHHHH
WHOOOSHHHH

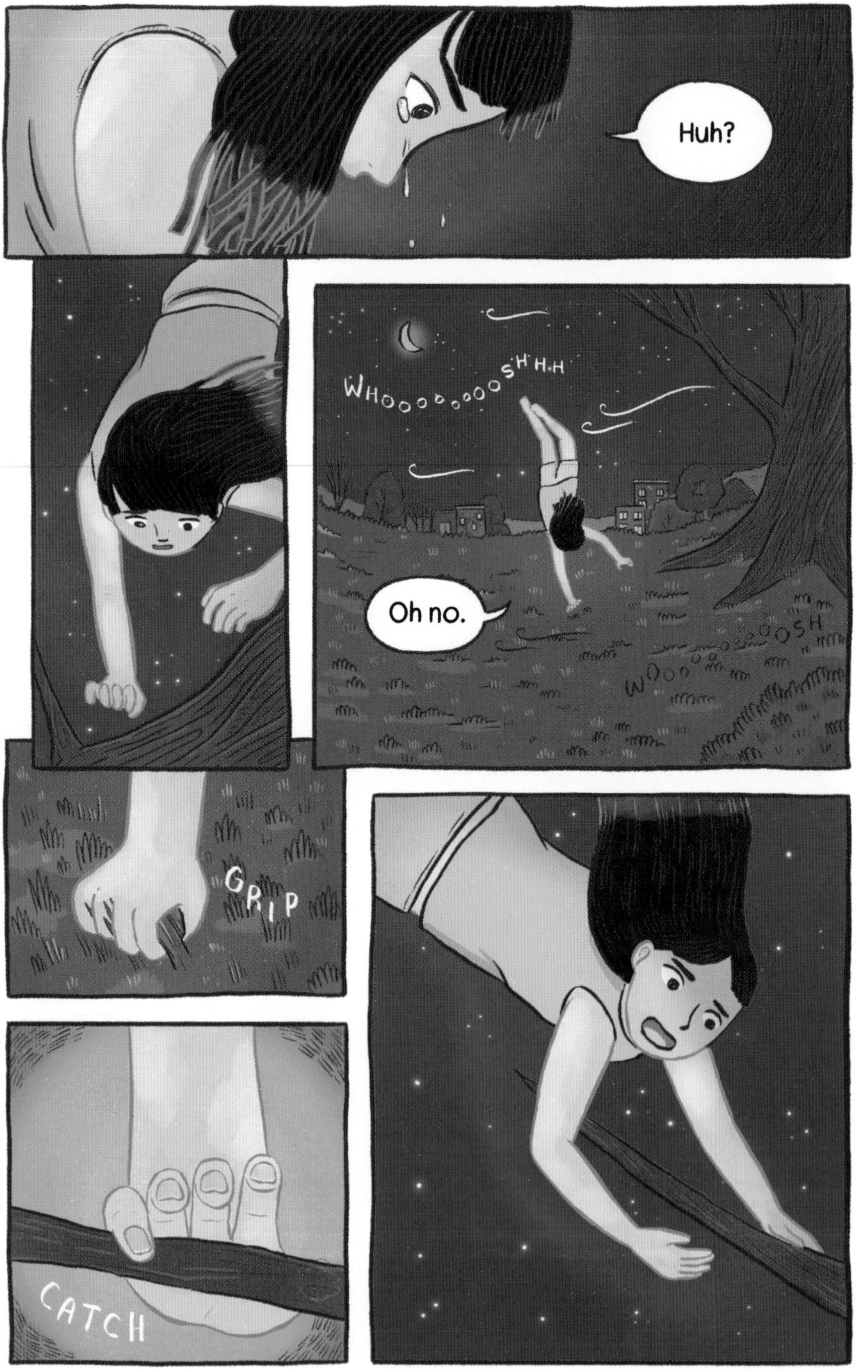
Huh?
WHOOOOOOOOOSHHH
Oh no.
WOOOOOOOOSH
GRIP
CATCH

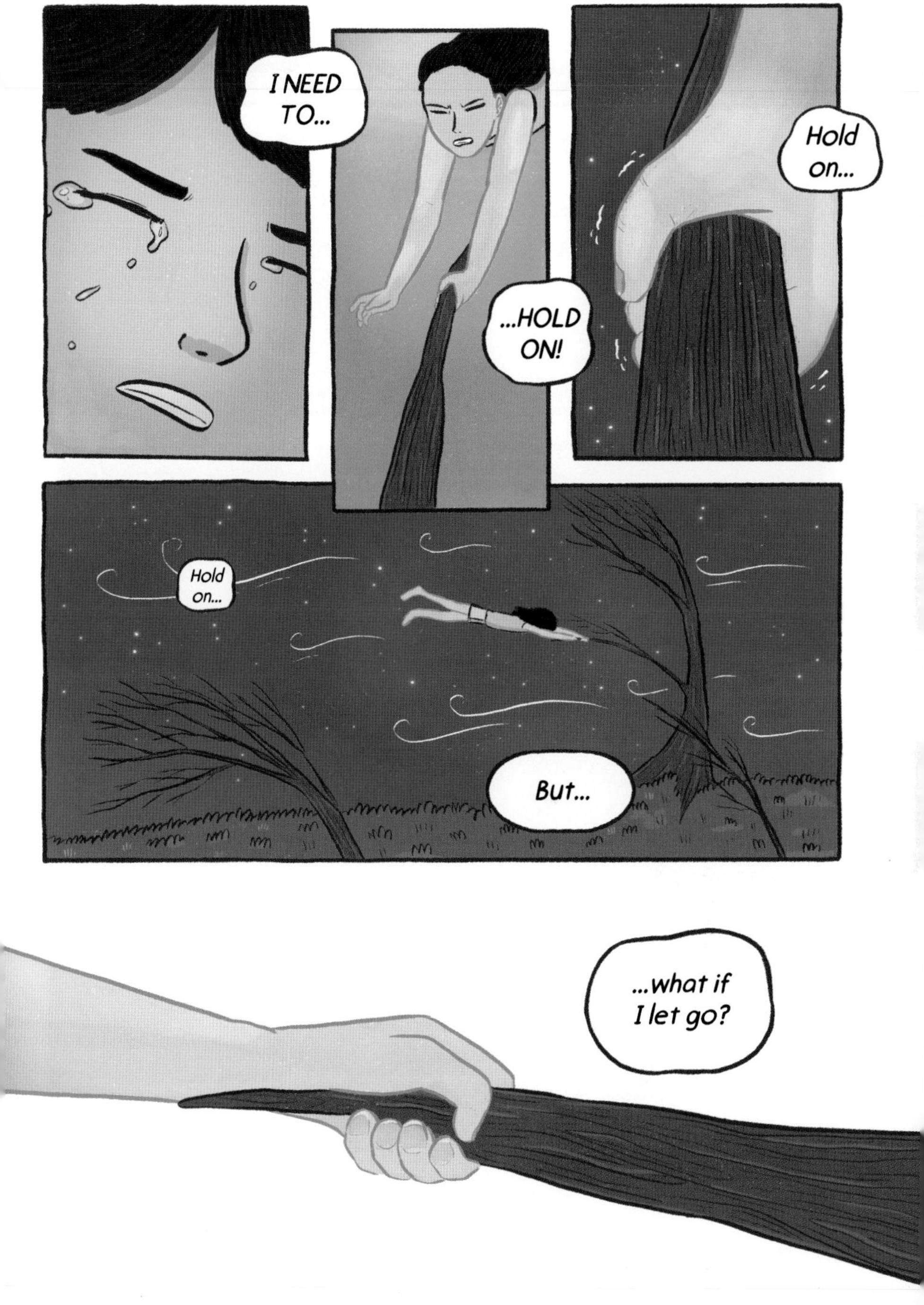
I NEED TO...
...HOLD ON!
Hold on...
Hold on...
But...
...what if I let go?

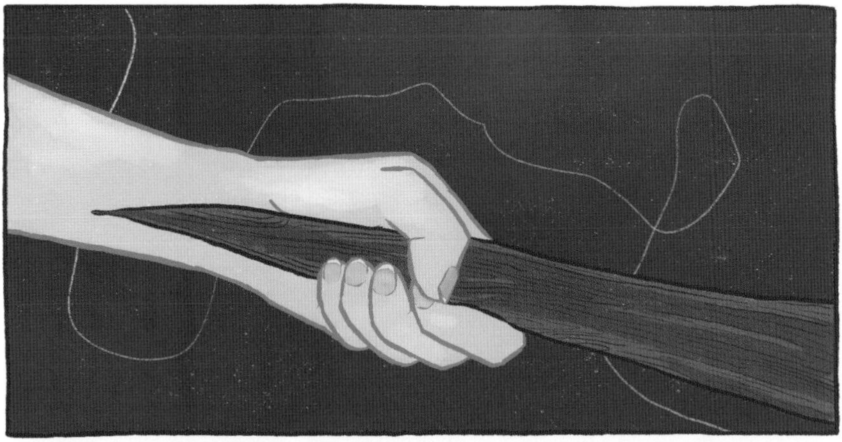

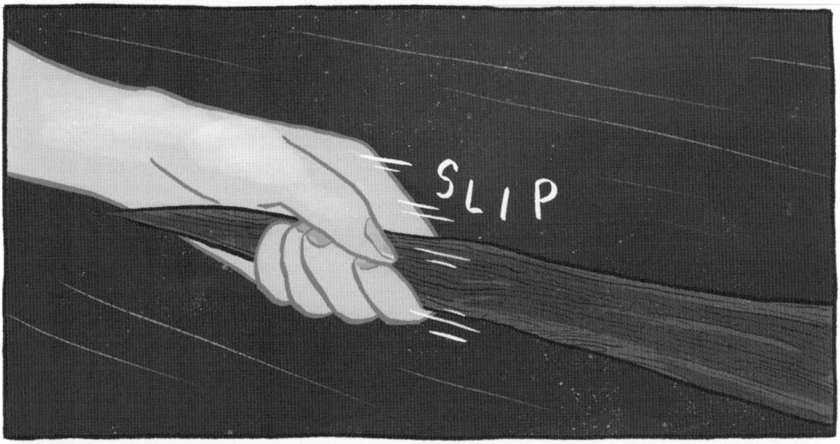
SLIP

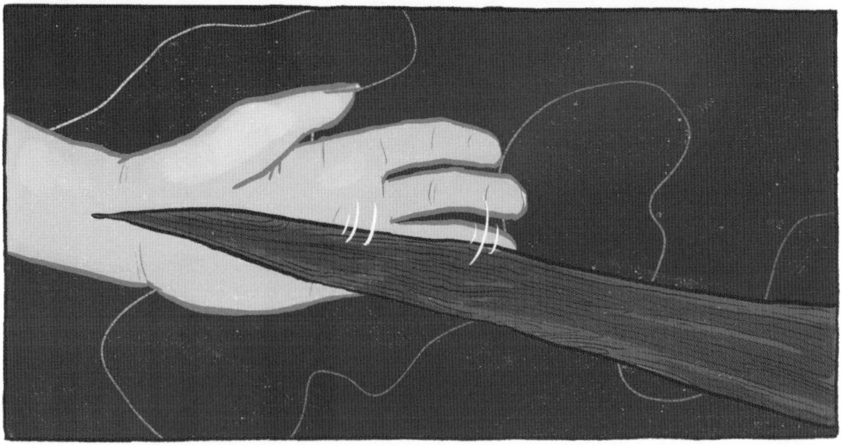

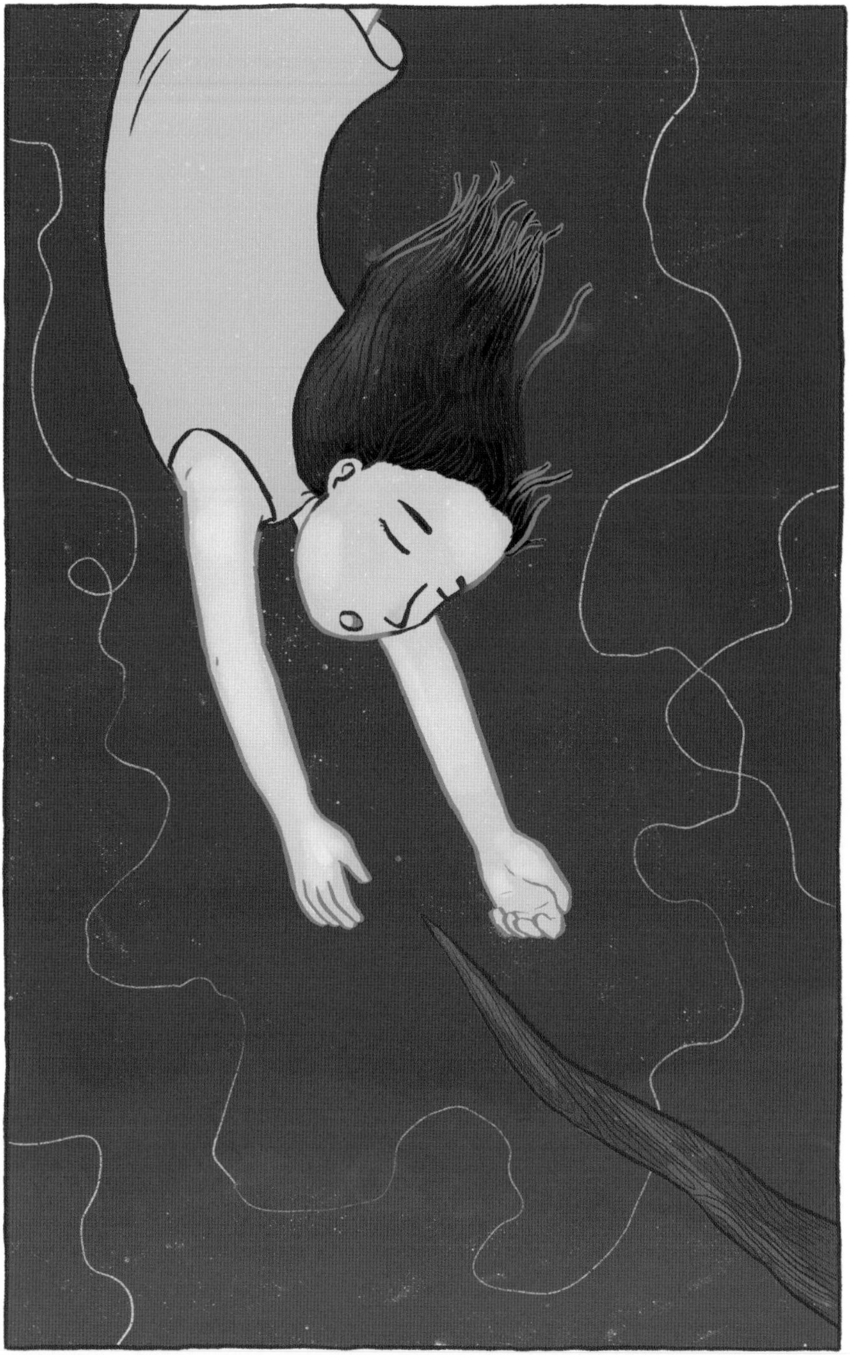

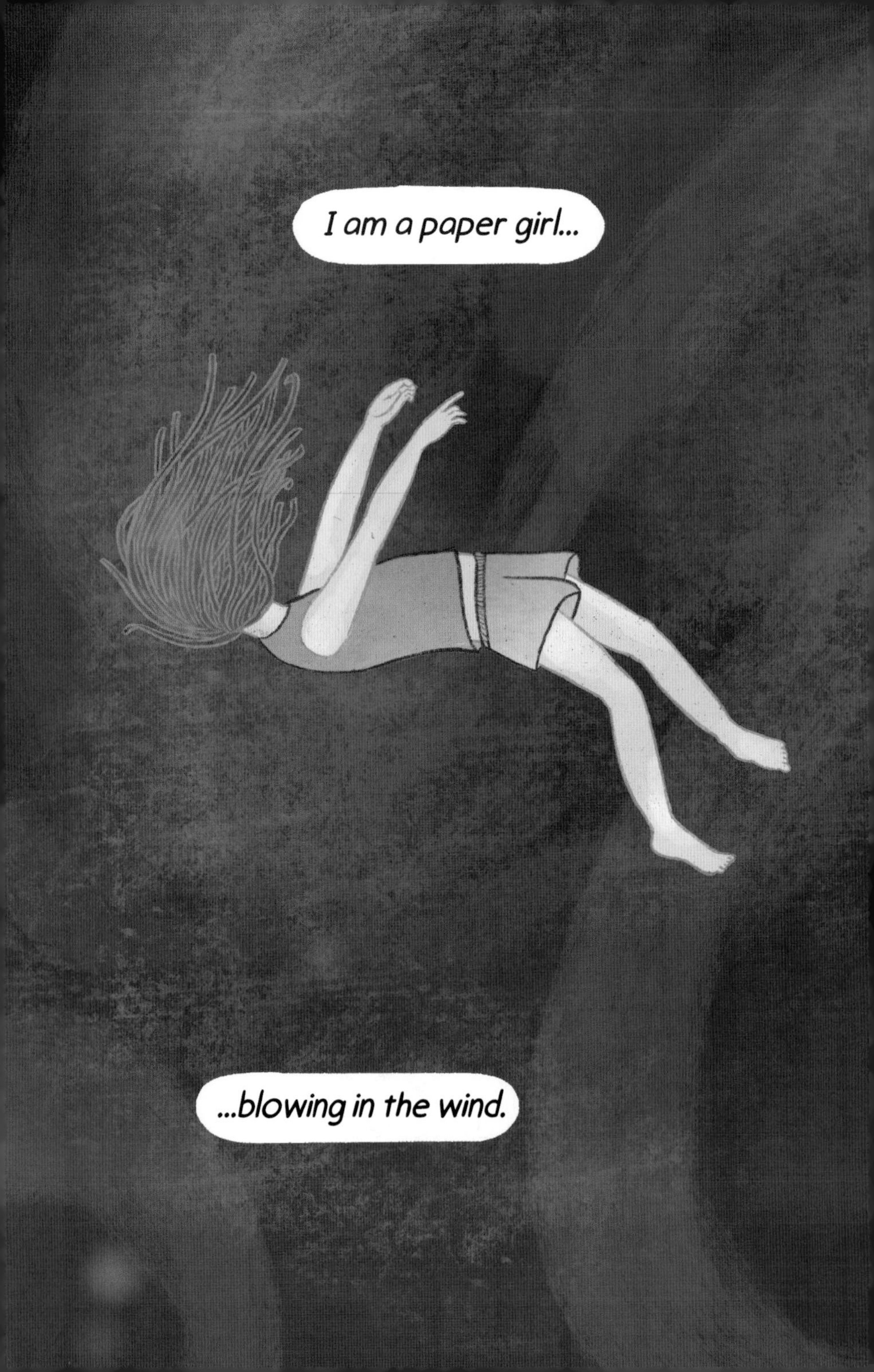
I am a paper girl...
...blowing in the wind.

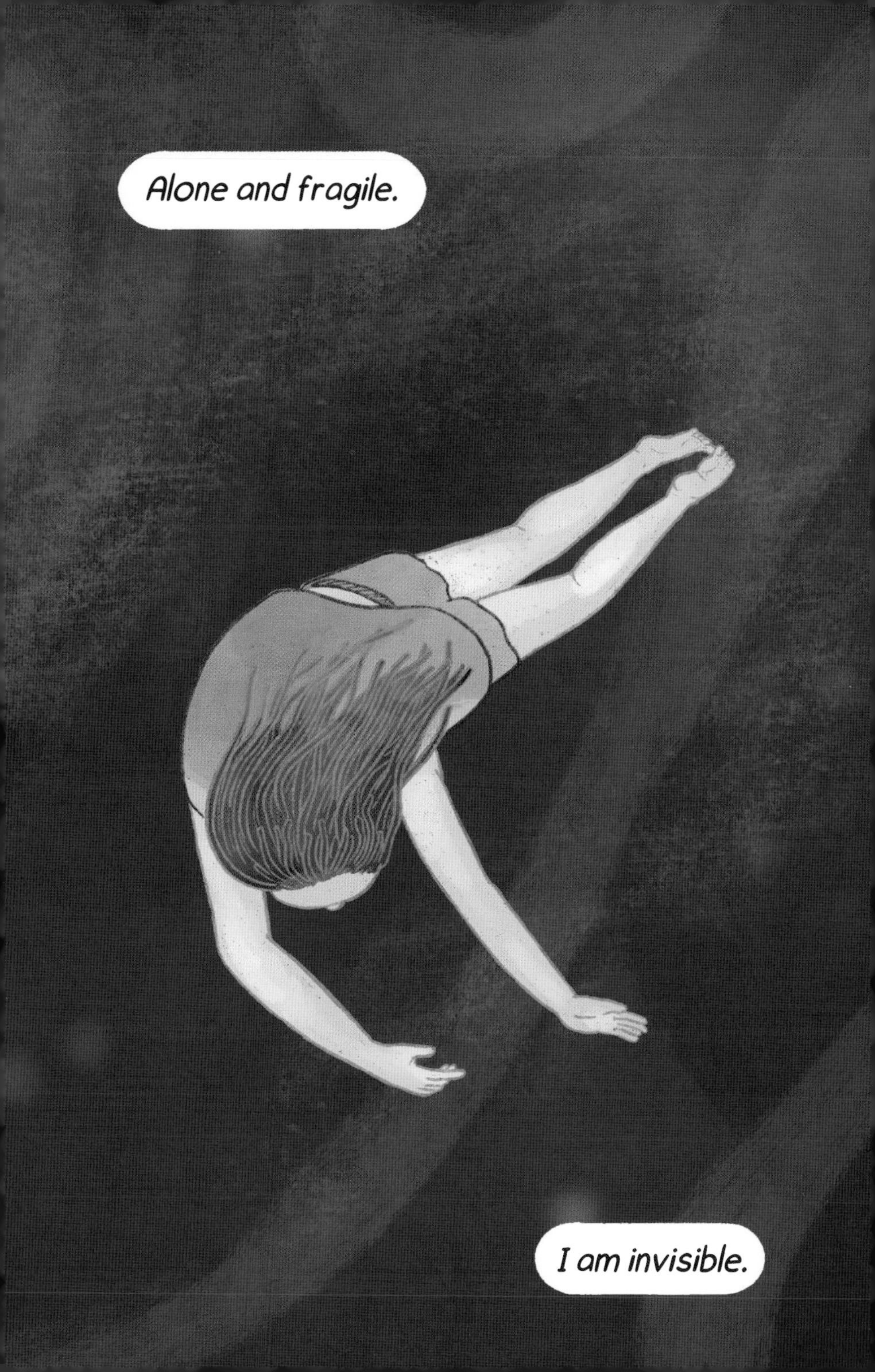
Alone and fragile.
I am invisible.

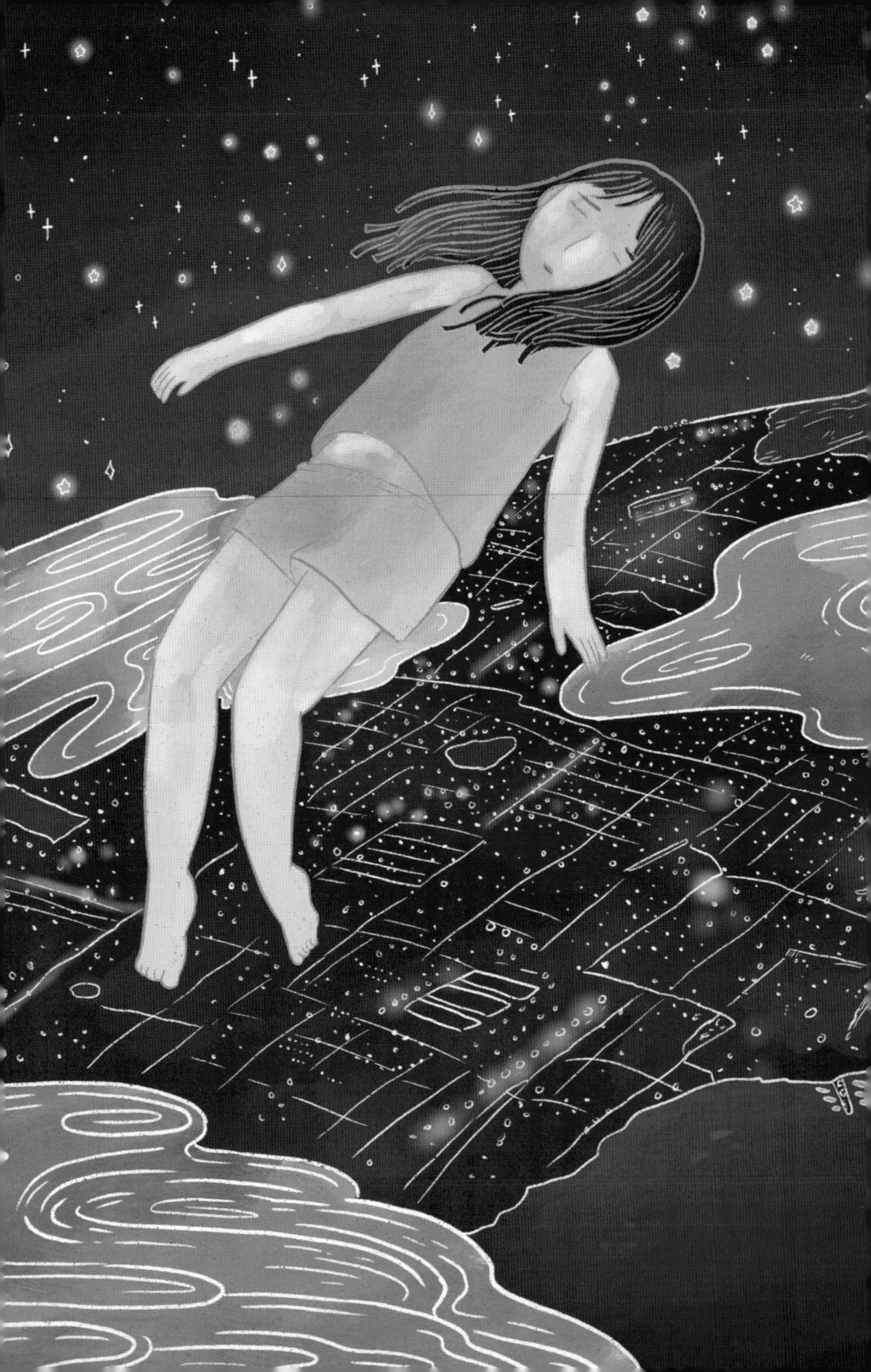

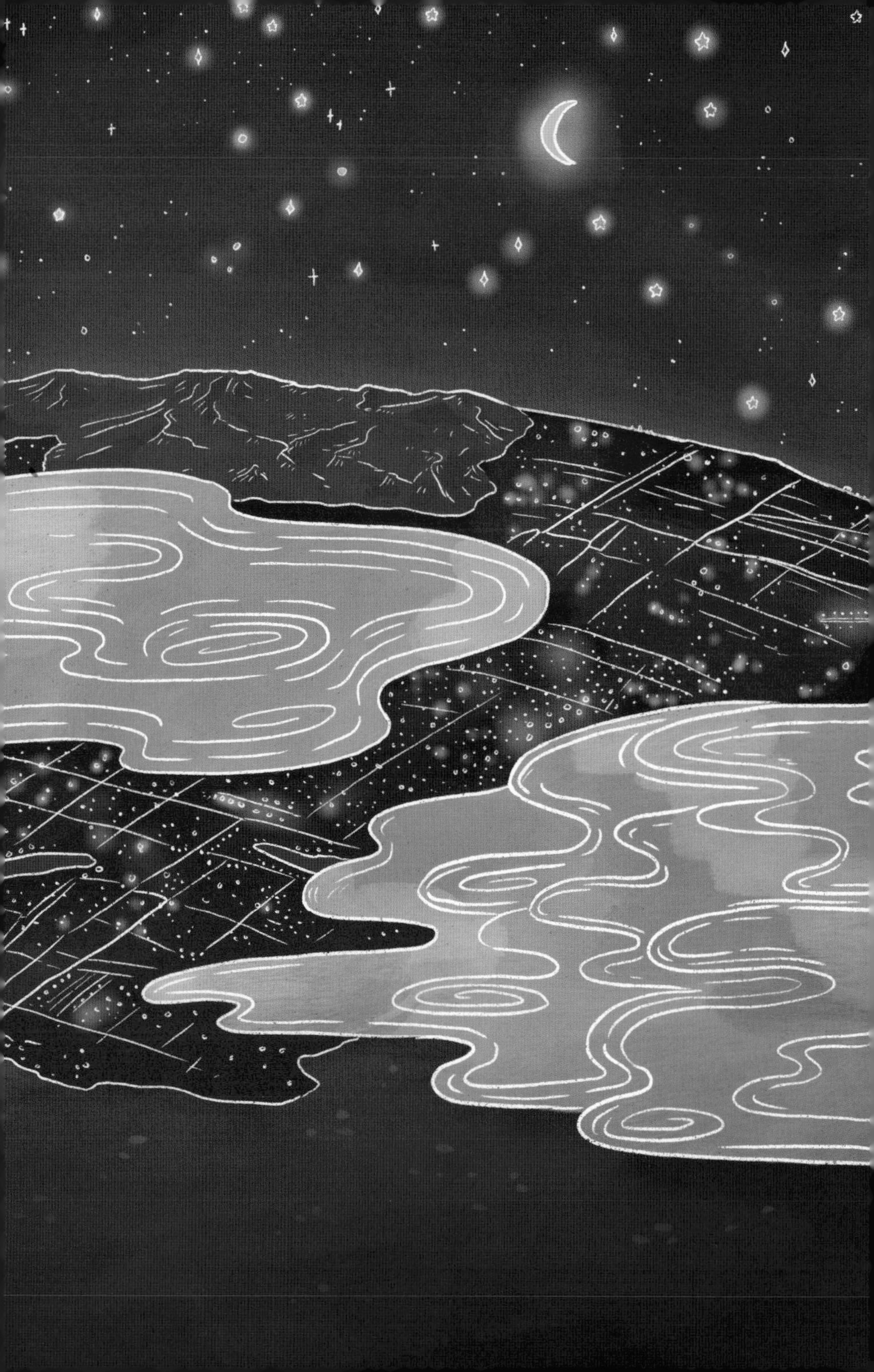

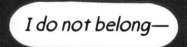
I do not belong—

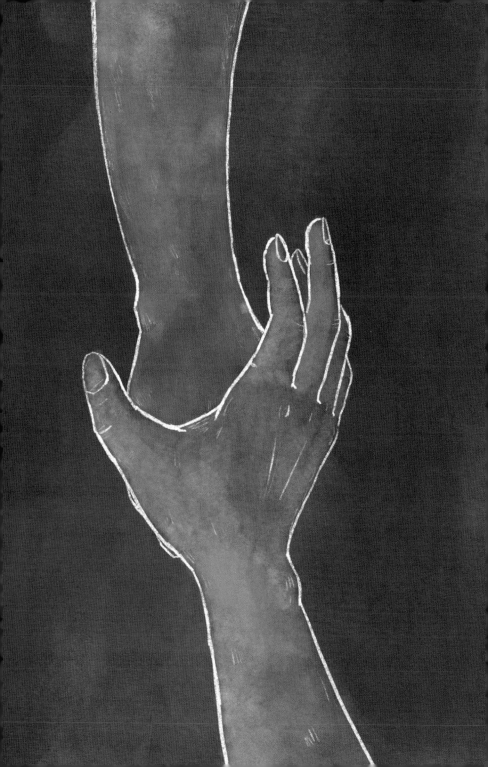

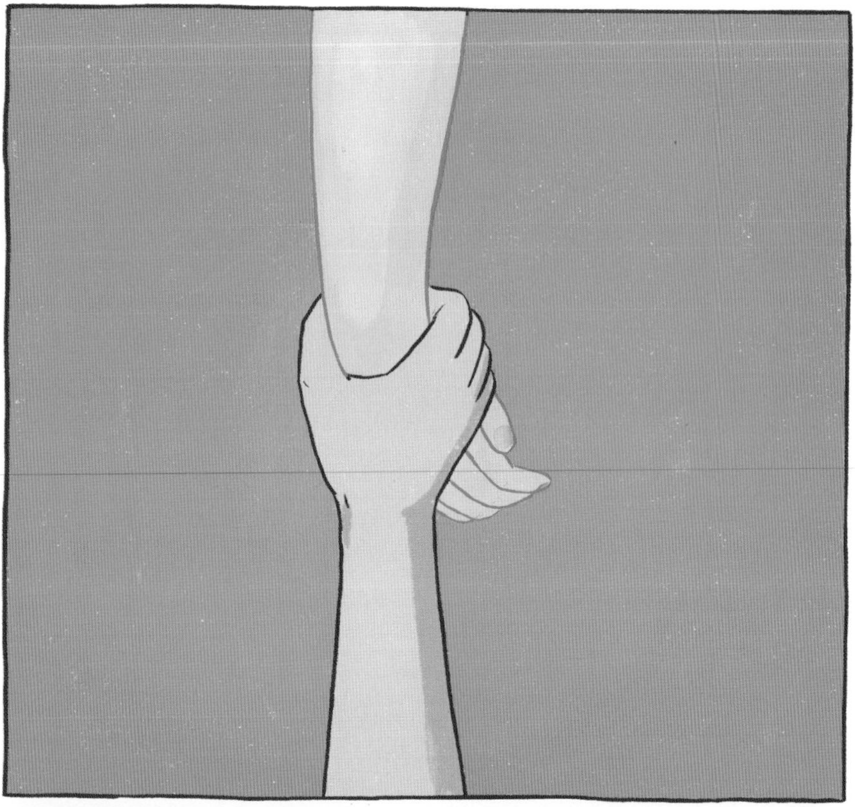

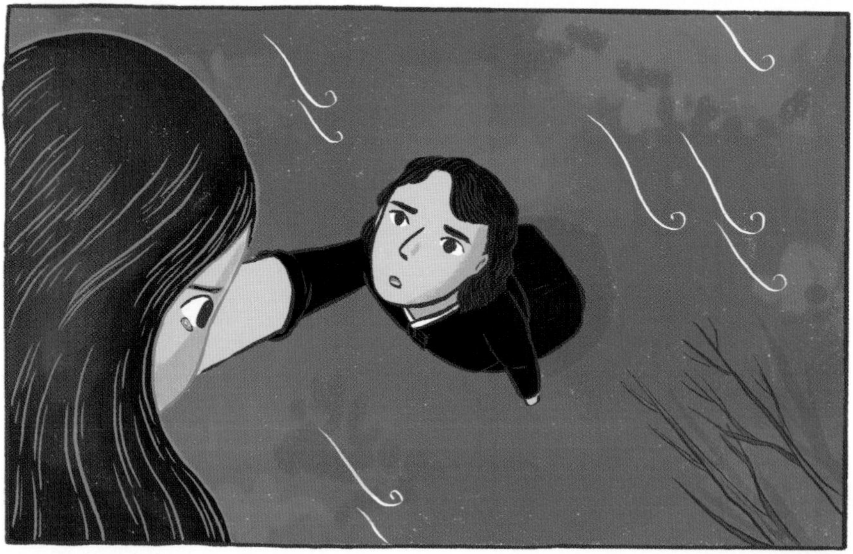

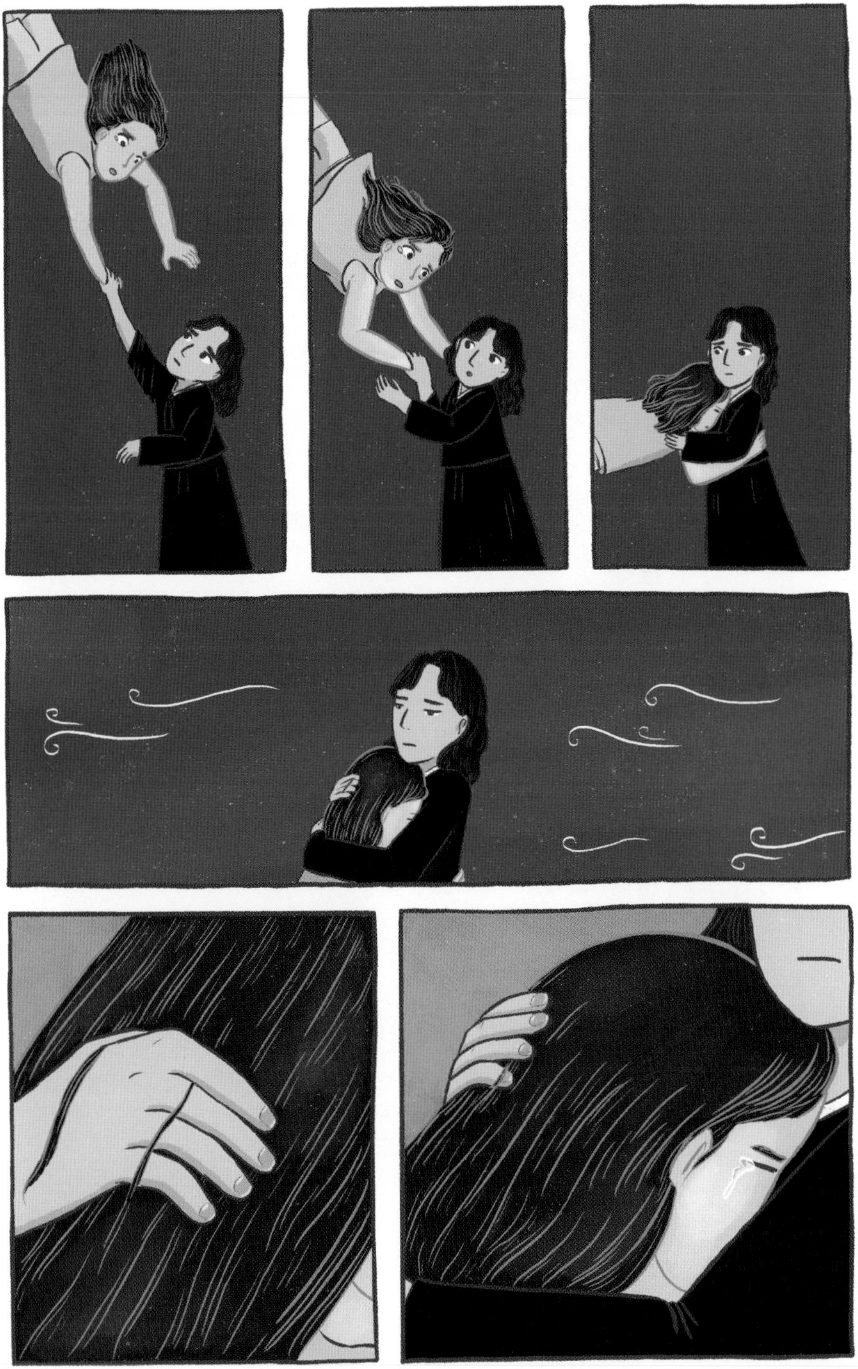

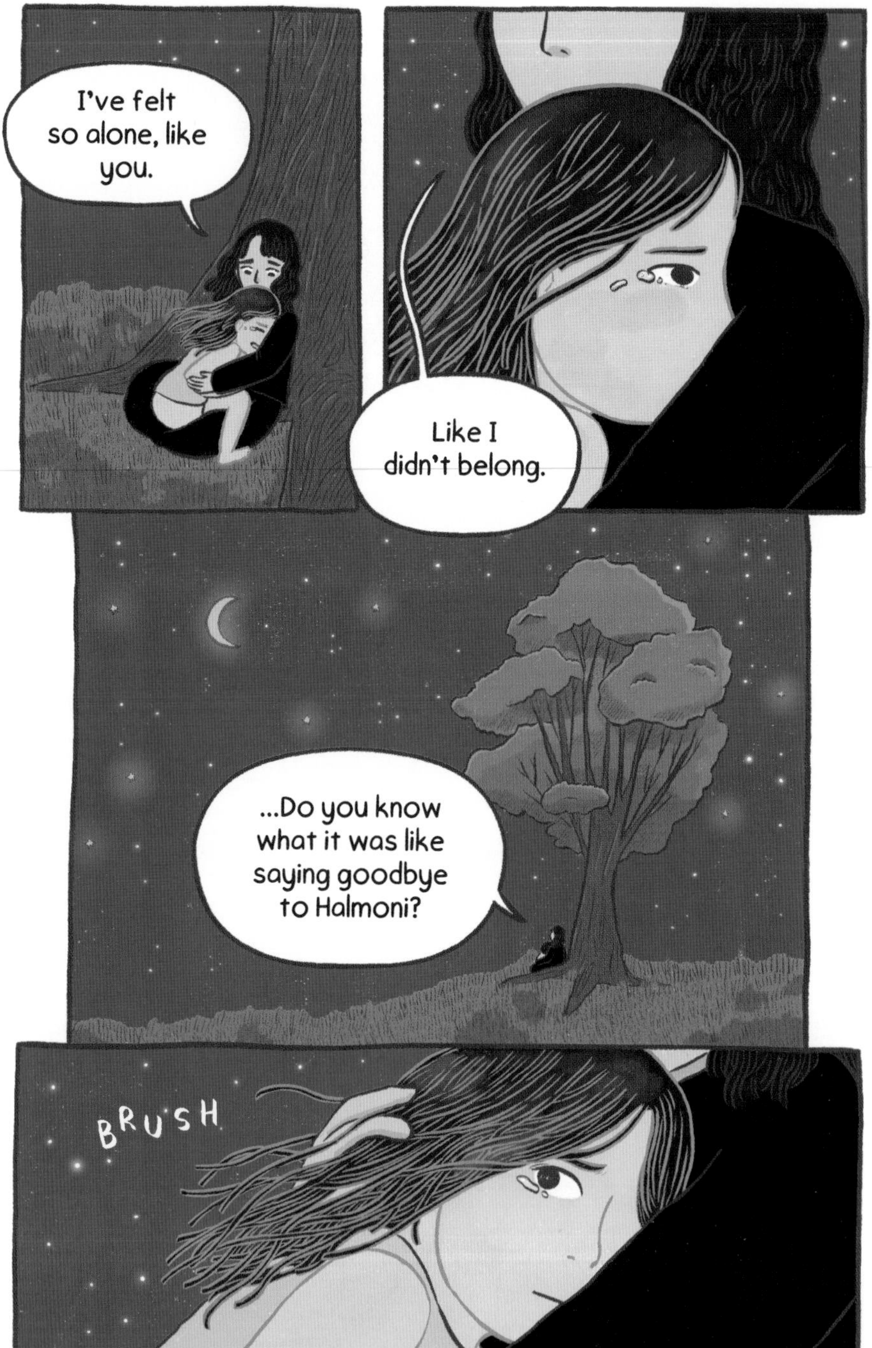
I've felt so alone, like you.
Like I didn't belong.
...Do you know what it was like saying goodbye to Halmoni?
BRUSH

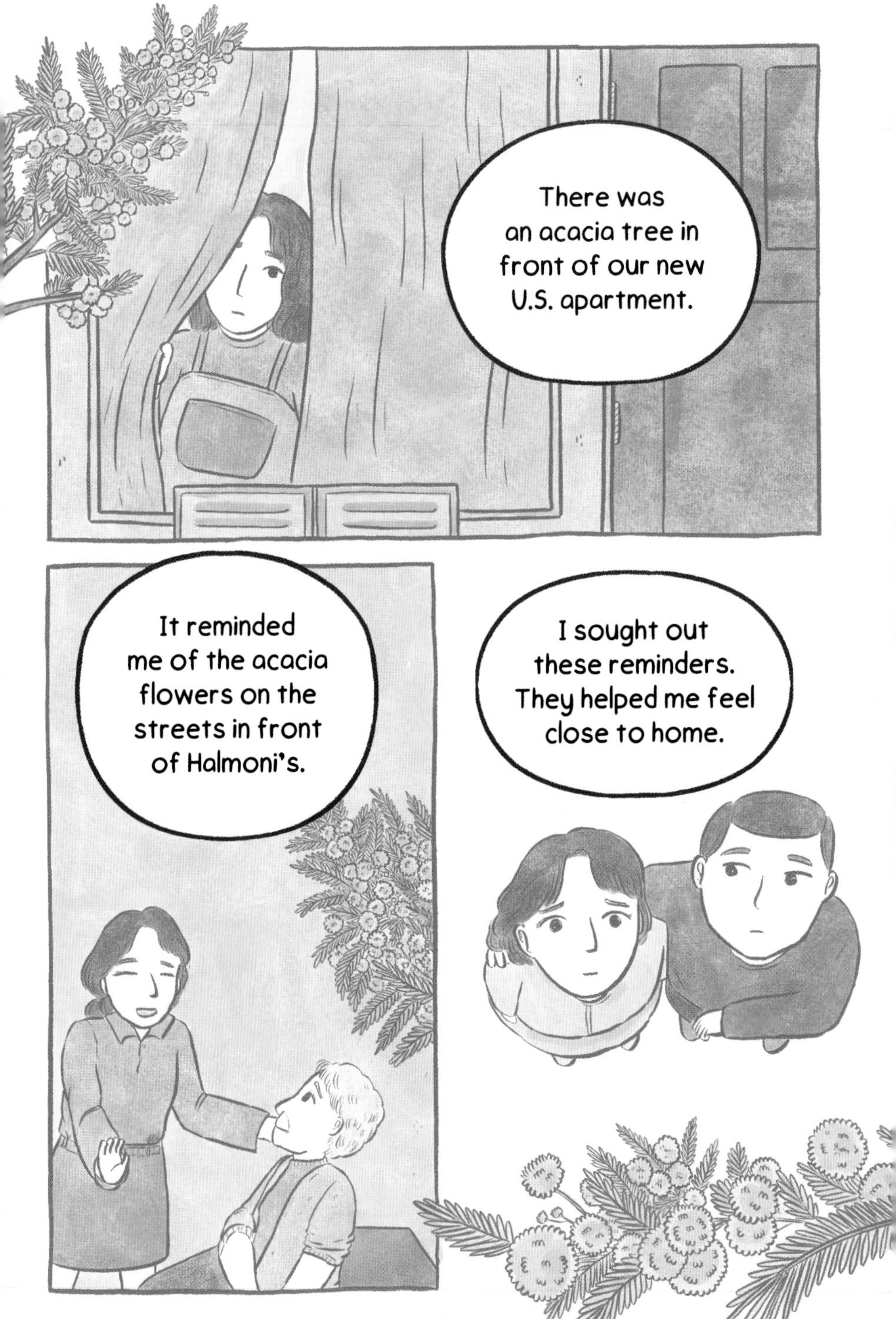
There was an acacia tree in front of our new U.S. apartment.
It reminded me of the acacia flowers on the streets in front of Halmoni's.
I sought out these reminders. They helped me feel close to home.

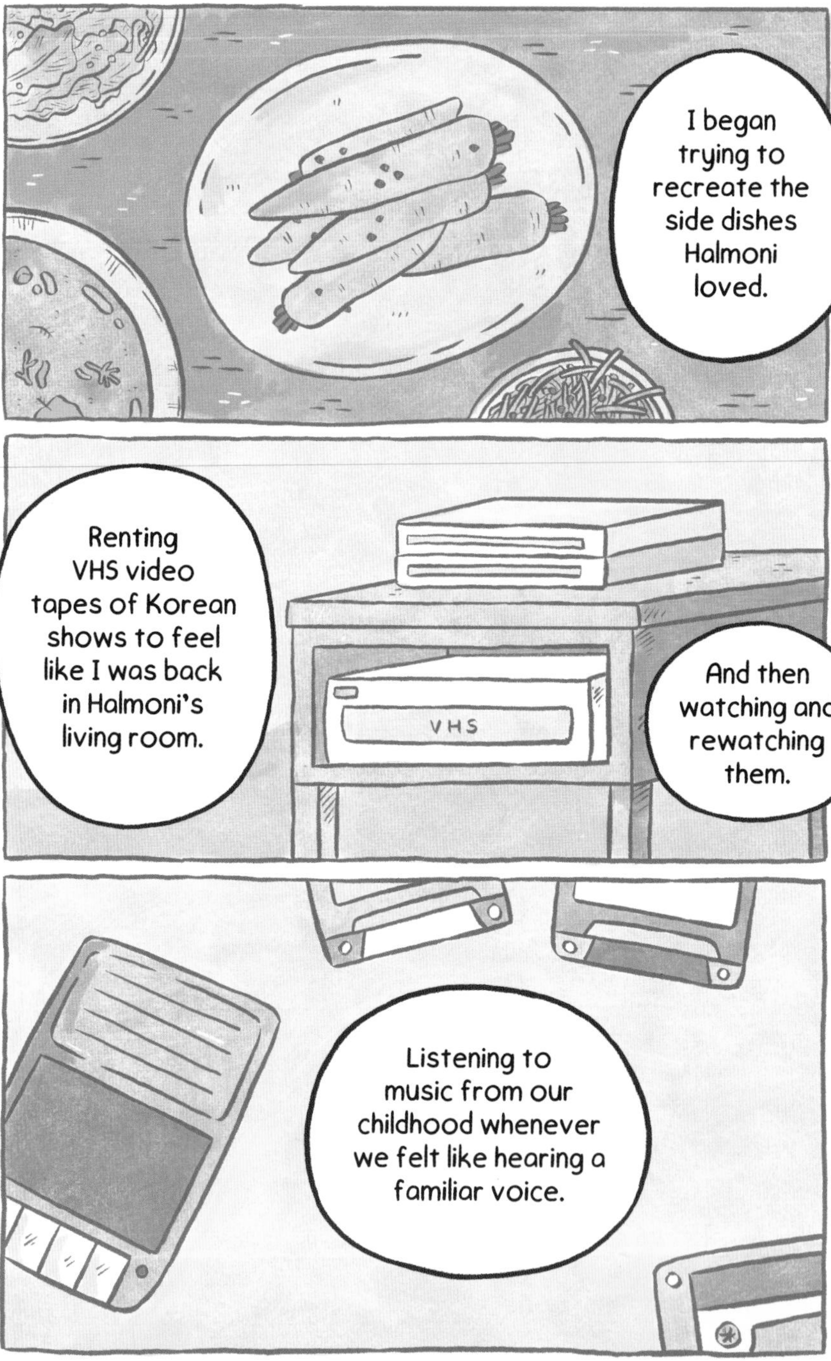
I began trying to recreate the side dishes Halmoni loved.
Renting VHS video tapes of Korean shows to feel like I was back in Halmoni's living room.
VHS
And then watching and rewatching them.
Listening to music from our childhood whenever we felt like hearing a familiar voice.

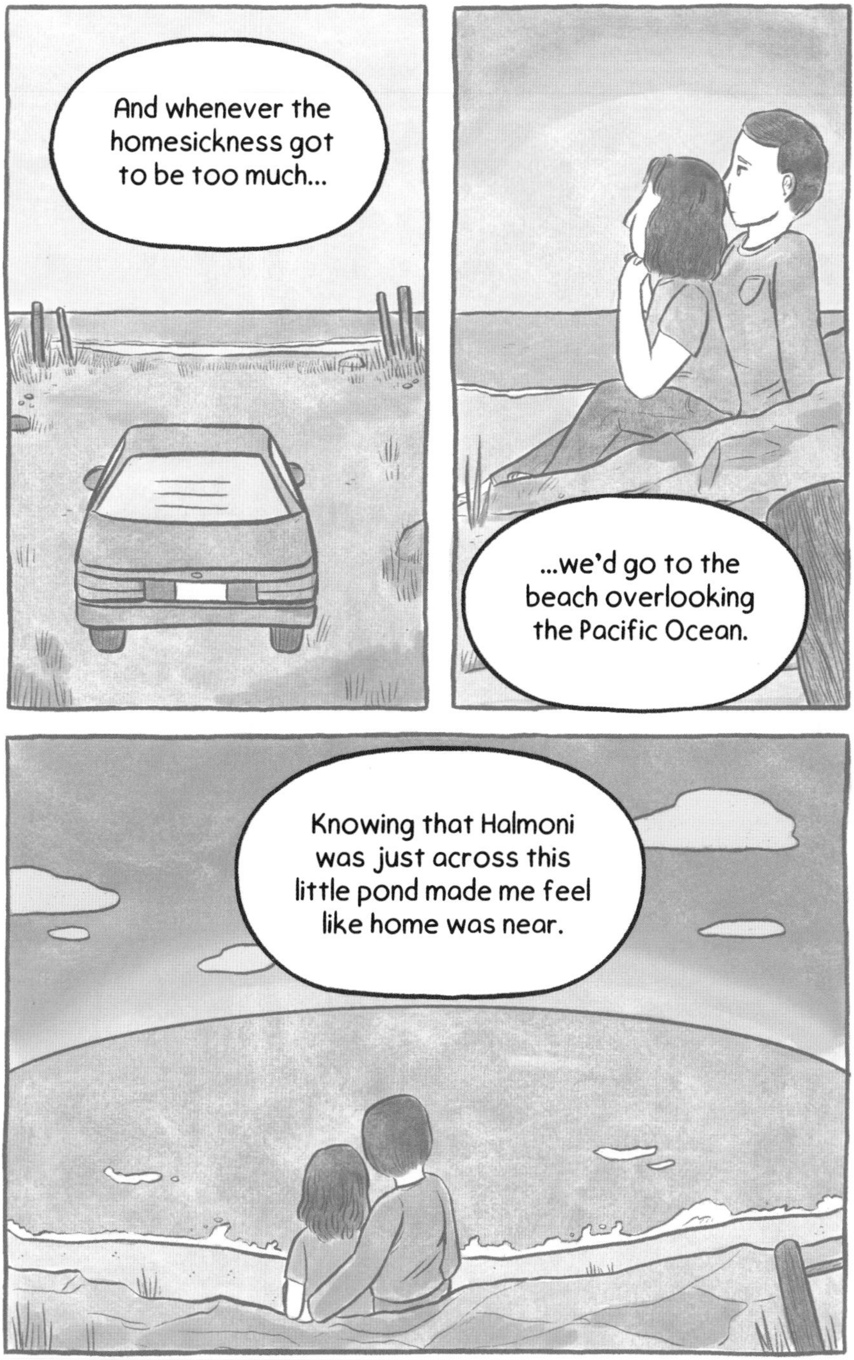
And whenever the homesickness got to be too much...
...we'd go to the beach overlooking the Pacific Ocean.
Knowing that Halmoni was just across this little pond made me feel like home was near.

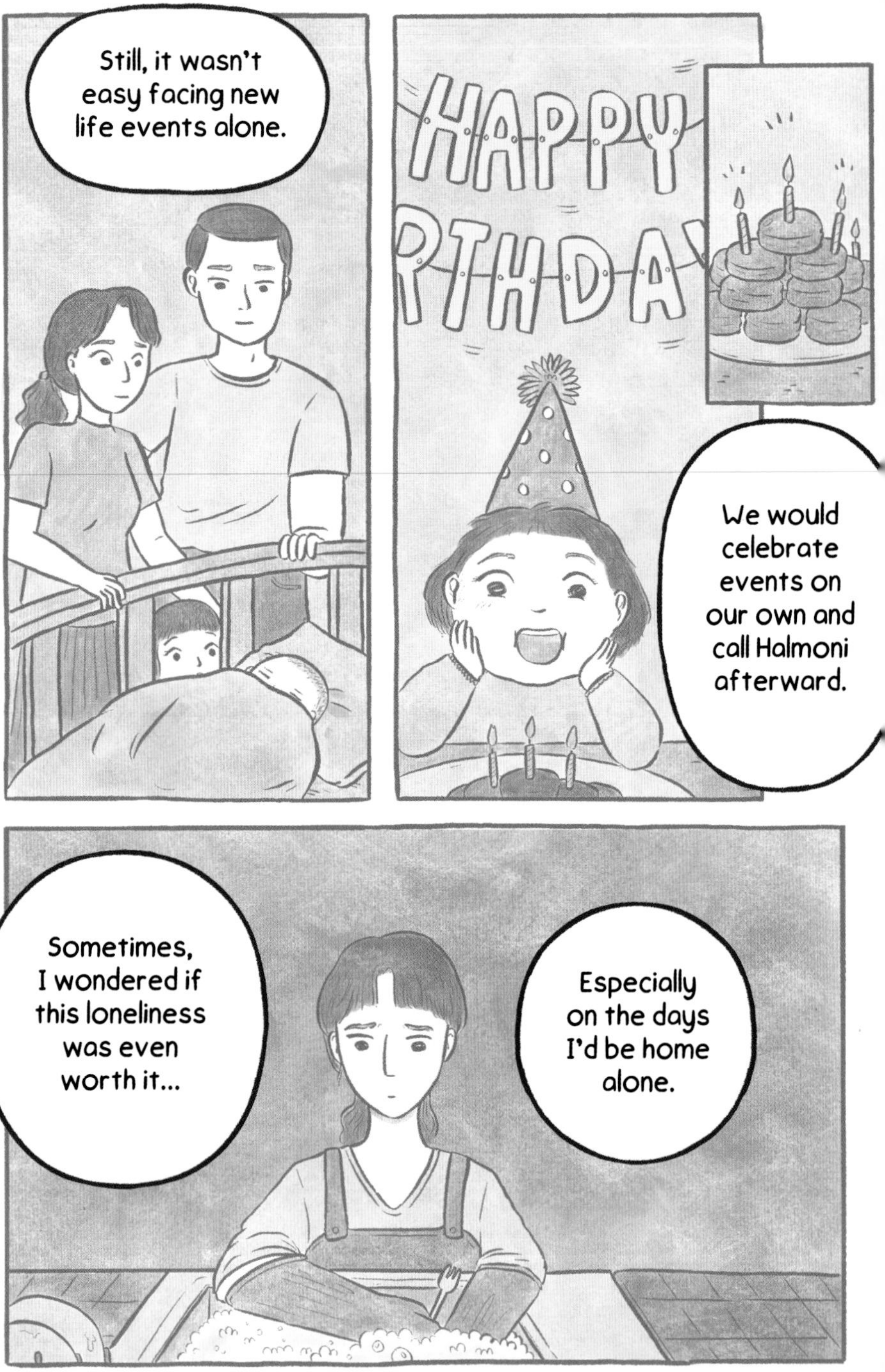

Still, it wasn't easy facing new life events alone.
HAPPY
RTHDAY
We would celebrate events on our own and call Halmoni afterward.
Sometimes, I wondered if this loneliness was even worth it...
Especially on the days I'd be home alone.

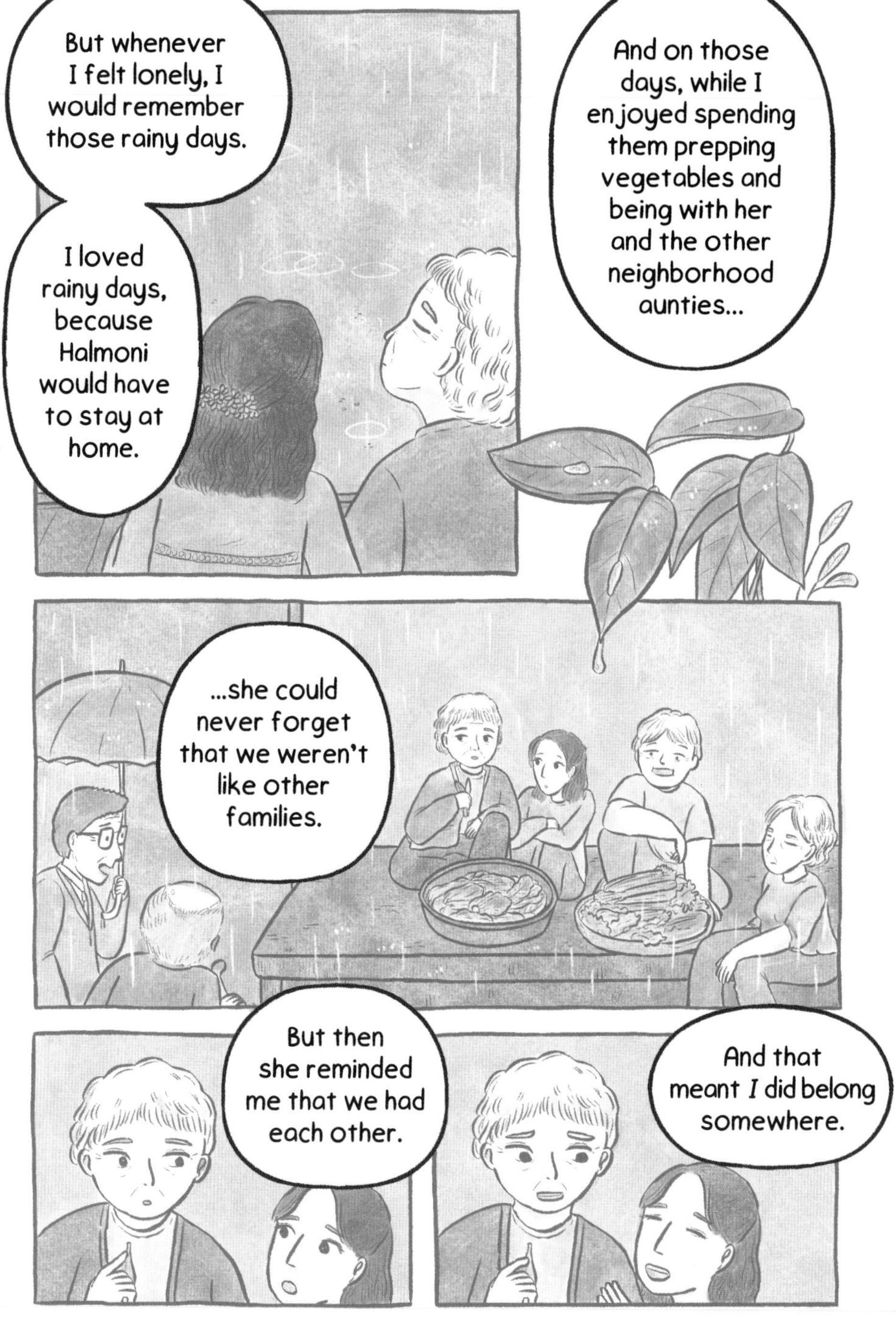
But whenever I felt lonely, I would remember those rainy days.
I loved rainy days, because Halmoni would have to stay at home.
And on those days, while I enjoyed spending them prepping vegetables and being with her and the other neighborhood aunties...
...she could never forget that we weren't like other families.
But then she reminded me that we had each other.
And that meant *I* did belong somewhere.

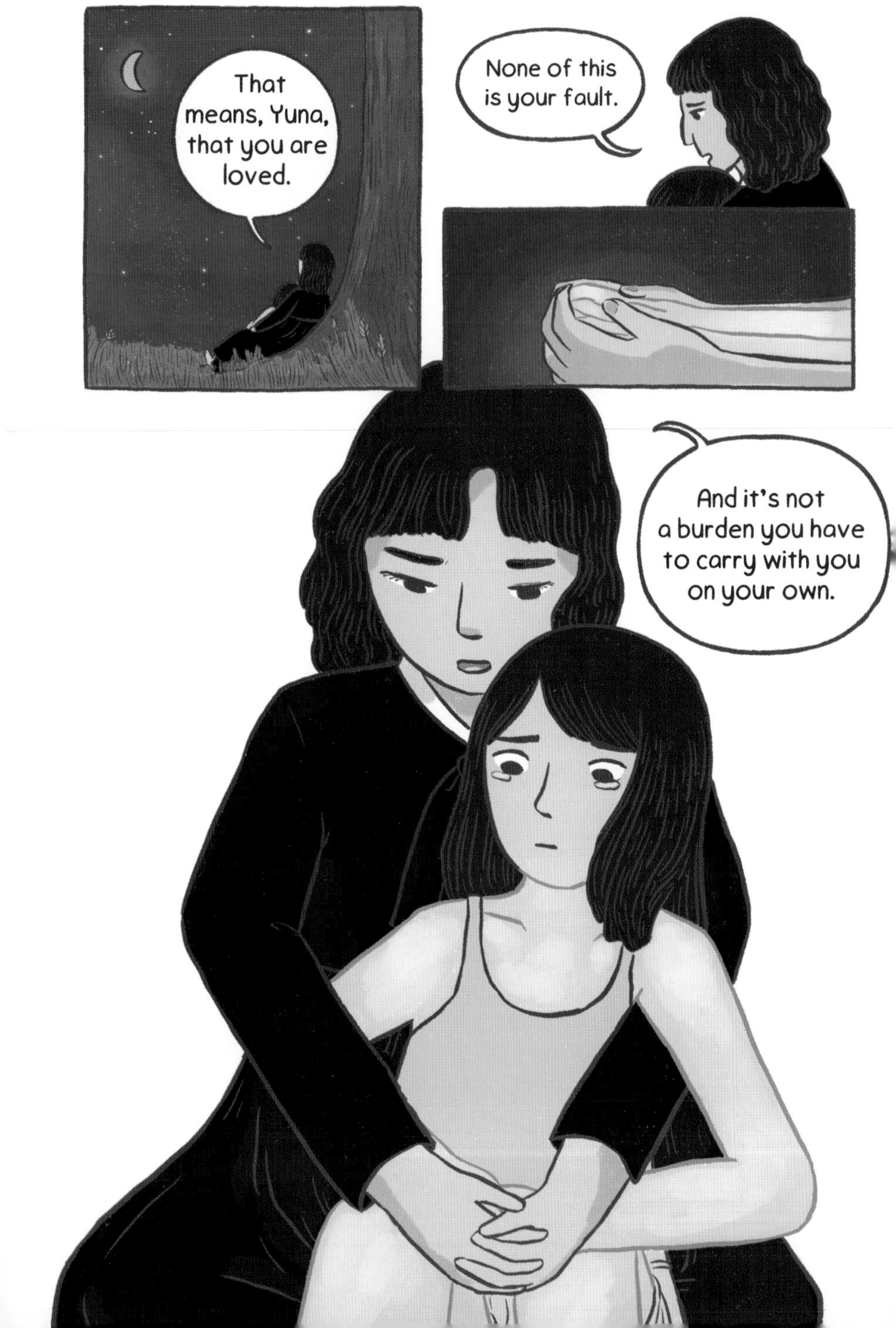
That means, Yuna, that you are loved.
None of this is your fault.
And it's not a burden you have to carry with you on your own.

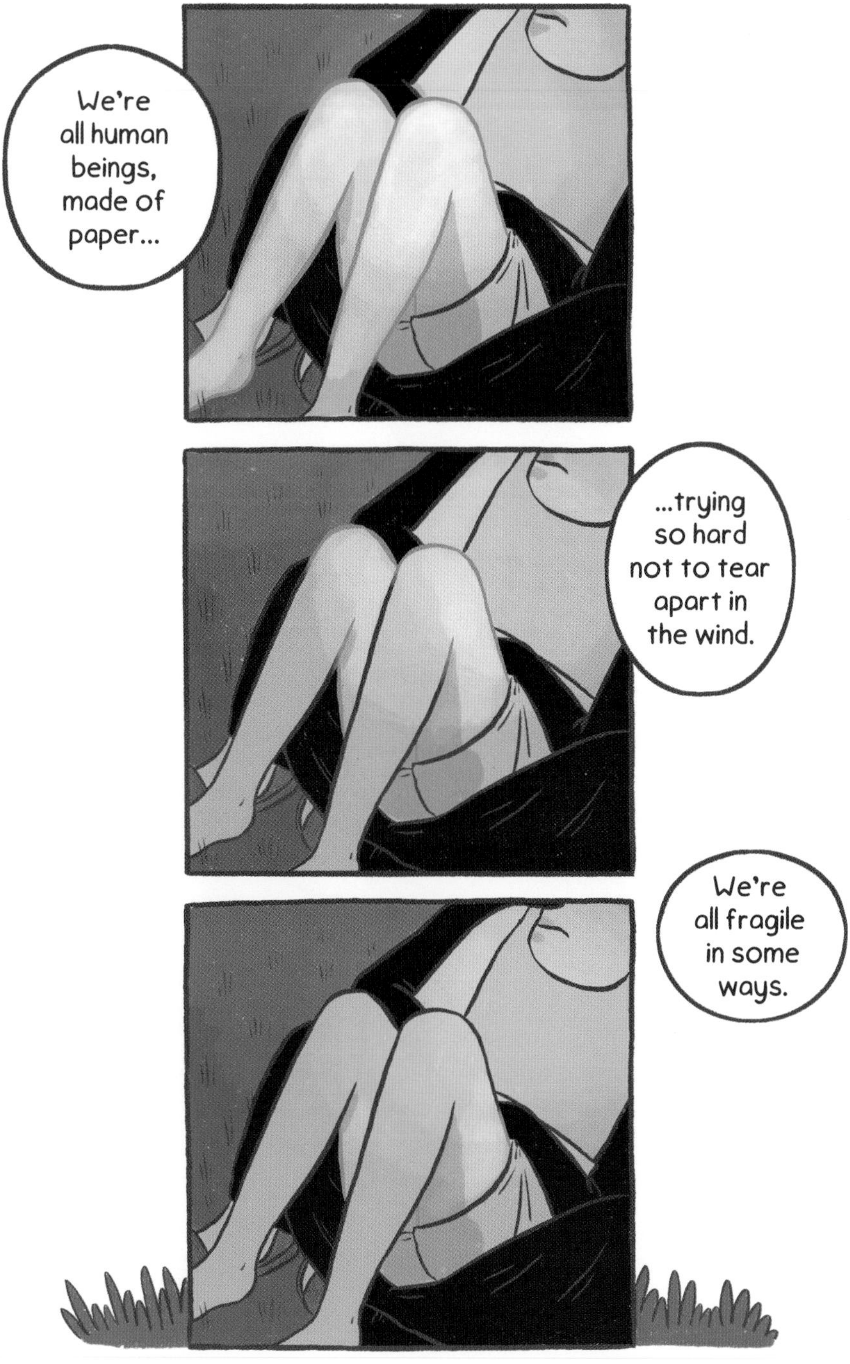
We're all human beings, made of paper...
...trying so hard not to tear apart in the wind.
We're all fragile in some ways.

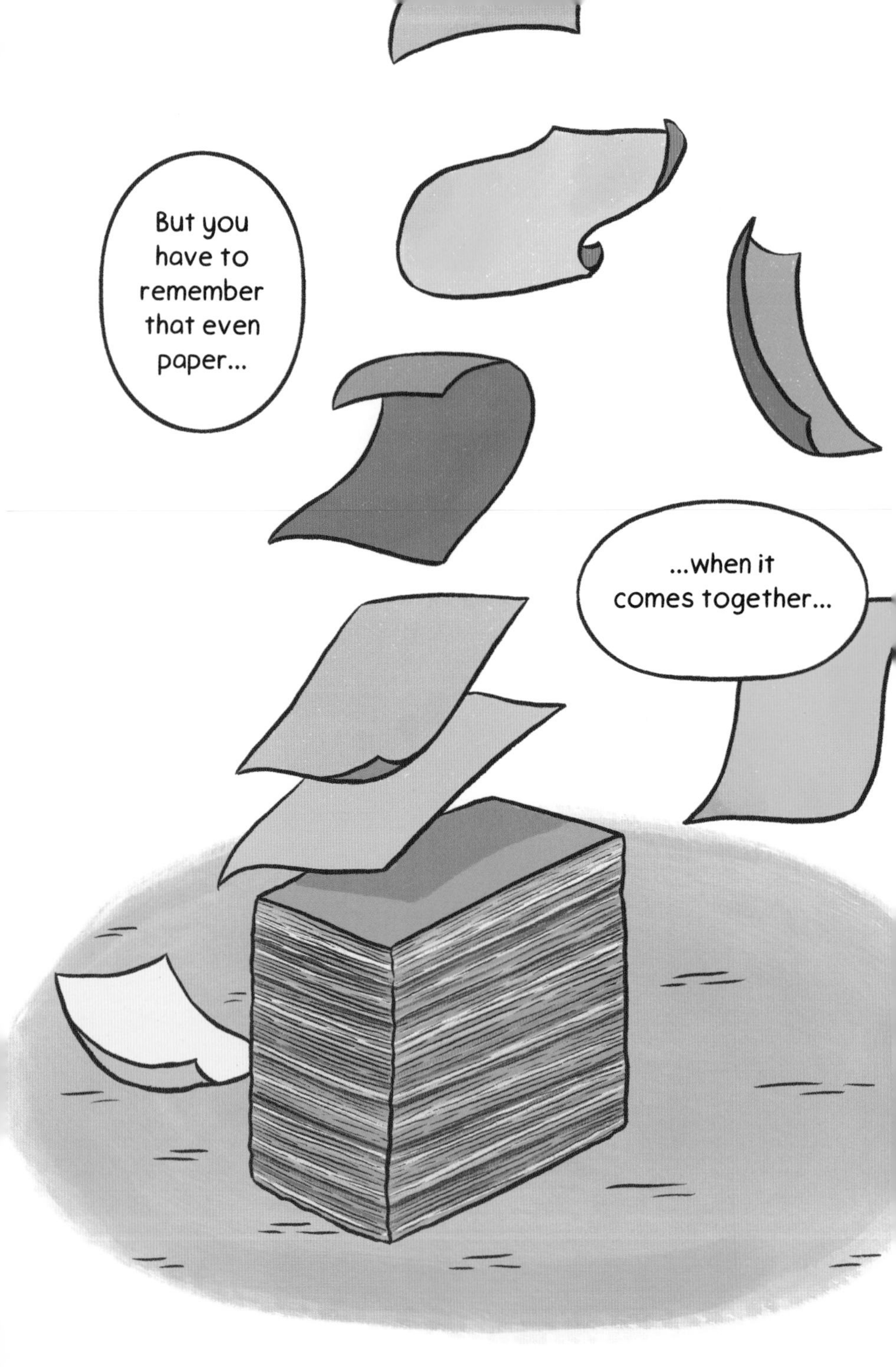
But you have to remember that even paper...
...when it comes together...

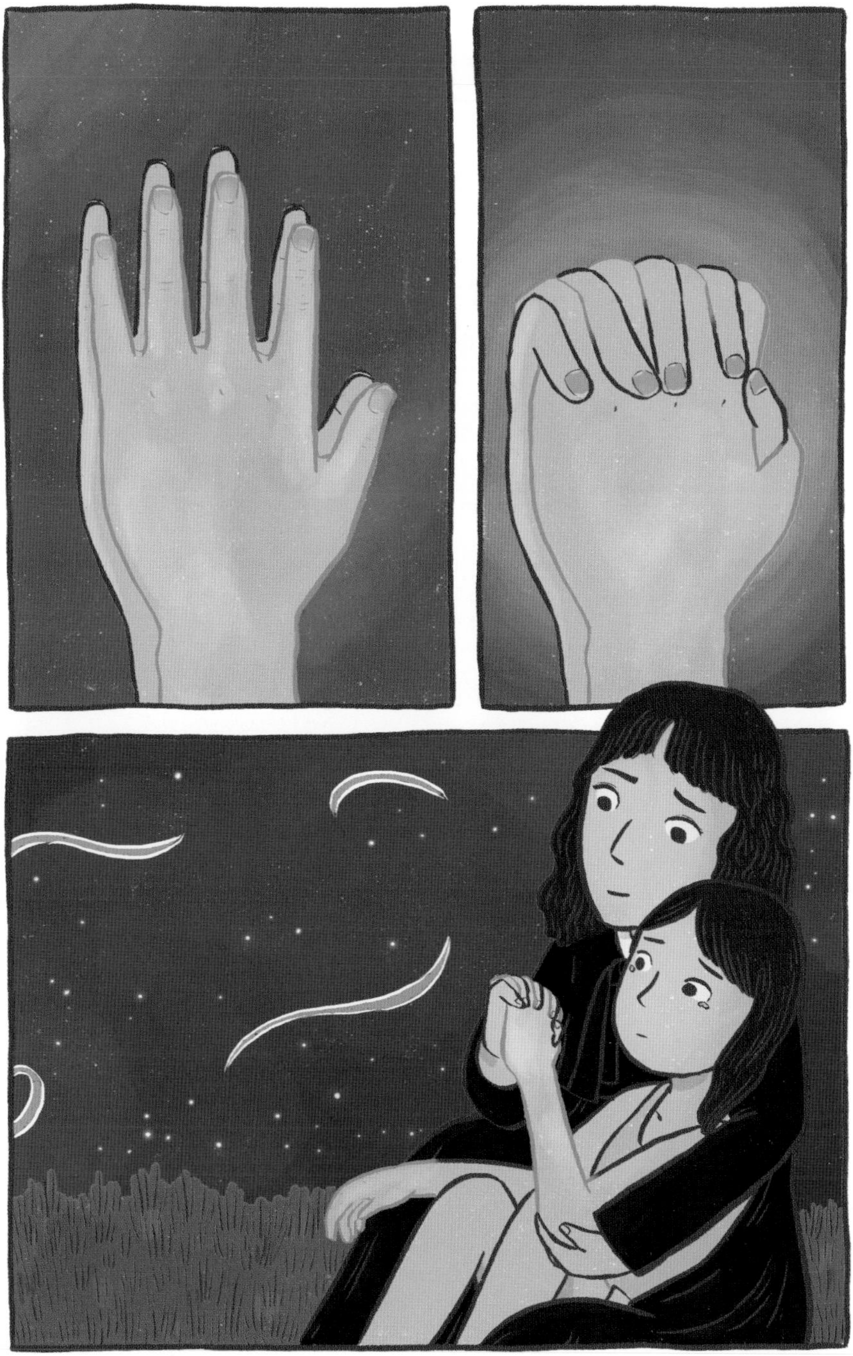

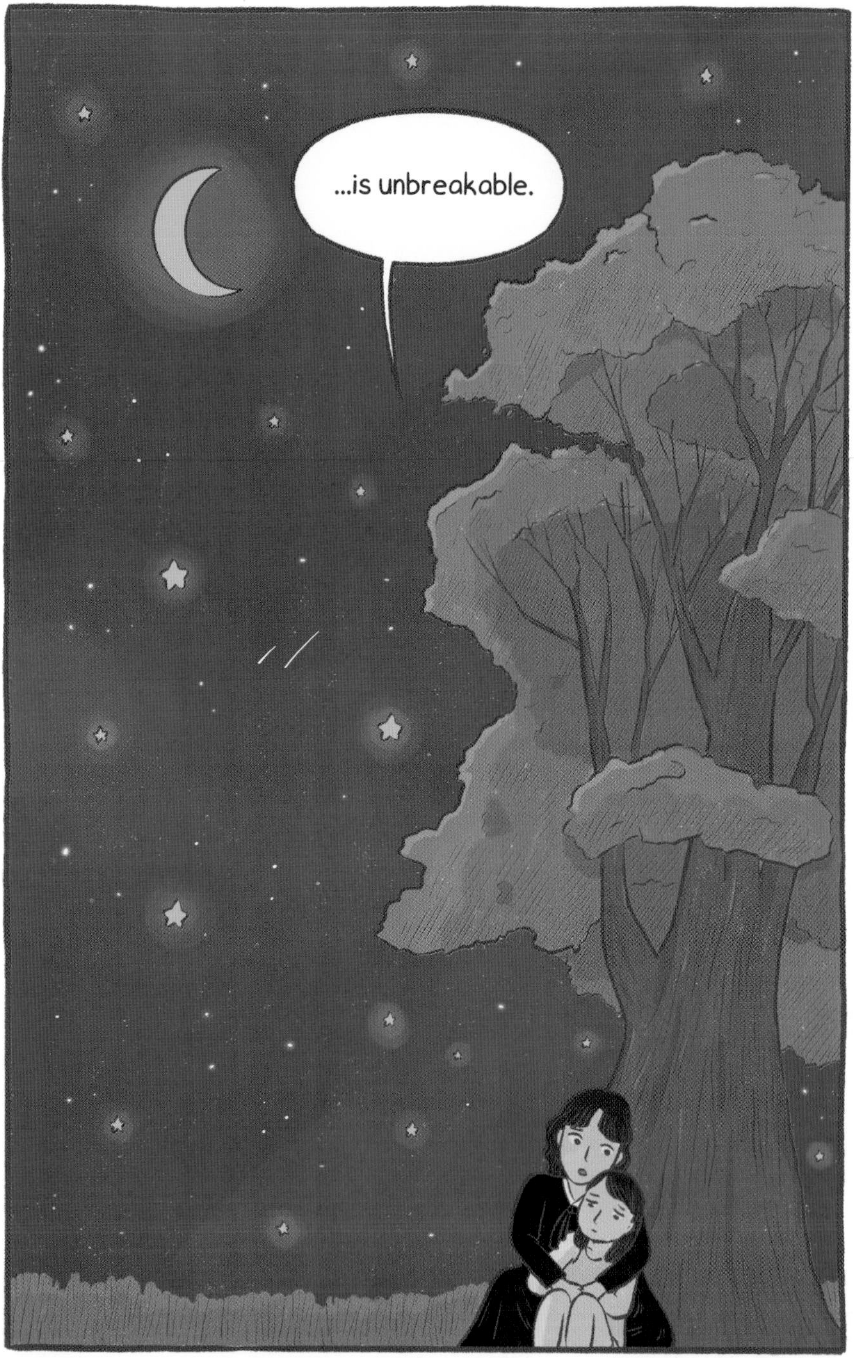
...is unbreakable.

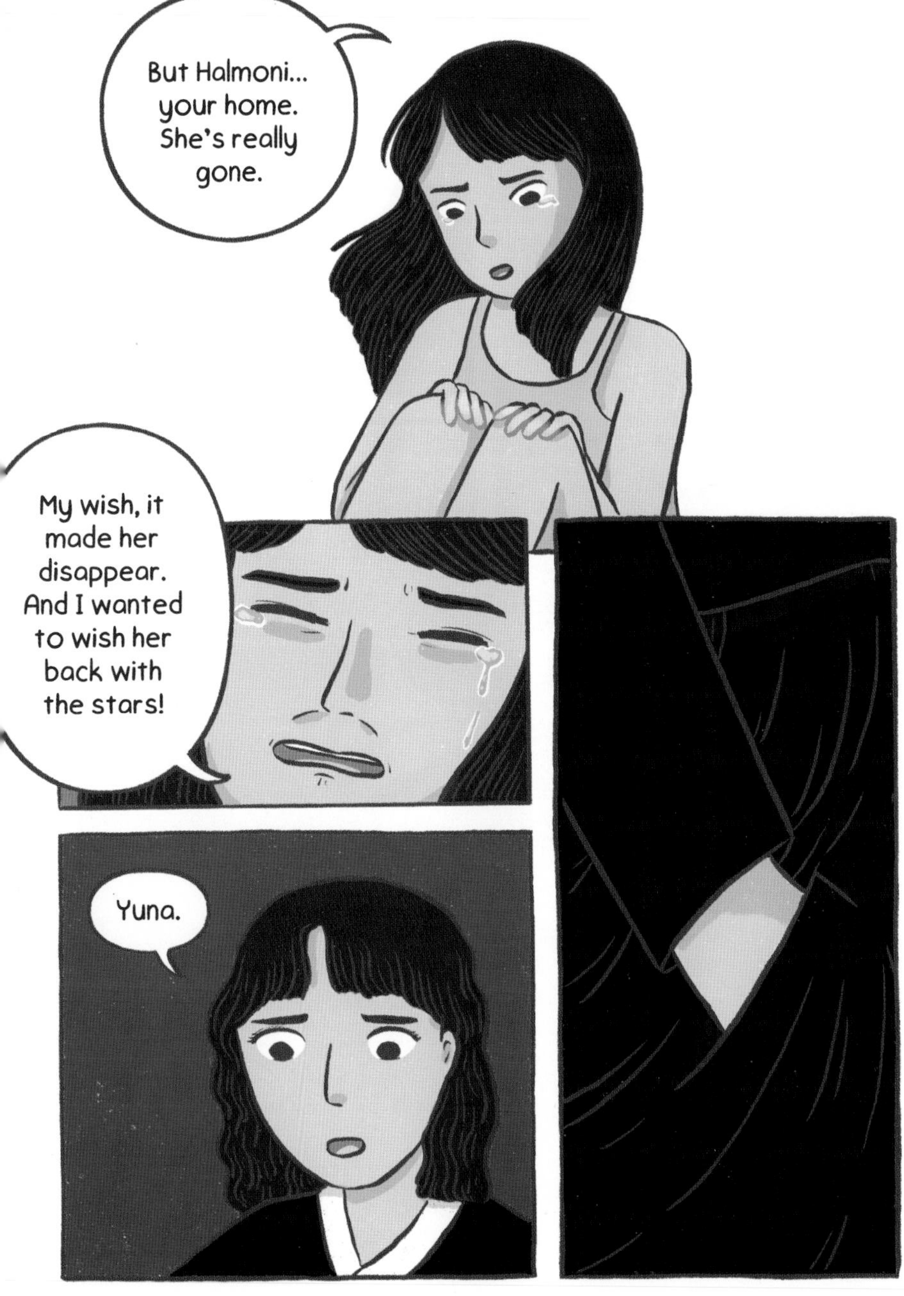
But Halmoni... your home. She's really gone.
My wish, it made her disappear. And I wanted to wish her back with the stars!
Yuna.

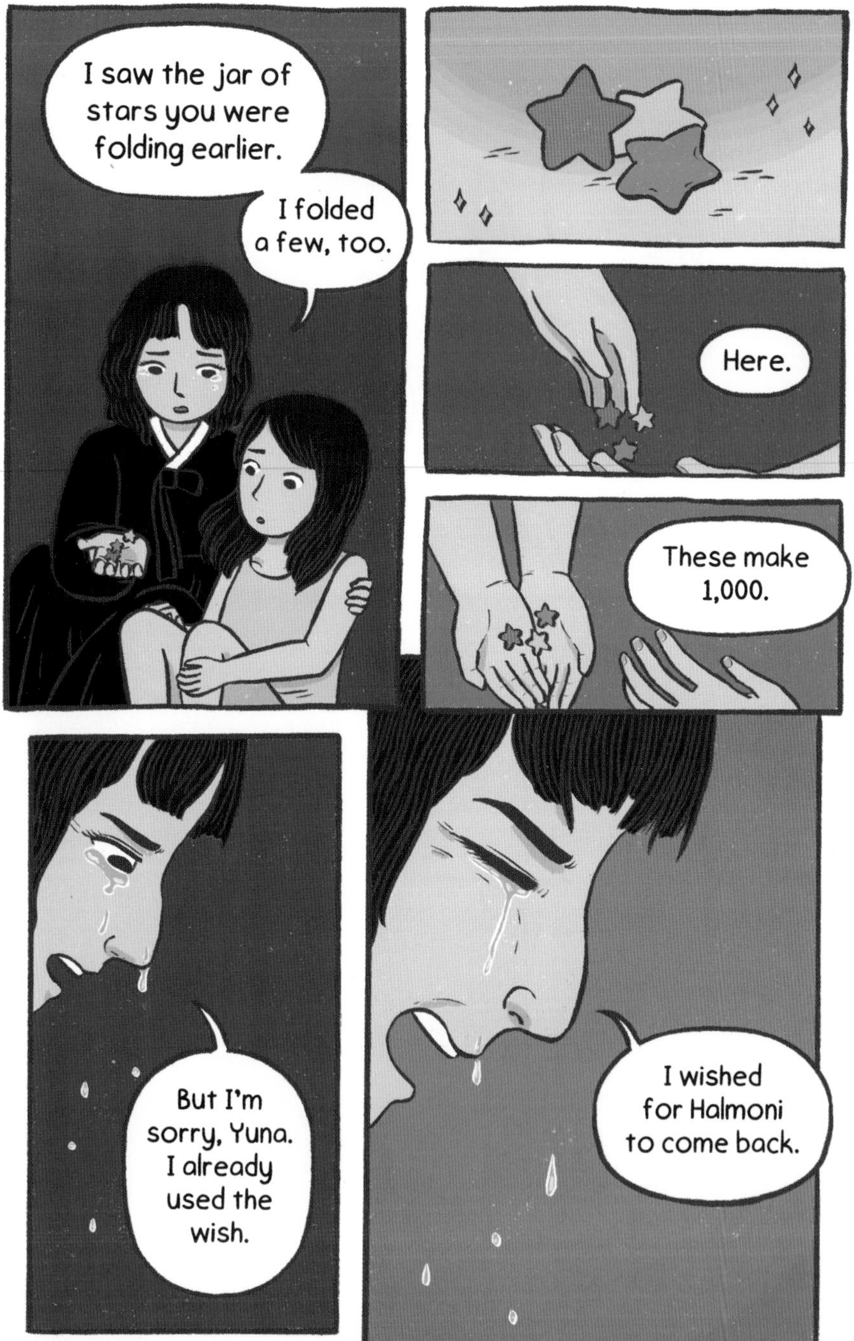
I saw the jar of stars you were folding earlier.
I folded a few, too.
Here.
These make 1,000.
But I'm sorry, Yuna. I already used the wish.
I wished for Halmoni to come back.

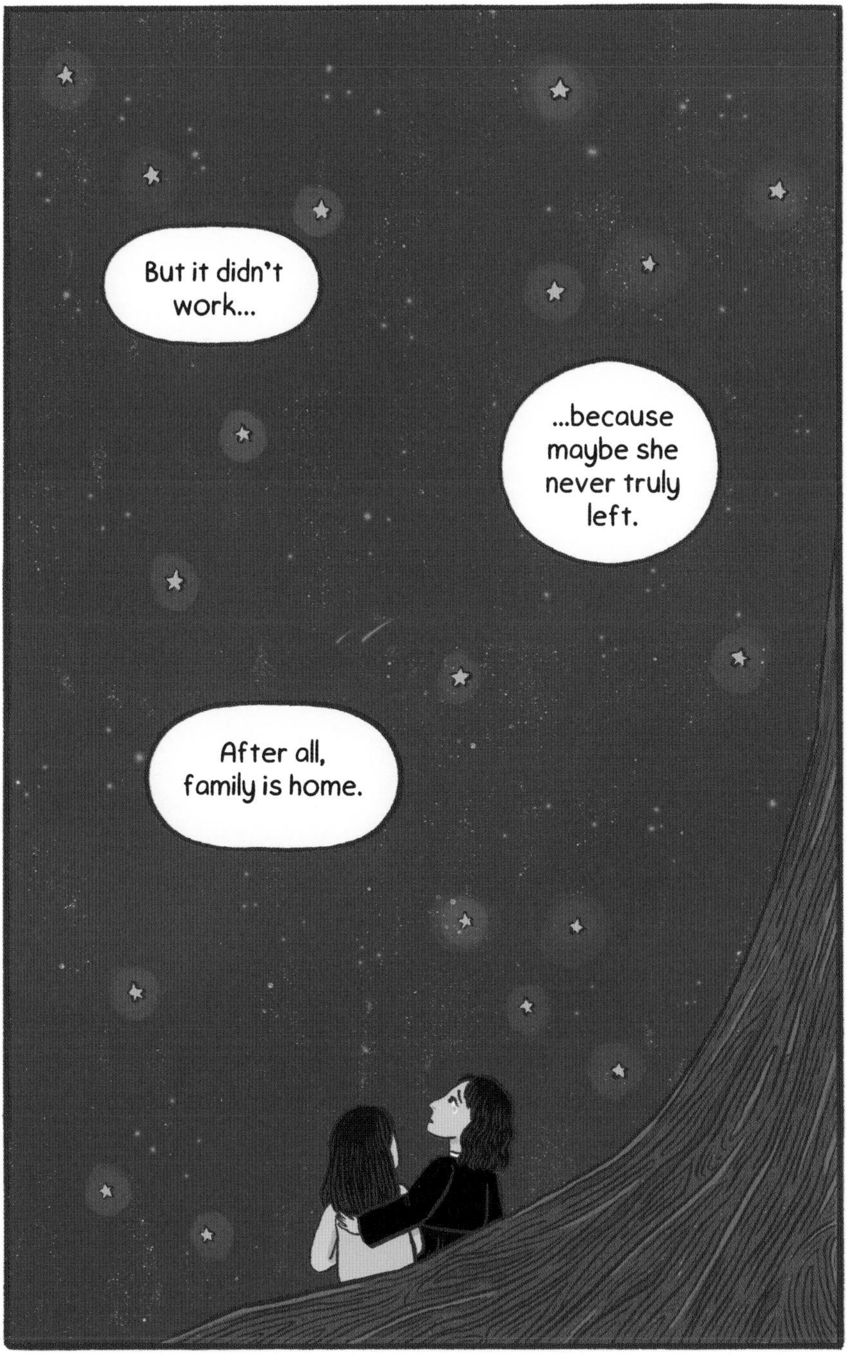
But it didn't work...
...because maybe she never truly left.
After all, family is home.

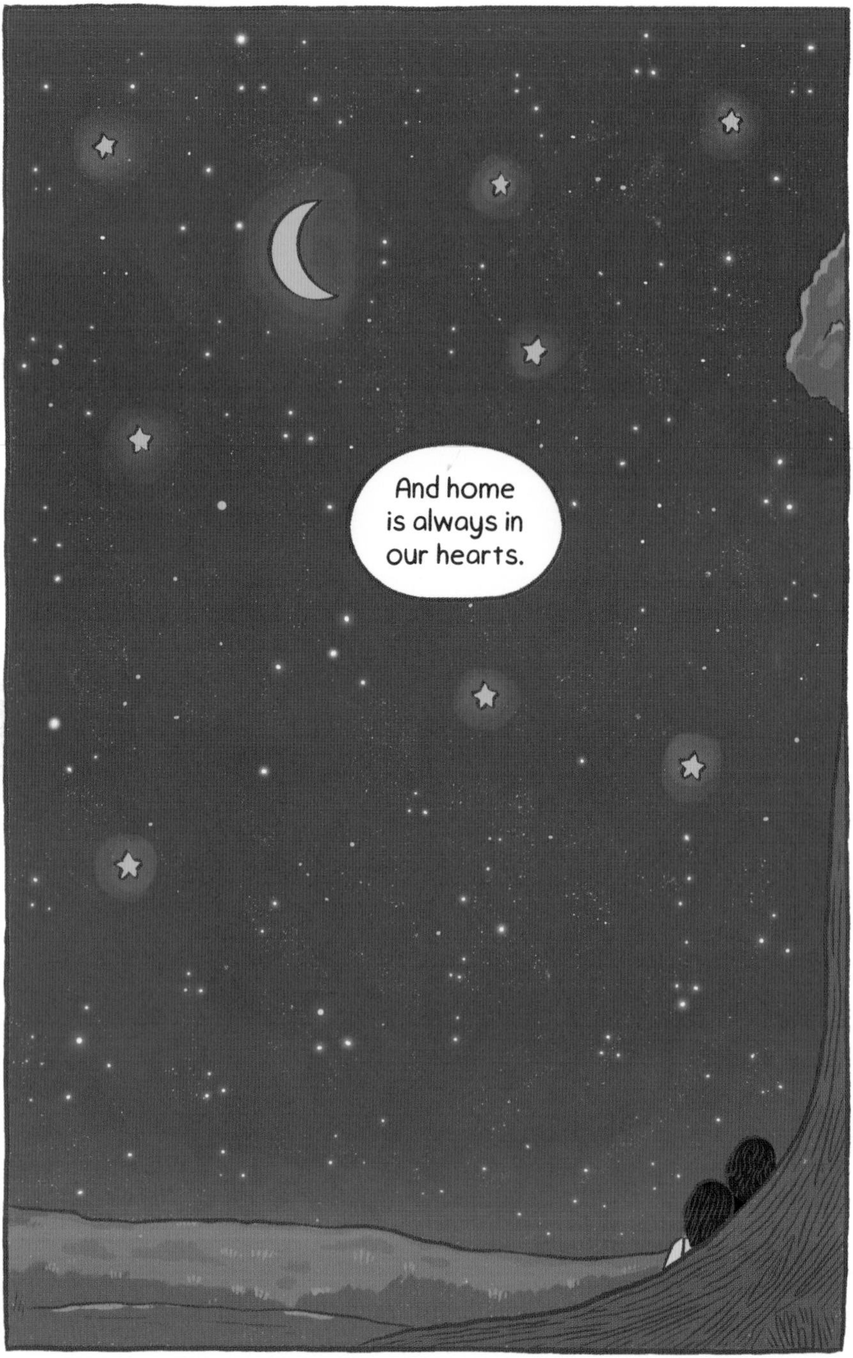
And home is always in our hearts.

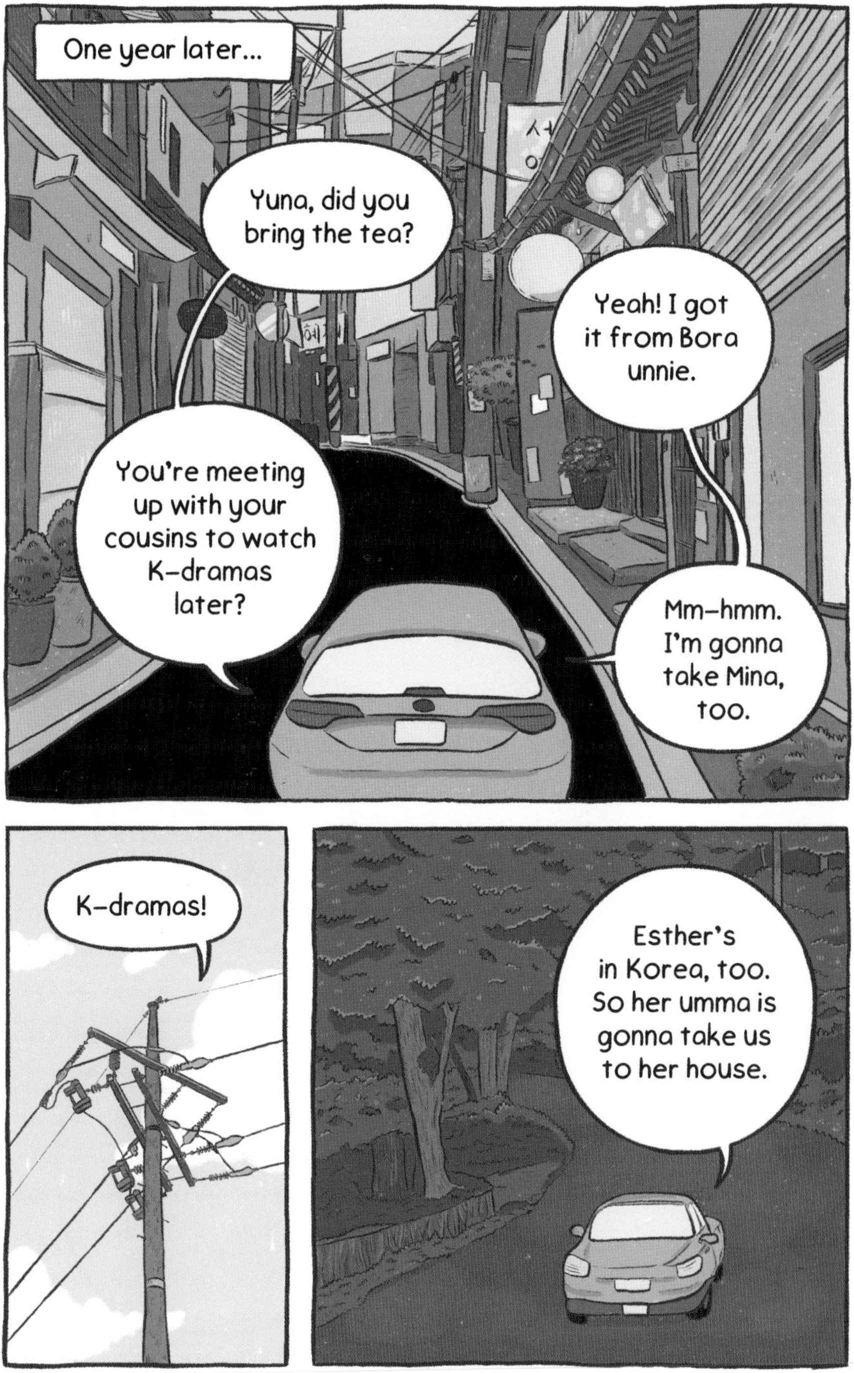
One year later...
Yuna, did you bring the tea?
Yeah! I got it from Bora unnie.
You're meeting up with your cousins to watch K-dramas later?
Mm-hmm. I'm gonna take Mina, too.
K-dramas!
Esther's in Korea, too. So her umma is gonna take us to her house.

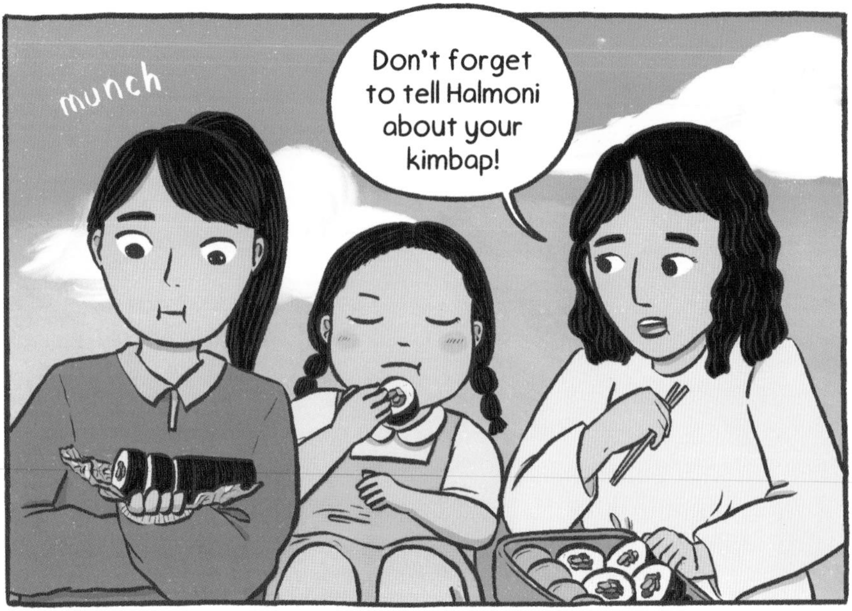
munch
Don't forget to tell Halmoni about your kimbap!

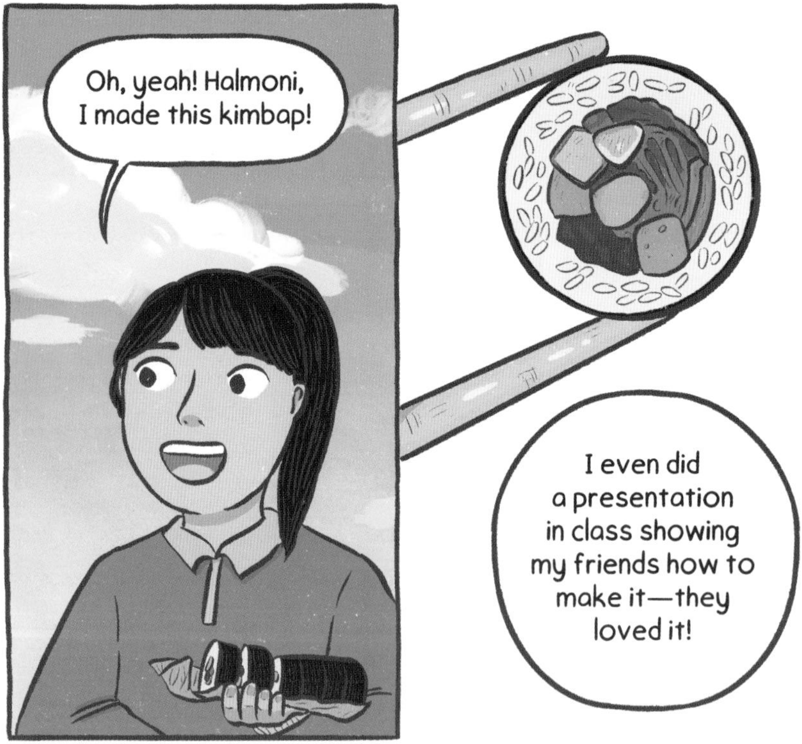
Oh, yeah! Halmoni, I made this kimbap!
I even did a presentation in class showing my friends how to make it—they loved it!

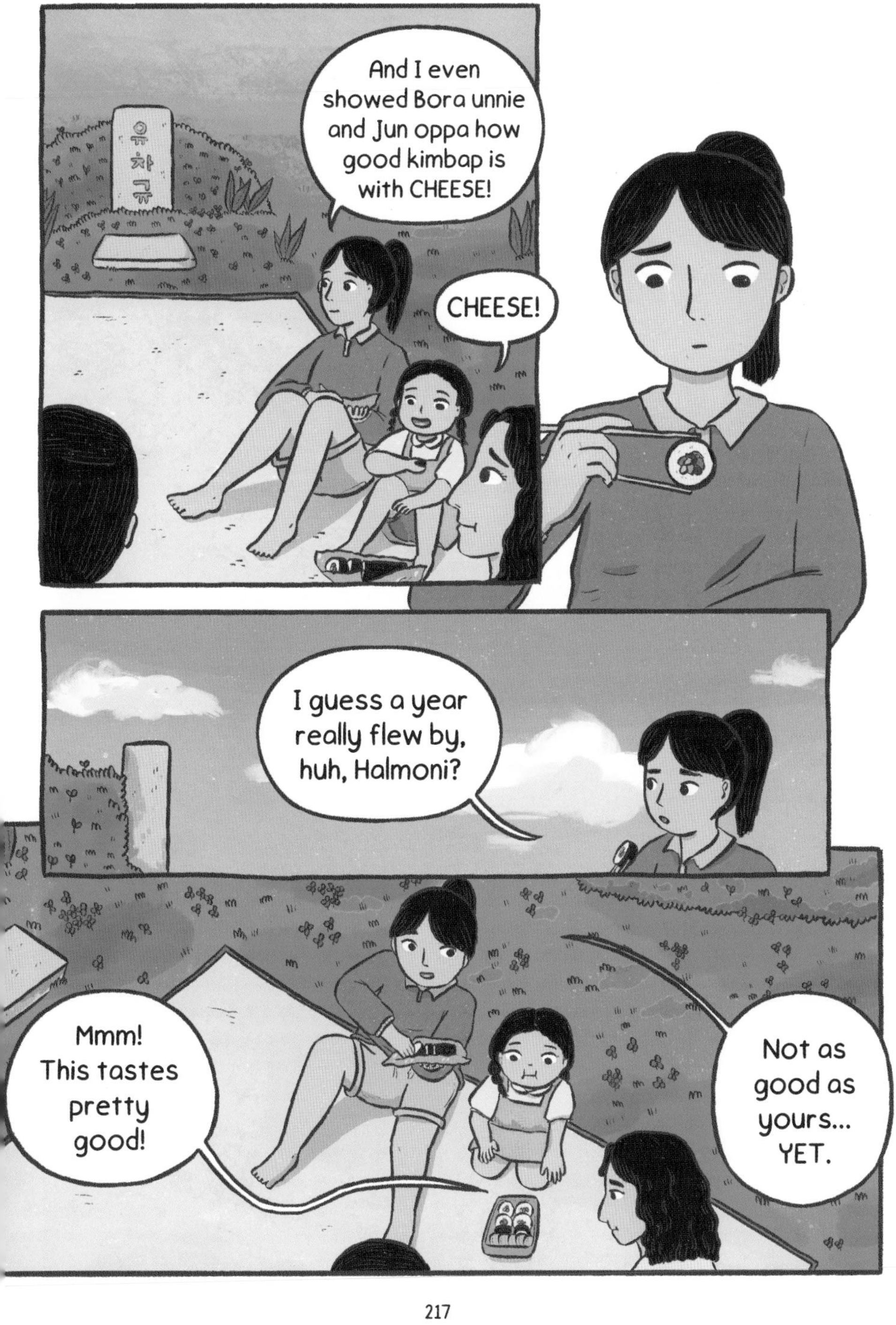
유
차
규
And I even showed Bora unnie and Jun oppa how good kimbap is with CHEESE!
CHEESE!
I guess a year really flew by, huh, Halmoni?
Mmm! This tastes pretty good!
Not as good as yours... YET.

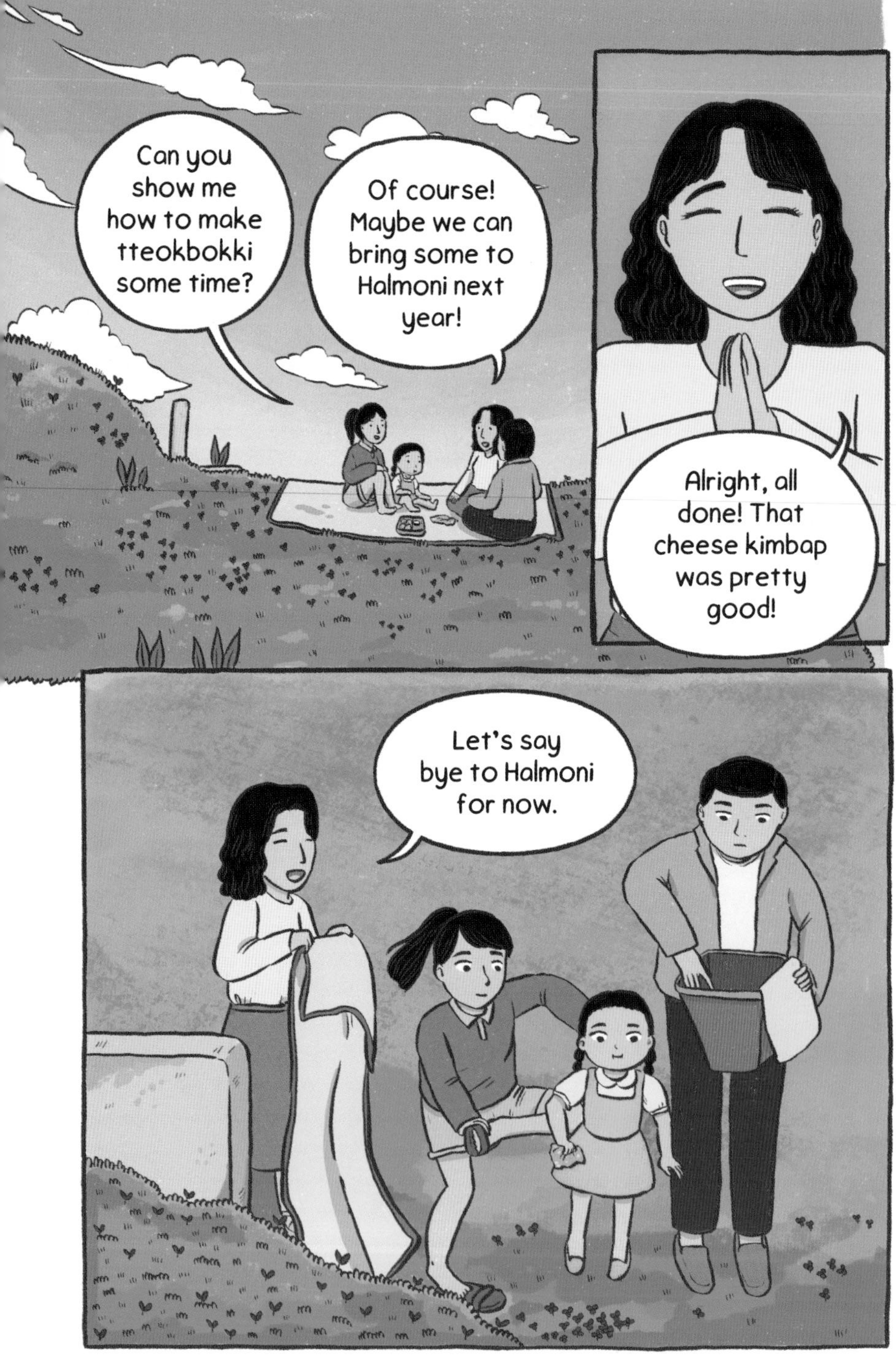
Can you show me how to make tteokbokki some time?
Of course! Maybe we can bring some to Halmoni next year!
Alright, all done! That cheese kimbap was pretty good!
Let's say bye to Halmoni for now.

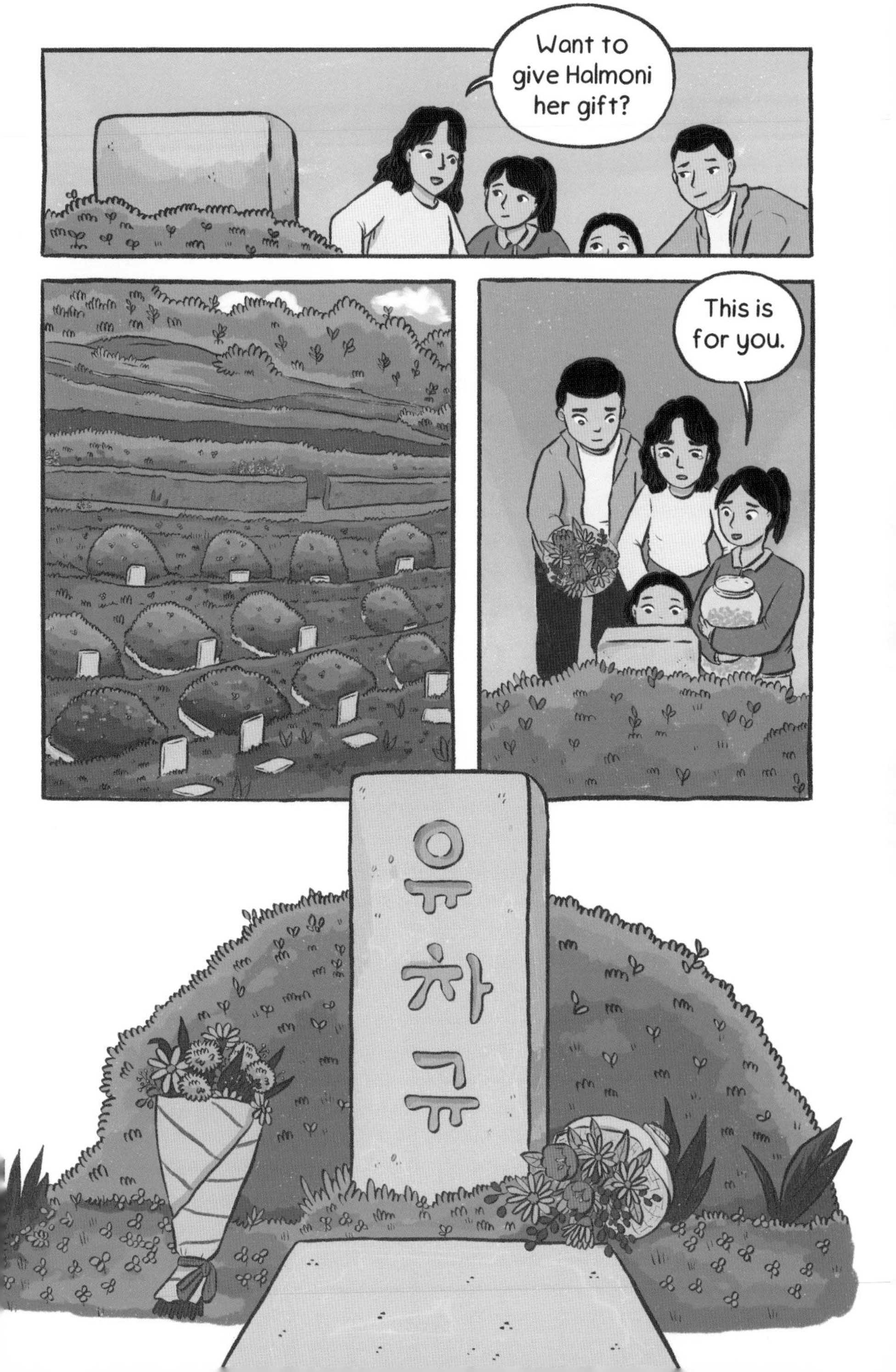
Want to give Halmoni her gift?
This is for you.
유차규

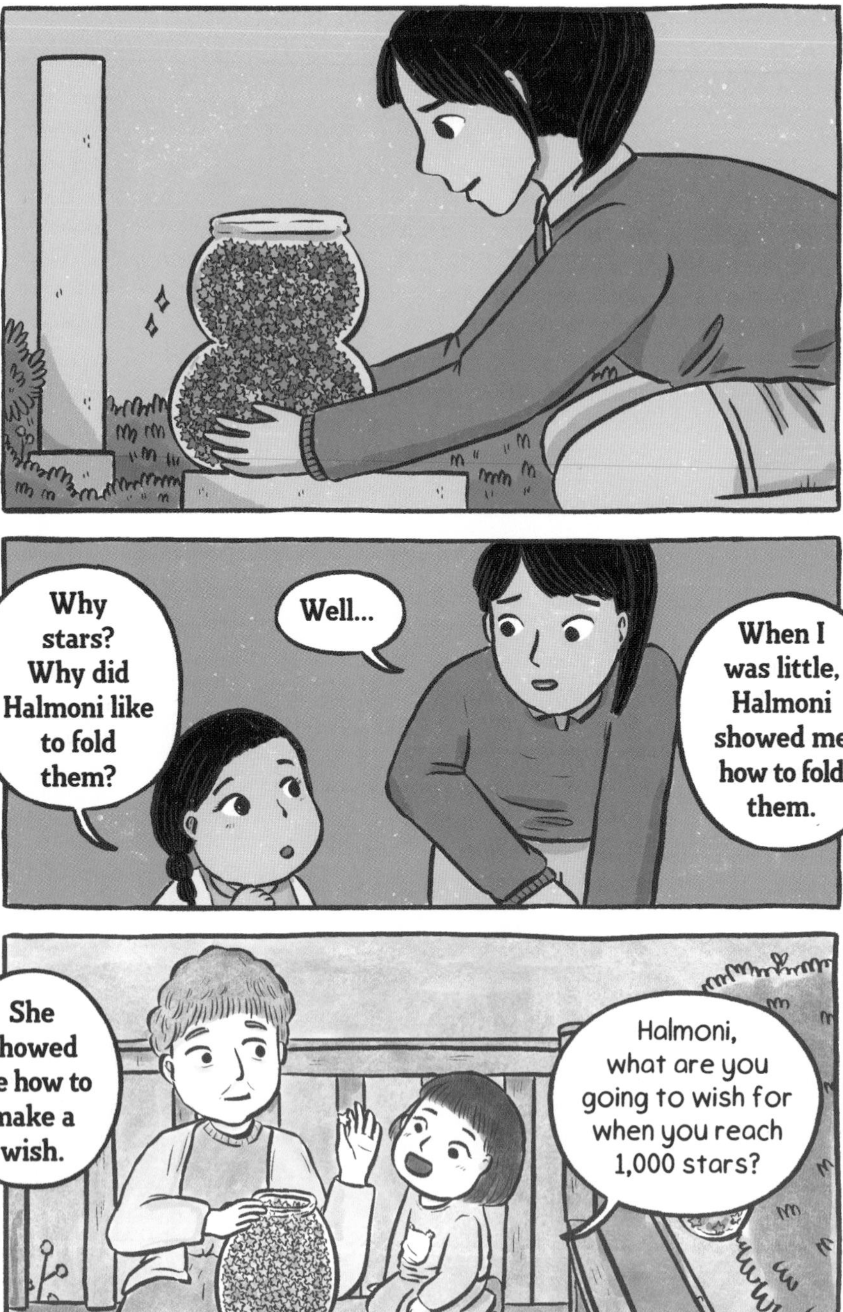
Why stars? Why did Halmoni like to fold them?
Well...
When I was little, Halmoni showed me how to fold them.
She showed me how to make a wish.
Halmoni, what are you going to wish for when you reach 1,000 stars?

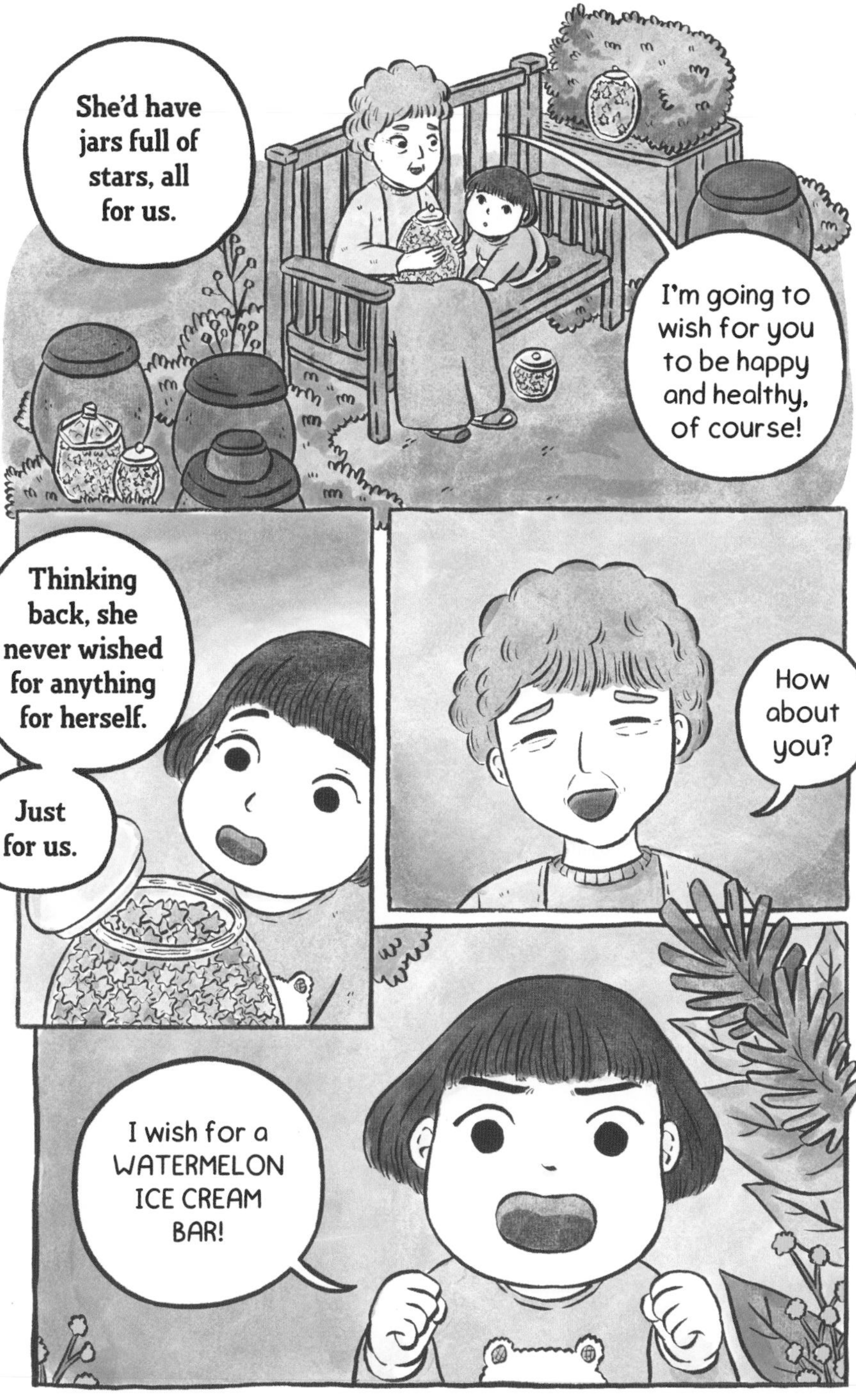
She'd have jars full of stars, all for us.
I'm going to wish for you to be happy and healthy, of course!
Thinking back, she never wished for anything for herself.
Just for us.
How about you?
I wish for a WATERMELON ICE CREAM BAR!

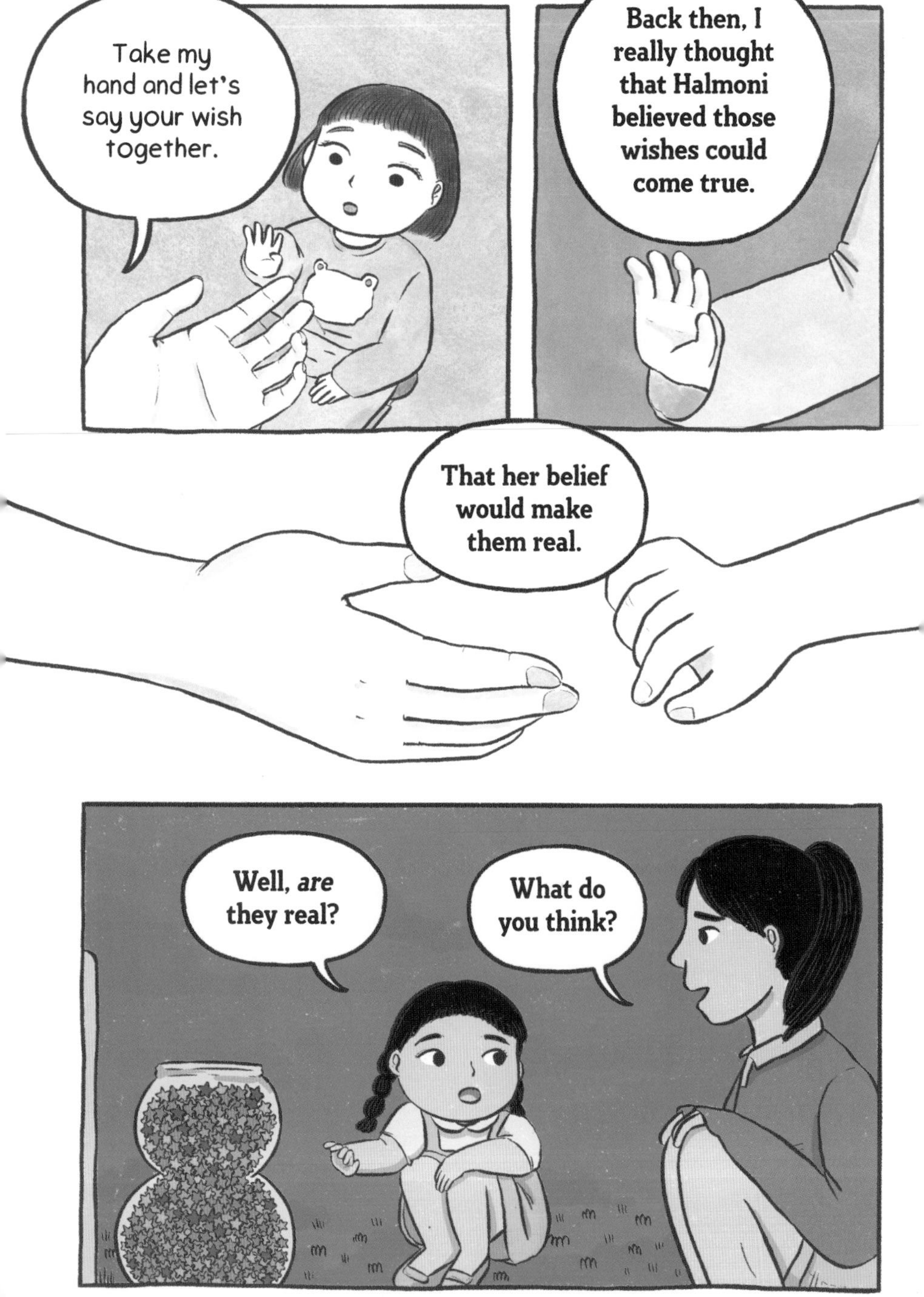
Take my hand and let's say your wish together.
Back then, I really thought that Halmoni believed those wishes could come true.
That her belief would make them real.
Well, *are* they real?
What do you think?

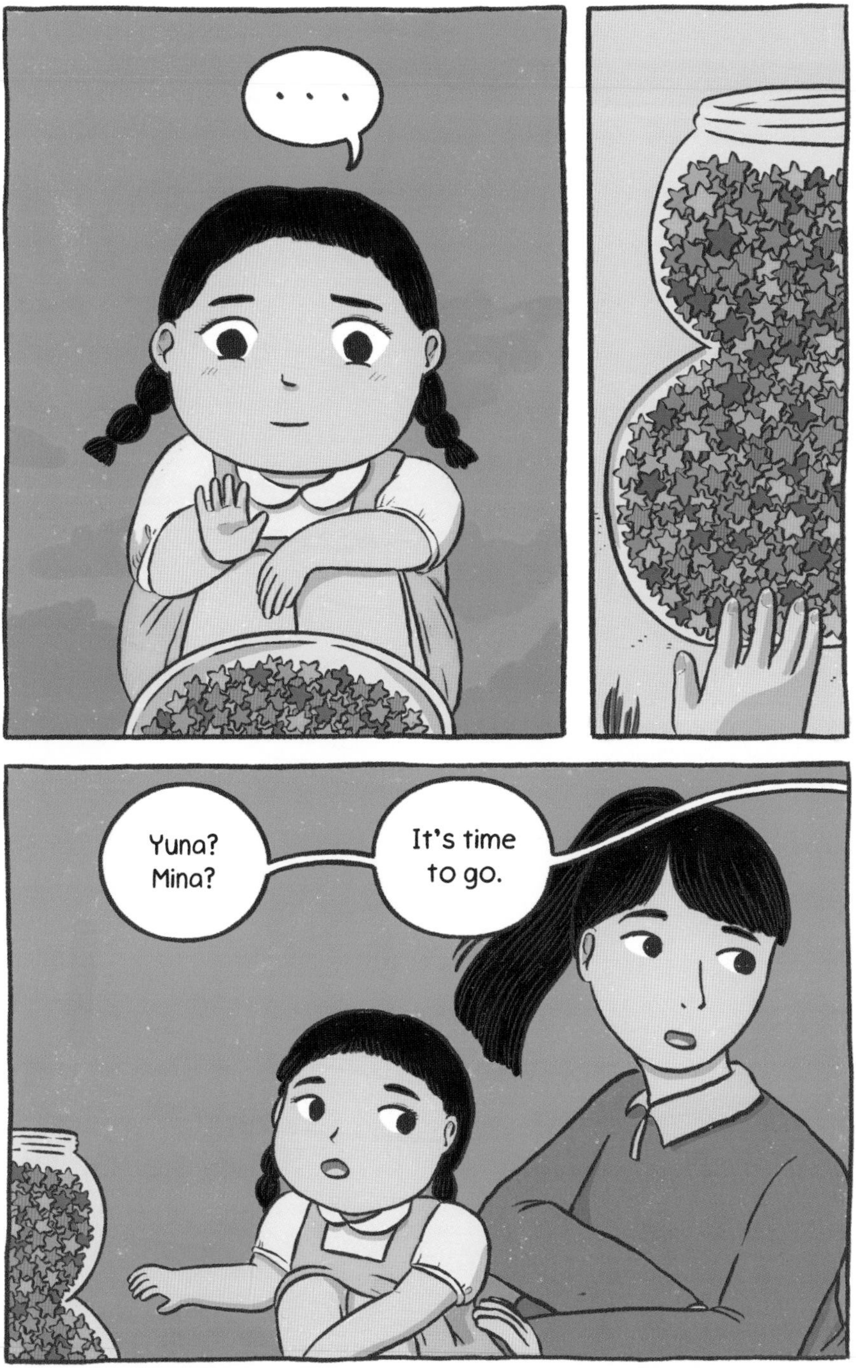
. . .
Yuna?
Mina?
It's time
to go.

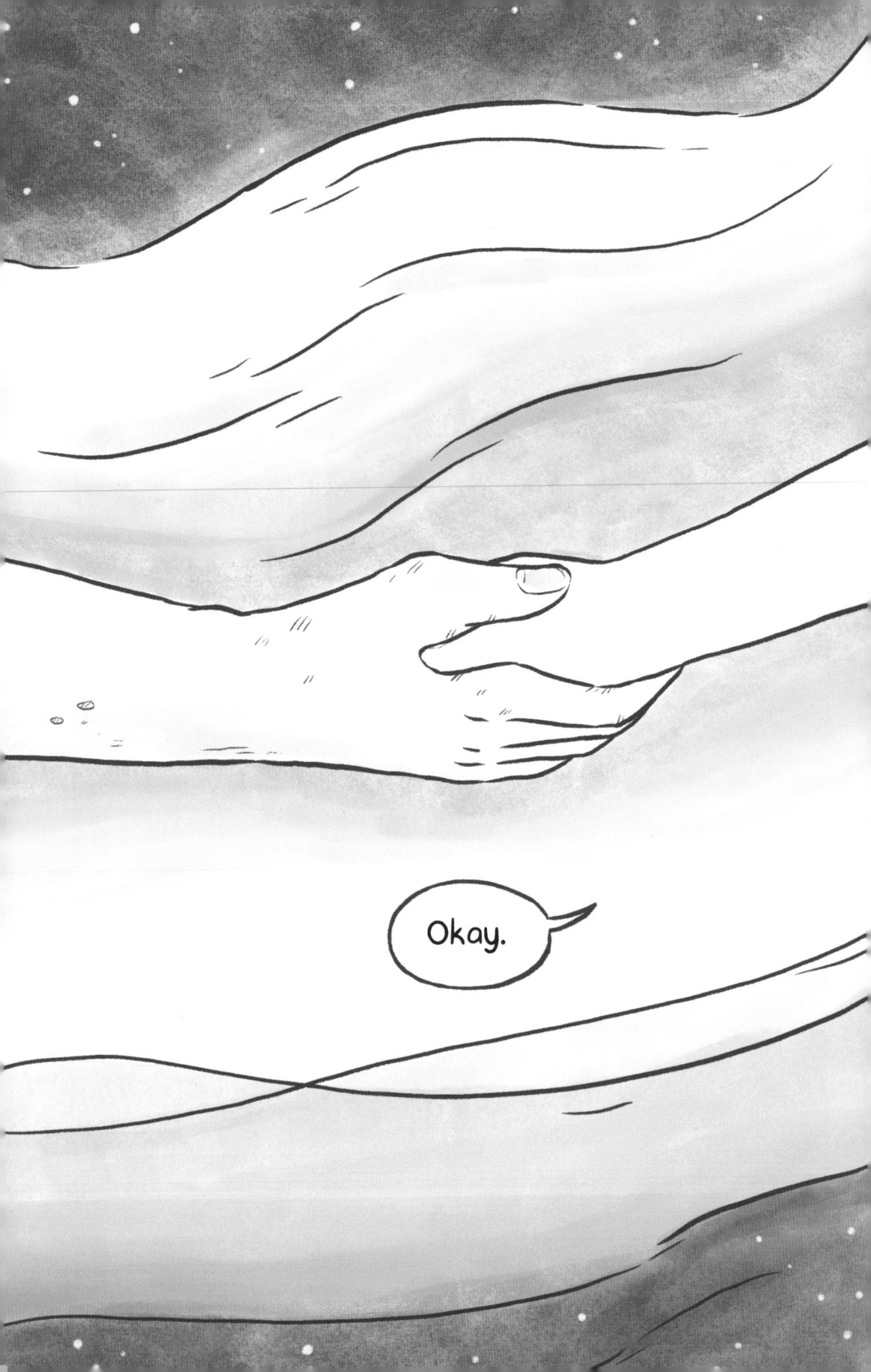
Okay.

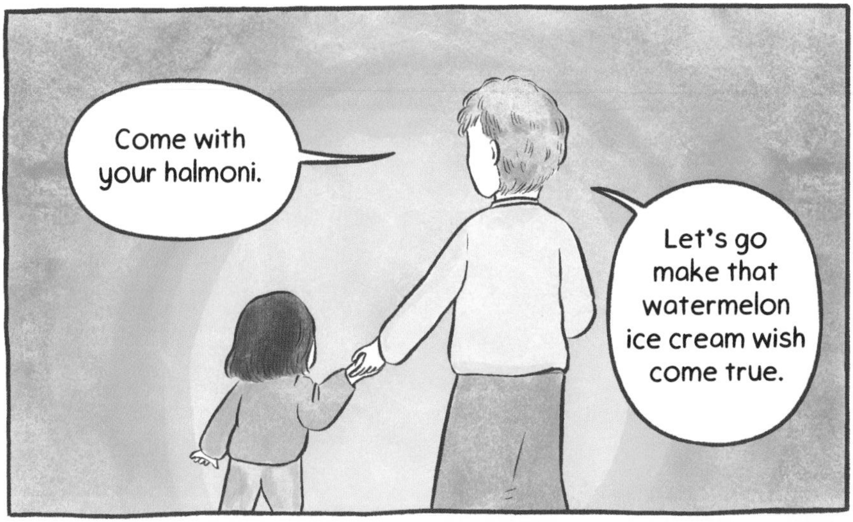
Come with your halmoni.
Let's go make that watermelon ice cream wish come true.

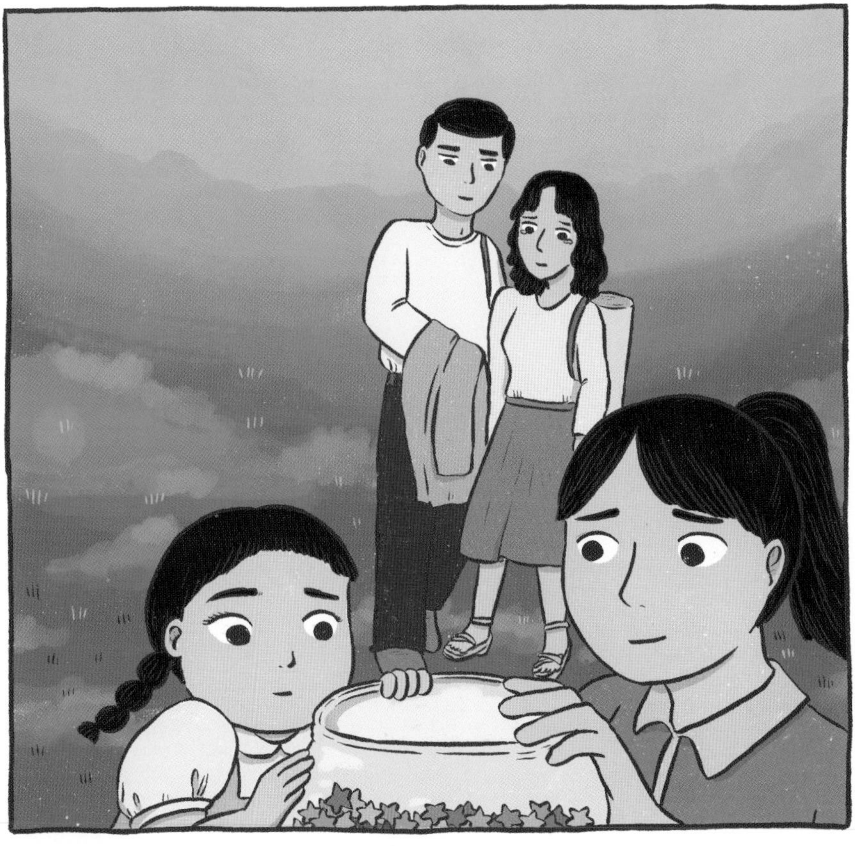

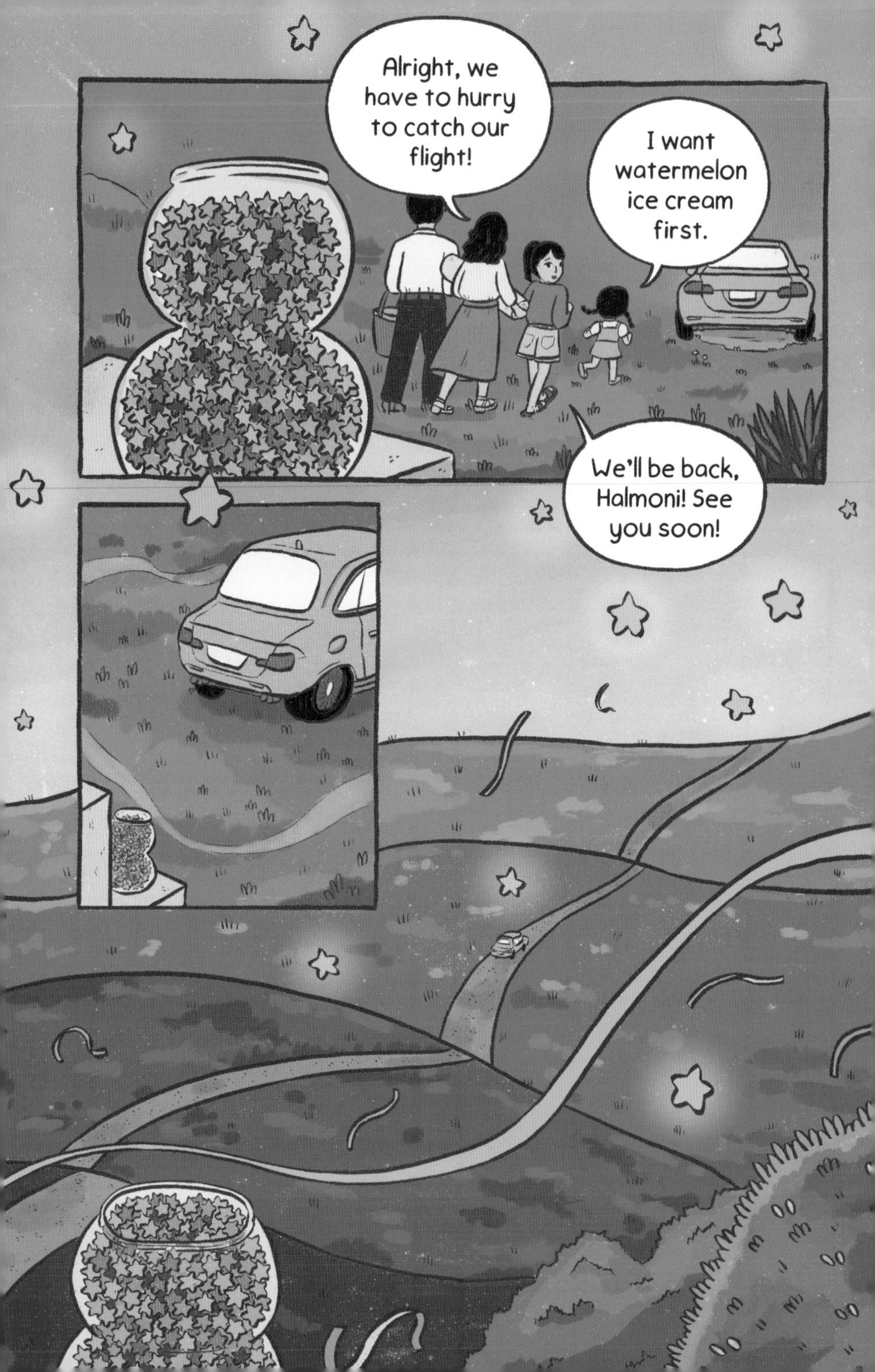
Alright, we have to hurry to catch our flight!
I want watermelon ice cream first.
We'll be back, Halmoni! See you soon!

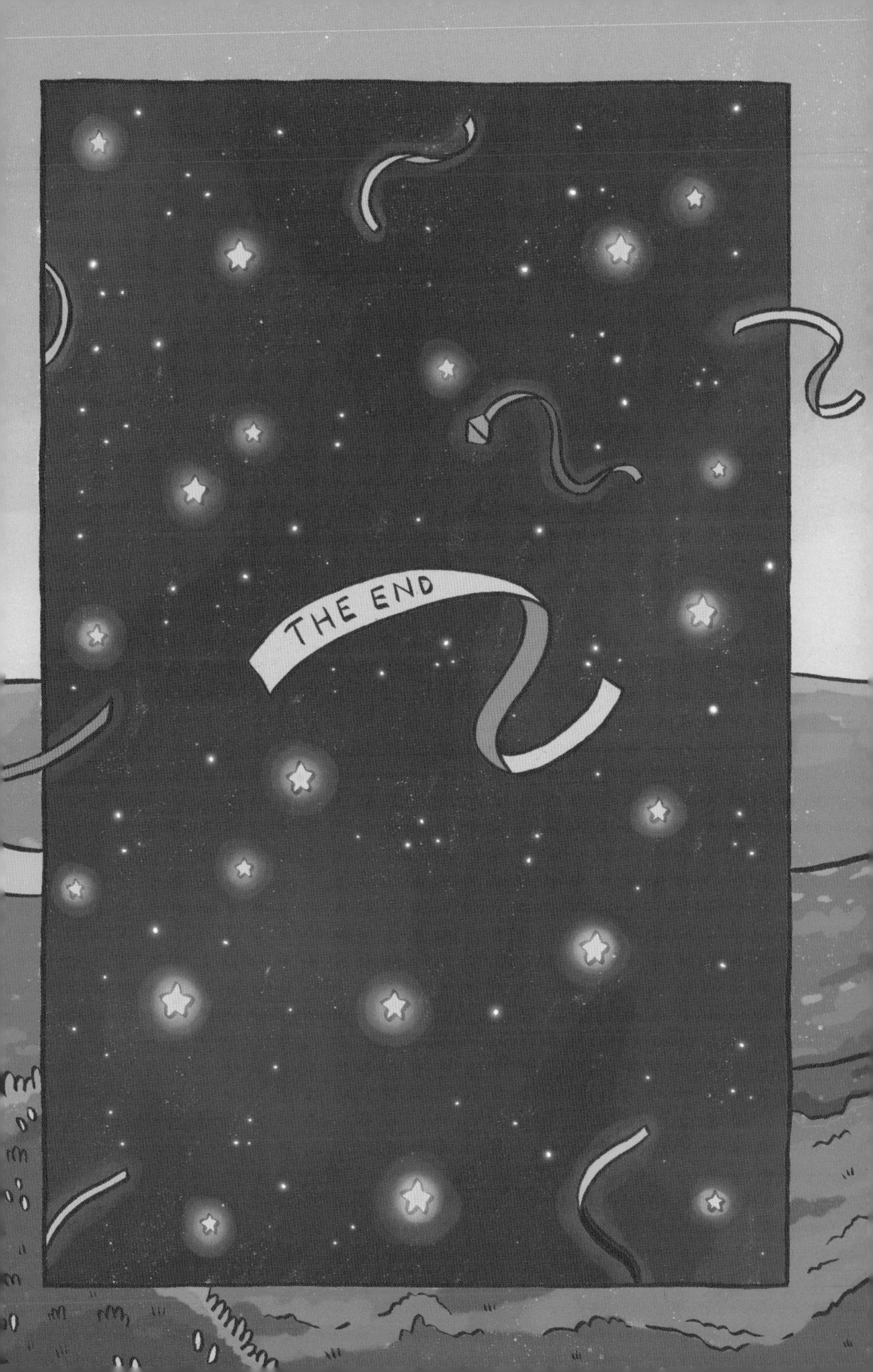
THE END

HOW TO FOLD A PAPER STAR

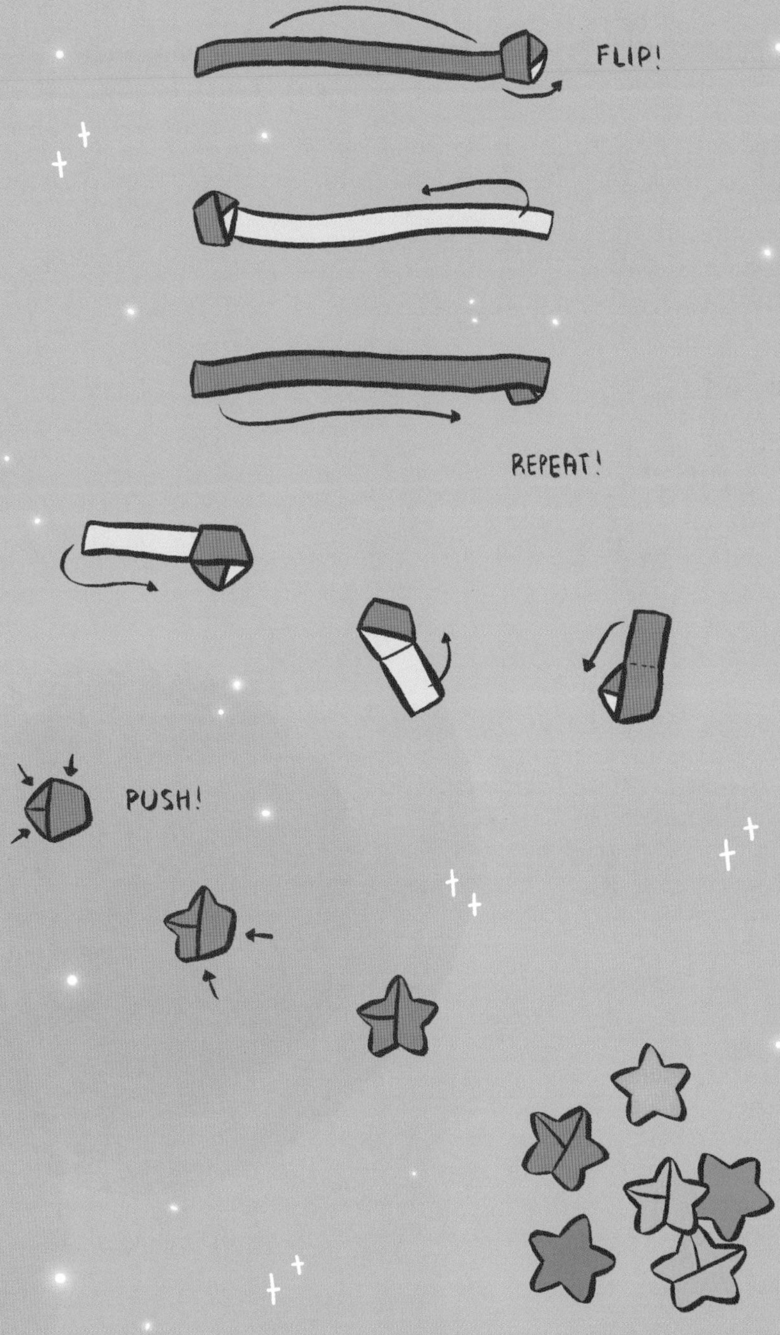
FLIP!
REPEAT!
PUSH!

Author's Note

This book is an ode to my umma's mother, my halmoni.

Growing up as the child of my immigrant parents, I had two homes: the U.S., where I was born and felt the most comfortable, and Korea, where most of my extended family lived. Every year, my parents would try to save up enough money to fly back home to Korea. Sometimes all of us could go, but other times, only one parent could go at a time.

Each time we landed, someone would greet us at the airport terminal, and we'd spend the next few weeks being with our family as much as we could. My halmoni was a single mother, raising my umma and her siblings alone. Like Yuna, I felt almost afraid of how thin, papery, and fragile she felt, and when she'd try to reach out and connect, I would retreat away. All of the stories in this book are based on true events, from the sauna to the last memory of waving goodbye.

When I was in middle school, I remember waking up one morning in the U.S. to my parents telling me we weren't going to school that day. My halmoni was in critical condition, and we'd be making a surprise trip to Korea. My umma had had a final phone call with her in the hospital, and my parents were rushing to buy plane tickets to see her before she passed, but ... we were too late. I could feel the helplessness my parents felt, fifteen hours away and unable to get there any faster.

This time in Korea, things felt completely different. Gone was the feeling of hominess, and instead, everything felt heavy and grim. Family members I didn't even know about had gathered together, and I felt so pointedly out of place. But more impactfully to my young self, I felt like I didn't know this Halmoni that everyone else was talking about. For the sake of this book, I simplified the funeral process, but it was so much more overwhelming and confusing, especially to me as a child.

Around this time, I had not only recently moved to a new city where there were very few Asians, let alone Koreans, but I had also skipped a few grades and was two to three years younger than everyone else in my class. In this period of feeling like I didn't belong even in the U.S., I felt like my own Korean blood was not genuine enough in Korea, among my family.

It was only later, after some years had passed and I'd grown older, that I started to learn about the Halmoni that my umma knew. My family would have a special little tradition, a treat of sorts for us, where the four of us would go to a local coffee shop every Saturday and chat about anything and everything. With me and my little sister drinking hot chocolates and my parents hot coffees, my umma would share with us stories of Korea, her life, and the things she and my appa experienced when they first moved here.

They told us about how they struggled to adjust to an English-speaking country, but the hope they felt was because so many opportunities seemed to be present for us, their children. Their place wasn't grand, but as they grew their family, it felt like they were creating warmth in a foreign place. We heard how my umma learned piano, how my appa would surprise my umma with drives to the beach whenever they missed Korea, and the road trips they'd take with us when we were toddlers.

And my umma would sometimes share stories of her own umma, my halmoni. As tears welled up in her eyes, she laughed as she told us about funny things or conversations she'd recall, how Halmoni came to visit a couple of times and what they did, and many of her childhood memories. These stories felt like precious nuggets to me, and I'd listen in awe at the lives that my parents and my halmoni lived. I held on to each tale like hands cupping water, transferring it into a safe well in my mind so that it would never disappear from my memory, even writing some down so that I'd always be able to cherish these, too. I could see just how important Halmoni was to their lives, and how I wished that I had more time with her now.

As I wrote *A Sky of Paper Stars,* I reopened that well of safely kept memories and poured some out onto these pages. They aren't all my own memories, but stories passed down through the generations, and I feel honored to be able to share these now with you.

My halmoni was a brilliant, resilient, honorable, and loving woman. She loved creating poetry, enjoying small moments of the day, and doing all she could for her family, giving her entire life to them.

I'm honored to be a part of my family and its history, the legacy that she has continued through her example. Like Yuna has realized, I realized, too, then, that I'll always have a place to call home—in my memories, with my family, and by sharing these snapshots with all of you.

Thank you so much for reading this book.

Thank you to my family for the direct inspiration in this story.

I also want to give a huge thank-you to Connie Hsu, my fantastic editor who understood my vision immediately and brought this story to life; Kathleen Ortiz, my amazing agent without whom this book would not have been possible; and of course the whole team at Roaring Brook Press, who worked tirelessly with me on all aspects of the book.

I hope these stories reach your heart as much as they reached mine.

About the Author

Susie Yi is a writer and illustrator based out of sunny Orange County, California.

Growing up, she would create little books out of printer paper and staples; write "news articles" about the latest things her sister, Heidi, and her stuffed animals had done; and draw in silly comics, and pass them out as weekly magazines for her family. Some notable stories include "Pony helped Heidi finish her homework faster" (Pony was a stuffed horse) or "Why Umma and Appa should let us watch more *Pokémon*."

Clearly, Susie always loved creating and telling stories and drawing art, doodling on anything she could find. But instead of going straight into a creative career, she took the long and winding road, studying biology and computer science instead in college (along with some animation and film courses here and there) and working in tech, until she finally decided to make one of the biggest decisions of her life and become a full-time author and illustrator.

Now, she spends her days writing stories about whatever strikes her imagination, and then drawing on her tablet to visually bring the words to life. Her goal in everything she creates is to move people's hearts, bring them joy and some kind of emotion, and inspire them to share and create their own stories. You can visit her at SusieYi.com.

Published by Roaring Brook Press
Roaring Brook Press is a division of Holtzbrinck Publishing Holdings Limited Partnership
120 Broadway, New York, NY 10271
mackids.com

Library of Congress Control Number: 2022920575

Our books may be purchased in bulk for promotional, educational, or business use.
Please contact your local bookseller or the Macmillan Corporate and Premium Sales Department
at (800) 221-7945 ext. 5442 or by email at MacmillanSpecialMarkets@macmillan.com.

First edition, 2023
Edited by Connie Hsu
Cover design by Kirk Benshoff
Interior book design by Sunny Lee and Casper Manning

Printed in China by RR Donnelley Asia Printing Solutions Ltd., Dongguan City, Guangdong Province

ISBN 978-1-250-84389-0 (paperback)
1 3 5 7 9 10 8 6 4 2

ISBN 978-1-250-84388-3 (hardcover)
1 3 5 7 9 10 8 6 4 2

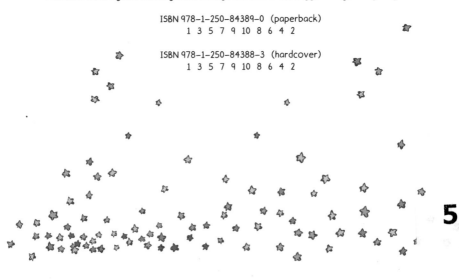